THE RIVEN LAND

THE RUPTURED KINGDOM
BOOK 2

ALLAN N. PACKER

LUMINANT PUBLICATIONS

THE RUPTURED KINGDOM SERIES

The Hard Edge of Magic (Book 1)
The Riven Land (Book 2)
The Weight of Interference (Book 3)
…other titles to come

Companion Novelette
The Renegade: A Prequel to The Hard Edge of Magic

Other epic fantasy by Allan N. Packer

THE STONE CYCLE SERIES

The Stone of Knowing (Book 1)
The Cost of Knowing (Book 2)
The Stone of Authority (Book 3)
The Struggle for Authority (Book 4)
The Stone of Vitality (Book 5)
The Hope of Vitality (Book 6)

Companion Novelettes
The Seer: A Prequel to The Stone of Knowing
The Rending: A Prequel to The Cost of Knowing

To Talitha,
In anticipation of journeying with you in life.
You're loved, you're wanted, and you're needed. May you discover you have a
voice. And may you use it to speak truth to your generation.

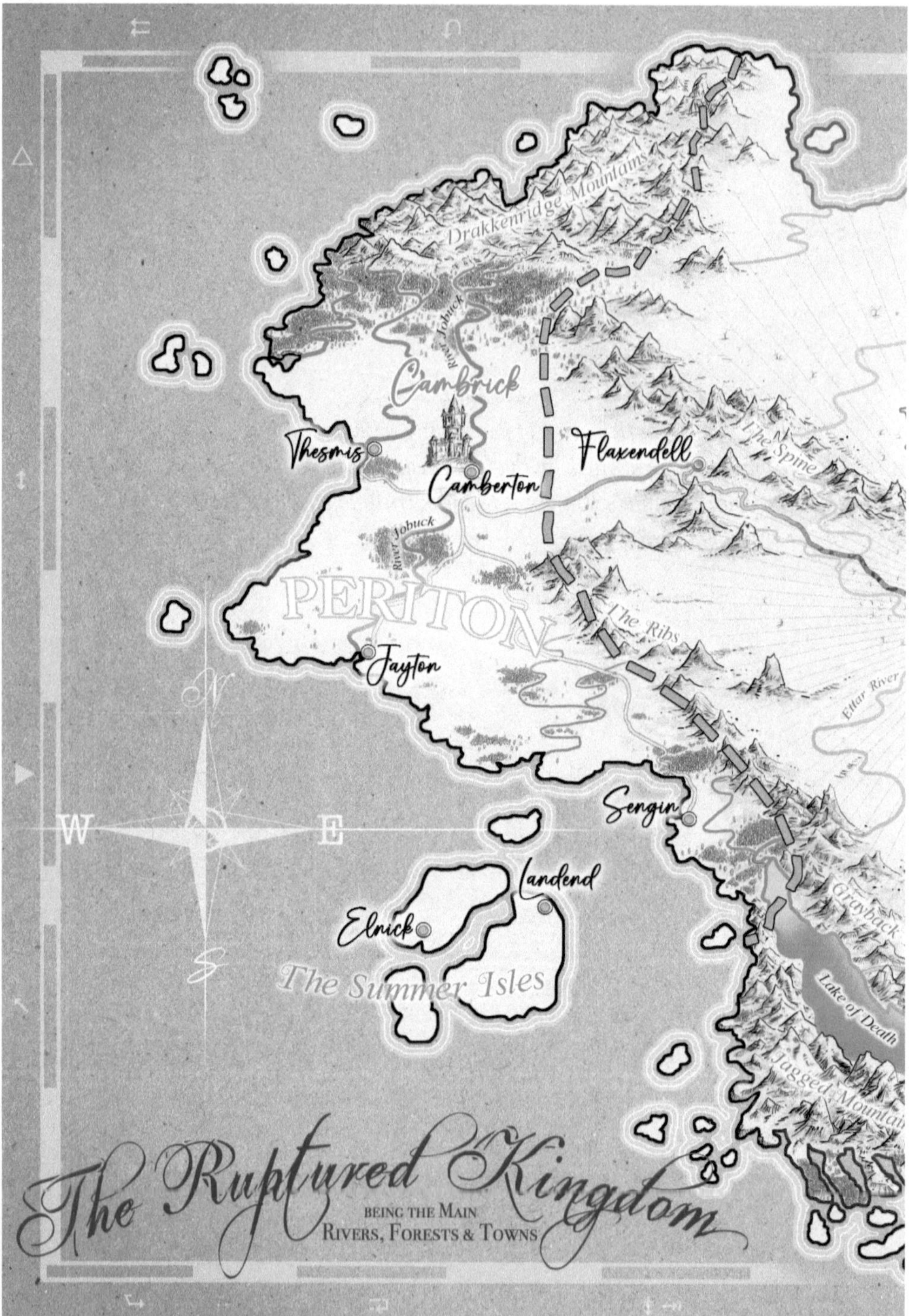

Drakkenridge Mountains
River Jobuck
Cambrick
The Spine
Thesmis
Flaxendell
Camberton
River Jobuck
PERITON
The Ribs
Jayton
Ettar River
Sengin
Grayback
Landend
Elnick
Lake of Death
The Summer Isles
Jagged Mountains
W
E
N
S
The Ruptured Kingdom
BEING THE MAIN
RIVERS, FORESTS & TOWNS

Northport
Forshem
MIETHESIA
Ruined Kingdom
Ellaran
Ellar River
Souther
Mountains
Brynford
Brynburn River
Firetip Mountains
Bane Mountains
TANTEL
Antilin
River Antil
Shelmar
Dynsdale
Naire H Sulp • Royal Cartographer & Geographer • High Street • Cambrick

VOLUME 1—THE FUGITIVE

CHAPTER 1

Skidding to a stop at the top of a ridge, the horse snorted, tossing its head wildly. Trisanna spun around in the saddle, staring back the way she had come. They hadn't caught her. Not yet.

The sandy shore of a lake lay at the bottom of the slope, barely a stone's throw away. Clicking her tongue, she urged the horse forward. Ears back, it spread its feet, refusing to move.

Sliding swiftly from the saddle, she spoke soothingly in its ear and stroked its neck. Then she led it trembling down the slope.

Three fishing boats lay idle on the sand, pulled well back from the water. Only one fisherman was anywhere in view. Standing beside a boat, he was working at his nets.

She hurried toward him, the horse trailing reluctantly behind her. "Greetings," she said, as cheerfully as she could manage.

"Mistress," he replied, bobbing his head respectfully before staring at her curiously. "What brings you to these ill-favored shores?"

"I would like to sail on the lake," she told him.

He chuckled. "You don't want to do that, Miss." He nodded toward her horse, still trembling at her side. "You should pay heed to your animal. It can tell the water ain't safe."

She cocked an eyebrow. "Yet you sail on it."

"Aye, that I do," he said with a sigh. "At times even I ask myself why. Precious few value my skin apart from me, and every one of them says I'm a fool."

When she didn't respond, he added, "There's good fishin' out there, 'tis true. And it's safe enough near the shore. But beyond?" A grim smile twisted his lips. "I won't trouble your pretty head with tales, but worse things than fish haunt the deeps!"

"Nevertheless, I would like you to take me out onto the lake," she said stubbornly.

He shook his head once again, more firmly this time.

Swinging a small pack from her back, she retrieved a bag bulging with coins and thrust it toward him.

He remained unmoved. "Don't let the stillness deceive you, Miss," he said, waving a hand across the water. "There's nothin' tranquil about this lake."

She reached for a fine chain around her neck and drew it out. A glittering jewel appeared from beneath her clothing. "This is yours too," she promised him. "All you have to do is take me out there."

After a long look at her hand, he transferred his gaze to her face. "Why?"

She shifted her feet awkwardly. "Someone told me I wouldn't dare to do it."

Throwing a glance at the slope behind them, she rummaged around in the pack a final time and produced a small bar of solid gold. "If we go right now, you can have this as well."

He drew back involuntarily. "That ain't stolen, is it?"

She shook her head. "This is my inheritance. But it's yours if you want it."

With a deep sigh he yielded at last. "Very well, m'lady. Only along the shoreline, mind."

His decision made, he swung the boat around and began pushing it toward the lake. He hesitated for a moment when he reached the water's edge, frowning as he peered off into the lake. Then, with a sigh of resignation, he pushed until the little craft was afloat.

While he was busy, she quickly removed the reins and saddle from her horse and slapped it on the rump. It immediately trotted back the way it had come. Seeing the look on the fisherman's face, she assured him, "Don't worry. She will return the moment I call."

The fisherman shrugged. Holding the boat steady, he waved Trisanna aboard.

"Thank you," she said with a thin smile, holding out the coins and the gold bar and reaching once more for the chain around her neck.

He shook his head. "I won't cheat you, m'lady. It ain't my way." Taking the bag of coins, he removed a few and returned the rest with the bag. "This will do me well enough." Then he jerked his head toward the boat.

A grateful smile on her lips, she stepped lightly aboard.

Climbing in after her, he poled the vessel away from the shore and set the sail.

A light breeze caught the sailcloth, and the boat glided away from the land. They hadn't traveled far when the fisherman swung the tiller to direct the little craft on a course parallel to the shoreline.

"So what's this about?" he asked. He gave her a wink. "Tryin' to impress an admirer with your boldness?"

She ignored his questions. "What do I need to pay you to sail me all the way across the lake?"

He looked at her sharply. "You agreed to a little run along the shoreline."

She shook her head. "You said that. I never agreed to it."

His face set hard. "I'm sorry, m'lady, but I ain't takin' you no deeper. No matter how much you pay me. We wouldn't make it halfway to the other side."

She subsided, content to bide her time. Occasionally she glanced at the water, but her main attention was on the ridge above the little beach.

Only a few minutes passed before gray-cloaked riders appeared, silhouetted against the sky. She counted ten of them. After a momentary pause they picked their way down to the lake, spreading out along the shoreline as soon as they reached it.

Distressed by such close proximity to the water, the horses neighed and stamped their hooves. Unmoved, the riders sat silently on their mounts, staring at the little boat.

The fisherman gazed at them for a moment. "Seems like everyone wants to visit our shores today," he ventured. He aimed an ironic look in Trisanna's direction. "D'you think they might want to sail as well?"

When she didn't reply, he peered at her thoughtfully. "They're chasin' you, ain't they? I can drop you further along the shore if you like. Somewhere well clear of them."

Even as he was speaking, the breeze began to die away. Frowning up at the sail, he tried to guide the boat closer to the shore. The little vessel refused to cooperate. As if running before a steady breeze, it began heading into deeper water. The riders lining the shore slowly began to shrink in size.

"What's happenin'?" he cried in alarm.

"They're doing it," she said bitterly, staring at the horsemen. "They're mages."

The sails began to slap limply as the breeze faded entirely. The boat continued to slide through the water, moving further from the land. Every attempt to steer it was futile. The tiller had no effect.

"How can we get back?" cried the fisherman in dismay.

"We can't," she told him. "Even if we reached the shore, they would push us out again."

"Then there's no hope," he moaned.

"Do not despair," she urged him. "We're not lost yet."

The breeze began to pick up again, and the fisherman peered eagerly at the sail. "We might yet make it back! Perhaps Providence might smile on us!"

She shook her head. "They'll never allow it," she said. "There is only one way for us to survive. You must set a course for Periton."

"Are you mad?" he cried. "We'd never make it!"

"We can't sit here and do nothing!" she insisted. "We must fight!"

After staring wild-eyed at her for a moment, he nodded dully. "You're right. If I'm goin' to die, I won't go unresisting."

The little craft responded immediately as he took the tiller and began to steer away from the beach. The horsemen dwindled in their wake, along with any prospect of safety.

She peered ahead, hoping for a glimpse of their destination, but the opposite shore was too distant to be seen. Bounded on both sides by mountains, the lake stretched away to the far horizon.

The wind began to pick up, and they raced forward, slapping through waves that were beginning to grow in size. Glancing back, she could see neither the horsemen nor the other boats on the shore.

A larger than usual wave crashed over the boat, drenching her. The wind had begun to howl, a wail of lament.

"What *is* that?" shouted the fisherman.

"It's the mages!" she yelled back. "We're out of reach of their pushing magic now, so they've turned the wind against us."

This latest attack seemed to spark new determination in the beleaguered sailor. "Keep your head down, Missy, and hang on," he called. "Looks like it's goin' to get rough."

For a moment she thought she sighted land beyond the bow of the boat, far off in the distance. But the spray and the wild tossing of the waves obscured it.

The fisherman shouted in terror, and she spun around to see a giant head emerging from the waves. Shaped like a misbegotten eel, the creature turned baleful eyes toward them. A huge maw opened wide, revealing multiple rows of razor-sharp teeth. The conjurings of her darkest nightmares had never rivaled the monstrosity before her.

It bellowed, and her heart skipped a beat. Mindless as the monster appeared, she heard meaning in its roar—a rage and hatred so visceral, so violent, that her strength abandoned her entirely. She collapsed in a witless heap.

The fisherman fared no better. Releasing the tiller to cover his face with his hands, he slumped to the bottom of the boat, gibbering mindlessly.

A second head appeared on the opposite side of the vessel, and the creatures howled at each other, bickering over the prize drifting helplessly between them.

In the midst of the madness, a memory came unbidden to her, reaching out from another place and time. The roar of the storm and the bellowing of the creatures faded, and she heard again in her mind the voice of the woman who had raised her. *Never fear the darkness, little*

Sanna, however scary it might seem. The tiniest flicker of light will always frighten away the deepest of shadows.

As her courage flickered into life, her will stirred as well. She had no powers that could defend them against the monsters, but there was one thing she could attempt. Reaching out with her mage ability, she stretched an illusion over the boat and its occupants, hiding every trace of them.

Ancient as the creatures and their malice might be, the magic was older. Confused by its power, they roared their fury, swinging their mighty heads around in search of their elusive prey.

The monsters could yet destroy the boat as they thrashed about. Realizing it, she crawled to the stern and took hold of the tiller.

The sail had been flapping uselessly with no one at the helm. Trisanna was no sailor, but as she gripped the tiller the wind caught the sail once more, driving the boat forward. They were heading in the wrong direction, but within moments they were clear of the creatures.

It wasn't the time or the place to be investigating a sailor's craft, but Trisanna had to at least try. Somehow executing a series of wild maneuvers, she managed to point the boat roughly in the direction of Periton. Too often the sail was barely filled. Her calls to the fisherman were lost in the wind.

She was almost ready to despair when the fisherman finally regained his wits. Glancing around, he saw that the monsters were gone, the howling gale had reduced to a steady breeze, and his passenger was in command of the boat.

He stared at her in awe. "Who are you?"

"An awful sailor," she replied, her voice trembling, "but one who refuses to give in."

A haunted look came to his eyes. "And those monsters?"

"They've disappeared."

He shook his head in wonder. "Then you and I are the luckiest people in the kingdom. No one swept into the deep has ever returned. Only wreckage blown ashore by the wind. I've never heard of any who faced the creatures and lived."

The fear hadn't left his eye, but he moved to the stern and took the tiller. Then he guided the boat westward, toward the landmass on the horizon she knew to be Periton.

Both of them lapsed into a long silence. Curiously, although the illusion around the boat remained intact, they could see each other and the little vessel. The fisherman seemed entirely unaware of anything unusual.

She preserved the illusion stubbornly, even though her mind was reeling, unable to shake off the terror of the creatures. Never could she have imagined such hatred.

With no further need to steer the boat, she gazed up at the sky, working hard at regaining her composure. She had barely managed to tame her emotions when the fisherman called to her quietly.

"I'm strugglin' to believe it, but we should be out of reach of the monsters now. They don't seem to go anywhere near land."

She nodded distractedly, her thoughts turning to the future. All of her energy had been bent on fleeing Tantel before they killed her. The idea of actually reaching Periton had seemed little more than an idle fancy. With the reality before her, she wondered what she would do when she got there.

She had never been a member of the mage council in Tantel. Her magical awakening had been kept secret from the mages belonging to the Compact. That was fortunate for her, because she would have been hunted down as a renegade if they had known she was a mage. Perhaps Periton treated independent mages more generously. She would find out before long.

What she needed most was to be properly trained. She knew so little about magic. Her own abilities had developed mostly by trial and error. She had discovered by accident that her magical ability involved illusion. The gift had never struck her as particularly useful. Not until the sudden appearance of the monsters. She couldn't imagine anyone overcoming the creatures with force, magical or otherwise. Illusion had saved her life and the fisherman's as well.

In any event, no one needed to know about her magical abilities when she first arrived in Periton. She intended to remain inconspicuous for as long as possible.

"The coastline ahead seems uninhabited," the fisherman reported.

"I'm happy to land there," she told him. "I'm not ready to face people just yet."

He seemed relieved. With a nod of agreement, he steered the boat toward a sandy beach a short distance away.

Closing her eyes in weary relief, she allowed her illusion to fade to nothing.

There was much to be grateful for. Leaving Tantel in their wake, they had set a course for Periton. And neither mages nor monsters had prevented them from reaching it.

CHAPTER 2

aster Inga stood in Chief Master Adrastas's reception room. He had offered her a seat, but she had refused it.

"You know why we can't let you go, Inga!" he protested. "We have four renegades out there, at least two of them extremely dangerous. Apart from you, we have three mages capable of detecting magical auras with farsense. Starting in a couple of months, I'm planning to send each of you in turn around the kingdom. Once every year per person. That should give us a way to flush out anyone hiding in a remote place. Of the four, your ability to detect glimmer is the strongest by far. You're more needed than ever."

"That's well and good, but I need a break. I'm tired, Adrastas! Weary in spirit. Right now I can't muster the focus to hunt anyone down."

"Why don't you have a day or two off here in Cambrick and spend some time with a friend? Emmela for instance."

She shook her head stiffly.

"You need to forgive her, Inga! The evidence she gave at the inquiry wasn't personal."

"I have forgiven her. That doesn't mean I want to spend time with her." She grimaced. "This place is becoming oppressive. I still have nightmares about Lars on the mountain—threatening to do to me what he did to your dog. And people have been avoiding me since we got back—since the trial, that is."

"It wasn't a trial, Inga! It was an inquiry!"

"This is me you're talking to, Adrastas. You know as well as I do that it was a trial, whether you call it that or not. Everyone else knows it too."

"Then I'll bring everyone together and set them straight!"

"That would only make it worse. People would talk of nothing else for weeks."

Adrastas was becoming distressed, but she didn't care. She'd only gone after Lars and Petria because he wanted her to. He'd ignored her warnings, then he'd let loose the baying hounds on her when she got back.

"You released Lars and Petria on much flimsier grounds," she told him, "even after Lars killed your dog. If it will help, I'm willing to kill your cat if you have one."

He groaned. "All right. I admit defeat. I'll give you four weeks." He took a deep breath. "You're not going to want to hear this, Inga,..."

"Then don't say it!" she said, cutting him off.

She hurried away before he had time to get it out.

HAVING BEEN RELEASED from her duties in Cambrick, Inga was free at last to visit her old Aunt Jemilla. She had a standing invitation to stay whenever an opportunity arose, and she'd been putting it off for too long.

Her aunt lived in the town of Sengin in the southeastern corner of Periton. The town had taken its name from the nearby Sengin Pass, the site of a crucial battle in the war that followed the Great Desolation. The battle had assumed great significance for any Peritonian who cared about history, since it secured Periton's independence from Tantel. Inga had no interest in history. She was interested in Sengin for one reason only: it was about as far as you could get from Cambrick while still remaining in Periton.

Sengin had become a thriving seaport, which meant that the road to Cambrick was well maintained. For most of the year it could reasonably be expected to be in good condition. Inga had therefore decided to take a carriage. It was expensive, but she had never been extravagant, and there was little else to spend her coin on.

She was on her way less than twenty-four hours after Adrastas agreed to release her. Emmela had stopped by to wish her a good journey. Inga had responded politely; she wasn't yet able to be warm. Adrastas had called on her as well, and she had thanked him sincerely for making time in his busy schedule. No one else acknowledged her departure in any way. Given the circumstances, it didn't surprise her that a surge of relief washed over her as she rolled through the gates of Cambrick.

As her destination drew ever nearer she admitted to herself that, thus far at least, her escape had been less than she hoped for. She had expected to find it relaxing to watch the Peritonian countryside roll by from the window of her carriage. Instead, it had been bumpy and uncomfortable. Before a day had passed she was telling herself that she would never rent a carriage again without first checking the springs thoroughly. Her overnight stays in country inns had been passable, but none of the beds had been as comfortable as her own.

Most disappointing of all, leaving Cambrick had not brought release from the endless cycle of her thoughts and memories. So much about the fateful trip to the mountain still haunted her. She had stared death in the eye and survived. But her life had hung in the balance, dependent solely on the whim of a power-hungry and self-centered fool.

Never would she forget the surge of relief she had felt at Dalthinir's arrival. Nor her delight in the uninterrupted time, however brief, she spent in his presence tending to his wounds.

Upon her return, she had been required to reveal everything she learned about him and his apprentice. Every last detail. The information was being gathered for the sole purpose of tracking them down and destroying them. And they expected her to play a leading role in the hunt.

It was more than she could bear.

. . .

WHEN THE CARRIAGE rolled into the town of Sengin at last, Cambrick and its bitter associations were far away. For a while.

It had been years since she visited her aunt, and she had retained no clear memory of how to get to her house. The carriage driver needed to stop more than once to ask for directions before they found it.

By the time they pulled into the lane that led to her house, the day was almost spent. Climbing down wearily from the cabin, she was greeted by her aunt.

"Inga! What an unexpected pleasure! I was picking some flowers when I looked up and saw you in the carriage."

"It's been too long since I've visited, Aunt Jemilla. I've come hoping you'll let me stay for a few days."

"Of course! I'd be delighted! Come on in."

Leaving the coachman to bring in her bags, Inga followed her aunt inside. "Have you been well?" she asked.

"Very well, thank you. I have my daughter nearby, of course, and the grandchildren. The little ones aren't so little any more—all of them are growing up. I can take you to see them whenever you're up to it. In the meantime, come and sit down! I'll make us both a cup of tea."

Bustling Inga into her parlor, she placed her in the best chair. Then she disappeared into the kitchen, reappearing a few minutes later with hot tea and cake.

Inga was soon immersed in an entirely different world. It was a simpler world, with few complexities and no life-or-death issues to navigate. For the first time since the trauma on the mountain, she allowed herself to relax.

"THE MOUNTAINS ARE IMPRESSIVE!" Inga exclaimed, pointing to the distant peaks lining the horizon.

"They are," agreed her cousin Felicia with a smile.

As Aunt Jemilla's only daughter, Felicia saw a great deal of her mother. That was also giving Inga plenty of opportunity to connect with her. It had only taken a single day before the cousins were eagerly making up for lost time.

Felicia and her husband ran a farm that included a small herd of horses. On that occasion, Felicia had been released from her duties to escort Inga on a tour of Sengin and its surrounds. Two of her horses were making the excursion possible.

"Sengin Pass is off in that direction," Felicia reported.

"The site of the battle? I'm afraid battles don't interest me."

"What about the lake? Have you seen it before? It's worth at least one look into its dark waters."

"You mean the Lake of Death?"

Her cousin laughed. "That title is mainly used by locals. And usually to impress visitors." She grew serious. "Supposedly, there *are* monsters in it, though. There's good fishing in the lake, but the fishermen never venture far from shore. Even so, some do occasionally go missing."

Inga nodded readily. "The only monsters I've met have been human. I'd be happy to see something different for a change."

"I certainly don't expect to actually see any monsters. I'd be keeping my distance otherwise."

After the two of them had been riding for a few minutes, they came in sight of a small beach. One boat was drawn up on the sand, and three more were on the lake. All of them were quite close in to the shore.

"We'll buy some fresh fish for our dinner," said Felicia. Clicking her tongue, she guided her mount down onto the beach.

Inga's horse became increasingly nervous as they approached the water. In the end, she dismounted and led it.

Busy negotiating with a fisherman, Felicia looked up when Inga arrived. "I'm sorry," she said apologetically. "I should have warned you about the horses. None of them want to go anywhere near the lake. People say it's because they sense the monsters. If so, it's the only evidence of monsters I've ever encountered."

"Every boatman knows that the monsters are real," the fisherman assured her before retrieving a number of fresh fish.

Leaving her cousin to conclude the negotiations, Inga led the horse away from the beach and sat down on a hill overlooking the water.

As she relaxed in the sunshine, a sustained surge of power startled her out of her musing. Immediately alert, she used her farsense in an attempt to identify the source. It was coming from the lake, a considerable distance away. She didn't recognize the smell, so it wasn't Lars or Petria. It had to be a mage she didn't know.

What could it mean? Was a mage at that moment battling the monsters? The very idea of it seemed far-fetched.

More importantly, who was it? It was hard to imagine any reason why Dalthinir or Kylen might be out there.

Powerful as the burst of magic was, it was much too far from Cambrick to be detected there.

The thought raised a number of alarming possibilities. With no Compact mages permanently stationed in Sengin, power could be used indiscriminately without anyone in Cambrick knowing. It would be an ideal place for renegades like Lars and Petria to base themselves.

Further, Tantel was on the other side of the lake. If the Tantellans sent mages into Periton, no one in Cambrick would be aware of it.

She immediately realized she had a duty to notify Adrastas. With renegades on the loose and too many unanswered questions, it was about time he stationed Compact mages throughout the kingdom permanently, whether they liked it or not.

Inga was becoming restless by the time her cousin finalized her purchase.

"Fresh fish!" Felicia exclaimed. "I can't think of anything better. I'm sorry to say it, but we'll need to return fairly promptly, while it truly is fresh."

"That suits me," Inga replied. "I need to send a message to Cambrick."

Thankfully, her cousin showed no curiosity about the message. When they returned to Sengin, they went their separate ways.

After preparing a dispatch to Chief Master Adrastas, Inga entrusted it to the town officials. Then she returned to her aunt's to enjoy Felicia's fish.

• • •

WITH GOOD FOOD and pleasant company, the meal should have been relaxed and enjoyable. But with her senses fully alerted, Inga couldn't prevent herself from trying to sense the unknown mage. The surge of power had ended before the meal began, but only after drawing near to Sengin. That left her feeling more responsible than ever.

She hadn't been able to detect the mage's aura. Unlike the use of power, which she could smell over long distances, she could only sense glimmer if a mage was relatively nearby. That either meant this partic-ular mage was beyond her range, or, unlikely as it might be, they were somehow able to mask their aura.

She lay down that night undecided about how to respond to the situation. There was no way to tell what kind of power the mage had been using on the lake. It seemed likely they were using mage touch either to attack or to fend off predators. If so, they might be capable of the kind of assault threatened by Lars on the mountain. Approaching an unknown mage alone and without support would be folly.

What could she do? Eventually she drifted off to sleep with the words of Adrastas in her mind. Sending her after Lars and Petria, he had asked her merely to 'keep an eye' on them. In the morning she would do some searching. If she found a mage, she would do nothing more than observe them. Then she would send another report to Adrastas.

CHAPTER 3

"This spot seems isolated," the fisherman told Trisanna as he steered toward the beach. "That suits me. People will raise a ruckus if they hear about our voyage. I'd rather keep it quiet."

"Will you stay in Periton?" she asked.

He nodded. "I won't risk the monsters a second time. I suppose I could return to Tantel by sea, but there's no real reason for me to go back. It will be a pity to give up my boat, but I'm not frightened to try somethin' different. What about you?"

"I'll be staying! This is my chance at a new start. I'm not sure what I'll do, but I'll find something. It will help if you stay in Periton too," she said frankly. "The mages who pushed us into the lake will think we perished, which means they might stop chasing me."

Before he could ask why she was being chased, she added penitently, "I'm truly sorry for everything I've put you through! I've upended your life and taken away your livelihood. I can at least give you the money and the gold bar when we arrive. That should help get you a new start."

Seeing his uncertainty, she added, "Don't worry about me! I'll keep a few coins—enough to last until I find something to do."

The moment he landed the boat Trisanna stepped nimbly onto the sand. Closing her eyes, she slowly released a deep sigh of relief.

Once he had pulled the vessel clear of the water, she fulfilled her promise and gave him most of the coins and the gold bar. The jewel she kept for herself.

"What's your name?" he asked.

"Trisanna," she replied. "What's yours?"

"I'm known as Zeke," he said with a bow. "I don't know if it will be safe for you to go wandering around on your own, Trisanna." He peered at her shyly. "We can be father and daughter if you like. You can go off on your own whenever you're ready, of course."

She brightened immediately. "Thank you, Zeke. Or perhaps I should say, Father," she added with a self-conscious smile. "You're very kind."

Zeke retrieved anything useful from the boat. Then, turning their backs on the lake and its horrors, they headed inland into Periton, daring to hope for better things.

REACHING the top of another hill, Trisanna paused to catch her breath. She felt tired. After leaving the lake they had headed west until the sun set. They had slept in the open among some trees.

She had never slept on the ground before. Having done so, she wasn't eager to repeat the experience. The ground had been hard and uncomfortable—nothing like the soft feather bed she was accustomed to.

Physical discomfort hadn't been the only reason she tossed and turned all night. Her restless mind had been reliving the trauma of fleeing on horseback from the only home she had known, followed immediately by the horror of her ordeal on the lake.

It was hardly surprising she had slept badly.

Zeke came to a halt beside her. He didn't have a lot to say, but she didn't mind. She was grateful for his willingness to listen to her steady flow of words.

"I miss my horse," she said ruefully. "I'm starting to become hungry too. Do you think we're heading in the right direction to find a settlement?"

He shrugged. "I imagine we'll find other people soon enough." From his tone, he seemed to think they might well regret it when they did.

THE SUN WAS RIDING HIGH in the sky when Zeke said to her quietly, "We're being watched." He jerked his head toward a ridge to the north of them.

Spinning around, she immediately began waving her arms excitedly.

"Apparently you never learned to be cautious around strangers," he mumbled, rolling his eyes.

"Surely you don't think we can be at any risk here," she said in surprise.

"That's coming from a person who saw no risk in sailing to Periton," he replied gruffly.

She blushed. "You're right, of course. I will try to be more careful in future."

"I meant no harm," he said hastily. "I just don't want to see you hurt."

"Don't worry," she assured him with a smile. "I'm more resilient than I probably look."

As they had been talking, a horse picked its way down from the ridge. A plainly dressed woman was riding it. She appeared to be middle-aged.

"Our greetings!" called Trisanna enthusiastically the moment the woman was within range. "Is there a market nearby?"

Hearing a groan from Zeke beside her, she abruptly fell silent.

"Where are you from?" the rider asked cautiously. "You seem new to these parts."

"We're from the Summer Isles," Zeke replied with a low bow. "Our accents must sound strange to you. My daughter and I were fishing when the weather turned rough. We were able to land near here. We have coin to pay for plain food and somewhere to lay our heads."

"My name is Trisanna, and this is my father, Zeke," Trisanna added brightly. After a furtive nudge from Zeke she subsided again.

The stranger had appeared very uncertain, but she seemed to reach a decision.

"Come with me," she said. "The town of Sengin isn't far away. You should be able to find what you need there."

"Thank you!" said Trisanna, making no attempt to hide her relief. She set off after the horse, Zeke close behind her.

"Do many people live in Sengin?" she asked.

"A few thousand," the woman replied.

"So many!" said Trisanna. "It must be a great city!"

The older woman was smiling in spite of herself. "It's small compared to Cambrick, our capital."

"Oh!" said Trisanna in wonder. She beamed back a smile of her own, grateful to find her mind moving in less gloomy directions at last.

"You look tired," said the woman.

She sighed. "We slept in the open last night. It was the first time I've done that. I didn't enjoy it very much."

"I'm sure something more comfortable can be arranged for tonight," the woman said kindly. Her initial stiffness had vanished entirely. "My name is Inga. I don't live in Sengin. I'm only visiting—staying with my aunt. She will be able to help you decide what to do. She baked a very delicious cake yesterday, too. Quite a lot of it still needs to be eaten."

Trisanna could feel her eyes widening.

Seeing it, Inga laughed cheerfully. "I think my aunt is going to like you."

INGA'S INSTINCT had been right. From the way Aunt Jemilla took to Trisanna, she might have been a long-lost niece. By the time they had put away two helpings of cake and freshly baked scones, washed down with plenty of hot tea, everyone had become very relaxed together.

"I didn't see much firewood on the pile," observed Zeke quietly.

"That particular task brings out the worst in me," sighed Aunt Jemilla. "These old bones don't enjoy chopping anymore."

With a quick nod, Zeke disappeared outside. Rhythmic sounds of chopping soon drifted in from the yard.

"He's a good man, your father!" the older woman exclaimed.

"He is indeed," confirmed Trisanna with a faint blush. "He's very kind."

It was becoming obvious to Inga that she'd been over-cautious when first searching for the unknown mage. She had quickly identified Trisanna's aura, and it hadn't taken long to find her. Once they met, she soon warmed to the girl. Trisanna's childhood must have been unusually sheltered. Sweet and unspoiled, she was clearly no threat to anyone.

According to Inga's best guess, she was a Compact mage from Tantel. Whether she was there with official approval or not, it was impossible to imagine any nefarious purpose behind her presence.

With her father busy chopping wood, a perfect opportunity had arisen to find out more. Inga rose to her feet. "Thank you, Aunt! You're a wonderful cook and a gracious host."

Then she turned to Trisanna with a smile. "Would you like to walk in the sunshine with me?"

"Gladly!" came the unhesitating reply.

The two of them set off, wandering through the fields near Aunt Jemilla's house.

Inga decided to come straight to the point. "Are you a member of the Compact in Antilin, Trisanna?"

The girl stared back at her wide-eyed. "Wh...why are you asking?" she managed.

Inga smiled. "It's obvious that you're a mage, and you're not from Periton. And I've never heard of mages in the Summer Isles."

A deep blush had covered the girl's face. It wasn't embarrassment. She was frightened.

Inga's smile faded. Something wasn't right.

"Are you a Tantellan renegade?" she asked bluntly.

"I'm no renegade," the girl protested. Then she added meekly, "Not by choice, anyway."

"Are you a Compact mage?"

She shook her head.

"Why are you here?"

The girl looked at her uncertainly.

"I'm not planning to harm you, Trisanna. And I can't help you unless I know what's going on."

After staring at Inga for a moment, she seemed to come to a decision. "They were trying to kill me. Not because I did anything bad! Just because of who I am. So I fled. There was nothing else I could do."

"Who was trying to kill you?"

"The mages in Tantel."

Inga covered her face with her hands. A new renegade was standing before her. Another person to be destroyed—not because of what she had done, but because of what she was. How could it all be happening again?

"How did you know I was a mage?" Trisanna asked, her voice trembling.

"You truly don't know?"

She shook her head.

"By definition, a mage is a person who can detect the use of magical power in others. I am a mage, so I detected your use of power on the lake. I happen to be one of the few mages in Periton who can also detect magical auras, which we also call magical glimmer, or just glimmer. That means I can detect the presence of magic in a mage, even without them having used magical power. That's how I found you earlier."

Trisanna was holding her head in bewilderment. "Just lately I've known about it when mages used power near me. But I haven't seen you using power. How can that be if you're a mage?"

"I could be the most powerful mage in the world, but until I use that power other mages won't be able to detect me. Unless it's someone like me who can detect magical auras. I'm unusual in another respect as well. Detecting both glimmer and the use of power is my only magical ability. The use of that kind of ability is undetectable by other mages. So you could say I'm an invisible mage. I can sense others, but no one can sense me. Not unless they can detect magical auras."

"I have so much to learn! Could you teach me?"

The girl's pleading eyes wrenched Inga's heart. But she couldn't do it. She'd been in trouble merely for talking to Dalthinir and tending his wounds. Even though he and Kylen had just saved the kingdom.

She sighed deeply. "I think you'd better tell me your story, Trisanna."

The girl nodded compliantly. Sitting down beside the older mage in a meadow, surrounded by wildflowers, she began.

"I grew up on a remote farm in Tantel. My parents loved me and provided for me, and I was very happy there. I once overheard a private conversation between my parents in which they bemoaned the fact that it would never be safe for me to raise a family of my own. I didn't understand what they were saying, but I was young enough that I didn't dwell on it. There was plenty to occupy me growing up.

"I might have remained on the farm until I grew old and died, except that something strange happened one night. I found out later I'd experienced a magical awakening.

"One day I was helping myself to some fresh cream when my mother came in. I was embarrassed because I hadn't asked first, and I wished she couldn't see me. To my astonishment, that's exactly what happened. I was amazed. I then wished she could see me, and she shrieked in surprise when I suddenly appeared. She was very alarmed by what had happened. I couldn't understand why—I thought it was exciting!"

She shook her head sadly. "My parents came to me that night and told me the truth. They said I'd become a mage, and that my magical ability was illusion. They said it would get me into serious trouble. I promised not to use it anymore, but they said it wouldn't make any difference. I didn't fully understand at the time. But I understand now, after what you told me. Sooner or later I'd have been found out even if I never used magic at all."

Tears came to her eyes. "That wasn't the end of it. They told me they weren't my natural parents. They said they couldn't have loved me more if I'd been their child. I believe them too! They were always wonderful to me. They said I was the daughter of the previous king of Tantel, King Nolan. He'd had a brief affair late in his life, and I was the result. He never knew he made the woman pregnant. For my own safety, she sent me away as soon as I was born."

Inga was wide-eyed now. "So you're the half-sister of the current king?"

She nodded. "I used to think my parents were overprotective, but I understand why now. They told me if the king ever found out he had a half sister, he would kill me without hesitation. Everyone knows he isn't a good man. That's why they thought it wouldn't be safe for me to have a family. Any children I had would be related to the king, and that would complicate things even more—for me and for them.

"That was only the beginning. They told me my birth mother was a mage. That's why I have magical powers. Apparently members of the royal family and mages aren't supposed to have children together. It threatens the stability of the kingdom or something. And it got even worse. It wasn't just the king who would want me dead. They told me the mages would want to kill me too—because they hadn't been involved in my magical awakening."

The tears were flowing now. "Not long after that people came looking for me. I don't know how they found out about me or where I was living. I hid myself using magic and they went away. I suppose none of them could have been mages, because they didn't detect what I was doing. But they said mages would be there soon. My parents gave me a horse and some valuables and told me to flee for my life. They'd try to cover for me as long as they could. I could see that I was putting them at great risk by staying there, so I left immediately. Hopefully they're safe now that I'm gone.

"I decided my only chance was to get to Periton, so I headed for the lake. I'd heard about the monsters, but I thought it was just talk.

"The mages must have arrived at the farm not long after I left, because they were never far behind me. When I reached the lake I met Zeke. He's a fisherman. He's also very kind. I convinced him to take me out on his boat. Then the mages arrived. When they saw us in the boat, they used magic to push us away from the shore. They must have expected the monsters would get us. And that's very nearly what happened!"

She had gone pale. "It was terrible! The monsters are worse than any nightmare. We only escaped because I hid us with illusion."

She peered at Inga with pleading eyes. "I came to Periton so people wouldn't chase me anymore. All I want is to live a quiet life. I'm not a bad person, Inga! Truly I'm not!"

Inga opened her arms wide and drew her in. Then she held her tightly. The unexpected sympathy undid the girl completely, and she wept loudly, her body shaking with her sobs. Inga continued to hold her. Her own insides were twisting unmercifully. She didn't doubt for a minute that the girl was telling the truth.

It was heart wrenching. To the royals of Tantel, Trisanna was a cast-off, an inconvenient disruption to the official bloodlines. To the mages of both kingdoms she was an outcast, a magical threat to the established order. She was another person with nothing but death to look forward to, a death she had done nothing to deserve.

Why did it have to be Inga who found her?

The more important question was why people had to be destroyed solely because of who they were. Her whole being rebelled against the inhumanity of it.

She could not and would not allow it to happen. She decided at that moment she would not rest until she found a way to save the Tantellan reject.

CHAPTER 4

Two months earlier

The night was well advanced when a loud voice startled the chief master of Tantel into wakefulness. Sitting up abruptly, he peered around in the dark. He saw nothing out of the ordinary. The isolation of his tower room made it unlikely that anyone had called from nearby. Had it been a dream?

Climbing out of his bed, Kharkin lit a candle and swung open the heavy wooden door of his room. He found no one lurking on the stairs. The air outside the room was bitingly cold, prompting him to hastily close the door again and reach for his robe.

Cold seemed to ooze perpetually from the tower walls in defiance of the seasons. Pulling his robe closer around him, he moved to one of the narrow windows and gazed down at the city of Antilin, the capital of Tantel. Heavy cloud cover made it the blackest of nights, with the darkness punctuated only by the tiny lights flickering below.

Turning his back on the window, he returned his thoughts to the mysterious voice, still clear in his mind. "Seek the amulet!" it had urged.

Where had the voice come from? What could it have meant? He wondered if his imagination had been playing games with him.

Only one amulet came readily to mind. The Amulet of Zinth was reputed to bestow great powers on the bearer. Any mage capable of mastering it could supposedly face a tidal wave without flinching.

But it had long been lost. To the best of his knowledge, it had not been sighted since before the Great Desolation.

Something was niggling away at the back of his mind, but he was unable to grasp hold of it and bring it into the open. It had something to do with an old document, but beyond that he could be certain of nothing. After wrestling with it for a few minutes, he shook his head in frustration. It probably just needed time, but he had never been a patient man.

It must have been two or three hours before dawn, and for a moment he considered returning to bed. But he quickly acknowledged to himself he had little chance of getting back to sleep. His ever-restless mind was hard at work, preoccupied with the amulet.

With a grunt of resignation he dressed and headed for the stairs. After reaching the bottom he set out for the massive building that housed the library of Tantel's Compact. It was closed and locked for the night, but as head mage he had a key that gave access through the rear entrance. As soon as he was inside, he snuffed out his candle and searched for a glow globe to replace it.

Candlelight was, of course, strictly forbidden in the library due to the risk of fire. Mages had instead devised a simple but effective alternative. Constructed from thick glass shaped into a sphere and mounted on a sturdy wooden stand, the glow globe emanated light from a radiant ball of fire within.

The luminance from his globe was noticeably feeble, but replenishing it was a simple task given his elements ability with fire.

The library had a basement that housed the oldest records, and he set off toward the narrow wooden staircase at the rear of the building. Holding his glow globe high, he slowly descended. Navigating stairs without handrails was always going to be hazardous, even with light to penetrate the darkness. He discovered he'd been holding his breath when he heaved a sigh of relief upon reaching the bottom.

The basement was large and only partially organized. Immediately before him, countless scrolls and stacked parchments sat neatly on shelves that reached to the ceiling. The rear section of the basement was a different matter. Strewn with old scrolls and parchments, it must have been the only part of the library untouched by the librarian.

Seeing the chaos once more, Kharkin shook his head. It was time he did something about it.

It wasn't difficult to guess at the reason for the disorder. This place almost reeked of the current librarian's predecessor. The man had been her mentor, and it was widely accepted that she revered him. He had died at a good old age, but with his mind undimmed to the end.

The oldest manuscripts lay in an untidy heap in the far corner of the room, and he decided to begin exploring in that location.

Many of the documents were difficult to read, either because the writing had faded, or because the paper—or animal skin in the case of parchments—had become fragile with age. He could almost hear the librarian fussing over the delicate condition of the records, even in her absence. He was extremely careful, so she would have had no reason to worry.

The task quickly became tedious. Too often, after a long struggle to decipher the writing on the latest document, he found its subject matter of no interest whatever. All he could do was set it down carefully and retrieve another. His biggest challenge was the lack of any clear idea about what he was looking for.

He'd been at it for a couple of hours when he finally called to mind what he'd been trying to remember.

Supposedly, the previous librarian had stumbled upon forbidden documents. Kharkin had been a young mage at the time, and he'd found the very idea of it tantalizing. Forbidden documents suggested dragon magic. It was widely accepted that human magic had its origin with dragons, and even in the absence of dragons, no one doubted that dragon magic held the potential to greatly magnify mage abilities. He felt sure there'd also been some mention of the Amulet of Zinth, although he had never heard more than that.

The fuss had quickly gone quiet. As head mage he well understood what must have happened. The chief master at the time would have immediately ordered the documents to be destroyed.

But what if that had never happened? If anyone had sought to preserve them, it would have been the librarian. Librarians had a reputation of abhorring even the notion of destroying documents, especially old documents. If they still survived, it would be because the librarian had hidden them somewhere.

After a couple of hours of searching, Kharkin discovered a manuscript authored by Master Arbilis. He had been chief master in the Methesian capital, Ettaran, at the time of the Great Desolation, when dragons had turned on humans. The writing was so faint it was barely legible. It was titled, *Magical Governance, by Master Arbilis*.

Kharkin began reading slowly.

> *A head mage is pressed upon by many challenges, not least the oversight of magical expression in a kingdom where magical ability is entirely absent in most of the population, including every member of the royal family. The question of bloodlines is a matter of cruciality. The prohibition of intermarriage between royalty and families with mage abilities has preserved the boundaries between political power and magical power. It has also been vital for stability in the kingdom. At the same time it has raised a number of challenging issues. For the sake of those who come after me, I have decided to record my thoughts on these and other key issues related to magical governance.*

As HEAD MAGE, such a document ought to be of interest to him. Nevertheless, he discarded it at once and returned to the search.

Three hours of frustration lay behind him when he stood up to stretch his legs. By then dawn must have been close. Wandering about aimlessly, he found himself in a corner of the room covered with old manuscripts. Pushing them aside moodily with one foot, he stepped into the corner and leaned against the wall.

As his foot landed, the floorboard creaked. Curious, he planted his foot again. The floor was definitely creaking. A quick check of the surrounding floorboards showed no such effect.

Greatly intrigued, he knelt to examine the floorboard. It was loose.

After trial and error he discovered a way to lever up the loose floorboard. With growing excitement he pulled it free and peered into the gap below. His glow globe revealed a small mound of documents. Reaching in carefully, he gingerly grasped the document on top of the pile and lifted it clear of its hiding place.

It was a parchment made of animal skin, cracked with age, with words still visible on its surface. With trembling hands, he brought it closer to the light, focusing his attention entirely on the spindly script before him. Unfamiliar at first, the words began to make sense once he recognized familiar characters in the flowery handwriting. The document opened with the following lines.

> *Ode to the Fallen One is a perilous tome. To open it is enough to release power beyond the comprehension of any human mage. Any who dares read it cannot emerge unchanged.*

THE DOCUMENT IT REFERRED TO, *Ode to the Fallen One*, was almost legendary. It was also very much banned. Kharkin felt certain he had stumbled on a treasure trove of forbidden documents, almost certainly the one that had caused so much consternation during his early years as a mage. As head mage his duty was to destroy them. He had no intention of doing so.

The faintest of glows had begun to penetrate the basement. Dawn must have broken.

He ground his teeth in irritation, knowing he could be disturbed at any moment. His only option was to come back to view these documents at a later time.

Replacing the parchment, he returned the loose floorboard to its original position. Then he did his best to return the corner of the room to the state in which he had found it.

He had no desire to explain to the librarian why he was there. Hurrying up the stairs as quickly as he dared, he extinguished his glow globe and unlocked the back door.

He was barely in time. Sunlight was shining brightly, and the librarian was arriving as he hurried away. She called to him cheerily. "You're up and about early, Chief Master!"

Waving without bothering to reply, he hurried back to his tower.

The day that followed couldn't end soon enough for Kharkin. His meetings felt interminable, and he became increasingly ill humored as the day progressed. Even after night had fallen he forced himself to wait.

He finally returned to the library at a little before midnight. Letting himself in, he headed for the basement.

He had barely arrived when he saw another glow globe waving up and down as it descended the stairs.

"Chief Master! I didn't expect to see you here at such an hour."

The librarian was smiling, but he was left in no doubt that she was there to keep watch over her domain. Her vigilance could only have been prompted by his unannounced visit earlier that day.

"Can I help you locate anything in particular?"

"I have vague memories of an old document on the topic of magical governance. I thought it might be of some interest. I couldn't sleep last night, and early this morning I decided to look for it. Without success, unfortunately." It was fortunate indeed that he had glimpsed this particular document on his previous visit.

She revealed no sign of suspicion at his smoothly delivered lies. "Perhaps I can help," she offered.

Stepping past him, she found her way to the right general area. After selecting and discarding no more than four or five manuscripts, she held one up. "Was it written by Master Arbilis?"

"It was!" he agreed, hoping he didn't look as disgruntled as he felt.

She handed it to him. "As you know, it isn't permitted to remove old documents from the library. I'm happy to wait while you read it, though."

Retrieving a stool, she parked herself on it and sat watching him.

Had his reason for being there been legitimate, he never would have tolerated her officiousness. He had the feeling she knew it, too.

He read the document carefully, even while his mind was busy working over possible plans. When he reached the end, he returned it to her.

"It was stimulating to read Master Arbilis's insights. He had some useful things to say," he observed.

"Which section did you find most illuminating?" she asked innocently.

"The passage near the end where he noted the slow but steady decline over many generations in the proportion of the human population exhibiting magical abilities."

She nodded. "If I remember correctly, he said the proportion of mages had decreased by one third over the previous hundred years."

"He said the decrease was by one quarter," he corrected her.

"Ah. I'm sure you're right," she said.

If she hoped to test whether he had given the document more than a cursory glance, she was wasting her time. He had an unusual gift— one that allowed him to visualize precisely any document he had seen. A single viewing was enough.

What was more remarkable was that she not only knew where to find the document he asked for, she had read it and remembered it well enough to recall its contents.

There was more to her than he had guessed. He felt sure she knew about the hidden documents. Why else was she hovering protectively in the basement? He didn't doubt she would check to see if he removed them.

Fortunately for him, removing them wasn't actually necessary. He only needed to view them. His exceptional memory would allow him to revisit them whenever it suited him.

The real risk was making her suspicious. If she thought he had discovered the documents, or even that he was likely to, she would almost certainly relocate them. He couldn't afford to let that happen.

He saw only one way forward. He would need to avoid the library completely until her suspicions faded.

CHAPTER 5

Although Kharkin desperately wanted to visit the library basement again, he knew he needed to back off. It was the only way he could allay whatever suspicions the librarian might be entertaining. Having made the decision, he left nothing to chance. Hiring someone to watch the building, he monitored the comings and goings of the librarian. He therefore had no difficulty identifying the moment when she began to relax her previously heightened vigilance.

He noted with considerable interest that the process had taken the best part of a month. There must surely have been a reason for her to show such dogged persistence. He became more certain than ever that she was aware of the forbidden documents and was determined to preserve them.

It would be a disaster if they were discovered, especially by the head mage. Although she could reasonably hope to avoid trouble by disclaiming all knowledge of them, the law required the documents to be destroyed immediately.

He had no intention of destroying them, of course, but she had no way of knowing that. And he couldn't tell her. It would undermine his position irretrievably if anyone found out what he was doing.

After allowing another two days to elapse for good measure, he crept to the library in the early hours of the morning. To his relief he found the documents still hidden in the same location. After removing and examining each of them in turn, he was confident he had committed them to memory. Returning them to their hiding place, he departed the basement after doing his best to leave it as he had found it.

Given the librarian's close scrutiny of his visits, it occurred to him she probably had her own ways of monitoring activity in the basement. Perhaps she left a parchment lying in a precise position. She would know someone had been there if she later found it moved.

With this in mind he returned to the library very early the next morning, keeping watch so he could enter at the same time as the librarian. Making his way to the basement, he was not surprised when she immediately followed him down the steps.

"How can I help you, Chief Master?" she asked in great alarm as he blundered about, picking up and discarding documents from one end of the basement to the other.

"I wanted to refer one more time to that parchment authored by Master Arbilis, but I can't seem to find it."

"Please stop! Let me do it!" It took her just moments to locate it and hand it to him. "I would be grateful if you would ask for help another time!" she said, frowning fiercely.

"My apologies!" he replied. "I will certainly call on you should I ever need to find something down here again."

After perusing the document briefly, he handed it back with a nod of thanks. Then he headed for the stairs.

If her reaction offered any indication, he had done a thorough job of covering his tracks. More than satisfied, he flashed her a genial smile as he departed.

A BUSY DAY lay behind the head mage when he finally retired to his room, eager to direct his full attention to his discoveries. Even without fully absorbing the detailed content of the documents he could see there was a great deal to be learned from them. His attention had been drawn at once to the reference to *Ode to the Fallen One*. The parchment had disclosed the location of the lost book in a remote corner of Periton, and it had also revealed that it could only be accessed during a total solar eclipse. He had found time to establish that the next occurrence would not occur for many years. It was disappointing, but there was plenty else to be excited about.

His search had originally been prompted by a desire to learn about the Amulet of Zinth, and incredibly, the hoard had included a document that spoke of the talisman. The document's revelations could only be described as startling. It described the amulet as surpassingly powerful, which came as no surprise. The most astonishing discovery was that it had not been lost at all. It had been entrusted to the first king of Tantel after the chaos of the Great Desolation. The monarch had in turn passed it down to his descendants.

Leaving such a talisman in the hands of royalty made no sense to Kharkin. Only a mage could use it, and no royal had ever been a mage.

A law had been enacted generations earlier, one that ensured no mage could wear the crown. The goal was to ensure stability by preventing political power and magical power from being concentrated in a single person. No one wanted to see an all-powerful despot on the throne.

He wondered if the purpose of handing the amulet to the king had been to prevent any mage from using it, perhaps reflecting a view that it was dangerous to concentrate too much power in a single pair of hands. If so, the goal had been achieved. Nevertheless, Kharkin intended to do everything in his power to gain control of the talisman.

The first challenge was to find out where the amulet was. If it was in the possession of King Garneth, the current ruler of Tantel, he felt sure he would have known. Was it locked away in a vault somewhere? Or had it been given to someone else? He intended to spare no effort in finding out.

It helped that Kharkin had been head mage for well over a decade. His tentacles were spread far and wide throughout the institutions of Tantel, and he moved quickly to put his contacts to work.

Within three days he knew that the amulet had last been seen in the reign of King Nolan, the father of Garneth, the current king. It took another two weeks before he uncovered information about the affair late in King Nolan's life that had resulted in an illegitimate daughter.

The baby had been well hidden. It proved necessary to resort to torture before he extracted the information that the amulet had been entrusted to her guardians. A woman had died in a vain attempt to conceal the truth.

Almost two months had passed since he heard the voice urging him to find the amulet. He now knew at least the general locality where King Nolan's secret daughter could be found. He fully expected to find the amulet at the same location.

There would be no question about her fate once he had retrieved the amulet. King Garneth would heartily approve of killing her. In fact, he would demand her immediate execution. Whether or not the law prevented her from taking the crown, he would regard her as having the potential to one day threaten his sovereignty.

He hastily called for Master Pernilla. Far from the most powerful mage in Tantel's Compact, she was nevertheless both capable and effective. She was also willing to be ruthless if necessary. People followed where she led, and if they didn't, she wasn't frightened to knock a few heads together. Over time she had become the most trusted of his deputies.

"Assemble a team, Pernilla, and do it quickly! I want your best people on it. I've received some disturbing news. Not only did the king's father have an illegitimate daughter late in life, she's still alive."

Shock showed on his deputy's face. "Does the king know about this?"

Kharkin shook his head. "He has no idea. The girl must be disposed of as a matter of urgency! But only after you've recovered an item of considerable value. An amulet—previously in the possession of the late king—was sent into hiding with her. I want it!"

"An amulet?" After a moment of incomprehension, Pernilla stared at him in disbelief. "You can't mean..."

"That's exactly what I mean! The Amulet of Zinth is not lost as has been believed. I've sent a small team into the region to find her exact location. Report to me as soon as you're ready to leave. I should have more information by then."

Pernilla hurried away after a brief nod.

A member of the team sent by Kharkin arrived not long after she had left.

"Did you find the girl?" the head mage demanded.

"We found the farm where she has been living, but she wasn't there. Someone must have warned her we were coming. She was probably hiding somewhere nearby."

Kharkin scowled. "Stay within easy reach. Master Pernilla is assembling a team of mages. You will guide them to the location."

The man withdrew with a bow.

The chief master would have gone himself if his health had allowed it. Nevertheless, he had appointed Pernilla for good reason, and his deputy pursued her preparations with energy. A formidable team of mages was on its way to the farm before noon the following day.

Their destination was located a considerable distance from the capital, and Kharkin did not expect to hear anything for a couple of days at least. For an entire afternoon he wandered about, restless and on edge. Eventually he gave up any attempt to find useful ways of occupying himself.

That night he fell into a deep sleep, and sometime in the early hours of the morning he dreamed. Even within its grip he knew it to be a dream, although it was unlike any dream he had experienced. It felt too real.

He found himself standing in the streets of an abandoned city. Spinning slowly around, he took it in. The city was expansive. Municipal buildings surrounded him on every side, and beyond them, dwellings stretched into the far distance.

Somehow he knew he was standing in the ruins of Ettaran, capital of the once-prosperous kingdom of Methesia. Long years ago a catastrophe had denuded the city of life—a disaster that came to be known as the Great Desolation. No living being had dared to cross its borders for longer than anyone could remember.

For reasons he didn't understand, almost every structure appeared to be intact. However, the city had by no means escaped the fabled desolation. No bird winged its way through the air, and no animal scurried across the empty streets. It was devoid even of vegetation. The emptiness and the silence overwhelmed and oppressed him.

"Enter the Great Library," said a dispassionate voice. He recognized the voice. It had urged him to seek the amulet.

Even in his dream state his heart skipped a beat at the prospect. The Great Library of Ettaran had been a glittering jewel, a source of wonder, not just for its architecture but for the treasures stored within it. Written records ancient and modern rested beside books and scrolls of every imaginable style, topic, and manufacture. It featured sculpture and art, zoological and botanic exhibits, relics from the past, and artifacts and memorabilia. No equivalent collection existed in the known world.

A separate wing maintained by the Compact boasted an unrivaled accumulation of knowledge on every imaginable aspect of magic, human and draconic. Mages in Tantel and Periton still mourned its loss.

Kharkin did not know his way about the city, but so great was the renown of the library that he was able to identify it without difficulty. Climbing the wide marble steps that graced the entrance, he stepped inside. The elaborately carved wooden doors that guarded the building gaped wide, as if careless of their duty.

Without needing to be directed, he followed a sign toward the library of the Compact. In the absence of lighting the corridor should have been dark, but in the dream it was illuminated by unknown means.

Reaching his destination he found everything in perfect order. It was as if the librarian had just left without closing the doors. Before he could reach for any of a large number of books that beckoned, the voice spoke again. "Go to the top level," it intoned.

Obediently he headed for a broad set of stairs off to one side that led upward. Light spilled freely down the staircase from above, and he ascended with considerable curiosity. Upon reaching the level above, he found himself in a huge reading room filled with desks and comfortable chairs. Large windows gave views of the city in every direction. At the far end of the room he saw more stairs, and he set off toward them, climbing them without the need for further instruction.

A large darkened room awaited him at the top of the stairs. A sign labeled it an observatory. Stepping into the room he was greeted by an unearthly glow, and almost without conscious thought he headed in the direction of its source. He soon found himself confronted by a huge glowing sphere, considerably taller than he was. Colors rippled across its surface in a mesmerizing pattern. He leaned slowly forward, reaching out to touch it.

"Keep back!" ordered the voice. "Touch it and die."

Drawing away hastily, he examined it more closely. It appeared to be a transparent sphere enclosing uncounted thousands of worms, no thicker than a twig and colored in every imaginable hue. The worms were racing about frenetically, as if desperate to find a way out.

"What is it?" he asked aloud.

The voice answered immediately. "It is pure magic, concentrated and contained." The voice seemed to sigh. "It was trapped here during the Great Desolation, prevented by dark forces from making its way throughout the world as it should. You may have wondered why mages today are weaker than their forebears, why their magic is unnaturally constrained. The magic before you is their birthright. Only by releasing it can magic fully permeate the world once more, as rain soaks the barren ground to bring new life."

"Who are you, and why are you telling me this?"

"One who desires only to see the world renewed. Some might be willing to watch passively until the sun grows cold and magic fades from the earth. But not I."

"How can I release the magic?"

"Only the Amulet of Zinth will give you the means. With it you can reach Ettaran unharmed and release the power. The amulet will awaken in your hands, and in your hands alone. You must bring it to the library in Ettaran! Embrace your destiny! Only you can restore the balance."

"I do not yet have the amulet. What if I am unable to retrieve it?"

The voice became a growl. "Spare no effort to recover it. Do not allow petty scruples to stand in the way of the greater good."

. . .

KHARKIN SAT UP WITH A START, the dream still clear in his memory. It could scarcely have been more real if he had visited Ettaran in the flesh.

He had been determined to find the amulet even before the dream. Recovering it now became an obsession.

CHAPTER 6

Inga's aunt had no hesitation in offering both Trisanna and Zeke a bed for the night.

Zeke had won Aunt Jemilla over completely. After chopping a substantial pile of wood, he noticed water stains in the kitchen ceiling. Before long he was on the roof repairing leaks.

She was no less taken with Trisanna. The girl had an innocent freshness about her that delighted the older lady.

As they were about to settle for the night Inga whispered to the young mage, "Sleep well. I'll do everything in my power to find a way to help you."

It was one thing to promise help, and another thing entirely to follow through on it. As Inga prepared to sleep she faced the difficulties confronting her. Trisanna couldn't simply settle in Periton as she had hoped for the simple reason that she couldn't hide her magical aura. Inga had long suspected that Dalthinir was capable of doing it. But if so, he was unique. As far as she knew no one else could achieve it.

Inga was not the only mage in Periton who could detect magical auras. If one of the others came upon Trisanna she would be exposed as a renegade, even if she never used magic again.

The situation had been further complicated by Inga herself. Before too many more days had passed, a strong contingent of mages was going to arrive in Sengin, ready to confront an unknown mage. If Inga hadn't found a way to help Trisanna by then, it would be too late.

A crisis was looming. What she could do to resolve it was far from obvious.

Inga woke to a day of cheerful sunshine. Before it came to an end, Aunt Jemilla had offered Zeke and Trisanna a permanent home. Zeke had already agreed to do some maintenance work for a friend of Jemilla's, and it was becoming apparent he would readily be able to support himself.

A small cottage lay behind Jemilla's residence. With a little work it could accommodate both Zeke and his daughter. They could join Aunt Jemilla for meals, and in return Zeke could help out on the property as needed. Zeke gratefully accepted the offer.

Trisanna was no less eager. With disaster drawing ever closer, Inga did the only thing she could. Taking the young mage aside, she told her that mages would soon arrive from Periton expecting trouble, that others besides Inga were capable of sensing magical auras, and that in Periton no less than in Tantel, Trisanna would be regarded as a renegade worthy of death.

"What can I do?" Trisanna asked in dismay.

"To begin with, you need to let Aunt Jemilla know that Zeke isn't your father. Tell her the truth—that you were vulnerable and he offered to pose as your father to protect you. Then you'll need to tell them both that you'll be leaving sometime soon. It isn't safe to explain why. Neither of them can know you're a mage."

Tears were running freely down Trisanna's face.

"We don't have much time," said Inga grimly. "It's far from obvious where you can go to be safe, and there's little I can do to help you in the longer term, much as I want to. I know of only one person we can turn to. I can't say where he is or how we can find him, but we need to make contact somehow. And it has to be in the next few days before the mages from Cambrick arrive.

"Like you, he's a renegade, and he doesn't deserve the title any more than you do. His name is Dalthinir."

THE RIDERS SPLASHED across a ford and spurred their horses onto the opposite bank. They didn't pause to rest when they reached it. Kothlar intended his group to reach Sengin as soon as possible. Chief Master Adrastas had emphasized the importance of responding at once to the magical incursion in Sengin reported by Master Inga.

Adrastas had also contacted his Tantellan counterparts in case a mage had arrived in Periton on legitimate business. It seemed highly unlikely. Protocol required either party to request official permission from the other kingdom before sending a mage into their territory for any reason.

If it wasn't a member of the Tantellan Compact, who was it? Had it been Lars or Petria, Inga would have recognized their magical footprint at once. Dalthinir and Kylen were less easy to identify, but Kothlar had a feeling that Inga would have known if it were them.

That suggested an entirely new mage—possibly a Tantellan renegade. Inga had no way of defending herself against aggressive magic, which was a key reason why Kothlar was leading a team that boasted a strong set of abilities.

They had been riding through the daylight hours and camping out overnight, and all of them were weary. The day had almost ended when they found themselves within reach of Sengin at last. Kothlar decided to allow them a good sleep that night in return for an early start in the morning. They didn't know what the morrow would bring, but it was better to face uncertainties fresh.

The first thing would be to locate Master Inga. He had no idea where she was staying, but the town officials must know, because she had arranged for them to send the dispatch to the chief master on her behalf. He would begin the search there.

Difficult as Inga's request was for Trisanna, she did what had been asked of her.

"It's time I told you the truth," she said to Aunt Jemilla, her face red with embarrassment. "Zeke isn't my father! He's a fisherman who helped me out. When he saw that I was vulnerable and needed protection, he offered to pose as my father. I'm sorry I lied to you," she said shamefacedly.

"Well now, that is a surprise!" Inga's aunt exclaimed. She dipped her head toward Zeke. "You did a very decent thing considering the circumstances, and it speaks well of you."

"It's wonderful to see Zeke so settled here," Trisanna continued. "He's a special person, and I think he has a lot to offer Sengin."

Aunt Jemilla responded without hesitation. "I think so too." Inga had the impression that Trisanna's revelation had raised Zeke even higher in her estimation.

"I wanted you to know I don't expect to stay in Sengin for long," Trisanna continued. "I hope you understand it isn't because I don't like it here!"

Inga's aunt and Zeke looked equally disappointed.

The older woman shrugged philosophically. "I'm sorry to hear it, but it's to be expected I suppose. There are so many opportunities for you young ones in the big city. I imagine Inga will look out for you."

"I certainly intend to do everything I can for Trisanna," Inga confirmed. "And no one's talking about leaving immediately. Both of us will enjoy your hospitality for a while longer if you're willing."

"Of course! You're welcome to stay as long as you like, Inga, as you well know. And the same applies to you, Trisanna. You'll always have a place to stay in Sengin."

A tear came to Trisanna's eye. "Thank you so much!" she said. "I can't even imagine anyone kinder than you."

"Oh, nonsense!" Aunt Jemilla replied, drawing the girl into a lingering hug.

After releasing her, she eyed them all seriously. "It's about time we all had a cup of tea, don't you think?"

• • •

INGA WAS BECOMING INCREASINGLY anxious as each new day passed. Securing Trisanna's safety for the long term was anything but straightforward.

However hard she tried, she couldn't think of a way to contact Dalthinir. She could ask Trisanna to create an illusion. But even if he were close enough to detect it, would he place a priority on investigating a surge of power in Sengin? She couldn't come up with a single reason why he should. It would be extremely dangerous for him to venture near other mages. And Sengin? It was so far away from anywhere Dalthinir was likely to be. He probably wouldn't be able to detect a surge of power in such a remote location even if he wanted to.

The only remaining option was to send Trisanna away, far from any mage with the ability to detect her. But any such strategy had no future. Adrastas was planning to regularly send mages around the kingdom specifically to identify magical auras.

Dalthinir had managed to remain hidden for ten years. Sending Trisanna away with him was the only viable solution for the longer term. But she had to find him first.

A part of her dreamed of him turning up unexpectedly, improbable as it might seem. But the days came and went without any sign of him.

She was no closer to a solution when she detected a cluster of magical auras one evening, not far from Sengin. There could only be one conclusion—Adrastas's team was about to arrive.

Many times she had regretted her hasty action in requesting support. But it had seemed reasonable at the time. How could she ever have anticipated the arrival of someone like Trisanna?

Only one uncertainty remained. If Adrastas had sent another mage with the ability to detect magical auras, there was no hope for Trisanna. It seemed unlikely. Such mages were in short supply, and Inga was already on hand. Either way, they wouldn't need to wait long to find out.

KOTHLAR SWUNG down from his horse. "Inga! I'm glad to see you well!"

His companions offered greetings of their own.

"Welcome, Kothlar." She nodded at the other members of his team. "Kaspra, Alexis, Emmela. It almost feels like old times." Her greeting seemed surprisingly cool.

She addressed Kothlar again. "Did you have a reason for doubting I would be well?"

Kothlar frowned. "Chief Master Adrastas led us to believe you were facing an unknown mage alone while lacking magical protection. He urged us to reach you without delay."

Inga softened visibly at his words. "I appreciate his concern, and I am sorry that you went to all this effort for no reason."

"What of this mage, then?"

She shrugged. "I hardly know what to say. After the sustained bursts of power on the lake, everything went quiet."

"So you've seen no sign that a mage came ashore?"

She raised her hands helplessly. "I have nothing useful to tell you. It's possible that the mage never intended to come ashore in Periton. It's also possible it was a mage leaving Periton—perhaps heading for Tantel."

Kaspra didn't hide her surprise. "Are you suggesting that the mage on the lake could have been Lars?"

"It wasn't Lars."

"What about Dalthinir?"

Inga shook her head emphatically. "It couldn't have been him."

"Because he would have made himself known to you?" Emmela asked quietly.

Inga turned to her with eyes narrowed, and the two of them stared at each other for a long moment. Emmela lowered her glance first.

"It isn't impossible that monsters took the mage," offered Alexis. "I've visited this region before, and the Lake of Death is called that for a reason."

"Are you aware of a mage coming ashore?" persisted Emmela.

Inga frowned. "I thought I had already answered that question."

Emmela shook her head. "You've deflected the question twice."

Inga flushed red, apparently with anger. "Then no, I'm not aware of a mage coming ashore. Are you satisfied?"

Kothlar would not have chosen Emmela for this mission, not least because her ability with illusion was of questionable value in these circumstances. But Adrastas had overruled him. He said that Emmela wanted to show support for Inga. If so, she had a strange way of demonstrating it.

"Have you found somewhere to stay?" Inga asked Kothlar, steering the conversation in a safer direction.

He nodded. "We will be staying in an inn. According to the town officials, it's one of the better ones. Would you like to join us there?"

"No, thanks. I'll continue to stay with my aunt."

"Would you like anyone to keep you company out here?" asked Emmela.

"No, thank you," replied Inga, a little too quickly. "Nothing personal, but my reason for coming here was to take a complete break from everything and everyone."

Kothlar nodded. "We will leave you in peace again, Inga. It's good to find you well."

"What are your plans from here?" asked Inga.

"We'll do some investigation and ask people if they've seen or heard anything unusual. Especially anyone new who arrived around the time of the power surges. We'll speak to you again before we return to Cambrick, but otherwise we'll try to leave you in peace."

Inga nodded. "Enjoy your time in Sengin. And stay away from the monsters!"

Once all of them had remounted, Kothlar led them back to the town.

He mused as they rode, reflecting on the visit. Inga hadn't been pleased to see them. He hadn't expected that, especially in view of her potential vulnerability. On the other hand, he was willing to acknowledge she had been treated badly during the inquiry into the expedition to monitor Lars and Petria. It had been obvious at the time she felt betrayed by Emmela in particular. But she was more sensible than most. He might have expected her to rise above it by now.

Of course the whispering behind her back couldn't have made it easy to return to normal. The nature of her relationship with Dalthinir had been the subject of a great deal of juicy gossip, and she must surely have been aware of that. Supposedly, all information related to the mission was restricted, but clearly someone had been unguarded in their talk.

The more he thought about it, the more readily he understood why Inga needed a break. As soon as his team had made their inquiries, they would return to Cambrick and leave her to the peace and quiet she so clearly needed.

KOTHLAR and his team left Inga restless and unsettled. She could at least be grateful they'd come without another mage capable of detecting glimmer. But why had Emmela joined them? There was no reason to include a mage with no ability apart from illusion. Her one contribution had been to force Inga into lying about a mage coming ashore.

Inga screwed up her face in frustration. No one had forced her to lie. It had always been her choice, and she couldn't reasonably blame Emmela for it. Emmela simply knew her well enough to recognize her evasion for what it was.

Hearing about Kothlar's plans had been no less alarming. No ships had docked on the day in question. There couldn't have been too many new arrivals in the town.

Zeke hadn't been hiding since he arrived. He'd been out and about doing odd jobs, and he'd told people he had just come from the Summer Isles. There were probably a few who also knew he had appeared with a young woman. How was it going to look when Kothlar discovered that the only new arrivals had settled with Inga at her aunt's?

In her experience, lying wasn't a safe strategy. Lies had a bad habit of unraveling when you least expected it. They also invariably multiplied, and it became more and more difficult to remember exactly what you'd said previously. But it was too late now.

She wasted no time calling together her aunt, Zeke, and Trisanna.

"Could you please do me a favor?" she asked. "Some of my mage colleagues just visited. They will be roaming around asking a number of questions in the next few days. Could you please say as little as possible to them?"

Her aunt's curiosity had clearly been roused by the request, but she trusted Inga completely, so she readily agreed, as did Zeke and Trisanna.

As soon as an opportunity presented itself, Inga drew Trisanna aside, leading her outside behind the main house.

"We're very fortunate that none of the mages sent from Cambrick are able to detect magical auras," she told the wide-eyed young mage. "Nevertheless, a lot could still go wrong. Could you please stay out of sight as much as possible for the next few days?"

Trisanna nodded.

As the two of them were about to re-enter the house, Emmela appeared around the side of the building. Was it possible she had over-heard some of their conversation?

"There you are," she said to Inga brightly. She smiled at Trisanna. "And who is this?"

Trisanna curtsied, blushing faintly. "My name is Trisanna," she replied. "Please don't let me interrupt you." With that she scurried away.

"A delightful child," offered Emmela. "Who is she?"

Inga ignored the question. "Why are you here, Emmela?"

The other mage returned a searching glance. "I've known you a long time, Inga, and something isn't right. I want to know what it is, because I want to find a way to help."

"I wouldn't ask for your help even if I needed it," Inga told her bluntly. "All I want is to be left alone."

Emmela refused to be put off. "Why did you lie earlier? Does it have something to do with Dalthinir?"

Inga was becoming annoyed. "Why are you so fixated on him?" she demanded. "If you must know, I don't see why he has to die, and I won't allow you or anyone else to bludgeon me into thinking otherwise."

"Whether it's Dalthinir or not, it's obvious to me you know more than you're saying about the mage you reported."

"And what? You've taken it upon yourself to expose me? You thought I should have been punished for helping Dalthinir. It didn't happen, so now you're looking for another opportunity to bring me down?"

Emmela looked shocked. "That isn't what's happening at all!"

"Then what is happening?"

"I told you. I want to help!"

"And I've told you, I don't want your help!"

Emmela threw up her hands. "What have I done to deserve this?"

Inga glared at her in disgust. "If you truly need to ask that, we have nothing worth saying to each other."

Turning her back on her former friend, she pushed through the door of the house, slamming it shut and locking it behind her.

Where would all this end? One step at a time she had been drawn into flouting the authority of the Compact. When it involved only Dalthinir, she had seen herself as compromised because of her feelings about him. The appearance of Kylen had shaken her, and Trisanna had finally tipped her over the edge.

The Compact existed to benefit the mages who formed its membership, and it also existed to ruthlessly destroy any mage who was not a member. Yet Compact membership provided no guarantee that a mage was virtuous and law-abiding, any more than independence gave certainty that a mage was not.

Emmela took Adrastas's view that the law must be obeyed without question and without exception. Inga had been slowly coming to see the Compact's position as a form of institutional oppression that must be resisted when it targeted those who didn't deserve death. How could two such positions ever be reconciled?

That didn't make her happy about everything she'd done. She'd turned into a shameless liar, coldly pushing away one of her oldest friends. But there could be no going back. Not when an innocent girl's life was hanging in the balance.

Leaning with her back against the door, she tried to stop herself from trembling.

CHAPTER 7

Kylen stood on a sandy beach, staring out at the water. From the day he had met Dalthinir his life had been filled with new experiences and new challenges. His own magical abilities continued to astonish him, and thanks to both the mage and the twins he had mastered a broad range of practical skills as well.

His most recent adventure had been learning to swim. They had made their way to the seaside for that reason.

He'd done it the hard way. Dalthinir had insisted he learn to handle himself in the water like any other person, and it had been unusually difficult to restrain himself from supporting his body weight with magic. Eventually he had become comfortable with dunking his head, treading water, and using simple strokes like overarm, sidestroke, and breaststroke to propel himself forward.

He had cheated in one respect only. The water had been bitingly cold, but a little elements magic easily dealt with the issue.

Jonno and Bella already knew how to swim, and they had enthusiastically monitored Kylen's progress from the beginning. They clearly regarded the operation as entertainment of the highest order. Not content to quietly observe, they delivered cheers of encouragement when he made progress and gales of laughter when he did something unusually inept.

At times it became impossible for Dalthinir to communicate with Kylen over the uproar. He was a patient man by nature, but as usual the twins tested him to the limit.

Achieving a basic level of proficiency might have been rewarding enough for Kylen, but something happened that transformed the experience into one of the highlights of his life. Swimming alone, he was startled when a head bobbed up beside him. The dolphin chittered briefly before disappearing underwater again. The experience itself was exhilarating, but nothing could have prepared him for the wonder of understanding the dolphin's communication.

"Strange looking fish! Such splashing, such flailing," it said, beaming its remarkable smile.

The creature was gone before he could respond, but he was ready when a head appeared a short time later.

"This strange looking fish envies the speed and grace of a dolphin!" he said. He was surprised to hear chittering instead of his own voice.

His attempt at communication had its effect. Before long, heads bobbed up all around him. In their excitement the creatures had so much to say he couldn't keep up.

Then the pod was gone, the dolphins gliding effortlessly through the water.

In his excitement Kylen felt like babbling about it with anyone who would listen. But he had been careful to avoid speaking of mage powers with the twins, not wanting to distance them. And would it help to draw attention to mage hearing when Dalthinir didn't share the ability?

In the end, he decided it would be inappropriate to continue to hide it from his mentor. But he would choose his timing. In the meantime, he treasured the moment, storing it away as a prized memory.

Precious as such experiences might be, he could never allow himself to fully delight in his growing proficiency in magic. The more his abilities developed, the more compromised he felt. His magic had its origin in direct contact with dragons. It was irretrievably tainted.

Much as he resisted the Compact's efforts to run him to ground, a part of him felt as if the fate the mages intended for him was fitting.

He couldn't turn to Dalthinir for comfort and advice either. His mentor might also be on the run from the Compact, but his magic had been awakened in a conventional manner. His abilities had never been contaminated.

Nor did the mage know that he had conversed with a dragon. Or how close he had come to opening *Ode to the Fallen One*. The consequences of yielding to the document's seduction would have been unimaginable, and the fact that he had almost given in to the temptation continued to haunt him. It only proved how blighted he had become. He wasn't at all sure he had the courage to reveal any of that.

He tried hard not to dwell on such matters. He had promised himself he would do everything in his power to use his tainted magic for good. What else could he do?

A FEW DAYS later they were on the beach when a fisherman brought in his vessel. Having helped him on an earlier occasion, Dalthinir knew the man a little, and they exchanged warm greetings.

"Would you all like a ride in the boat?" the sailor asked. "I've got nothing to show for my efforts today, so I might as well find something useful to do."

The twins climbed in without hesitation. Before long all of them were sailing away from the shore.

Spotting dolphins, Kylen leaned over the bow. As soon as one came close enough, he chittered, "Are there any fish nearby for this fisherman?"

A few moments later a head appeared, chittering, "Follow." It then proceeded slowly out to sea.

Kylen called at once to the fisherman. "Can we follow that dolphin?"

"If you like," he replied, steering the boat in the indicated direction and holding the course for several minutes.

After a while the fisherman called out excitedly, "Look! Seabirds ahead! When they dive into the water like that it means fish are around."

Bringing the vessel about, he threw his net into the sea. Flapping fish covered the bottom of the boat the moment he hauled it in again.

"Dolphins have always been lucky for me," he told them. "You lot seem to be lucky as well!"

In the days that followed they often went out with the fisherman. On several other occasions dolphins guided them to shoals of fish. No one else knew of Kylen's role in it.

They helped scale and clean the catch, and the fisherman gave them fish in appreciation for their help.

To Kylen, scaling and cleaning was a tiresome and messy job. As with so many practical matters, the twins proved much more adept at it. Each of them could scale and clean two fish in the time it took him to do one. They weren't slow in pointing it out, either.

A morning came when they were all out in the boat, fishing in deeper water. To the fisherman's frustration, the fish had disappeared.

"I think I can see seabirds further out," he called, pointing out to sea. "Let's go take a look."

As they were helping to pull in the nets, a head appeared near Kylen. "Big storm comes. Safest deep down," it chittered before disappearing abruptly.

"I think there might be a storm coming," called Kylen. "Perhaps we should head toward land."

The fisherman waved a hand dismissively. "No need to worry, I see the clouds. It shouldn't get rough for a while yet. We'll try our luck one more time."

Dalthinir leaned closer to Kylen. "What makes you think a storm is coming?"

For a moment he hesitated. Then he decided the time had arrived. "A dolphin told me."

His mentor's startled eyes stared back at him. "You have mage hearing ability?"

He nodded. "I'm sorry I didn't tell you sooner. I...I felt embarrassed."

Dalthinir rolled his eyes. "You and I are not in a competition," he said. "I'm here to help you." He grinned. "It's suddenly obvious why we've been so lucky at finding fish!" He cast an eye toward the sky. "Perhaps I should encourage the fisherman to turn back."

Kylen shook his head quickly. "I'm not sure we need to be too alarmed. He's aware that a storm is coming, and the dolphin didn't mention timing."

After a moment's consideration, Dalthinir nodded and drew back. But his eyes were increasingly drawn upward to a sky that was growing darker by the minute.

The waves were becoming choppy by the time they reached a place where the fisherman was willing to cast the nets. When they hauled them aboard again, they were empty of fish.

By then the waves had grown in size alarmingly. "It's time we were gone!" the fisherman shouted. Bringing the boat about, he steered it toward land.

At first they made good headway, but progress quickly slowed to the point where they were scarcely moving forward at all. The waves had become mountainous, and the little craft was tossed helplessly about.

"This wind will shred the sail if I don't reef it!" shouted the fisherman as he began hauling it in. The worsening conditions made the task extremely challenging, but he managed to complete it. Rigging a storm jib, he allowed the boat to run before the wind.

How long they were driven before the storm Kylen couldn't tell. After being tossed about for a few hours he felt too ill to care. He was dimly aware that swimming wouldn't keep him alive for long if he was washed overboard or the boat capsized, but he wasn't worried about drowning. Magic would keep him afloat. The challenge would be for them to stay together.

At some point he rallied long enough to notice that all of the boat's occupants were still there. And that the storm jib had been shredded.

He almost roused himself when a series of huge waves threatened to dash the boat onto some rocks. But he wasn't needed. Somehow the crisis was averted, presumably thanks to Dalthinir. He sunk once more into the bilges.

Calls from the fisherman eventually made him aware they were about to be washed ashore onto a beach. Clambering unsteadily over the side, he saw the twins helping each other and the fishermen helping Dalthinir. He staggered forward through the waves and threw himself onto the sand. He was dimly aware of the fisherman beaching the boat. How the man found the energy to do it was a mystery.

After an unknown period of time had passed, someone approached him.

The tall figure of Dalthinir overshadowed him. The mage was peering down at him. "Are you hurt?"

"No. Just a bit queasy." He sat up slowly, looking around. "Where are we?"

"We've been blown south. That's all I can say with any certainty."

Kylen frowned in concentration. "There are several mages not far from here."

Dalthinir started in surprise. "Where? And do you know who?"

He waved a hand toward the east. "Kothlar and Emmela, with two other mages. I don't know their names, but both of them were on the mountain with us. Inga is a bit closer to us. With another mage— someone whose glimmer I haven't seen before."

A startled look came over Dalthinir's salt-streaked face. He stood brooding for a few moments. "They're here for a reason," he finally said. "We need to find out what it is."

AFTER A FEW MINUTES on dry land Kylen felt well enough to get up and move around. He was in time to catch a conversation between Dalthinir and the fisherman.

"The boat still seems structurally sound," the fisherman was saying, clearly relieved. "The rudder has been damaged and some of the sails are torn, but I'm confident I can do the repairs myself. I just need access to tools."

"Will you be able to sail it home on your own?" asked Dalthinir.

The fisherman nodded confidently. "Yes, once it's properly repaired."

He looked at the mage uncomfortably. "I'm sorry I subjected you to this." He nodded in the direction of Kylen. "I should have headed to shore when your youngster suggested it."

Dalthinir waved it away. "There's no reason to blame yourself. No one can predict the weather with any certainty."

The fisherman looked relieved. "What will you do? I'm guessing some of your party might think twice about another sea voyage, but you're welcome to return with me if you would like to."

Dalthinir dipped his head in appreciation. "Thank you for your offer. We'll stay here, at least for a while. We don't have many possessions. We can collect whatever we left behind next time we're in the area."

He peered hopefully at the fisherman. "Would you be willing to avoid mentioning us when you talk about what happened? Before long word will get around that we survived a shipwreck, and people will become very inquisitive. None of us likes a fuss—we'd rather keep to ourselves."

Fortunately, the fisherman was more than willing to accommodate them. "Of course!" he replied without hesitation. "I'll be off now. I'm going to look for a farm or a village where I can borrow what I need. All the best, and thanks for helping with my fishing!"

As soon as he was gone, Dalthinir eyed his companions tentatively. "Are you up to some walking?"

All three of them nodded.

"Then it's time for us to go. Kylen, you'd better lead the way."

As they walked, the twins began a conversation.

"What do you think it is?" asked Jonno, jerking a head toward Dalthinir.

Bella eyed the tall figure of the mage thoughtfully. "A bear walking upright after a swim?"

Jonno frowned. "I was thinking more like a scarecrow after a thunderstorm."

"Do you think she'll recognize him?" asked Bella.

"Inga? Recognize a scarecrow in a bearskin?" Jonno shook his head firmly. "Not a chance. She'll be too busy trying to figure out how it got a magical aura."

Both of them burst into laughter.

The mage didn't open his mouth, but his scowl said plenty.

Kylen paused long enough to take a close look at the mage and the twins. Finally he glanced down at himself.

"None of us are fit to be seen at the moment," he acknowledged. "We'll draw attention to ourselves without the fisherman saying a word."

Throwing up his hands in frustration, Dalthinir stopped walking. "Very well," he grumbled. "Next time we come across a stream, we'll pause long enough to clean up a bit."

The twins winked at Kylen, and he grinned back.

Finding a stream didn't take long. After rinsing their garments with fresh water as best they could, they settled down to allow them to dry in the late afternoon sun. Jonno used the small knife at his belt to trim Dalthinir's beard and hair. Bella did whatever she could to improve his appearance.

"She won't be able to resist you," Bella told the mage with a grin.

He pretended he hadn't heard her.

By the time they were finished, the sun was about to set.

"How far away are we?" the mage asked Kylen.

"We're probably close enough to reach them soon after dark," he replied.

"Then we'll keep going. Lead on."

Setting off once again, Kylen led them into the growing dusk, proceeding ever more cautiously the darker it became.

CHAPTER 8

An entire day had come and gone without contact from Inga's fellow mages. She tried to tell herself they'd decided to leave her and Trisanna alone, but it was wishful thinking and she knew it.

With a feeling of impending doom hanging over them both, she ought to be planning something. But she felt paralyzed. Her instinct was to hide away, like a fox in its den hoping the hounds would pass by without sniffing it out.

The arrival of Kothlar crushed her hopes once and for all.

"Inga, do you have two recent arrivals staying here with you and your aunt? A middle-aged man and a young woman?"

Realizing this was no time to dissemble, she agreed at once. "We do. From the Summer Isles, I believe."

"By boat?"

She nodded. "I believe so."

"Is it possible that one of them is the mage you detected on the lake?"

"Neither of them is a mage, as I've already made clear to you."

"They might be capable of masking their magical auras," he suggested.

"I don't believe it," she said simply.

"Is there a reason you didn't mention their arrival when we last spoke?"

"I didn't see it as relevant."

He sighed. "I don't understand why, Inga, but you seem to have decided to be obstructive. I was hoping we could finish our investigation and leave you in peace, but that clearly won't be possible. Representatives of the town authorities came here with me, and they intend to bring your two guests in for questioning. People can't simply arrive in the kingdom without seeking official approval, no matter where they're from. As for you, members of my team have made it clear they believe you have a responsibility to be direct and honest with us, especially when something as significant as a mage incursion is involved. I'm hoping you'll come willingly."

She stood shaking her head at him. "I've been tried twice. I suppose I should have expected a reason would be found to try me a third time," she said bitterly.

Kothlar didn't rise to the bait, but he didn't look comfortable either. Nevertheless, he had always been one to place duty above other considerations. He wasn't going to make an exception for Inga.

Pointing to the door, he gestured for her to precede him. She went meekly, resigned to her fate, whatever it might be.

Two carriages waited down the lane. Zeke and Trisanna were already getting into one. She was ushered into the other one, Kothlar climbing in behind her. Aunt Jemilla had seen them go, and she stood outside the door of the house wringing her hands.

Inga's carriage moved off with a sudden lurch. Kothlar had seated himself opposite her. She glared across at him, but he looked out the window, unwilling to meet her eyes.

As they rolled into town, her main concern was for Trisanna, not for herself.

Kothlar joined his colleagues with a heavy heart.

"Is she in custody?" asked Emmela.

"She is," he confirmed grimly.

"And the other two?"

"They're in the town lockup."

Kaspra stared at him in alarm. "Surely Inga isn't in the lockup, is she?"

Kothlar looked uncomfortable. "They don't have any other secure accommodations."

"This is for her own good!" insisted Emmela. "We won't leave her there for more than twenty-four hours, whatever happens. I'm convinced she's been with Dalthinir. I don't know if she came to Sengin to be with him, or if he came here to be with her. It doesn't matter. What matters is that he'll never allow her to remain locked up. This is our best chance of flushing him out of hiding! Removing him permanently is in her best interests."

"None of that makes sense!" objected Alexis. "If the two of them met by choice, why would she have sent a report to the chief master?"

"Perhaps she did it in a moment of clarity—before he could convince her not to follow through with it. Or, more likely, she didn't discover who the power surge came from until after she sent the report."

Both Kaspra and Alexis were frowning.

"We have no evidence of wrongdoing on Inga's part," asserted Alexis. "There is no legal basis whatever for locking her up! What right do we have to sully her name and reputation in this way without cause?"

Kaspra's face showed her disgust. "I didn't sign up for this!"

"I will make sure she is released first thing in the morning," said Kothlar placatingly.

"She should be released now!" exclaimed Kaspra.

"In the morning," he repeated firmly.

Leaping to her feet, Kaspra stormed out of the room. Alexis wasn't far behind her.

"You've done the right thing!" Emmela told him. "There are guards constantly on duty around the lockup facility, and I for one will be watching through the night to see if Dalthinir appears. I trust you'll be ready for action if he does! The sooner he's out of the way, the sooner we'll have the old Inga back."

He returned a sour look before leaving the room himself.

KYLEN CREPT forward in the darkness, Dalthinir beside him.

"I've been to Sengin before," the mage whispered. "I remember the layout of the town. They're holding Inga in the town lockup!"

"We should break her out now!" hissed Kylen.

He felt a restraining hand on his arm. "Not without understanding a lot more about what's going on here."

Both of them moved away silently until the town buildings were out of hearing range.

Dalthinir summed up the situation. "Inga is in one section of the building, and the other unknown mage is in another."

"And Emmela has positioned herself near Inga's cell," added Kylen. "I didn't see her, but she was using power. That probably means she's hiding herself with illusion."

"I wonder who she's hiding from," said Dalthinir. "Any mage will know immediately that she's there."

"Where is this invisible mage?" asked Bella. "Emmela, isn't it? She was on the mountain, but we didn't actually meet her."

"Outside the main entrance to the town lockup," Dalthinir replied.

"There are probably guards about," said Jonno. "There usually are when dangerous prisoners are in the lockup."

"Inga dangerous? Surely no one would think that," said Kylen disbelievingly.

"Most people think all mages are dangerous," Bella informed him.

"What are we going to do?" asked Kylen.

"The first question is why is she being locked up?" said Dalthinir. "The second question is who is the other mage, and why are they being locked up?"

"That's three questions, not two," said Jonno reasonably.

There wasn't enough light to see anything, but Kylen felt sure Dalthinir would be glaring at Jonno in the dark.

"Why don't we go and ask?" said Bella.

"Excellent suggestion," said Jonno cheerfully.

"Don't even think about it!" said Dalthinir.

He was too late. The twins were already gone.

After a moment's hesitation, Kylen set off in the same direction. Chances were someone would need to rescue them before long.

Hearing Dalthinir moving to follow him, Kylen paused for a moment and said quietly, "I'll make sure I don't wander too far away from you, because I might need you to mask my use of power. But it's probably safer for you to stay out of sight." Dalthinir must have accepted the suggestion, because Kylen moved forward alone.

Sauntering up to the town buildings, the twins parked themselves on the steps leading to the main entrance.

"I heard that some people have been locked up in here," said Bella ominously.

"Who?" asked Jonno eagerly.

"I don't know."

"Who locked them up?"

"Mages from Cambrick."

"Why?"

"Because they like throwing their weight around."

"Who told you that?"

"The usual lot. They probably had a few too many ales. A whole mob of them were talking about coming here and busting the prisoners out."

"Aren't there guards?"

"I expect so, but that won't bother them. They like a good fight. They just need to convince themselves there's a reason for it."

"Did you tell them to crawl back into their holes? You're better than anyone at talking them down."

"How could I? I don't know anything about who's been locked up or why."

"Sounds like it might be entertaining! Let's stick around and see what happens!"

They didn't have long to wait. A woman appeared from around the corner of the building and approached them directly.

"What are you two up to?" she asked.

"Just sitting," Bella replied innocently.

"I wouldn't suggest staying here. There might be trouble. A mage is locked up inside."

"A mage?" asked Jonno in alarm. "A dangerous one?"

"Nowhere near as dangerous as the mage who's going to try to free her. It won't be safe to be anywhere near here when that happens."

"We heard other people were locked up too. Are they dangerous mages too?"

She waved a hand dismissively. "They're just people who came into the kingdom without permission. The town officials locked them up so they could question them."

"It sounds like there's no real reason for anyone to get upset," suggested Bella.

"You're right. It will be safer if everyone stays away from here."

"Thank you!" exclaimed Jonno. "We'll pass on the good news!"

"You do that," agreed the woman.

"Bye!" they said, running off into the night.

All of them returned to Dalthinir.

"There. That wasn't hard," said Bella with a grin. "Emmela was happy to tell us what we wanted to know."

"What happened?" asked the mage impatiently.

"Jonno and Bella nudged Emmela into showing herself and telling them who was locked up and why," Kylen told him. He briefly reported the interaction.

"She must have been using illusion to hide herself," Dalthinir told them. "I sensed it when her power stopped. She's using power again now you're gone."

He sighed. "The two of you have done well. As usual. It sounds like Inga is being locked up in the hope it will bring me into the open, although it isn't clear why they think I'm in the region. It also seems they don't realize they've detained another mage as well."

"What should we do?" asked Kylen.

"If I'm right, they'll probably release Inga if I don't appear."

"And if they don't?"

"Then we'll have to do something. Based on what we've just heard, though, it makes sense to wait, at least until tomorrow."

They headed out of town to find somewhere to sleep.

. . .

THEY ROSE with the sun the next morning.

"I've been thinking about the situation," said Dalthinir. "They locked Inga up for a reason, and it has something to do with me. I can't imagine Inga's done anything to deserve imprisonment. She's probably there on suspicion of connecting with me, although I have no idea why they would think that. At the same time, they don't realize they have another mage in the lockup. I'd like to know who the person is, and whether he or she is dangerous."

"If they release Inga, we can ask her what she knows," suggested Kylen.

The mage nodded. "We'll watch from a distance."

INGA LOOKED up as Kothlar approached her cell with a guard. "Time for the execution?" she asked sardonically.

The guard opened the cell and stepped aside.

Kothlar waved her to the door. "You're free to go. There's a carriage outside to return you to your aunt's."

"I was imprisoned without any charge being laid, and now you're just letting me go?" She glared at him. "Don't expect me to simply ignore what's happened here."

The normally unflappable Kothlar looked unusually disconcerted. "Please don't make this any more difficult than it needs to be."

"Difficult for me, or difficult for you?"

Turning away with disgust, Inga left the building and headed for the carriage.

Emmela was holding the door open for her. As she opened her mouth to speak, Inga stopped and stared at her. Seeing the look on Inga's face, Emmela immediately clamped her mouth shut.

Turning her back on her former friend, Inga climbed into the carriage. She barely moved until the horses pulled into the lane leading to her aunt's house.

65

Aunt Jemilla came running as soon as she saw the carriage. "What's been happening?" she asked anxiously.

"I'll explain later, Aunt. I hope you don't mind, but I need some time alone for a while."

"Of course! Take as long as you need!"

Inga set off briskly, heading toward the sea. She wanted to be far from everyone. Once she was truly alone, she meandered aimlessly, trying to clear her head.

Perhaps an hour had elapsed when she saw a slight figure walking toward her. Her first reaction was annoyance, but then she realized there was something familiar about the figure. She came to an abrupt halt, her mouth gaping with astonishment.

"Bella!"

Seeing her arms opened wide, the girl ran forward, throwing herself into Inga's embrace.

"What are you doing here? Are you well? Are you...all well?"

"Yes, we're all well, Inga. And Dalthinir misses you too."

Inga felt the color rising up her cheeks, but she was past caring about such things.

"It isn't safe for Dalthinir here. Or for Kylen. What brought you here?"

"We're only here by accident. But Dalthinir realized something was wrong when he and Kylen located you in the town lockup."

"It isn't me he needs to worry about! There's a young woman they've locked up as well. She's a mage, although no one realizes it yet. She'll be in real trouble if they find out. Dalthinir has to rescue her!"

"He's aware there's another mage there, and he's guessed that the other mages haven't realized it yet. He wanted to find out if the mage is dangerous."

"Come and sit with me. I'll tell you everything. But first I want to hear about you. Surely we can spare a few minutes for that."

The two of them sat together chatting contentedly, putting aside the troubles of the world for a time. A few quiet minutes with Bella was balm for Inga's soul. She slowly began to relax, the tension easing out of her.

Best of all, Dalthinir was here. He would make everything right. Trisanna would be safe at last.

CHAPTER 9

Trisanna found herself confronted by a town official who stared sullenly at her and Zeke.

"Why have you come here?" he demanded.

"My daughter and I are from the Summer Isles," said Zeke. "We were fishin' when the weather turned rough. We were blown to the mainland."

"Where is your boat now?"

"On the bottom of the ocean," Zeke replied regretfully. "It broke up on some rocks. We were fortunate to reach the shore alive."

"You've been staying with an old woman and doing odd jobs. Why?"

The fisherman seemed puzzled by the question. "How else could I provide for us?"

"Did it occur to you to seek permission to live and work in Periton?"

He shook his head. "I didn't realize somethin' like that would be necessary."

"Ignorance of the law is not a valid excuse," said the official grimly.

He waved a hand. "Take them back to their cell!"

Escorted to the lockup, they were soon securely confined once more.

Trisanna wondered if Inga had been released, and if she would try to do something for them. As the day dragged by, though, it became increasingly clear they would need to fend for themselves. All of it was her fault, of course. Zeke was only in trouble because of her. The responsibility of it began to weigh heavily on her.

Then it occurred to her that they had escaped the monsters using illusion. Could she use it again? Perhaps if the guards saw that the cell was empty, they would unlock it and come inside to investigate. That might allow them an opportunity to slip away unobserved.

Zeke didn't know she was a mage, and he needed to be protected from knowing that. But she had used an illusion on the lake without him realizing. He'd still been able to see her and the boat. Presumably that meant he wouldn't be aware of an illusion this time either.

Apart from Inga, no one else knew she was a mage, and she was keenly aware it would go badly for her if she were to be discovered. Inga had made it clear it wasn't safe to use magic if other mages were around because they would sense it. But if she could find a way to escape, maybe they could be clear of the area before other mages arrived.

If she and Zeke were gone, they wouldn't know what to conclude from the use of power. She supposed they would assume an unknown mage had helped them break out of the lockup. But it shouldn't get Inga into trouble. Inga had said her only magical ability was to sense the use of power and magical auras.

She understood so little about magic, but she knew enough to suppose that many things could go wrong if she decided to act. However, they were already in trouble with the officials, and she couldn't begin to guess at the consequences. Torn between bad outcomes, she decided she had a responsibility to at least make an attempt to resolve the situation.

The next time she heard a guard approaching the cell, she wrapped herself and Zeke in an illusion. The guard arrived to an apparently empty cell. Astonished, he immediately called for assistance. Other guards came running. They were soon calling out in alarm. To her dismay, none of them entered the cell to try to understand how they had escaped.

Perhaps if she ended the illusion before other mages arrived, they wouldn't know who had done it. But she had no intention of suddenly appearing when they were watching. As soon as the guards left she would do it.

She waited in vain. One guard remained, stationed by the cell.

In the end, she gave up and ended the illusion when his back was turned. Gaping in astonishment to see them in the cell again, he ran off to call the other guards.

"What was all that about?" asked Zeke in bewilderment.

She shrugged. "I imagine we'll find out before long."

KYLEN LISTENED open-mouthed as Bella reported everything she had learned from Inga.

Dalthinir was frowning. "So if I understand it correctly, this Trisanna is the illegitimate daughter of the previous king of Tantel from an affair with a powerful mage. She was recently awakened magically and has strong illusion abilities, but she's untrained. Since she's a renegade and a threat to the current king, a group of mages attempted to kill her, but she escaped over the Lake of Death, using illusion to hide herself and the fisherman from the monsters."

Bella nodded.

"Then we clearly need to rescue her." He grimaced. "Now would be a good time to have some illusion ability available. I'm not sure how we'll break her out with lockup guards on duty."

"Do you smell that?" asked Kylen, sensing a sudden burst of power.

The mage looked up in alarm. "It's coming from the direction of the jail. And it isn't a scent I recognize. Trisanna must be trying to find her own way out. Even if she succeeds, she risks exposing herself as a mage. We need to get down there!"

Both of them sprinted toward the lockup, the twins right behind them.

"You need to stay out of sight!" called Kylen. "I'll do whatever's needed—you can mask me!"

Dalthinir was panting for breath, but he managed, "There isn't time for subtlety! Others are there already."

The mage was right. Mages were converging on the prisoner. Kylen recognized their glimmer.

It was the worst possible outcome. There was no time for plans. And Dalthinir needed to stay out of sight. If he appeared, there would almost certainly be consequences for Inga as well as for him.

It meant Kylen needed to take the lead. He hurried on, determined not to think about it.

The lockup came into sight. It was positioned behind the town hall, away from the main street, with no other buildings near it. Four mages stood on the far side of it. As he ran toward it he sensed power pouring out of them.

He soon discovered a magical shield surrounding the building, denying physical access to it. After pausing for a moment to think, he thrust out his own power, shaking the earth beneath the mages. The shield wavered as the four of them were thrown to the ground. It was all he needed.

The magical aura of the imprisoned mage showed him exactly where he needed to be. Pushing forward, he reached the building, throwing up a shield of his own before the others could block him again. They quickly wrapped a shield around his to prevent his escape. He didn't let it trouble him. He would worry about escape when the time came.

Sweeping his hand in a wide arc, he traced a person-sized opening in the building. Drawing upon his mage touch ability, he pulled back his arm. The area he had outlined crumbled, leaving a gaping hole in the wall. Inside he saw a young woman and an older man. He was close enough to confirm that the glimmer belonged to the young woman. Inga had said her name was Trisanna.

"Quickly!" he urged, waving them forward.

Neither of them moved. Puzzled, he called to them again. "I've come to rescue you, Trisanna. Hurry!"

Her eyes had widened at the sound of her name, but both of them seemed rooted to the spot. Something was preventing them from leaving.

Stepping in through the hole in the wall, he approached them, frowning. They stood in a cell with metal bars beyond them. Guards on the other side of the bars stared in utter amazement.

The imprisoned pair stared at him with no less astonishment. "How did you do that?" asked the young woman.

Looking back the way he had come he saw only the hole in the wall. There was no time to resolve the mystery. With neither of the prisoners showing any inclination to move, he grabbed Trisanna's hand and pulled her outside. As he did so, the man grabbed hold of her as well.

He managed to get her almost completely outside before her fellow prisoner could prevent it. By then both of them were gasping in amazement. Letting go of her, the man hung back, refusing to follow.

She immediately turned to re-enter the cell. When Kylen resisted, she said, "I'm not going without Zeke! And don't worry—I understand what's happening now! I'll bring him out." Disappearing inside, she emerged a moment later pulling him behind her.

Wide-eyed and extremely reluctant, Zeke was astonished to find himself outside of the building.

"The wall looks intact," she told him, "but it's just an illusion. Our new friend here knocked a hole in it."

Kylen understood at last. It was Emmela's work, of course. Seeing him knock a hole in the wall of the building, she had magically restored its original appearance to confuse the prisoners. She had achieved her goal. They hadn't tried to escape because they couldn't see the hole he'd created.

Strangely, Emmela's illusion hadn't affected him. The confrontation on the mountain came to his mind. She had successfully used an illusion to hide herself and Inga. Lars and Petria hadn't been aware of their presence until a blow to her head interrupted the illusion. Yet he had noticed them from the moment he entered the rock-enclosed room.

There wasn't time to ponder it now. He needed to find a way through the magical barrier surrounding his shield. Before he could do anything, the ground beneath them shook.

Belatedly realizing that Kothlar was copying his earlier action in an attempt to distract him, he reinforced his shield. But he wasn't quick enough to protect himself from a large block of stone shaken loose by the tremors. Falling from above, it struck a painful blow to his arm, drawing blood and causing him to cry out.

For a moment he saw red. As he prepared a counterstrike, he abruptly remembered the behavior of Dalthinir in the confrontation on the mountain. Even with Lars threatening to end Inga's life, Dalthinir had satisfied himself with putting the rogue mage to sleep.

Kothlar didn't deserve to be attacked. He was doing what he believed to be right—what the law demanded. Abandoning any thought of revenge, Kylen concentrated on breaking through the shield that surrounded them.

Wrapping a new shield tightly around himself and the escaped prisoners, he pushed against the barrier established by his opponents. At first it resisted him, but as he added magical force to his efforts, he felt it begin to give way.

At the same moment, he heard the young woman murmur determinedly, "If they want to play games, I can do it too."

Abruptly a voice called out, "They've disappeared!"

Trisanna was demonstrating that illusion didn't belong solely to Emmela—she had the same magical ability herself. She had created an illusion of her own to hide Kylen, Zeke, and herself.

"Nicely done," he told her. She responded with a grave nod.

Another voice answered immediately. "It doesn't matter if we can't see them! We can sense their power!"

"We need help right now, Dalthinir," he mumbled to himself.

For Inga's sake he was glad the mage had refrained from showing himself in any way. And until now there'd been no real reason to mask Kylen's use of power. But the time had come for him to lend a hand.

Almost immediately the second voice called out in frustration, "Where did their power go?"

Dalthinir must have understood what was happening. He was masking the power used for both Trisanna's illusion and Kylen's shields. Invisible and untraceable, they were free to make a clean escape.

Trisanna's illusion did not affect Kylen. He could still see her as well as Zeke. He hoped they could see him as well. Just in case, he grabbed her hand again and began pulling her in the right direction. She came unresisting, Zeke trailing behind.

They hadn't gone far when Dalthinir appeared ahead of them.

"You can drop the illusion now," Kylen murmured to his companion.

She must have responded immediately, because Dalthinir greeted them with a smile. "You must be Trisanna. That was a timely effort with the illusion. Welcome to our ragtag band!"

The twins arrived, Jonno whistling appreciatively when he saw Kylen holding Trisanna's hand.

Suddenly aware of what he had been doing, he dropped her hand as if it were a hot coal. Releasing it seemed to affect her no more than when he took it in the first place. He couldn't pretend to be quite so indifferent. He felt his face glowing red.

"This is Zeke," she said seriously, pointing to her companion. "In the short time I've known him he has been unfailingly kind and a good friend. I don't want to see him get into trouble because of me."

"And this is Jonno and Bella," said the mage. "But there'll be time for introductions later. The entire town guard will be on us soon."

As they hurried away, Jonno called, "Come with us! Bella and I have arranged some transport."

Kylen wasn't sure whether to be impressed or to roll his eyes. Either way, he wasn't surprised. Following Jonno across a field, he saw a farmer on an open wagon waiting patiently.

"Thank you, kind sir!" said Dalthinir as they all piled into the back.

"Glad I can help!" the farmer replied. "Got talkin' with your young lass here. She was admirin' me cows, so I told her me tale of woe. Then she tells me you just got some friends out of the lockup."

Dalthinir glanced at Bella in alarm.

"No need to trouble yourself!" the farmer continued. "I won't tell no one. They've locked up me Bessie three times now, and I would've happily got her out if I could. Supposedly, she was in for trespassin'. It were more like envy, I reckon. Bessie's me prize cow, in case you're wonderin'. She's took first prize from the head guard's scruffy beast five times so far. This little jaunt is me way of payin' the beggar back for pickin' on Bessie."

The twins had done it again. Kylen decided they definitely deserved some kind of award.

With the drama behind them at least for the moment, his arm began to throb. Noticing him wincing, Dalthinir examined the wound, cleaning and binding it.

The farmer drove until it was dusk, avoiding roads and settled areas. By then Sengin lay far behind. The smell of sea air suggested they were near the coast.

All of them thanked him many times as he drove away.

"Don't you be mentionin' it now!" he called back. "It were a pleasure."

Jonno and Bella produced fresh bread and cheese. After eyeing it with a raised eyebrow, Dalthinir shrugged wearily and waved permission for them to pass it around.

"I'm guessing all of us need sleep," the mage ventured when they had eaten their fill. "Find yourselves somewhere comfortable to lie down. We can talk in the morning."

CHAPTER 10

Lifting high a burning torch, Master Pernilla ascended the final flight of steps and stepped onto the landing. The room before her stood at the very top of the tower. Breathing heavily, she paused to catch her breath.

No one had ever accused the slender mage of faint-heartedness. She nevertheless allowed plenty of time to prepare herself. Although her report would not satisfy the chief master, she refused to be discomposed by it. She reminded herself that he hadn't placed her in authority as a favor to her. More powerful mages were available—a fact that irritated her more than she cared to admit—but she was his best leader, and both of them knew it.

After a few moments she grasped hold of the iron door knocker and rapped twice.

"Enter!" came a gruff reply, barely audible through the thick wood.

Lifting the latch, she pushed the door open.

"Well?" The voice sounded menacing without a barrier to screen it.

"The girl has been disposed of, Chief Master."

"In what manner?"

"She fled the farm on horseback just before we arrived. Two of our number remained there while the rest of us chased her all the way to the Lake of Death. She was on the water when we arrived. She'd convinced a fisherman to take her out. We pushed the boat out into the lake, then raised up a storm. The creatures took them both."

"How can you be certain?"

"No one has returned from the middle of the lake. Not ever."

A frown twisted the gray brows of Chief Master Kharkin, but he didn't argue.

"Have you recovered the amulet?" he demanded.

Pernilla shook her head.

"Then return to the farm and find it! Tear the place apart if you have to."

SEVERAL DAYS HAD PASSED before Pernilla made her way once more to the tower room of the head mage. She was not looking forward to the interaction.

"Did you find the amulet?" growled the chief master.

She shook her head. "We tore the place apart as you ordered. We found no sign of it."

"What of the people at the farm—the ones who raised her?"

"We extracted a great deal of information before we disposed of them."

"And?"

"They were well aware of her ancestry. They had been hiding her from the king from her infancy. There were surprises, though..."

"Well?" demanded the dark cloaked figure sharply.

"They seemed to think she had been magically awakened."

Kharkin scowled dismissively. "How could that be?"

"Her mother was a mage."

"Impossible!" scoffed the chief master. "Such a thing could never have been hidden. Next you'll be telling me she rode away with the amulet."

Pernilla stared back at him, unmoving.

The dark eyes of the head mage widened, then narrowed threateningly. "Don't even think about hiding the truth from me."

Pernilla schooled her features into some semblance of a calm demeanor. "They gave her a number of valuables as she was preparing to flee. They claimed the amulet was among them."

Kharkin snorted disbelievingly. "So you're telling me the monsters now have it?"

"We would have forced her back to the shore if we'd known. We knew nothing about it until later."

"There are many things you don't know, Pern," growled the other. "Like the fact that we've just received word from the Peritonians that a mage was detected at their end of the lake. It wasn't anyone they know. They're asking if it was one of ours."

It was Pernilla's turn to be shocked. "You're suggesting she made it to the other side? I don't believe it!"

"It had better not be unbelievable. I want that amulet! I'm greedy, and I've never pretended otherwise. But there's a lot more involved than that. And I want the girl dealt with. You've done enough guessing. Go and find out the truth."

"To Periton?"

"It's been too long since the Tantellan Compact sent a goodwill mission to the fools in Cambrick. I'll furnish you with the necessary papers. Tell them an extremely dangerous renegade has escaped to Periton and you're there to track them down. They have a renegade of their own—you could offer to deal with him while you're at it."

"Who else are you proposing to send on this mission?"

"Your veterans. All of them. And this time make sure you include a mage who can detect magical auras."

Pernilla's eyebrows went up. "You see this girl as that important?"

"The amulet is that important! If I didn't trust you implicitly, Pernilla, I'd be going after it myself. As for the girl, you're not seriously questioning her importance, are you?" From the look on the chief master's face, he might have been speaking with an imbecile. "The king was shocked to discover he has a half-sister. Worse, you're now telling me she's also a mage. And if that wasn't enough, the Peritonians are now fully alert to an unknown mage at their end of the lake."

His brows drew together. "In case you're too dull-witted to understand the significance of this, let me spell it out for you. The king wants a half-sister even less than we want a renegade mage. If you're right, she's the most dangerous person imaginable, because she has the blood of both mages and royals mingled in her veins. Do I have to remind you that the king has no heir and no other siblings? The next in line to the throne of Tantel is a royal renegade! That's the last thing we need! And it certainly isn't going to help us if the Peritonians get their hands on her."

Kharkin hardened his expression. "Don't let me detain you. You have a lot of preparation to do. Never forget that I have high expectations of what you'll achieve. And I promise that you will be well rewarded if you succeed."

He stood watching tensely as she left. He had told her he would go himself if he didn't trust her implicitly. The truth was he trusted no one implicitly.

The only reason he wasn't going himself was his health. His physician had made it clear nothing could be done about the steady deterioration in his heart condition. These days he couldn't make it to his tower room without pausing for a rest. He could relocate, of course, but he was too stubborn. And he didn't want people to think he was losing his edge.

The Amulet of Zinth had the potential to change everything. He knew of at least one document that credited the amulet with a range of physical cures. Perhaps it could heal his heart.

He needed the amulet, and he needed it urgently.

Chief Master Kharkin stood uncomfortably at attention before King Garneth of Tantel.

If the sovereign knew of Kharkin's health challenges he had never revealed it. Whether he knew it or not, he hadn't been known for showing consideration to his subjects. He had never yet offered the chief master a seat.

"The girl appears to have been dealt with, Your Majesty," he said evenly.

The king eyed him shrewdly. "Are you sure about that, Kharkin?"

Taken aback by the question, the head mage hesitated. To his own annoyance, he saw that the king would see his hesitancy as having provided an answer.

Attempting to recover, he conveyed details of what was known about her disappearance.

His mind was racing as he spoke, trying to understand the implications of the king's question. Either he had superior sources of intelligence, he was learning how to read Kharkin when he was lying, or he was simply good at guessing when to call someone's bluff. Whichever it was, it was irritating and unnerving.

"What are your plans, Chief Master?" the king demanded.

"With your permission, I will send a goodwill mission to Periton."

"To Periton, eh? You botched the first attempt, so now you want to try a goodwill mission?" The king rolled his eyes. "The idea actually has merit. Make it happen. Your people should be in no doubt that their key priority is to deal with the girl."

"Of course, Your Majesty. We will not rest until we are certain that she has been dealt with."

"While they are there they can take a good look around," added the king.

The chief master bowed an acknowledgment.

"Your...goodwill mission, Kharkin. Does it include any other agendas I should be aware of?"

"No, Your Majesty," he lied, hoping his face wasn't betraying him. It seemed ironic to hear such a question from a man who was famous for his hidden agendas.

The king drew his lips back in the semblance of a smile. "Then you are dismissed."

He bowed low. On the surface the meeting had proceeded remarkably smoothly, even taking into account the king's pointed comments and questions. However, he was well aware that the sovereign was a dangerous man to cross, however trivial the matter might be.

As he was leaving the room, the king called after him, "Never forget that I have high expectations of what you'll achieve."

The door shut behind him, leaving him rooted to the spot. Weren't those the exact words he had used with Pernilla?

It could only have been a bizarre coincidence. He couldn't imagine how the king's minions could possibly have overheard their conversation. And Pern would never be stupid enough to report it to anyone.

Even so, such things were not easy to dismiss. He walked away more unsettled than usual, never doubting that was exactly what the king intended.

CHIEF MASTER ADRASTAS stood on the dock at Thesmis, the port city nearest to the capital, waiting to welcome the mage delegation sent by the Tantellan Compact. The ship had arrived in port, but as yet no one had disembarked.

Three other mages stood at his side. Masters Kothlar, Dibson, and Pellistri had ridden in a carriage from Cambrick with him. Kothlar had been less than enthusiastic, but he had come. The other two were clearly flattered and a little overwhelmed by the invitation.

In happier times he would have included Inga, and he felt a pang of disappointment at her absence. She was still in Sengin. After the drama of her detention—a measure that Adrastas regarded as both unlawful and unnecessary—it wasn't hard to imagine she would be reluctant to return at all. He couldn't bring himself to blame her.

Allowing Emmela to accompany the party had been a major miscalculation on his part, and he heartily regretted approving it. Emmela remained unrepentant. As far as she was concerned, the appearance of Kylen confirmed her instinct that Dalthinir was in the area, even though there was no evidence to support it. She was still insisting that Inga had gone to Sengin solely to meet with Dalthinir.

Kothlar was not at all convinced, and neither was Adrastas. If Inga had gone to Sengin to meet Dalthinir, she would surely have left with at least some sense of anticipation. Adrastas believed he knew her well enough to have spotted signs of that. But there'd been nothing even vaguely hopeful about her demeanor. She had left in a very depleted state—*weary in spirit*, as she had put it.

Emmela was proving remarkably stubborn. She still claimed that Dalthinir had been the mage referred to in Inga's initial report. That made no sense to anyone apart from her. Inga had been secretly watched after her release from the lockup. No renegades had approached her at any time, which clearly undermined Emmela's position. Nor did Emmela have an explanation for the sudden appearance of a new and entirely unknown mage—the young female known as Trisanna.

The mission had been nothing short of a disaster. After Kylen—an untrained youth—had successfully extracted Trisanna from the town lockup, the pair of them had simply disappeared. It became apparent during the breakout that Trisanna's ability was illusion. But Kothlar and the others had been left bemused when every trace of power disappeared along with the two renegades. No one had any idea where they were now, nor how they had managed to escape from the region.

One mystery remained. Inga had said she was not aware of any mage coming ashore. And yet Trisanna and her father had been staying with Inga at her aunt's. Had Inga lied to protect Trisanna, or had she failed to detect that Trisanna was a mage? She must have been aware of the truth—unless Trisanna was able to mask her glimmer. Such a thing would be both alarming and completely unprecedented.

Adrastas's difficulties had been steadily growing. Periton's renegade mage count had now increased to five. He had no idea where any of them might be. And with Inga absent, he was missing a senior mage he had come to rely upon.

A boat was finally separating from the ship, prompting him to push aside his gloomy thoughts. It had been a very long time since a delegation of Tantellan mages last arrived in Periton. He needed his wits about him.

Having left the ship, the boat moved slowly toward the pier, the rowers straining at their oars. Adrastas turned to Pellistri with his eyebrows raised.

"There are six mages in that boat," she told him.

Her report confirmed the evidence of his eyes. Tantellan mage garments were almost indistinguishable from those of their Peritonian counterparts, and six of the passengers sitting in the little craft were dressed in the distinctive robes.

He hadn't expected the Tantellans to send more than three or four mages.

A second boat left the ship. "It seems they've brought another six mages," Pellistri informed him.

He frowned. Inga would have been able to detect magical auras while the mages were still on the ship. He'd known Pellistri's ability was considerably weaker, but experiencing it in practice was confronting.

The bigger concern was the arrival of twelve mages. Why had they sent so many?

The first boatload reached the dock, and the new arrivals climbed out.

"Welcome to Periton," said Adrastas with a tight smile. "I am Chief Master Adrastas. His Majesty King Durvaryn has asked me to convey his welcome as well."

One of the mages stepped forward and bowed. "Thank you for your welcome, Chief Master. I am Master Pernilla of Tantel, and I bring greetings from His Majesty King Garneth of Tantel and Chief Master Kharkin."

"I have arranged for carriages to escort you to your lodgings where you will have an opportunity to rest and freshen up after your voyage. You are formally invited to a welcome dinner this evening."

Having exchanged further introductions and pleasantries, the Tantellan mages climbed into the carriages and rolled away to their accommodations.

As soon as they were gone, Adrastas leaned toward Kothlar and asked, "What do you make of them sending twelve mages? What could be the purpose of it?"

Kothlar seemed unsurprised. "Having eyed them, I think we can safely assume they're not here for a goodwill visit. This will be a hunting trip."

"Hunting? Who or what?"

"Most likely the new mage. Trisanna."

When Adrastas didn't respond, he added, "We're the ones who

prompted it. You let them know that Inga had sighted a mage that wasn't one of ours. I suspect we're about to hear their version of who she really is."

He was almost certainly right.

"I'm already regretting sending that dispatch," Adrastas admitted.

"It's too late for regrets, Chief Master. Our task now is to find a way to turn this visit to Periton's advantage."

Adrastas nodded, doubly grateful he had pressured Kothlar into coming on this trip.

CHAPTER 11

With the welcome dinner behind them, and a new day having dawned, Adrastas wasted no time in sitting down with Pernilla. He had also invited Kothlar to the meeting.

"I will be frank, Master Pernilla. I was not expecting a dozen mages. Not on a goodwill visit. Is it possible you have come to Periton with a different agenda in mind?"

"You are candid as well as perceptive, Chief Master, and I welcome that. I believe there is little to be gained in dancing around the issues, so with your permission I will be equally frank."

Adrastas nodded stiffly.

"If I have been reliably informed, the Compact in Periton is acquainted with the challenges posed by renegade mages."

The chief master hesitated for a moment before nodding again.

"I regret to say that a renegade mage from Tantel recently slipped through our guard and escaped. Your recent dispatch left us with the impression she might have found her way to Periton."

"Can you describe this person?" asked Adrastas.

"Gladly. She is a young woman who goes by the name of Trisanna. She is extremely dangerous. The threat she poses cannot be overstated."

Adrastas couldn't resist shooting a glance at Kothlar.

Pernilla did not miss it. "You have already encountered her?"

"We have," he acknowledged.

Pernilla's face appeared drawn. "Is she in your custody?"

"She was, briefly. She escaped with the help of another renegade."

The Tantellan was making a concerted effort to appear impassive, but Adrastas felt certain she registered alarm at this news.

"Was it Dalthinir?" she asked.

He shook his head. "No. A different renegade. A young man." Adrastas decided to reveal no more than he needed to.

"Did she leave anything behind when she escaped?"

Ah. So she had something the Tantellans wanted. Adrastas couldn't help wondering what it might be.

"No. She escaped before we had a proper opportunity to examine and question her."

"I am truly sorry to hear that." Pernilla's demeanor gave the lie to her statement. She seemed mightily relieved.

She immediately continued. "We have reason to believe she means great harm to your kingdom and our own. An important purpose behind our visit is to deal with the renegade before she is able to follow through with her plans. Our hope is that Periton will allow us to energetically pursue her, wherever she may be."

"King Durvaryn can hardly be expected to permit a large company of Tantellan mages to roam freely around the countryside unattended!" Adrastas retorted.

"Of course not!" replied Pernilla. "It need hardly be said that we will take no action of any kind without first receiving the approval of His Majesty. And while we would prefer to operate independently for the sake of efficiency, we would be willing to work closely with some of your number if that is your preference. Perhaps while we are at it, we can help you deal with your own renegades. Especially if the person we seek has thrown her lot in with them."

"I will convey your proposal to His Majesty," Adrastas promised. "That will take time. In the meantime, I trust you and your companions will make use of the opportunity to enjoy the many attractions of Thesmis."

After a respectful bow, Pernilla departed, leaving Adrastas and Kothlar alone.

"What do you make of all that?" asked Adrastas.

"They might be our best hope of dealing with our renegades. Assuming that's what we want to happen."

Adrastas looked at him sharply. "What do you mean? Why would you suggest we mightn't want our renegades dealt with?"

Kothlar shrugged. "We were out of our depth with Dalthinir's new friend Kylen. He made us look like children with toys. I haven't seen this Tantellan group in action, but I suspect we might find them just as difficult to handle if it ever came to that. They'll keep their eyes open while they're wandering around. It's possible they might decide Periton is ripe for the plucking."

"And you believe we might not be able to resist them effectively without Dalthinir and Kylen's help?"

He shrugged. "It's a possibility."

Kothlar was not known to be given to wild fancies, yet he was apparently serious. And Adrastas hadn't forgotten he had guessed correctly about the Tantellans' purpose in coming to Periton.

Adrastas frowned. "Dealing with the security of the kingdom is King Durvaryn's responsibility. My responsibility is to eliminate renegades. It astonishes me to hear you even contemplating the idea of recruiting them!"

"I know the law as well as you do, Adrastas. What I don't yet know is what these Tantellans are capable of."

And with that he excused himself and departed.

Adrastas was left shaking his head in bewilderment. Why did the two people he most relied upon have to lose their perspective at the same time?

THE MEETING with King Durvaryn was proving to be more challenging than Adrastas anticipated.

The king glared at him. "I will certainly not allow twelve Tantellan mages to spy out every nook and cranny in Periton! Don't expect me to consent to any such thing!"

"I understand your concerns, Your Majesty. But they will not be unaccompanied. Some of our mages will be with them at all times. And our troubles with Tantel are in the distant past. We mustn't forget the many years of peaceful relations between the two kingdoms."

"I have met King Garneth, Adrastas. Once. And it was once too many! I wouldn't entrust a rabid dog to the man."

"It might be seen as a provocation to simply send them all home. And there is a chance they might be able to help us deal with our own renegade problem. We currently find ourselves with no fewer than five renegade mages to deal with."

"I concede your point about the risk of being seen as provocative, much as I resent Garneth placing me in this position. It's easy to guess how he would react if twelve Peritonian mages arrived on his doorstep expecting free access to his kingdom. How many of our own mages are you proposing to attach to this mission?"

"I had two or three in mind, Your Majesty."

"Two or three! How could so few be expected to keep an eye on them?"

"How many would you want me to assign?"

"Twenty, at least."

Adrastas was aghast. "Twenty? That isn't practical, Your Majesty. We simply don't have enough mages to withdraw twenty of them from their usual commitments for an unknown period of time. It could have a major impact on the kingdom."

The interaction sputtered on, with the king eventually agreeing to approve the mission, but only on the condition that twelve Peritonian mages accompanied the Tantellans.

Adrastas was now faced with finding twelve mages who were willing to go and could be released.

Kothlar would have to lead the Peritonian contingent. He wouldn't even be vaguely interested, of course. Not after everything that had happened in Sengin.

Adrastas wasn't looking forward to discussing it with him.

To the astonishment of the chief master, Kothlar was not only willing to lead the mission, he actually seemed eager to do it.

His immediate response was, "Someone needs to keep an eye on the Tantellans. I have one condition though—I don't want Emmela to be involved."

"Of course. She was never under consideration anyway."

"I think you should appoint Alexis as my deputy. He's shown he has a cool head in a crisis."

"Gladly," Adrastas replied. "You'll need someone who can detect magical auras too. In the absence of Inga I'm going to send Pellistri."

The team membership was settled in a remarkably short time.

"Do you have any idea of the Tantellans' real agenda?" asked Kothlar. "I'm aware of no evidence to suggest that Trisanna is an imminent threat to both kingdoms, either from her time in Sengin or when Kylen broke her out."

Adrastas nodded slowly. "It's a crucial question. Our interaction with Pernilla was instructive. You might remember she asked if the girl had left anything behind in the lockup when she escaped. She seemed relieved when I said she hadn't."

"So you believe this Trisanna has something they want?"

"Almost certainly. Although I have no idea what it is."

Kothlar seemed satisfied. "It's good to have been made aware of it. When do we start?"

"As soon as I've informed the others. We need to get back to Thesmis as soon as possible. The Tantellans will be getting restless."

"Twelve mages? That will mean a party of twenty-four!" Pernilla was aghast. "It will be impossible to hide a group of that size. Any renegade will sense us coming from miles away!"

Adrastas was unyielding. "King Durvaryn was willing to approve the mission only under that condition. I wonder how your king might react if the situation were reversed."

Pernilla nodded tightly. "You have a point," she acknowledged.

"Twelve is a large group already," Adrastas continued. "That many people can't expect to be invisible."

The Tantellan looked at him strangely for a moment before throwing up her hands in resignation. "Very well. I suppose we will have to do the best we can in difficult circumstances."

"Master Kothlar will lead the Peritonian mages. All of them will have assembled in Thesmis by tomorrow. You can expect them to be ready to leave immediately. Horses have been provided for everyone in the party."

"Thank you for your help, Chief Master. I am grateful for it, and I am confident King Garneth will be equally gratified."

Adrastas left feeling a nagging unease about the mission. There was a great deal he didn't understand about the intentions of the Tantellans, and the more he pondered it the more grateful he was that the king had insisted on sending an equivalent number of Peritonian mages.

He also took comfort in knowing that Kothlar would be leading the Peritonians. There was no one he trusted more for such an important assignment.

There was one thing Kothlar knew that Adrastas hadn't revealed to Pernilla. The king would be sending a substantial squadron of mounted guards to shadow the expedition. They would keep their distance, but they would be available at short notice should Kothlar ever need them.

"We will begin our search in the south," Kothlar announced.

"Why?" asked Pernilla in a tone bordering on rudeness. The Tantellans clearly saw the large group of locals as an intrusion, and strains were already beginning to emerge.

"Because Trisanna arrived in the south, and it's unlikely she will have been able to move far since then."

Pernilla nodded curtly. "Lead on, then."

Kothlar headed southeast across country, intending to intersect with the main road that ran from Cambrick to Sengin in the southeastern corner of the kingdom. From there he planned to head north-west along the coast.

As they rode they naturally separated into two groups—the Peritonians leading and the Tantellans following. Both groups likewise kept to themselves when they paused for a midday meal. Kothlar briefly joined the visitors and made an attempt at drawing them out, but every effort was firmly rebuffed.

When they set out again Kothlar waved Alexis over. Leaning closer, he spoke to him quietly. "Before long our guests are going to look for a way to strike out on their own. I don't intend to let them get away from us. Make sure everyone is ready to move quickly."

Alexis nodded. Over the next few minutes Kothlar saw him spreading the word. Thus far he had every reason to be satisfied with his choice of a deputy.

On the morning of the third day out from Thesmis, their path led them through the outskirts of an extensive forest. An hour before noon, Alexis rode up to Kothlar.

"The Tantellans are falling behind," he said. "I'm wondering if they might be about to make a move."

Kothlar nodded. "Come with me," he said. Turning his horse around, he rode back along the path. A considerable gap had opened up between the two groups, and the two men rode for several minutes before they reached the second group.

The look on the faces of the Tantellans made it clear their presence was not welcome. Ignoring it, Kothlar headed for Pernilla.

"Is there a problem?" asked Pernilla coolly.

"Could I request that your group remains in close contact with ours?" Kothlar said frankly. "The king's soldiers routinely patrol the kingdom, and he has sent word of our party and its size. If we are inadvertently separated, neither group will be recognizable to the soldiers. I wish to avoid any possibility of trouble."

Pernilla didn't seem surprised. She nodded casually. "We will do our best."

Over the next few hours the Tantellans did indeed remain in close contact. Nevertheless, for reasons he couldn't articulate Kothlar remained dissatisfied. He recognized there was little he could do apart from keeping a watchful eye on them.

The afternoon was drawing to a close when they reached a river. No ford was in sight, so Kothlar signaled his riders to find a place to camp. The timing seemed right to end their journey for that day. By the time they prepared food and established a campsite, it would most likely be dark anyway.

Kothlar spotted Pernilla riding behind, and waved to her. He made no direct attempt to speak to the Tantellan. It seemed unnecessary. He fully expected Pernilla to take her cue from the Peritonians. He was therefore taken completely by surprise when the Tantellans rode past them toward the river.

He had dismounted, but he hastily climbed back into the saddle, calling for Alexis. The two of them hurried after the visitors, arriving at the water's edge to find no sign of them.

The river was flowing swiftly between steep banks, and any riders who entered the water would have quickly been swept downstream. No obvious landing place was visible anywhere downriver.

"Pellistri!" he shouted. "I need you. Urgently."

He turned to Alexis. "Get the others mounted. Start searching downriver. This is a dangerous place to have attempted a river crossing. I want to know what's become of the Tantellans!"

The moment Pellistri arrived, the two of them set off following the river, keeping as close to the water as they were able.

"Can you detect their glimmer?" Kothlar asked.

"No," she replied. "There were traces at first, but now there's nothing."

"Is it possible they've been swept out of your range?"

She shook her head. "That isn't likely to be the issue. It isn't surprising I can't sense them—water is the one thing that masks magical auras."

"You would also lose sight of their glimmer if they all died at the same moment."

Pellistri refused even to acknowledge the possibility of such a disaster.

"The only thing we can do is keep searching," Kothlar conceded with a sigh.

A frustrating couple of hours passed before Kothlar called the search to a halt. There was no point continuing in the dark.

The river bent in several broad sweeps downriver, providing multiple locations where horses could easily have reached land, or more grimly, where bodies of men or horses might have been snagged by fallen branches along the riverbank. But no trace of the missing Tantellans or their magical auras could be found.

Twelve riders and their horses had simply disappeared.

CHAPTER 12

An exhaustive search conducted by Kothlar's mages the following morning drew the same conclusion as before. It was as if the Tantellans had vanished from the face of the earth.

"I'm placing you in charge of the party," Kothlar told Alexis. "Make contact as soon as you can with the soldiers who've been trailing us. See if you can discover anything that might indicate what's become of the Tantellans."

"What are you planning to do?" asked Alexis.

"I'm going to make some inquiries of my own," he replied. "I'm leaving immediately. You can inform the others."

His deputy looked at him strangely but didn't question his decision.

Kothlar set off at once, following the river. He held out no hope of discovering anything connected with the Tantellans' disappearance, although his path did at least allow him a final opportunity to look for any sign of them. Having expected to find nothing, he wasn't disappointed.

As soon as he found a suitable ford, he crossed the river and made for the main road. Reaching it, he turned his horse south, away from the capital.

He would need to return to Cambrick eventually, but he saw no reason to hurry back. There would be no answers for him there, only questions, and he had more than enough mysteries to contend with already.

An extraordinary situation called for an unconventional response. He was taking his questions south. He was going to find Inga.

PULLING out weeds could be very satisfying. However hard the weeds resisted, they eventually succumbed to the inevitable. And best of all, they didn't argue about the process.

Having starting the task not long after dawn, Inga had already made an impressive difference to the appearance of the lane leading to her aunt's house. Hearing a horse approaching, she allowed herself to pause and look up. The horse slowed as it drew nearer, coming to a complete stop when it reached the entrance to the lane.

Getting to her feet, she squinted into the bright light silhouetting the animal, struggling to recognize its rider. When he dismounted and removed the hood from his face, her heart sank.

"Kothlar." Her face formed a glower all by itself. "I presume you've come to put me back in the lockup. What have I done this time?"

He winced. "I'm sorry I did that to you, Inga. Emmela was insistent, and I allowed her to convince me. I was a fool. The others were not happy with the decision. They saw it was wrong, and it should have been obvious to me as well."

"You did me a favor. That night in the lockup brought everything into perspective for me. I'm finished with the Compact."

Her statement was provocative, but he didn't allow himself to be deterred. "I need your advice."

"If you want my advice, you can have it for free: leave right now!"

Kneeling down once more, she resumed her weeding.

"We have a problem," he persisted. "With the Tantellans."

When she continued to ignore him, he added, "They're hunting Trisanna."

She was in the act of tugging at a weed when he said it. He'd been smart enough to raise one of the few subjects she cared about. The news stopped her cold.

Climbing slowly to her feet once more, she scowled at him. "You never were much good at taking a hint, were you?" She jerked her head toward the house. "You'd better come with me. You look as if you haven't slept in days."

Trudging wearily behind her to the house, he somehow found the energy to remove the horse's saddle and replace its bridle with a halter. Tying the halter to a post, he followed her inside.

She served him fresh bread and preserves along with hot tea. Judging from the way he attacked it, he hadn't eaten in a while. His eyes were drooping by the time he finished. He sighed deeply.

"You need to sleep before you try to say anything," she told him.

He shook his head firmly. "This can't wait. Where can we speak privately?"

"Come outside. We can walk while we're talking. You'll go to sleep if you don't keep moving."

He must have already decided what to say, because the moment they were outside it all poured out in a rush. "You have a part in what's going on. Everything that's happened was prompted by your dispatch to Adrastas. He sent a message to the Tantellans asking if the mage you detected on the lake might have been one of theirs. He wanted to offer them a chance to own it from the beginning if they were responsible. They responded with a proposal for a goodwill visit to Periton. Adrastas agreed after discussing it with the king. They had no other option—it would have been perceived as an insult if they'd refused. I went with Adrastas to Thesmis to greet them. They sent twelve mages."

Her eyebrows rose up. "Twelve? Why so many?"

"It soon became obvious they hadn't been sent to Periton because of their diplomatic skills. Their leader announced that a dangerous mage had escaped from Tantel, someone who posed a significant threat to both kingdoms."

"Trisanna," she said flatly.

He nodded. "They wanted permission to scour the kingdom until they'd tracked her down and dealt with her. The king agreed on condition that twelve of our mages accompanied them. They weren't happy about it, but they weren't given a choice. Adrastas asked me to lead our group."

"I'm sure you were suitably excited."

To her surprise he said, "I agreed without hesitation. I wasn't at all convinced she was such a threat, and I wanted to keep an eye on what they were up to. It wasn't until we were underway that I got a proper look at them. There are nine men and three women."

"What are their abilities?"

"They never spelled them out. But they're not the kind of people who do parlor tricks at parties. Every one of them would as soon cut your throat as speak to you. My cousin is a member of the king's personal guard, and I've watched him train. These Tantellans look about as hard-bitten as him."

Seeing the grimness of his expression, she began to feel the cold grip of fear. And not just for Trisanna. For Dalthinir and Kylen as well.

"When we set off, I had the feeling they'd break away from us at the first opportunity. It didn't take long. We reached the River Jobuk just before dusk on the third day. There was no ford nearby, so I halted our party. The Tantellans simply kept going. The river was flowing swiftly at that point. They apparently rode straight into it."

"That's madness!"

His brows furrowed. "Madness or not, it was carefully planned. Within moments, there was no trace of them."

"Was Pellistri with you?"

"She was. She said their magical auras suddenly vanished."

"The water would mask their glimmer. Assuming they hadn't died."

He shrugged. "They could have drowned, but I doubt it. I have a feeling that's what they intended us to think. Something tells me they're alive and well. And completely unsupervised."

"Did you look for any sign of them downstream?"

"We searched until it was dark, and more thoroughly the next morning. We found nothing. You could be forgiven for thinking they'd never been there."

He fell silent.

"You seem to have your own opinion about their real agenda," she suggested.

He peered thoughtfully at her. "When Trisanna was with you, did she have anything unusual on her?"

"What kind of thing do you mean?"

"Something valuable, maybe."

Inga frowned. "She had some coin and a few other valuables. But nothing the Tantellans would send twelve mages to recover."

"She wasn't wearing ornaments or jewelry of any kind?"

"Why are you asking?"

"We had a couple of meetings with the Tantellan leader, a mage known as Pernilla. Adrastas got the impression from her she has something they want. I've been wondering if recovering it might be the real reason for their mission."

"Trisanna did have something around her neck," Inga said, straining to remember details. "I didn't get a good look at it—I caught a brief glimpse of it on one occasion. Whatever it is, though, it isn't the only reason they want her. She's King Garneth's sister. Or half-sister to be more accurate—she was born illegitimately."

He stared at her wide-eyed.

She shrugged. "Now you know why they're so eager to kill her."

He peered at her in complete bewilderment. "I can't believe you kept everyone in the dark about something this important! Why didn't you tell me?"

"Tell you? And what would you have done?"

"I would have informed the king. This kind of thing is his responsibility."

"Both of us know where that would have ended. He would have handed her straight back to the Tantellans. She's next in line to the Tantellan throne! Any other decision would amount to a declaration of war."

"None of that is my responsibility."

"The person who turns her in doesn't get to pretend they're not responsible for what happens next!"

He had nothing to say.

She planted her hands on her hips. "You wanted to sanction me simply for *talking* to a man who had just saved the kingdom! There was no way I would have entrusted this kind of information to you!"

He didn't know what to say. That didn't surprise her in the least.

She glared at him. "Having her true identity announced to the world was the last thing she wanted. Her fondest hope was to stay out of sight and live a quiet life! And she probably would have managed it if you and Emmela hadn't shown up and had us all arrested!"

"You can't take it upon yourself to make decisions about issues like this!" he sputtered.

"Arrest me, then. The moment I saw you I knew you'd come to lock me up again."

He was holding his head. "I don't know what's worse," he moaned. "The fact that you took it upon yourself to suppress information of monumental significance, or the fact that I think you did the right thing."

"Maybe there's hope for you yet," she said dryly.

"I'm in an impossible position now," he protested. "If I pass on this information, you'll be in big trouble. If I don't, no one else will know what's motivating the Tantellans."

He suddenly stood stock still, frowning. "She isn't just the Tantellan king's half-sister, is she? She's also a mage!"

"How could she be?" asked Inga calmly. "Her father was a king."

"But who was her mother? What if he got a mage pregnant?"

"Royals have always been prohibited from reproducing with mages," she reminded him calmly.

He ignored her comment. "Please tell me it isn't true!"

She gave nothing away.

"She *was* the one you detected on the lake. Then you met her and heard her story. You couldn't bear to see her killed for no other reason than an accident of birth. Oh, Inga!"

She looked at him coldly. "Feel free to raise your theories with her directly next time you see her. In the meantime, speculate all you like, but don't expect me to pay any attention to your ramblings."

His shoulders had slumped. "She's a renegade mage with royal blood in her veins. It's no wonder the Tantellans want her dead!" He groaned. "Why did she have to come to Periton?"

He stood staring off into the distance for a few moments, his eyes glazed. Then he ran a hand over his face. "Bad as it is, I need to put all of this aside. None of it is the reason I came to talk with you. Your ability is detecting magical auras. Are you aware of any way of masking glimmer?"

"Where are you going with this, Kothlar?"

"This isn't about Trisanna. It's about the Tantellans and their disappearing act."

She stared at him, rapidly considering the potential implications of such a conversation.

Then she shrugged. She was tired of juggling secrets. "Dragons reputedly were able to hide their auras. So it's possible."

"Are you aware of any human mage who's capable of it?"

After a moment's hesitation she answered him honestly. "No. But I have my suspicions."

"Dalthinir?" he asked.

She nodded. "I don't see how he could have lived under our noses in Cambrick without being able to hide his glimmer."

"Do you think it might be possible to hide someone else's aura as well?"

She pursed her lips. "It might be," she said noncommittally. She had definite opinions on this topic, but she had no intention of sharing them. Dalthinir could keep his secrets as far as she was concerned.

He took a deep breath. "Much as I dislike the idea, I think it's possible the Tantellans have at least one mage capable of doing it. It would explain why their glimmer disappeared so abruptly."

"Perhaps." She wasn't entirely convinced. "Why choose a river for their disappearing act if they could have done it anywhere? It added a significant element of risk."

"Because there would be no valid reason for their glimmer to disappear anywhere other than in water."

She didn't offer comment. She had believed for some time that Dalthinir was capable of hiding his magical aura. Was she simply unwilling to accept that other mages might be equally capable of doing it?

Kothlar's thinking had moved on. "It leads to the next question. Can someone hide the use of magical power?"

"I have no certain knowledge, but I have my suspicions about that as well."

He didn't seem surprised. "When Kylen broke Trisanna out of the lockup, they both disappeared."

"You mean you couldn't see them anymore?"

"Right. We could still track the use of power, but that soon stopped as well."

"Perhaps because no one was using power."

He shook his head. "I think it more likely they were using a combination of illusion and some kind of masking capability. It didn't occur to me at the time, but I'm beginning to see it's the only plausible explanation for what happened."

Inga hadn't been present, and she hadn't heard exactly what had happened. Clearly Trisanna had used illusion to hide them, and either Dalthinir or Kylen must have hidden their use of power. It wouldn't have been necessary for them to hide magical auras, because none of the mages present could detect auras. But they were probably capable of doing that as well if they needed to.

"This is worse than a nightmare," said Kothlar miserably. "Our renegades are now able to hide their entire group using illusion. They're apparently able to hide their glimmer and their use of power as well. It doesn't seem unreasonable to suppose that the Tantellans are able to do the same. It places the rest of us in a frighteningly weak position."

"How ironic. It sounds like you need Dalthinir's help," she said, her mouth twisting in a wry smile.

"I suggested something similar to Adrastas. He didn't take it too well."

She stared at him open-mouthed. "Are you telling me you actually proposed working with renegades instead of killing them?"

He ignored her question. "I need to return to Cambrick."

"What are you going to do when you get there? What will you tell Adrastas?"

"I don't know. I need to make him aware of our vulnerability. But you needn't worry, Inga. I'll find a way to do it without exposing all your secrets."

He looked at her sharply. "I do need to understand one thing, though. When I first arrived you said you're finished with the Compact. What did you mean by that?"

She sighed. "I wasn't announcing I've become a renegade if that's what you're asking. I'm still willing to come under the authority of the Compact as long as no one expects me to return to Cambrick."

"We've already seen the importance of having someone in the border region. Would you be willing to be the eyes and ears of the Compact in Sengin?"

"Yes. I'll gladly monitor and report the movement of Tantellan mages. Don't ask me to turn in Trisanna, though. Or Dalthinir or Kylen for that matter."

He nodded dully. "I'll suggest to Adrastas that we need to leave you here. It's the least I can do given my past indiscretions."

She nodded gratefully. "Thank you."

His eyelids were beginning to droop again.

"You need to rest before you go anywhere!" she told him.

"Perhaps for an hour or two..."

Taking him back to the house, she pushed him into a spare bedroom and made sure no one went near him. He didn't emerge until dawn. He'd slept through an afternoon and an entire night.

He wanted to leave immediately, but she wouldn't hear of it. While her aunt was serving him a hot meal with second helpings, Inga saddled and bridled his horse.

"Be careful, Kothlar," she said as he mounted.

"You too, Inga." After a quick wave, he urged his horse forward. Reaching the end of the lane he turned onto the road and was gone.

He'd been the last person she wanted to see when he arrived. Now, she'd wished him well and meant it. She could only wonder at her own fickleness.

But these were uncertain times. Every one of them needed all the friends they could get.

VOLUME 2—DANGERS MULTIPLY

CHAPTER 13

The morning after escaping from Sengin with the help of the farmer, Kylen woke to find his companions already stirring. Once they had shared a simple meal, they cleared away every sign of their presence and prepared to move out.

"Where to next?" Jonno asked Dalthinir.

"We'll head for the coast," he replied.

Zeke brightened visibly at the news, and it was obvious to Kylen that both Dalthinir and Trisanna had noted it.

They hadn't been walking long when they came upon a small village. Normally they were careful to avoid towns, but this settlement was nowhere near big enough to include a market square. It was so tiny it didn't even boast a tavern. It was the kind of place that was too insignificant to be worth avoiding.

The village consisted of a few rough cottages, positioned on either side of a small road that was little better than a path. Passing through it they glimpsed few faces, and none of them were friendly.

With no reason to linger, they kept moving steadily westward in the direction of the sea.

Some time after leaving the village Kylen caught sight of a boy heading toward them. A large basket was perched precariously on his head, and he was walking strangely. Peering at him, Kylen saw that the soles of his feet were not making contact with the ground—his weight was carried entirely on the sides or the balls of his feet.

The moment he noticed them, the boy lowered his head and tried to move faster. In his haste he more than once appeared to be in danger of losing his load.

"Good morning," offered Bella as he passed.

The boy didn't answer. Shuffling forward as quickly as he was able, he was soon lost to sight around a bend in the road.

Kylen had been walking beside Zeke. "What's wrong with him?" he asked curiously, jerking his head back along the path behind them.

"He has clubfoot." Zeke shook his head sadly. "Not much of a life for him, I'm guessing."

The sound of angry voices soon reached them from the direction he had gone.

"Freak!"

"No one wants you here! You bring bad luck on the whole village!"

The words were punctuated by cries of pain.

Without pausing for a minute, the twins sprinted back the way they had come.

Filled with curiosity, Kylen hurried after them, the others close behind him.

Turning the corner, he saw the clubfoot boy on the ground, surrounded by three boys who were jeering at him while kicking him mercilessly. He lay helpless with his head cradled protectively in his arms.

"Stop it!" Bella yelled fiercely.

Looking up, the three tormentors paused in their assault on the victim. They turned to face the two figures bearing down on them, their body language suggesting they were more than willing to fight. Then, registering the larger group behind the twins, the three of them hastily exited the scene.

The boy's basket had been knocked to the ground in the scuffle. Its contents, an assortment of clothing, lay strewn across the path. Some of the clothing had been trampled in the dirt.

"My mother will have to wash it all again," the boy muttered miserably.

Then he scowled up at his would-be rescuers. "What did you have to do that for?" he demanded. "It's going to be worse for me now! Much worse!"

"We couldn't stand by while they bullied you!" Bella retorted.

The victim was not impressed. "And what about next time? And the time after that?"

Shaking his head, he got up and began gathering the garments. Jonno tried to help him, but the boy pushed him away. As soon as he had filled the basket, he turned and headed back the way he had come. He didn't look behind him.

Jonno threw up his hands in frustration. "What were we supposed to do?"

"Bullying like this doesn't happen on impulse," Dalthinir told him. "It's a pattern of behavior. You broke the rules when you rescued the boy, and the bullies will demand payback. They'll be wanting to demonstrate that the system is still in place. That means they'll come down on him even harder next time. He obviously understood that."

"There must be something we can do!" exclaimed Bella.

Dalthinir stood musing for a few moments. After a glance at Trisanna he nodded his head. "Perhaps we can find a way to help. These boys would be very superstitious. We might be able to take advantage of that."

"What are we going to do?" asked Jonno.

"We'll discuss it later," promised Dalthinir with a mysterious smile.

Kylen was no less puzzled than the others, but Dalthinir had nothing further to say.

"Let's find somewhere to camp," his mentor suggested. "As soon as we're settled we can start making plans."

RELAXING in the shade of a tree with the others, Trisanna spotted the lean figure of Bella heading their way.

Bella's eyes were alight. "He's coming!"

Surging to her feet, Trisanna felt her heart skip a beat. Dalthinir's plan was about to be put to the test.

They had chosen a spot where they could overlook the road without being seen. The location was very close to the place where the bullies had accosted their victim two days previously.

Peering down the path, she saw him coming. Once more a basket was perched on his head. And once more a group of boys gathered further down the path. The bullies were not far from her position.

This time the group must have numbered seven or eight. The new additions were bigger and older than the original three, and every one of them was brandishing a crude club. They intended to make a statement.

The boy with clubfoot saw them waiting, but he didn't falter. He must have known that a beating was coming sooner or later. Perhaps he simply wanted to it get it over with.

Seeing his raw courage, Trisanna swallowed convulsively, fighting back tears. A part of her wanted to run into the open and stand beside him. Instead, she stayed hidden, biding her time.

The group of boys remained silent as he approached. When he reached them they parted and flowed around him.

"So you thought you could get help, did you?"

"Where are your rescuers now?"

When he didn't react to their taunts, they moved closer, raising their clubs purposefully.

At that moment, a dark shape swooped low, passing so close over the heads of the startled boys they all ducked involuntarily.

"It's a raven!" one of them exclaimed. "It's unlucky to meet a raven!"

A hare appeared, hopping slowly onto the path and passing through the group before disappearing into the undergrowth on the other side. It was so close they could have grabbed it if they'd dared.

"Something bad's going to happen," moaned one of the younger boys. "It always does if you meet a hare on the road."

"Something bad is definitely going to happen," scoffed one of the older boys. "This little freak is about to get what he deserves."

Before any of them could move, a huge shape abruptly blotted out the sun. Enormous wings beat slowly as a great dragon dropped from the sky and settled beside the startled boys.

Several of the bullies turned and bolted, but one by one they were lifted into the air by unknown means and deposited back where they had begun.

"Run again, and you die," growled the dragon, smoke billowing from its nostrils.

The boys cowered before it, trembling with terror. Then the massive creature shifted awkwardly, and their eyes were drawn to its feet.

"IT HAS CLUBFOOT TOO!" blurted one of the boys incredulously.

The dragon lifted its head to the heavens and roared. Fire poured from its nostrils.

The bullies covered their ears, and several of them howled in fear.

"Do you dare suggest something is wrong with me?" demanded the fearsome beast.

A pathetic chorus of whimpers was the only reply.

Throughout it all the clubfoot boy had remained on his feet, watching wide-eyed. The dragon now glanced in his direction.

"If even a hair of this boy's head is harmed—by you or anyone else —I will come for you! I will take each of you when you least expect it and bear you away to unending torment!"

With this warning, the dragon disappeared abruptly.

As the boys sat stunned, the raven reappeared, flying low over them once more before flapping slowly away into the distance.

Picking themselves up one at a time, the boys slunk off. Their intended victim was left standing alone. The path stood empty. Nothing remained, except the clubs discarded by the bullies.

After peering around in bemusement for a while, he shrugged and resumed his journey.

TRISANNA STOOD among the others as they celebrated their success. The twins were barely able to contain their excitement.

"That was nicely done," offered Dalthinir with a smile. He clapped Kylen on the back and grinned at Trisanna. "You both performed your roles admirably. Your illusions were remarkable, Trisanna! And you were perfect, Kylen. I'll never forget the looks on the faces of the boys when you picked them up and sent them sailing back to the dragon."

Trisanna felt herself blushing with the praise.

"In case you're wondering," Dalthinir added, "I hid all use of your magic. Even if another mage had been nearby, they would have detected nothing."

Kylen seemed no less impressed than the others by the illusions. Nevertheless, he turned to her with a frown. "A clubfoot dragon?"

She looked at him calmly. "Why not? Dragons might have clubfoot for all we know."

He shook his head stubbornly. "No they don't. And they don't speak our language, either."

Dalthinir was staring at him curiously. "You're right, Kylen. What makes you so sure, though?"

Kylen blushed. "I must have read it somewhere," he sputtered. Hurrying to change the subject, he asked, "Do you think they'll leave the boy alone now?"

"Are you serious?" chortled Jonno. "They won't dare to go anywhere near him!"

"I expect that Jonno is right," agreed Dalthinir. "We've left them in a difficult position. If they try to tell the adults what happened, no one is going to believe them."

A delighted laugh burst out of Bella. "It was a beautiful touch to have the dragon say it would come after them if *anyone* harms the boy. They'll be falling over themselves to protect him now!"

Zeke was no less complimentary. It was clear that he was especially proud of Trisanna.

The celebrations might have continued for longer if Dalthinir hadn't called them aside. "I think it would be better if we're not seen in the area. We can continue heading west." He winked at Zeke. "I suspect I'm not the only one eager to see the coast again."

No less satisfied than the others by the outcome, Trisanna nevertheless couldn't relax. And as time passed her discomfort only continued to grow.

Dalthinir must have noticed, because he came alongside her as they walked. "Were you unhappy about something that happened?" he asked tentatively.

"Not at all!" she replied hastily. "I'm delighted that we were able to help the boy."

"Is it Zeke?" he persisted.

She was grateful for his concern and pleased that he had offered her an acceptable reason for her uneasiness.

"I am concerned about him," she replied. "He's gone out of his way to help me, and I've ruined his life in the process."

"I don't think he minds."

"But I do!" She glanced at the fisherman, walking ahead of them. "This isn't the kind of life he would choose for himself. Fishing is the life he loves. But I don't know what to do!"

Dalthinir nodded. "Leave it to me, Trisanna. I'll give it some thought."

"Thank you!" she breathed as he moved away. She was grateful to him for sensing her concern and doing what he could to ease it.

He had no way of knowing what was really troubling her.

From the moment she had first witnessed the bullies, it had felt as if the amulet was tugging at her. It had become increasingly intrusive as she proceeded with her illusion. She had almost felt like the amulet wanted to join in on the action—even that it had wanted to give the dragon the power to consume them entirely. And not because it was eager to exact justice. Inflicting pain and suffering was what it cared about.

And yet the dragon wasn't real. How could it consume anyone? And the amulet had no sentience of its own. How could it have independent wishes and desires of its own?

None of it made any sense.

Could it be that she was becoming hardened herself? Was she merely trying to avoid responsibility, shifting the blame for her thoughts and desires to the amulet instead?

She had no answers to these questions, and she wasn't ready to raise them with Dalthinir. Not until she'd had time to think it through for herself.

Pushing down her discomfort, she plodded on behind the others.

CHAPTER 14

Kylen stood beside his companions gazing down at the seaside town of Jayton. It had taken barely a day to reach it, even though they had gone well out of their way to stay clear of farms and other people.

The previous evening they had sat together around a fire, recalling their experiences in Sengin and beyond. Although they hadn't known each other long they clearly felt relaxed together, and there had been plenty of laughter.

Kylen had sensed it might prove to be a farewell of sorts. Before they settled for sleep, Dalthinir had addressed Zeke directly. "I hope you know you have no obligation to remain with Trisanna. You understand enough of her story to be aware that life will never be normal for her."

"I know that," the fisherman replied. "But it ain't my way to desert someone when they're in trouble."

"There's no need to worry about her," the mage assured Zeke. "We'll do everything in our power to take care of her."

"I've seen that already," he acknowledged. "I couldn't have freed her from the lockup."

"I owe you more than I could ever repay," Trisanna had told him self-consciously. "I'll be forever grateful to you! But I can't forget that your whole world has been upended because of me! I don't want to ruin the rest of your life. I'll never be at peace if you're constantly at risk on my account."

Zeke had offered no response, and they ended the conversation with nothing finally resolved.

Now, after a brisk walk the following morning, the sea was within reach. Zeke couldn't keep his eyes away from it.

"It's obvious to all of us where your heart lies," Dalthinir told him gently.

The fisherman didn't try to deny it. He sighed. "I didn't sleep a lot last night. I was thinking about our conversation. If Trisanna truly needed me, I wouldn't hesitate to stay. But I know she'll be safe with you. And you're right about where my heart lies. I get restless when I'm too far from the wind and the waves."

He gazed uncertainly toward the horizon. "What am I going to do if I leave you all?"

"After everything that's happened I don't think it will be safe for you to stay in Periton," Dalthinir replied. "For a time you posed as a fisherman from the Summer Isles. Perhaps you could turn the story into the truth. Find someone who'll take you there. Once you've arrived, I imagine you'll discover a local fisherman who would appreciate your help."

"You still have what I gave you, don't you?" asked Trisanna.

He nodded. "I do, but I can't keep it! It's too much!"

"I want you to have it!" she insisted. "You lost your boat and your livelihood because of me. Maybe it will go partway toward getting you a new start."

For a long moment he hesitated, but eventually he yielded to the pull of the ocean. After embracing Trisanna wistfully, he set off down the hill toward the town. When he reached its outskirts he turned around and waved once. Then he resumed his journey without looking back. Before long he had disappeared among the buildings.

Trisanna was clearly sorry to see him go, but at the same time a weight seemed to have lifted off her.

She turned to the mage. "Thank you for your kindness to Zeke," she said. "It's such a relief to know he has a chance to make a new start." Then she included all of them in her glance. "And thank you for putting yourselves at risk to rescue me!"

"Think nothing of it," Dalthinir replied. "We might have helped you, but it doesn't mean you're safe. Every mage who doesn't belong to the Compact is under sentence of death." He softened his words with a smile. "I don't want you to be too discouraged, though. We seem to manage somehow."

She smiled in return.

"I decided it was safer for Zeke, as well as for us, that he didn't know more than he needed to about our future plans," Dalthinir continued. "We can talk freely now."

Seeing an understanding nod from Trisanna, he pressed on. "You've probably been wondering how I came to be a renegade. I won't bore you with details, but I left the Compact ten years ago, and I've been on the run ever since. It isn't because I set out to harm anyone. But that makes no difference to the authorities."

Seeing the puzzled look on her face, he added, "You have many questions, I'm sure. I won't try to answer them now, but we'll get to them in time."

He pointed at his apprentice. "I met Kylen just after his magic had been awakened. Because it happened without the Compact's involvement, he's on the run too."

"Kylen is a rescuer," Bella told her. "He likes rescuing strays of various kinds. Most recently it was you, of course, but he also rescued us from the streets in Cambrick."

Feeling the blood creeping up his face, Kylen looked down hastily.

Dalthinir resumed his introductions. "You've already seen the twins in action. They're incredibly quick-witted, which has saved us more times than I can easily describe. Unfortunately, I haven't entirely been able to cure them of their old habits yet. They're still light-fingered at times, as I'm sure you've already noticed. It will be the death of me one day. But I haven't given up on them! And we truly couldn't manage without them."

"Bella and I don't only come with quick wits and our obvious charm and good looks," said Jonno seriously. "We also bring intelligence to the group."

"Which is fortunate since the rest of you have little more than magic to rely on," added Bella.

Both of them burst out laughing.

Kylen laughed along with them. Dalthinir was right. Even without the faintest hint of magic, the company had come to rely heavily on them.

"I don't have a lot to offer," said Trisanna, blushing self-consciously.

"That isn't true at all," Dalthinir insisted. "Given your ability with illusion, I expect you will help us as much as we can help you. There are likely to be occasions when it will be very useful for all of us to disappear."

"There are often times I would like to be invisible," said Jonno. "Especially when borrowing things."

"By which he means stealing," corrected the mage, his brows furrowing reproachfully. "I really will turn you into a toad one day."

At that instant Jonno disappeared. In his place sat an ugly toad, croaking mournfully. Kylen's jaw dropped, and Bella shrieked in horror.

"Let that be a lesson to you!" guffawed Dalthinir, aiming a wink at Trisanna, who blushed at the attention.

Jonno suddenly reappeared.

"That was...incredible!" gasped Bella.

Jonno stared at them, bemused. "What happened?"

"Trisanna just turned you into a toad," said Kylen casually. "Only an illusion, of course." He mightn't be giving anything away, but he was incredibly impressed.

"If it was an illusion, it was a very convincing one!" Bella exclaimed.

Trisanna faced Jonno, wincing with embarrassment. "I'm so sorry, Jonno. That was uncalled for. I shouldn't have done it."

"Nonsense!" Jonno replied. "It didn't hurt a bit. I didn't even see the toad. But if you truly want to make amends, you can turn Dalthinir into a horse. I'm sick of walking."

"While you're at it, you might as well turn Kylen into a horse as well. Then I can ride too," added Bella solemnly.

Both of them began laughing again.

This time Trisanna joined in as well. "I can see why everyone appreciates you both so much," she said with a big smile.

"It's nice to be joined by someone smart enough to recognize our true worth," Bella returned.

"Entertaining as this might be," said Dalthinir, "it's time we were gone from here. For Zeke's sake—and for our own as well—we need to put distance between us. But before we do, I'm hoping you might be willing to indulge my curiosity, Trisanna."

She looked at him uncertainly.

"Once or twice I've caught a brief glimpse of your necklace," he continued. "I'm aware you keep it out of sight, and I don't want to pry. But would you be willing to show it to me?"

After a moment's hesitation, she reached for a chain around her neck, pulling it from beneath her clothing to reveal a large blue jewel. It was mounted on a backing of what appeared to be gold. The mount hung from the chain.

Dalthinir's eyes went wide. "How did you come to have that in your possession?"

"My mother...my foster mother gave it to me as I was about to leave the farm. She didn't say what it was, but she said it was valuable. She made me promise to keep it safe."

Seeing her eyes beginning to grow moist, Kylen turned to the mage. "Do you know what it is?" he asked.

"I think I can hazard a guess," Dalthinir replied. He glanced at Trisanna. "Have you ever sensed any hint of magic about this amulet?"

"Yes," she confirmed, "although not until quite recently."

He didn't seem surprised.

"What do you think it is?" asked Trisanna.

He didn't want to be drawn. "I can't be certain. I need to ponder it for a while. In the meantime, we've been here long enough. It's time we were gone."

Setting off again suited Kylen. He couldn't sense magical auras nearby, so there should be no risk from mages. But it was unusual for them to stay in the open for so long when they were near a town, and he had begun to feel restless. "Where will we go?" he asked.

"East," Dalthinir replied vaguely. Seeing the quizzical looks on the faces of the twins, he forestalled them by adding, "We can talk tonight around the fire."

Kylen had at least as many questions as the twins, but it was clear that Dalthinir was not willing to be drawn further at that moment. There was nothing any of them could do, except wait.

EVENING FOUND the little group huddled around a small fire hidden within a thick stand of trees. By then the twins were almost bursting with curiosity.

"I can't remember the last time you looked so serious, Dalthinir," prodded Bella.

"You promised answers!" Jonno insisted. "What's the story with Trisanna's necklace?"

Dalthinir regarded them wryly, one eyebrow raised. "Curiosity can get people into a lot of trouble."

Seeing that an explosion was imminent, he waved his hands placatingly. "Patience! If you give me half a chance I'll tell you what I know." He took a deep breath. "I've been trying to call to mind everything I've read and heard that might be relevant. Only one conclusion makes any sense. I suspect Trisanna's necklace might be the Amulet of Zinth."

"What's that?" asked Jonno.

"It's a magical artifact. One with quite a reputation."

"What kind of reputation?"

"The very least that can be said is that the Amulet of Zinth is believed to have great power. No talisman is more greatly desired by mages who lust after dominion and influence."

Dalthinir redirected his gaze to the fire. "I once saw a reference to it among some papers belonging to a mage who died ten years ago. He was doing prohibited research into dragon magic. I caught little more than a glimpse, but the document that mentioned the amulet also referred to Master Arbilis, a mage who lived at the time of the Great Desolation."

As he mentioned Master Arbilis he shot a glance at his apprentice.

Kylen discovered he was holding his breath.

"Is there any way to confirm that my necklace is the amulet?" asked Trisanna. She had gone pale.

"I can't be certain without consulting the library in Cambrick. Even there I might not find a definitive answer. Ettaran would have been the best place to research such things."

His brows furrowed. "The Compact library in Cambrick preserves many old documents, and some of them almost certainly contain references to the amulet. I imagine the same could be said of the equivalent library in Antilin. However, for obvious reasons, neither of those libraries are accessible to us. As I mentioned, the best place of all to search would be Ettaran—in the Great Library."

"There was a library there?"

"Oh, yes! The building itself was said to be a glittering wonder, and it housed treasures beyond price, not the least of which was the accumulated knowledge of centuries, written down in scrolls and books. Supposedly, people walking into the library for the first time could only hold their breath." He shrugged. "Unfortunately, we can't expect to go there and retain our sanity."

He continued before any of them could comment. "There might be one other option open to us, though. The town of Flaxendell is supposed to have maintained quite a sizable library. I'd like to explore it, assuming it's still there."

"Where is Flaxendell?" asked Trisanna.

"Across the border."

"The border? With the ruined kingdom?" asked Bella, her eyes wide.

The mage nodded. "I imagine we're not likely to meet too many other people there. Searchers included."

"Crossing the border is dangerous," said Jonno. He sounded unusually serious.

Dalthinir shrugged. "Everywhere is dangerous for us. More so than ever now."

All of them took his meaning, not least Trisanna. She was downcast. "I'm bringing trouble on you."

The mage was as unruffled as ever. "Please don't let it distress you. As I said earlier, you bring an important ability to our company. You've already given us a diverting demonstration of your mastery, and from what I hear you managed to escape the monsters on the lake. That's nothing short of astonishing."

A shadow passed over her face at the mention of the lake, but she managed a weak smile of her own.

"The amulet must be important if you're convinced we need to cross the border," ventured Jonno.

The mage smiled grimly. "We need to understand what we might be carrying around with us. Perhaps I can explain it like this. Imagine a lone traveler in the wilderness who hears sounds of snuffling approaching his campfire. Before settling down to sleep, he might reasonably be expected to confirm that the sounds are coming from a lost dog eager for human company rather than a hungry lion on the prowl for supper."

"Can't you tell us more?" prodded Bella. "If you're comparing the amulet to a hungry lion, you must know something about it."

Dalthinir shook his head firmly. "I'm not going to say more. Not until I can confirm its identity. Are you willing to risk a visit to Flaxendell? Even though it's inside the border, the twins should be in no danger there. That won't be entirely true for the rest of us, but there shouldn't be any need to stay there for long."

Both Kylen and Trisanna nodded immediately. The twins, normally the first to embrace any new adventure, hesitated before agreeing.

"In that case, we'll head east and then north," said Dalthinir calmly. "Sooner or later we should come upon the old road that connected Cambrick with Ettaran. The road runs through Flaxendell. For the moment we'll keep going until we find somewhere secluded, then we'll break our journey for a while."

He regarded them seriously. "Up to now, we've responded to crises as they've arisen. That's worked only because the Compact has underestimated us. They've also been less than effective with their searches. All of that could change at any time. We should also remember that

Lars and Petria are out there somewhere, and they seem to have few scruples. We need to be thoroughly prepared before we ever stumble upon them."

"What do you have in mind?" asked Bella curiously.

"While we're taking a break I would like us to practice a maneuver. It's something we need to master before trouble finds us."

A twinkle had come to Jonno's eye. "Do we get to suggest maneuvers?"

One of the mage's eyebrows went up. "No, thanks. If I know you at all, you'll want me turned into a horse. I think I'll be the one to suggest maneuvers."

Jonno contented himself with a wink at his twin.

They set off immediately, heading east, away from the ocean. The mage set a brisk pace, limiting their rest stops. They reached the outskirts of an extensive forest late in the afternoon. Plunging at once into its shadows, the mage led them in deeper. He didn't pause until they came to a large clearing near a bubbling stream.

"This will do nicely," he said.

He turned to Kylen. "Is anyone nearby?"

Kylen couldn't sense magical auras anywhere within range. But the mage would want to know the likelihood of others interrupting them. Gazing upward, he watched until a hawk came into view. Like them, it was heading east. Borrowing its eyes, he looked down intently as it glided over the forest. Crossing a river, it continued across open country. A road appeared below, but only a single farmer's wagon moved on it. He detached himself as the bird wheeled north.

"There's nothing much happening in the direction we're going," he reported. "The forest goes on for quite a while. There's a river at its eastern border. A road lies beyond that. There's nothing significant moving on it."

The mage nodded. "The river would be the Jobuk. The road beyond it is the main road between Cambrick and Sengin."

Clearly bemused by what had just happened, Trisanna was trying not to stare at Kylen.

Bella leaned in her direction. "He borrows the eyes of birds. Other creatures too."

Jonno nodded solemnly. "Nothing's safe from his prying eyes. It's all very distasteful really."

Dalthinir got in before they could start laughing. "It sounds like we can risk a small fire. Let's eat and then settle for the night. We can start working on our maneuver in the morning."

CHAPTER 15

They rose with the dawn. As soon as they had broken their fast, Dalthinir gathered them together.

"The first step in preparing a response to danger is to understand the tools we have at our disposal. I'll begin with a question for Trisanna. Does your ability with illusion include sound and smell?"

She looked at him quizzically. "I'm not sure I understand."

"Some mages with the ability to form illusions are able to extend the illusion to cover all of the physical senses, not just sight. An example might help. Suppose we become aware of a wildcat heading in our direction. Disappearing from sight won't keep us safe if the wildcat can still smell us. Similarly, if we're hiding from people, it will give us away if one of us sneezes."

She stared back at him wide-eyed. "Oh! That had never occurred to me! I have no idea if I'm capable of doing that."

"When you came up with a toad yesterday, it croaked," Kylen pointed out.

The mage smiled encouragingly. "That's true. Why don't you try something to find out what you're capable of?"

"I'm happy to do that, but I'm not sure how."

"I can think of a simple way to check," suggested Jonno. "Turn

Dalthinir into a skunk. We'll let you know if he smells like one as well."

Bella considered the suggestion thoughtfully. "We might not be able to notice much of a difference from how he smells normally."

Leaping at once to Dalthinir's defense, Trisanna protested, "I'll do no such thing! I do have a question of my own, though. Hiding things seems less complicated than making something appear that isn't there. There were toads on the farm where I grew up, so I'm familiar with them. If I want to create an effective illusion, am I limited to things I know well?"

"An excellent question," Dalthinir told her. "I understand that illusion is more subtle than that. The illusion triggers a response in the minds of anyone or anything affected by it. I imagine all of us knew what toads looked like, so our minds were able to help out with details."

His answer fascinated Kylen. "So if each of us described the toad, the descriptions would have been different?"

"Almost certainly," the mage replied.

"What if I'd never seen a toad, and I'd never heard a description of one either?" asked Bella.

"In that case, details would be provided by the person shaping the illusion. You would still see a toad. Or, more accurately, whatever the mage thinks a toad looks like."

Trisanna nodded. "That must have been what happened with the clubfoot dragon. I'm sure Kylen was right when he said that dragons don't actually look like that."

Another question had intrigued Kylen. "I've been present twice when Emmela created an illusion that worked on other people—once on the mountain, and once at the lockup in Sengin. But I wasn't affected by it in either case. Why was that?"

"Did you see the toad yesterday?" asked Dalthinir.

"Yes, I did."

"That hints at the answer," the mage told him. "Emmela's illusions weren't strong enough to convince you, but Trisanna's illusion was. That suggests Trisanna's ability is much stronger."

"Does it matter how close you're standing to the person making the illusion?"

Dalthinir shook his head. "I don't believe so."

As they were talking, Kylen caught sight of something out of the corner of his eye. He'd never seen a skunk, but the creature strolling casually toward the little group must surely have been one. A white stripe featured prominently on its black body, and its bushy tail was waving lazily in the air. It wound its way around Bella's feet, flicking its tail back and forth across her legs.

Then, approaching Jonno, it turned its back on him and let loose a stream of liquid.

Kylen immediately reeled from the assault on his senses. He had never imagined anything could smell so bad.

"Ew!"

"Disgusting!"

Everyone was reacting at once. Then, incredibly, both the skunk and the smell were gone.

Bella was still covering her nose. "That was horrible! I take back everything I said about Dalthinir's odor!"

"I think we've answered the question about the illusion providing smell," said the mage with a grin. "And the toad croaked, so we already know your illusions are capable of producing sound. That means sound and smell are at least half covered."

Trisanna's eyebrows drew together. "Half covered? What do you mean?"

"When you've made us invisible, will others nearby be able to hear us? Or smell us?"

Trisanna turned to Kylen. "It's a good question," she said with a smile. "I've just made the two of us invisible. We'll soon find out whether they can hear us."

"Where did Trisanna and Kylen go?" asked Jonno, peering around in surprise.

Dalthinir put a finger to his lips. "Ssh! I think we're supposed to be listening. She'll want to know if we heard them talking."

A smile quirked Trisanna's lips. "He's smart, your Dalthinir."

"We can hear them, but they can't seem to hear what we're saying," said Kylen admiringly.

Dalthinir's face lit up in a sudden smile. "Trisanna and Kylen are back again."

"That was weird," breathed Jonno.

"Could you hear us talking?" asked Trisanna.

The twins and the mage shook their heads.

"Testing whether our smells are hidden might be more difficult," said the mage. "But I'm confident we'll find that smell is covered as well."

He exhaled happily. "Your ability is going to make a huge difference," he told her. "Even when you're hiding us we'll be able to talk freely."

"If we can still see and hear each other, how will we know we're invisible to other people?" asked Kylen.

"She can tell us she's done it. All we need to do now is to agree on a word or phrase to alert her that she needs to hide us."

"What about a bird call?" asked Jonno. He gave a trill. It didn't sound like any birdsong Kylen was familiar with, but it certainly sounded like it came from a bird.

"The idea is good. But can anyone else do it?" asked the mage.

They shook their heads.

"You'll all be doing it by the end of the week," Jonno promised them. "I'll make sure of it."

"If we're hiding from mages," Dalthinir concluded, "then I'll hide Trisanna's use of power as well as any power Kylen might need to use. I'll also hide our magical auras."

He smiled with satisfaction. "I'd say we have our maneuver in place now. I think we can afford to take a break."

THE BIRD'S eye view of the region had left Kylen with unrealistic expectations of how long it would take to trek through the forest and cross the river. In practice it had taken far longer. As they headed east, the forest had become dense to the point of being impenetrable, forcing them to backtrack more than once.

When they eventually broke through to the river, they found them-selves confronted with water flowing swiftly between steep banks.

Dalthinir scanned the river in both directions. "Crossing here won't be possible."

Jonno wasn't dismayed. "Couldn't you turn us into fish, Trisanna?"

She laughed. "Looking like a fish wouldn't help very much." She pointed downward. "This is what we need."

Following her gaze, Kylen was astonished to see that the river had been replaced by a gentle stream. No more than ankle deep, it bubbled merrily around large stepping stones that neatly spanned the gap between the two banks. Orange and yellow flowers floated slowly down downstream, drifting past a duck paddling lazily ahead of eight fluffy ducklings.

Bella's hands were clasped before her. "Oh! That's beautiful!"

Dalthinir looked uncomfortable. "I'm sorry to spoil the fun, but you'll need to let me know before you use power, Trisanna. I need to mask it, or we'll risk exposing our presence to any mages who happen to be in the area."

Trisanna's hand flew to her mouth. "I'm so sorry!" she said, her eyes wide. The gentle stream disappeared in an instant, replaced by the harsh reality of the river.

With no easy way of climbing along the riverbank to find a ford, they headed back into the forest. Three more days passed before they finally found a way across the river. They waited for nightfall to cross the north-south road from the capital, then they kept going until they found a suitable place to camp. When they finally settled for what remained of the night, they weren't far from the border region.

Jonno was as buoyant as ever in the morning. "All this back and forth through the forest hasn't been entirely wasted," he said. "Your attempts at birdsong have almost driven me mad. But at least all of you can now do something that sounds vaguely like it."

He rolled his eyes at Trisanna. "Almost all of you, anyway." Even after days of trying, her best attempts still sounded like a strangled cat.

They all needed to be able to make the sound. Any of them could use the alarm to alert the others to imminent danger. After Trisanna had established an illusion, she would use the sound to let the others know they were hidden. Having masked her illusion, Dalthinir would inform everyone the same way.

"It's a pity we're not using the warning bark of a fox," she said. "I can do that quite well." Opening her mouth, she delivered a sound remarkably similar to the squeal-like call used by foxes in the wild.

Jonno held his hands to his head. "Why didn't you tell us that in the first place? You'll be the death of me yet," he lamented, delivering a very passable imitation of Dalthinir complaining about the twins.

Dalthinir ignored him. "That will do nicely as your warning, Trisanna. We'll keep an ear out for it."

After glancing around the group, he added, "I imagine we're all tired. We'll take a rest day before heading north."

"How close to the border region are we?" asked Kylen.

"Close enough," Dalthinir replied. "The border isn't clearly defined. But if we kept going east we would find it harder to live off the land. It gradually becomes more barren."

"Is that the only reason people stay away?" asked Trisanna.

Dalthinir shook his head. "It isn't safe for people to travel there for any length of time." He was clearly choosing not to say more.

KYLEN FOUND himself in the unusual situation of being alone with Dalthinir. Moving alongside his mentor, he decided to make the most of the opportunity.

"How do mages from Tantel have their magic awakened?"

Dalthinir eyed him curiously. "What makes you ask?"

Kylen shrugged. "I was just wondering."

After a searching glance the mage nodded knowingly. "I see. Well, it's an interesting question. The answer is that I don't know. Mages from the two kingdoms get on reasonably well for the most part, but there are some things that are never discussed. Magical awakening is one of them. Tantellan mages have always been surprisingly secretive about their awakening rituals. So Peritonian mages don't talk about them either."

Kylen pushed down his disappointment. From the little he knew, Trisanna's magic had been awakened unexpectedly. That suggested the

Tantellan mages weren't involved. How had it happened, then? He couldn't believe that a dragon had done it. She seemed too...unspoiled.

Much as he wanted to know, it wouldn't be appropriate to ask her. Not if the topic was off limits.

Everything about Trisanna fascinated him. She was big-hearted, she had a sense of humor, and she was a mage with strong ability. There was no use pretending he wasn't drawn to her. But she was above him in every way. She was the daughter of a king, and he was a nobody.

All of that paled into insignificance, though, in light of the fact that a dragon had been responsible for his magical awakening. His magic was tainted. He was damaged beyond repair. The kindest thing he could do would be to stay away from her.

Dalthinir seemed to sense his mood. "We haven't spent much time on your training lately," he said brightly. "As soon as we're somewhere relatively safe we can resume our sessions. Trisanna can join us. She has a lot to learn."

Kylen nodded dully. For him, truly relaxing in her company wasn't an option. Not when he could never afford to let her discover the truth about him.

Away from the company collecting firewood, Kylen was startled to suddenly detect a large concentration of magical auras. They weren't far away, and they were heading roughly toward the clearing where he and his companions had established a campsite.

Running frantically back the way he had come, he attempted between gasps of air to sound out the agreed birdsong. He could only hope Trisanna would hear it and make them invisible. Glimmer was of no concern—Dalthinir routinely masked the auras of all three of them. Invaluable as the ability was, it seemed to cost him little effort.

The mages were rapidly drawing closer. At the rate they were moving they could only be on horseback. As he ran he wondered who were they and where had they come from. More importantly, how had they remained undetectable until they were almost upon the little band?

Bursting into the clearing, he found the others on high alert, hiding among the trees.

Dalthinir waved him to his side. "Don't worry, Kylen. Trisanna and I both detected them in plenty of time. She's hiding us." Trisanna and the twins hurried over to join them as he was speaking.

The clearing lay very near an animal trail. The riders had apparently stumbled upon the trail and decided to follow it. It only remained to be seen whether they would remain on the trail and ride past or veer off into the clearing.

The question was quickly answered. The clearing filled with snorting horses and dark-clad riders.

"Get some wood and build a fire," ordered a woman with a commanding voice. The riders immediately scattered among the trees, one of them passing alarmingly close to where Kylen and his companions were standing.

Dalthinir's eyes had gone up in surprise. "Based on her accent, they're Tantellan," he mused, speaking normally. He clearly had complete confidence in Trisanna's ability to hide sound as effectively as sight.

Glancing at her, he saw she had gone pale. Had she recognized one of the mages? Or had she concluded that these mages were in Periton searching for her? Whatever she was thinking, it was hard to understand how they'd found their way to the very location where she was hiding.

The leader drifted closer to their position, another of the mages beside her. The other mage featured a black beard and a shock of black hair.

"I'd love to be able to hear what the Peritonians are saying right now!" crowed the other mage. "They must think we all drowned. Except they won't be able to find our bodies."

"Don't get too excited," warned the leader. "They might not be as stupid as you think. Sooner or later they'll realize exactly what happened. And they'll know we're avoiding them intentionally."

"What difference does that make?"

"We're not here to start a war! We're here to find the girl."

"And to retrieve the amulet from her."

"Be very careful," growled the leader. "Information like that could get you into a lot of trouble."

"Don't think you can hide it from me!" protested black beard. "I was the one who found out where it had gone! But you needn't worry. I know how to keep things to myself."

"If you ever do talk, I'll fry you from the inside out."

Kylen drew back instinctively at the tone of the speaker. Whether or not the threat was empty, she didn't sound like someone to cross.

It was beyond strange to stand beside another person who was entirely unaware of your presence. His natural instinct was to remain silent and rigid, holding his breath anxiously. Glancing around he saw that only Dalthinir was behaving normally.

The two Tantellans moved away, their conversation apparently at an end.

"It looks like they'll be here for a while," said the mage. "We might be wise to remove ourselves elsewhere. Something tells me we'll find it hard to relax while we're sharing the clearing with them."

Gathering their few possessions, they prepared to leave.

Jonno had something he wanted to do first. Sprinting to the center of the clearing, he spun around slowly, wagging his head and leering at the intruders. Then he ran back to rejoin the others.

Dalthinir had watched the performance with one eyebrow raised. "Satisfied?" he asked.

Jonno took a deep breath and slowly released it. "Very," he replied with a grin.

Shaking his head, the mage turned and led them away from the clearing. He kept them walking briskly for several hours, pausing only for brief breaks.

As they traveled, Kylen glanced up at the sun from time to time. They were heading in a northeasterly direction.

He swung in beside the mage as dusk was falling. "Have we crossed the border yet?"

His mentor didn't immediately answer him. "We'll camp over there for the night," he called, pointing ahead to a stand of trees just beyond a stream. As they splashed across the stream, he twisted around to speak to Kylen. "If you don't mind waiting, I'll answer your question when we're all settled. I imagine others might want to know as well."

Having no objection, Kylen replied with a simple nod.

As soon as they were sharing some food, Dalthinir cleared his throat significantly. Once he had their attention, he began.

"There are a number of important issues we need to consider. I'm sure all of us are wondering about the mages we encountered earlier. And Kylen asked a while ago if we'd crossed the border yet. I'm afraid that neither subject comes with easy answers, but I'll make an attempt at answering Kylen's question."

He gazed off into the east. "It's impossible to say with any certainty whether we've crossed the border. Maps exist, but they're of limited use, since the border isn't exactly a fixed line. It can't be. That's because the effects of the devastation aren't instantly obvious. To begin with, they increase slowly the further in you go. That isn't all. The area affected by the devastation isn't static. It seems to grow and shrink for no apparent reason. It's a key reason why people keep well away from the border. It's no good trying to farm land that's safe one day and unsafe the next."

His face became grim. "The one thing I can say for certain is that the further east we go, the greater the risk."

Kylen stared at him. "What happens when people go in there?"

"They go crazy," said Bella at once.

Jonno nodded. "When we were growing up there was a man from a neighboring farm who went into Methesia. People used to say there was treasure in Ettaran, the old capital. Jewels lying around in the streets, supposedly. Our dad said it was all nonsense."

"This man went with three others," Bella told them. "No one knows what happened to his companions. But someone found him wandering near the border. They must have figured out where he came from and brought him back."

"What was wrong with him?" asked Trisanna.

Bella tapped her forehead. "He'd gone completely mad. He looked normal physically."

Kylen frowned. "What kind of things did he do?"

"You don't want to know," said Jonno with a grimace. "Some of it was quite disturbing."

"It was like he could see people who weren't there, and talk with them too," Bella added. "He acted as if he was somewhere else."

Jonno shrugged. "In the end, he fell into a river and drowned." Considering how close to the border they were at that moment, he seemed surprisingly matter-of-fact about it.

Trisanna looked alarmed. "We're not going there are we?"

Dalthinir didn't try to hide the truth. "We can't get to Flaxendell without crossing the border. But as I've already said, it will be quite safe for Jonno and Bella in Flaxendell. Even mages usually aren't too badly affected. It gets worse when you get closer to Ettaran."

Bella seemed intent on changing the subject. "Who were those people who appeared out of nowhere?" she asked.

"They were mages," Kylen replied.

Dalthinir nodded in agreement. "From Tantel, it would seem. Some of what they said wasn't easy to make sense of, but it sounded like they're hiding from Peritonian mages." He gazed sympathetically at Trisanna. "I'm sorry to say it also sounded like they're here in Periton to look for you. And they seem aware of your amulet."

She shook her head in bewilderment. "I can't begin to guess how they know about it. If I knew it would make them leave us alone, I'd just give it to them!"

"Don't be too quick to decide such things," cautioned Dalthinir. "As long as we make sure we keep away from them, it won't be an issue."

CHAPTER 16

Something roused Kylen from a deep sleep. Surfacing reluctantly, he struggled to grasp what had disturbed him. Almost nothing was visible in the dark and no unusual sounds could be heard.

Then all at once he knew.

Leaping up in alarm, he called to the others. "Wake up! We're about to have company!"

Even while he was sleeping, his farsense had registered the presence of new magical auras. A large cluster of them was near at hand and rapidly drawing closer. He had enough time to briefly wonder how the Tantellan mages could have found Trisanna not once, but twice. Then their horses were upon them.

He caught a glimpse of Trisanna awake and on her feet before he dimly heard the bark of a fox through the clamor of the arriving party. He heaved a sigh of relief knowing she must have hidden them with an illusion.

"I didn't want to be awake," grumbled Jonno.

Bella tugged at Trisanna's arm. "Can you add some wasps to your illusion?"

"I suppose so."

"Good!"

Bella pulled out her slingshot, drawing a grunt of satisfaction from Jonno. The two of them were soon busy collecting stones.

Almost immediately, the cries of horses and the shouts of people filled the night. The interlopers tried in vain to swat the wasps that buzzed noisily about, stinging them relentlessly.

"Move out!" yelled the Tantellan leader.

Within minutes the campsite was quiet once more.

"Let's get back to sleep!" said Jonno.

Dalthinir had other ideas. "We can't risk staying here. We need to move."

A chorus of moans from the twins didn't shake his resolve. "Hurry up!" he insisted, continuing to prod until they were underway.

In the dark it wasn't easy for Kylen to tell which direction they were taking, but he suspected it might be due east. They didn't travel for long. No more than an hour had passed when Dalthinir decided to let them settle again.

It felt like Kylen had barely drifted off to sleep when the mage shook him awake. "They're back," he muttered before hurrying away to wake the others.

They drew aside together into the shelter of some trees and watched bemused as their latest campsite was overrun by the foreigners.

"We'll stop here for the rest of the night!" called the woman who was leading them.

Kylen's companions watched bleary-eyed as the Tantellans put halters on the horses and hobbled them. Then they rolled out blankets and prepared for sleep.

As their companions were settling, the leader approached black beard.

"Why here?" the mage asked her. "This location looks no better than the last one."

"Instinct," replied the leader gruffly, although she sounded less than certain about it. "And there are no wasps here."

"I hope this girl's worth all the fuss," said black beard.

The leader pinned him in an unsmiling gaze. "You were at the farm where she grew up. Are you certain the people who raised her gave her the amulet before she left?"

The other grunted an affirmative. "That's what they said."

"They might have been telling you what they thought you wanted to hear."

"Not a chance. They weren't faking it. They were tight-lipped at first, but once we went to work on them they became pathetically compliant. We squeezed every last drop of information out of them. They were begging to die by then. They told us everything before we ended it."

A long, lingering wail startled Kylen. Looking at Trisanna he saw her face twisted in anguish. Wide-eyed, he stared helplessly at her.

Bella knew exactly what to do. Hurrying to her side, she threw her arms around the wailing girl and drew her close. Burying her face in Bella's shoulder, Trisanna sobbed uncontrollably.

None of the intruders reacted in any way—incredible as it seemed to Kylen, her illusion remained intact through it all.

With nothing more to say to each other, the two Tantellans joined their companions in settling for what remained of the night.

Dalthinir had been looking on thoughtfully. "I don't understand how they found us again," he said, a puzzled frown on his face.

Before Kylen could say a word, he heard Jonno calling.

"Kylen! I need your help!"

Following the sound of his voice, he headed into the trees.

"Grab hold of these," said Jonno, thrusting a handful of halters toward Kylen.

With no experience of horses, he took them nervously. Thankfully, the animals ignored him.

"Bella! Bring her over here!" called Jonno.

The two of them appeared out of the darkness, Bella leading her by the arm. Trisanna seemed to have recovered herself at least in part.

Dalthinir had followed them to find out what Jonno was up to.

Seeing him, Jonno nodded in satisfaction.

"These Tantellans just won't take a hint!" the twin exclaimed. "I'm sick of them constantly appearing out of nowhere. It's time to do something about it. Can all of you ride?"

Each of them responded in the affirmative except Kylen. Having spent almost his entire life in Cambrick, his exposure to horses had been close to nonexistent.

"You can ride behind me," Jonno told him. "All you have to do is hang on to my waist."

He addressed the others. "I've saddled and bridled horses for Trisanna and me." He handed halters to Bella and Dalthinir. "You'll need to saddle your own," he told them. "Each of us can lead two other horses. When you're ready, take two halters from Kylen and secure them to your saddle."

It felt like an eternity, but probably no more than ten minutes had elapsed before they were ready to go. Bounding up onto the horse, Jonno beckoned Kylen up behind him. It didn't prove quite that straightforward. In the end, the twin was forced to dismount and help Kylen up before remounting himself.

Dalthinir led them into the night. Kylen later discovered they had been riding northward.

They continued with occasional breaks until a couple of hours after dawn.

By the time the mage brought them to a final halt, Kylen was heartily sick of being bounced up and down. His rear felt bruised and uncomfortable. The moment they stopped he slid awkwardly from the horse's back.

"I'll be delighted if I never see a horse again," he muttered to no one in particular.

"The first time on a horse's back is the hardest," Bella told him sympathetically.

Dalthinir smiled down at him. "I think you could use a distraction, Kylen. See if you can borrow some eyes. I'd like to know what the Tantellans are up to. They'll be aware the horses are missing by now. I used a bit of magic to cover our trail, although I'm not sure how much it will help. They keep managing to find us somehow. At the least, though, we should have put a bit of a distance between us."

Kylen stopped wincing long enough to peer into the sky in search of a bird of prey heading in the right direction. He eventually spotted an eagle riding the thermals southward. Borrowing its eyes, he maintained contact until well after the eagle was out of sight. Eventually he caught a glimpse of a party of people trudging slowly on foot.

"I've found them," he told the mage.

"Where are they?"

"A long way off. But they're heading north, directly toward us."

Dalthinir shook his head in bewilderment. "It makes no sense! They're finding us so easily, even though they themselves don't seem to know how it's happening. I'm sorry to say it, but if they're heading our way we need to keep moving."

"Where will we go?" asked Kylen.

The mage looked grim. "To Flaxendell, as we intended. Maybe they won't follow us east."

He trained his gaze on Jonno, an eyebrow raised. "I wouldn't normally condone you stealing horses from anyone, much less mages. But on this occasion I'm grateful to you for your initiative. I'm sure we all overheard the riders say they were concealing themselves from their Peritonian counterparts. I don't doubt that the Peritonian mages provided the horses. They would also have been charged with keeping an eye on the visitors."

He dismounted. "We'll release the horses. I expect they'll find their way home. Losing their mounts will slow down the Tantellans, and that has to be a good thing for the kingdom since they appear to have gone rogue. There's another piece of good news, too. If your saddlebags are anything like mine, you'll find them well stocked with provisions. We'll be glad of them where we're going."

He faced the twins sadly. "Trisanna and I will remove our saddles and bridles and leave them here, but your horses need to remain saddled. We're heading into great danger, so it's time for you to leave us. I don't know where to suggest you should go, but the two of you have proven repeatedly that you're resourceful enough to manage on your own."

Jonno dismounted. "I'm not going anywhere," he said.

"Me neither," added Bella stubbornly, climbing down from her horse.

"But you know better than anyone what will happen if you keep going!"

Jonno shrugged. "So do you. You're still planning on doing it."

"I'm not leaving Trisanna," said Bella flatly.

Jonno cocked an eyebrow in imitation of the mage. "I wouldn't normally condone you leading people to a horrible death. But on this occasion I know you're doing it for Trisanna's sake, and I'm grateful to you for it. We're coming with you. And that's that."

"I can't bear it!" cried Trisanna. "All of you are only in danger because of me! The Tantellans wouldn't keep following you if I wasn't with you. It's time I took responsibility for myself. I'll meet with them, and they can have whatever I've got!"

Kylen shook his head vigorously. "We heard what they've done already. They'll kill you, and we won't let that happen! We were being chased before we met you. The only thing that's changed is who's chasing us. And we're better off than we were. Having you with us gives us a way to avoid them."

As they were talking, Jonno and Bella had dismounted and removed the saddles and bridles from their mounts. Bella quickly stripped the provisions from the four saddlebags and put them into a sack.

The twins slapped their horses on the rump. They trotted off with their ears back, the other animals not far behind them. They were smart enough to head due west.

Jonno looked expectantly toward the mage. "Let's go!" he said.

Kylen approached Dalthinir quietly. "The Tantellans have changed course."

His mentor raised his eyebrows inquiringly.

"They were heading north, directly toward us. Now that we're heading east, they're heading a little east of north."

"So they're on an intercept course."

Kylen nodded.

The mage stood silently for a moment, musing. "It's almost as if they're being drawn to us."

"That isn't all. While I was watching them they suddenly disappeared."

"Disappeared? Do you mean they were hidden in a forest?"

He shook his head. "They were in open country. One moment they were there, and the next moment they weren't. And they didn't reappear."

Dalthinir's brows drew together. "I can only conclude that they're also capable of hiding themselves magically. Presumably they didn't do so sooner because they weren't aware they were being observed. It must have set them thinking when we stole their horses."

Then he called, "Trisanna!"

She came to him immediately.

"It seems that our hunters are capable of hiding themselves too. That means we won't have any warning when they next catch up with us. Do you think you can make us invisible all the time?"

She nodded.

"While you're asleep?"

"I'm not sure."

Dalthinir didn't seem concerned. "We'll test it, then."

He gazed back the way they had come. "It's just become more important than ever for us to identify your amulet. If it is what I think it might be, I can understand why they want it so much. It will also be crucial for us to do everything in our power to prevent them from getting it."

His demeanor made it clear he had nothing more to say on the subject.

At that moment Jonno approached them. "Bella and I have been looking for places to set traps. From all the indications, there aren't too many animals in the region."

"We can safely say we've crossed the border, then," the mage told him. "All of us should fill our waterskins as soon as possible. It's impossible to guess how safe it will be to drink the water further in."

He sighed. "Even with the provisions from the four saddlebags, all of us are going to need to tighten our belts."

CHAPTER 17

Kothlar stood in the chief master's reception room, still clad in the clothes he had traveled in. He hadn't paused to sleep, eat, or bathe since returning to the capital.

"Where in the ruptured kingdom did you disappear to?" demanded Adrastas. He appeared more agitated than Kothlar could remember seeing him in a very long time. "You picked a spectacularly bad moment to abandon Alexis and your team! The king is furious! Either a dozen Tantellan mages have died through our negligence, or they're wandering around the kingdom doing whatever they like after slipping away from us. I don't know which is worse!"

"Has there been any sign of them?"

"No! How could you lose them like that? Alexis found no sign of them having been drowned." He thumped the table angrily. "Where have they gone, and what have you done about it?"

"If you settle down, Adrastas, I'll try to answer your questions."

"I'm waiting! What do you have to say for yourself?"

"Which question do you want me to answer first?"

Adrastas went red in the face. He looked like he was about to erupt.

Kothlar abruptly decided he'd had enough of the chief master's attitude.

"I suggested that you settle down, Adrastas. Since you ignored my suggestion, it's my turn to get worked up!" He jabbed a finger at the head mage. "You sit here in your tidy little office and send us off to deal with your messes. Some of them are messes you've made worse! I've been riding for days in an attempt to find answers. I've had very little to eat or drink and nowhere near enough sleep, and I can't remember the last time I had a bath. And the best you can do is yell at me! I've had it! If you're not willing to behave like an adult I'm leaving! Come and find me when you're ready to have a sensible conversation!"

With that he spun on his heel and strode toward the door.

"Wait! Please don't leave, Kothlar! I'm perfectly calm now."

Interrupted in the act of opening the door, he glanced behind him. Adrastas appeared visibly calmer. He had seated himself at the ornate table in the center of his room, and he was gesturing toward a seat opposite.

Kothlar glared at him, a grunt of irritation passing his lips. Releasing the door, he turned and headed back to the table.

"I'm delighted to hear you've been working so hard to find answers," Adrastas said reasonably. "What have you learned?"

After viewing him with narrowed eyes for a few moments, Kothlar recognized that he needed to calm down himself. He took a deep breath.

"I wanted to understand how the Tantellans had managed to disappear so completely. So I went to Sengin to consult with Inga."

Adrastas's eyebrows rose up in surprise.

"The Tantellans disappeared completely," Kothlar continued. "There was no sign of them. Pellistri's farsense detected no hint of their magical auras, and none of us detected any use of magic."

"The obvious conclusion was that they had allowed the river to sweep them out of sight while using the water to mask their glimmer," said Adrastas.

"Perhaps," conceded Kothlar.

"The other possibility is that they were dead."

Kothlar shook his head. "That's unlikely. There was no sign of them or their horses downstream. It reminded me of the incident in Sengin, when Trisanna was broken out of the lockup. The same thing happened. She and her rescuer visibly disappeared. All trace of their magic then disappeared as well."

"What are you suggesting? That the renegades and the Tantellans both have a way of disappearing physically and magically?" Adrastas was shaking his head dismissively.

"It's one possible conclusion."

"What did Inga have to say?"

"She didn't witness either incident. But she has long suspected that Dalthinir is able to hide his magical aura. Maybe his use of magic too." Before Adrastas could argue, he added, "How else do you think he was able to live right here in Cambrick without us ever becoming aware of him?"

The blood had drained from the chief master's face. "If you're right..."

"Then we have a serious problem. We can reasonably assume we're at a big disadvantage compared to the renegades. That might also apply to the Tantellans. Emmela has our strongest illusion capability, and her strength is medium at best. We have no one who can hide either magical auras or the use of magic."

"Have you figured out any kind of a solution?"

"Not one that you'll ever agree to."

Adrastas glowered at him. "Don't expect me to go soft on the renegades. That isn't going to happen!"

"I hardly need to point out to you that the Tantellans will now be fully aware of our capabilities. And our limitations. That gives them an advantage. At the very least we have to acknowledge that they slipped away from us with contemptuous ease. I'm more than happy to leave the politics to you, but I can't help wondering how excited the king is going to be about all this."

Adrastas's eyes had narrowed. "The renegades aren't going to help us even if we wanted them to."

"How do you conclude that?"

"Surely it's obvious."

"It isn't obvious to me."

"They're not going to share their secrets with us if we offer nothing in return. The only thing they're likely to want is a full pardon, and that's something we'll never agree to."

"Even if the independence of Periton depended on it?"

"Don't be ridiculous! What reason is there to think the kingdom is at risk?"

"Explain the facts to the king, and see if he shares your confidence."

Adrastas went quiet. "What are you proposing?" he finally asked.

"Do you remember when Lars and Petria demanded that everyone stop what they were doing to find Dalthinir? This is a stop-whatever-you're-doing moment. Some mages can't be released, for obvious reasons—we need to adequately protect the royal family, and there are some tasks that can't be interrupted. But whoever's available should be dedicated to tracking down the Tantellans."

"You're asking a lot. Why do I have the feeling you haven't finished yet?" asked Adrastas suspiciously.

Kothlar fixed the head mage in a determined stare. "The abilities of the Tantellans appear to outstrip our own. We have to find a way to close the gap."

"And?"

"That means you need to turn a blind eye if some of us get an opportunity to consult with Dalthinir and his friends."

"This is treasonous talk! Don't expect me to go crawling to renegades! There's no place for them in this kingdom."

"Even if they can help us protect ourselves against potential enemies?"

"Don't push me, Kothlar."

"Then stop tying my hands behind my back!"

The two men glared at each other.

Kothlar broke the silence. "If I lead an expedition to find the Tantellans, then I'll be doing so on the understanding that I can do whatever I need to do to protect the kingdom."

Adrastas didn't comment. To Kothlar, that amounted to an unspoken acceptance of his position. It was all he was likely to get, and better than he'd expected.

"Anything else?" growled the chief master.

"Yes. You need to leave Inga in Sengin."

"Why?"

"She will provide us with useful eyes and ears in the southern border region."

He snorted. "What's the real reason?"

"If you tell her to return to Cambrick she'll refuse."

The chief master's face darkened. "Why should she get special treatment?"

"Because you owe her. Both of us do. We've treated her abominably. Between us we've given her more than enough reason to stay away."

Adrastas didn't look happy. "I'll think about it."

"Will you release the mages I need to go after the Tantellans?"

"I'll think about that too."

KOTHLAR STOOD on the steps of the Compact's Auditorium, surveying the mages assembled before him. He pushed down the frustration gnawing at him. Reaching this point had taken longer than it needed to, but he couldn't afford to dwell on that.

Days had passed before arrangements had been made for a large number of the kingdom's mages to be released from their usual occupations. Organizing the logistics for an extended expedition consumed several more days. Now—finally—mages, horses, and supplies were ready to leave.

"Our mission is to find the Tantellan mages," he called. "Once we've tracked them down, we will escort them to Thesmis and put them on a ship back to Tantel. You're undoubtedly asking yourselves why a group this size is needed to track down a dozen foreigners. It isn't simply because we have a large kingdom to search. Never underestimate these people! We have reason to suspect they command unusual abilities. Before this is over I expect there will be times when we need to call upon our combined strength. But for now, find your horses and mount up! We'll be leaving in ten minutes."

The party finally mounted and moved out. The sight of so many mages riding through Cambrick was sufficiently unusual that crowds were soon lining the streets, craning forward for a better look. Kothlar, leading the column, ignored them, staring straight ahead.

Alexis guided his horse alongside. At Kothlar's request he had once again been appointed second-in-command.

"Where are we going to start looking?" he asked quietly.

"We'll be heading east."

"Why east?"

"There's been a breakthrough—the one good thing that's come from the interminable delay in getting this expedition ready to leave. The horses have been found. Just yesterday."

"The ones used by the Tantellans?"

"Yes. The description of the animals matches exactly."

"Doesn't that mean the Tantellans are all dead? Surely they wouldn't have abandoned their mounts by choice."

"There's certainly mystery around it. But the saddles and bridles had been removed."

"Thieves?"

"Unlikely. Why would anyone steal the saddles and ignore the horses? The animals are worth a lot more than the equipment."

"Where were they found?"

"East of the capital. Wandering westward."

"Which suggests they were even further east when they started."

Kothlar nodded.

With the gates drawing closer, both men fell silent. Once they were clear of the city, a group of ten riders approached, Ramond at their head. Kothlar had specifically requested the mercenary captain, and it was one request Adrastas hadn't quibbled about.

Kothlar dipped his head. "It's good to have you and your men with us, Ramond. Have you been briefed?"

"I have."

"Including the news about the horses?"

Ramond nodded.

"Then you know where we're heading. I would be grateful if you and your men would lead the column. As you are aware, the size of our party means we will need to camp out during our travels. Could you choose a suitable campsite each evening when dusk is approaching? You may also be aware that the king has provided a squadron of his guards. They will be protecting the rear of our column. I will introduce you to their leader at the first opportunity."

After agreeing to the requests, Ramond called his men forward.

Just south of the city a road branched eastward. At one time it had been the main road to the long-abandoned Methesian capital of Ettaran. In recent days it had seen little use. Thankfully it was still in surprisingly good repair, even after many years of neglect. Ramond turned onto the road as soon as he reached it.

The entire column followed him eastward.

WHETHER THE CHIEF master approved or not, making contact with Dalthinir was high on Kothlar's agenda. The idea of any renegade going anywhere near such a large group of mages might seem implausible, yet Dalthinir seemed to have developed an uncanny knack of showing up in the right place at crucial moments.

For that reason Kothlar had been extremely reluctant to include Emmela in the party. Her animosity toward Dalthinir had undermined her objectivity in the past, leading her to extreme views and unhelpful behavior. Worse, she'd refused to own her mistakes, even when proven wrong.

Unfortunately for him, he couldn't afford to leave her behind. From the moment he began to guess what the Tantellans and the renegades were capable of, Kothlar had placed a high value on illusion skills. Every available person with the smallest mage taste ability had therefore been attached to the expedition. It was widely accepted that none of the other mages had strength to equal Emmela's. That made her a necessary inclusion.

When the expedition halted to make camp for the first time, Kothlar decided he could no longer ignore the one task he had been putting off. With Alexis at his side, he summoned Emmela.

"Master Kothlar," she said, dipping her head.

"Master Emmela," he grunted. "I have a practical matter to raise with you. Are you able to hide the members of our party?"

She frowned in disbelief. "All of them?"

"All of them," he confirmed coolly.

She stared back at him. "I very much doubt it. Not with a party this big. I expect I could hide Ramond and his men."

"Please do it."

"Now?"

He nodded curtly.

After gazing at him with narrowed eyes, she turned her attention to Ramond. At that moment he was with his men, conferring with them. All of them abruptly disappeared.

"How long can you keep it up?"

"I'm not sure. It's tiring! A couple of hours at most."

"Will the illusion continue when you're asleep?"

"Certainly not!"

"Please gather every mage with illusion capability. I want you together to work on hiding the entire group."

Emmela looked stunned, but she nodded before leaving.

Next, Kothlar called for Kaspra and Ellis to join him and Alexis.

"Can you hide magical auras?" he asked.

They frowned back at him. "That isn't possible."

"Just because no one in the Compact can do it doesn't mean it's impossible."

"Are you saying it *is* possible?"

He nodded tightly. "Find three others—choose people with strong mage touch abilities—and figure out how to do it."

They hurried away with eager looks on their faces.

Alexis was staring at him incredulously. "What makes you so sure it's possible?"

When Kothlar didn't immediately answer, a knowing look came over his face. "You've spoken to Inga! That's where you went after the Tantellans disappeared!" He frowned. "If she knows this can be done, why hasn't she reported it to anyone? It's significant information!"

"Don't get too carried away," Kothlar told him. "You've made some intelligent guesses, but you're still wide of the mark. Inga didn't tell me it's possible."

"But she thinks it might be possible," suggested Alexis shrewdly.

He stood musing for a few moments. "Why did you tell Kaspra and Ellis it's possible if you're not certain it is?"

"I want them to be able to figure out how to do it."

"...and you think they're more likely to succeed if they believe it can be done."

"I can see I chose my deputy well," acknowledged Kothlar with a smile.

Alexis was looking thoughtful. "If the Tantellans are able to hide their glimmer, it would certainly explain how they succeeded in disappearing so completely."

Kothlar nodded. "Especially if they combined it with illusion."

Alexis didn't appear satisfied. "That isn't the only explanation. The river would have hidden their auras until they were out of range of Pellistri. And they didn't need illusion. The river was flowing fast enough that they would have soon been lost to sight anyway."

"All of that is true. But there was no river on hand when Trisanna escaped from the lockup."

A light had come to Alexis's eyes. "So you think Dalthinir can do all this, even if the Tantellans can't." He nodded to himself. "It would certainly answer a number of questions."

"I believe Dalthinir is capable of hiding not only magical auras, but the use of magical power as well. And it seems logical to assume that Trisanna has powerful illusion ability. Working together, they can effectively make their little party completely invisible."

Alexis's jaw was hanging wide. "It won't be good for us if the Tantellans are capable of doing that," he finally said.

Kothlar nodded with satisfaction. "Now you understand what we might be up against. And you can see why it's crucial for us to figure out how to do it ourselves."

CHAPTER 18

"What's that?" asked Kylen, pointing to a line of trees stretching as far as he could see into the distance.

Dalthinir squinted toward it. "Ahh. Now I know exactly where we are. That's the main road between Cambrick and the old capital of Ettaran. Trees were planted on both sides of it along its entire length. I'm happy to see they've persisted. Finding it is good news. We'll make better time if we're following a proper road. And I don't expect we'll meet any other travelers."

He looked like he was about to say something more but changed his mind. It wasn't hard for Kylen to guess what he might be thinking. The Tantellans were the only other travelers they had any likelihood of meeting, and Dalthinir would be doing everything in his power to make sure that didn't happen.

When they reached the road they found it still in good condition. Turning their backs on Periton, they followed it eastward.

After about an hour they came upon a bridge that soared over a deep ravine. The river flowing gently at the bottom of it appeared to be unremarkable apart from the complete absence of waterfowl.

"I wonder if there are any fish down there," ventured Jonno.

"I wonder," murmured Dalthinir.

Whatever his views on the state of living creatures in this vicinity, he seemed to have no doubts about the engineering prowess of his forebears. Stepping onto the bridge, he headed confidently across it.

Kylen followed after only a moment's hesitation. All of them reached the other side without incident, and they continued their journey.

Up to that point he had seen nothing that even vaguely hinted of danger. Not as far as he could tell, anyway. Yet something wasn't right. The countryside around them appeared entirely empty of animal life. He would normally have expected a steady accompaniment of birdsong as they traveled, especially with trees on both sides of the road. But birds were absent, leaving the land with a silent, brooding feel. Most likely the silence accounted for Kylen's growing sense of unease.

He could only guess at the location of the Tantellans. With birds of prey absent in these regions, he was left blind. However, eyes in the sky might not have helped. Not if the foreigners were invisible.

A couple of hours before sunset they caught sight of houses ahead.

"We appear to have arrived in the outskirts of Flaxendell," Dalthinir told them. "In the heyday of Methesia it was a major town, and travelers used it for overnight stops. It was a popular place to break the long journey between Ettaran and Cambrick."

"Perhaps we can sleep with a roof over our heads tonight for a change," offered Bella hopefully.

"Perhaps we can," agreed the mage. "Provided we can find a place that's still structurally sound."

Soon they were passing houses on both sides of the road. A few of them were overgrown with vegetation, and roofs had collapsed in some cases. But many looked almost normal, and he couldn't help expecting to see people emerge from them. The further they went, the more unnatural the absence of life began to feel. The silent emptiness began to fray his nerves.

The sun was sinking low in the sky when they reached the center of the town. Municipal buildings stood around a large and now empty town square. Kylen's first impressions suggested the town hall, justice building, and administration chambers remained intact.

Dalthinir hurried past them without a second glance. He cared about nothing except the library.

Locating it was not difficult. A tall and imposing building, it boasted a columned facade. Kylen stood gazing up at it admiringly.

Dalthinir was visibly relieved. "It looks remarkably well preserved," he said. "The sun won't set for a while. I'm going to take a quick look inside in case any documents of interest are easy to locate."

"We'll see if we can find somewhere to sleep tonight," offered Jonno.

Waving an acknowledgment, Dalthinir set off for the library entrance. Kylen followed him, curious to see what might await them there.

Two big wooden doors guarded the building. One was closed and the other stood ajar. Pushing it wide, the mage stepped inside, with Kylen at his heels. Leaves and dirt had blown in through the partially open door, littering the floor in the large entrance hall. Beams of light from high windows streamed down upon row after row of tall shelves, all of them filled with books and scrolls. It seemed untouched by time. Looters appeared to have ignored the place. Apparently they saw little value in books and parchments.

Striding along the central corridor, Dalthinir turned off into an aisle to examine the books more closely. Kylen wandered where his feet took him. He found himself looking at a shelf labeled, 'Dragonnes and their Wayes'. Selecting one of the volumes at random, he blew decades of accumulated dust from the top of it and gingerly opened it roughly in the middle of the book. His eyes fell on the following words.

Until recent years, Dragonnes were a common sight in the sky above Methesia. The superstitious among the common folk set great store by them. The merest glimpse of one was regarded as the best of good fortune. The reason for their vanishment has been and remains a matter of great dispute. Some say that the unbridled folly of humankind has driven them away. Others claim that dragonnes have turned against humankind and

> *cannot be trusted. My own limited dealings with the ancient creatures disposes me to think favorably of them.*

At this point Kylen caught sight of something out of the corner of his eye. Turning his head he glimpsed a girl, perhaps twelve years of age, standing at the end of the aisle staring at him. She was plainly dressed in a brown smock. A single glimpse of her appearance was enough to send the book tumbling from his nerveless fingers to land heavily on the floor. He stood rigid with his eyes bulging as a shiver went up his spine. He was staring at a wraith. The fading light from the windows shone right through her.

She peered at him, a forlorn look in her eye. Then she turned slowly and headed toward the rear of the building, following the corridor that ran along the far wall.

"Dalthinir?" he called in a quavering voice.

He was still trembling when the mage's face appeared around the bookshelves a couple of minutes later.

Seeing Kylen's state, the mage hurried to his side. "Whatever's the matter?"

He pointed. "There was a girl. Or a ghost! I can't say. I could see through her. She looked at me, then went to the back of the building."

Dalthinir hurried to where he was pointing and stared along the corridor. "There's no sign of her now," he reported.

With the daylight fading, the building was beginning to go dark. Noticing the volume on the floor, the mage bent to pick it up. He glanced curiously at the title, then he replaced it on the shelf.

He took Kylen's arm. "It's time we left. It will be dark soon. I didn't find anything useful, but I can try again in the morning."

They couldn't leave quickly enough as far as Kylen was concerned. Hurrying along beside the mage he exited the building, releasing a deep breath when they emerged into the open. Dalthinir closed both doors behind them, then headed into the square.

There was no immediate sign of the others, but it wasn't long before all three of them returned.

A strong breeze had sprung up, bringing a ruddy tinge to Trisanna's cheeks and setting her hair dancing about her face. Kylen had never seen a girl who looked so appealing. Even so, he couldn't help glancing back over his shoulder toward the library. To his relief, there was no further sign of the phantom girl.

"You look like you've seen a ghost, Kylen!" exclaimed Bella.

"He did see an apparition in the library," Dalthinir told them calmly. "It's a reminder to be especially alert for possible danger."

Seeing the others staring strangely at him, Kylen said, "She was about twelve years of age, and she had a sad look on her face. I could see right through her. After she turned away she disappeared."

Even to him it sounded feeble, nevertheless the twins immediately went pale. Knowing how superstitious they were, Kylen felt bad about stoking their fears. He knew what he'd seen, though. He hadn't imagined it.

"Did you find anywhere suitable to spend the night?" asked Dalthinir.

Trisanna nodded. "There's an inn that seems in reasonable condition. Back the way we came. Some houses too if you'd prefer one of them."

"Lead on," he told her.

Reaching the inn, they filed inside. Kylen glanced around apprehensively, desperately hoping there would be no return visit from the girl in the library.

A wide wooden bar faced them, a few stools still positioned in front of it. Approaching it, Dalthinir ran a finger over its surface, releasing clouds of dust to drift lazily in the dim light.

Several small tables with bench seats stood to one side of the bar. One of the benches lay on its side, but apart from that and the ever-present dust, it might have been any normal inn after closing time.

On the other side a few chairs stood before a huge fireplace. Remarkably, a pile of old wood remained stacked neatly beside the hearth.

"This will do," said the mage.

The breeze had strengthened considerably, and it fiercely resisted their efforts to close the inn door against it. With an effort they succeeded in shutting out the wind, and with it the forsaken emptiness of the once proud and bustling town.

Kylen worked with his companions preparing a fire. They had no fresh food that needed to be cooked and it wasn't especially cold inside the old inn, but there was something comforting about a crackling blaze in the fireplace. And, if the wind rattling the shutters offered any indication, the temperature was likely to drop as the night progressed.

With their preparations complete, they settled into the long-abandoned chairs and sat before the fire, sharing a little food and drinking sparingly from their waterskins.

Trisanna had almost nothing to say. In spite of her past, she had seemed remarkably cheerful when he first met her. She rarely smiled now. For a brief moment he wondered if he had done something to offend her, but she seemed equally withdrawn with the others, with the possible exception of Bella.

He didn't need to ponder for long before he remembered the revelation about the fate of her carers. It left him feeling very foolish. For her, the news must have been devastating. It was more than enough to account for her behavior.

Making an attempt to empathize with her, he tried to imagine what it must be like to lose the people who had loved and nurtured you. It was a struggle. He had never experienced a mother's tenderness.

There had been people who cared for him though—Olatiren at first, and more recently Dalthinir. The circumstances were far from equivalent, but it was the closest he could come. He had felt the loss of Olatiren keenly, and he knew it would hit him very hard if anything happened to Dalthinir. Even if he couldn't fully comprehend Trisanna's situation, he could still make an effort to be especially thoughtful and considerate toward her in future.

Before long any lingering light in the sky was gone. By now the wind was howling eerily, and they threw more logs into the fireplace. Then they sat immersed in their thoughts as they stared at the flickering fire.

They themselves would be entirely invisible to any watchers, with even their smell and their sounds hidden. Further, Dalthinir was masking the three magical auras. Nevertheless, with pursuers behind and ghostly visitors lurking in the town, they didn't settle for the night until many wards had been set about them.

Sleep offered escape from the strangeness around them, and Kylen welcomed it. It wasn't long before he sank into a deep slumber.

ONCE MORE KYLEN found himself in a vision. The setting was like the one he had experienced after hitting his head on the way up the mountain. Alone in the dark in a vast cavern, he crept carefully forward, uncertain about what lay beneath his feet. The atmosphere of the place felt oppressive, as if fresh air had not been admitted in eons.

As before, a dim light gradually grew in strength, revealing nothing apart from the characterless walls of stone around him.

Again he reached the underground lake, and once more a small craft skimmed the dark waters until it came to rest at his feet. Ignoring his uncertainty he climbed into the boat, watching without curiosity as it whisked him away from the shore and toward an island that loomed ahead in the semidarkness.

When the boat deposited him onto the sandy beach of the island, he headed inland at once, climbing to the summit.

The wooden staff, carved at its tip in the shape of a dragon, lay before him again. A voice boomed, this time addressing him by the name given to him by the dragon. "Take it, Kalmithien!"

He stared at it dispassionately for a few moments before reaching down slowly to pick it up.

As his hand closed over it, a mighty flash shattered the darkness. The cavern cracked wide to reveal settled lands around it on every side. He somehow sensed he had caught a brief glimpse of Periton, Tantel, and distant kingdoms unknown to him.

Far out at sea a tidal wave rose up, mountainous in size, poised to sweep across the land to wipe every trace of humankind from the earth. Unnumbered voices shrieked in terror. The cry of the old woman on the hillside rose above them all. "Doom! Doom upon us all!" she wailed.

An ancient voice swelled in evil delight, growing in volume until its demented laughter blotted out every other sound.

Detached as Kylen was in his vision, distress still overwhelmed him. He buried his face in his hands.

ALL TRACES of the vision were swept away as the sound of screaming startled him into wakefulness.

Climbing unsteadily to his feet he peered around, trying to reorient himself.

Trisanna was calling out in great distress, "I'm sorry! I'm sorry! Forgive me!"

Forgetting his own nightmare, he ran to her side. He tentatively reached out a hand to comfort her before drawing back, overcome with awkwardness.

While he hesitated, Bella appeared, enfolding Trisanna in her arms and drawing her head to her own breast. For several minutes Trisanna wailed inconsolably.

Feeling foolish, Kylen moved away. In doing so he encountered Dalthinir. The mage was standing rigid, a haunted look on his face.

"Did you have dreams as well?" Kylen asked him.

Dalthinir stared back at him, glassy eyed. "Not dreams," he murmured. "Nightmares. Visions of dragons and the end of the world."

Registering the startled look on Kylen's face, he turned away, unwilling to say more.

Surprisingly, neither Jonno nor Bella appeared to have been affected.

The night was still and dark. Dawn must have been several hours away. But there was no question of anyone sleeping.

When Trisanna finally calmed down, she avoided the others. Sitting off to one side, she tolerated only Bella's presence.

Jonno and Kylen built up the fire, and Dalthinir joined them before it once more.

Jonno broke the silence. "Do you realize how long the three of you slept for?"

The two mages looked at him blankly.

"You slept through a night, a day, and the best part of another night," he informed them.

"We were very worried," said Bella. "We couldn't wake any of you!"

Kylen looked at them blankly. "Why do I still feel tired, then?" he asked.

With no explanations on offer, they fell silent.

The hours dragged on. Kylen felt a huge surge of relief when the sun finally appeared. But his unease grew with the sunlight. It was clear that none of them belonged there. The land itself seemed determined to drive them away.

CHAPTER 19

For Kylen, the gloominess of the inn evoked the horror of his vision. He longed for the brightness of day.

To his relief, he had passed the night without a further sighting of the phantom girl. He had a feeling that she was too insubstantial to appear in the daylight, so once the sun had risen high enough to banish the half-light, he pushed outside.

The wind had died away in the night, and a gentle breeze tugged at the hair hanging around his face. His feet took him further along the road to the central square. Civic buildings still towered proudly, battling neglect and the slow decay of time. But it was a desolate place. There was something haunting about walking through empty streets that had once thronged with people like himself. Hurrying away from the square, he made his way onto the main road to Ettaran.

Trisanna had spoken of houses near the inn, and he soon found rows of dwellings just beyond the square as well. The front door of the second house stood wide open, and on impulse he crossed the overgrown path that led to its porch and poked his head inside. The silence within seemed peaceful rather than threatening, and he stepped across the threshold into the front room of the house.

A faded rug lay on the floor, with armchairs still positioned around it. Beams of light flooded in through a window on the eastern side of the house, softened by their passage through the leaves of a nearby tree. He stood for a moment, captivated by the dappled shadows dancing on the rug.

A door at the western end of the room led into the kitchen, and he peered curiously inside. An unusual object lay on a bench just inside the door and he bent to examine it. It resembled nothing he had ever seen, and he stared at it in bemusement. Then with a flash of insight he recognized what it was, or rather what it had been.

He was looking at the remains of a doll. Upon closer examination, faint traces of a blue dress were still visible. Whoever made the doll had apparently used seeds of some kind as a filling. The seeds must have sprouted, puncturing the body in many places and forever altering its shape. Without soil to sustain them the shoots had died off, rotting away to leave only withered stalks.

He shuddered involuntarily. The doll spoke of the decay that was slowly wearing down this once-thriving settlement. They had barely passed the borders of the ruined land. What would they find if they continued into the heart of the desolation?

Pushing such bleak prospects from his mind, he turned his attention to more immediate problems. What had become of the Tantellans? He wondered how they might respond to ghosts in the half-light and nightmares in the dark. Perhaps they would be sensible enough to abandon their pursuit.

Unable to find more encouraging topics to dwell upon, he pushed through the door and back into the daylight. Releasing a deep sigh, he set off along the road, enjoying the warmth of the sunshine.

Not far ahead of him an unusually grand house came into view with a large park opposite it. The park held no attraction for him. Even from his current position he could see that vegetation had run rampant. With no one to tend it, such an outcome was inevitable.

The mansion was another matter. Having grown up on the streets, stately homes had always been well beyond his reach. When the houses and buildings in Flaxendell had been abandoned, they seemed to have been left largely intact. This might be his first real opportunity to get a glimpse of what life was like for the fabulously wealthy. Hurrying forward, he headed for the abandoned home.

Then a movement caught his eye. Something was lurking in the shadows of the last house before the mansion. He froze, not daring to breathe. It was the wraith in the brown smock, and she was looking directly at him. He stared at her wide-eyed.

After regarding him for what seemed like an eternity, she pointed slowly at the mansion. Then, her face stern, she raised her hand as if barring the way.

The meaning was clear. She was warning him away from the mansion.

Abruptly she ignored him, turning her back on him and peering carefully around the building in the direction of the grand house.

Recovering his wits, he sucked in a long, shuddering breath. He realized that if she was hiding from something it might be wise for him to do the same. Scurrying into the shadows of the previous house, he peered forward nervously. She was still there.

Her attention was focused on the mansion ahead. More interested in her than in anything she might be looking at, he noticed at once when she glanced back toward him. Seeing that he had hidden himself, she nodded in what appeared to be satisfaction. Then she pointedly raised a finger to her lips.

For the first time he made an effort to see what she was warning him about. He could see nothing. As he continued to stare forward, he thought he heard something. Straining his ears, he began to hear snatches of speech. Fully alert, he drew back deeper into the shadows.

The voices were louder now, as if the speakers were coming closer, yet he could see nothing.

"There's no sign of them!"

"According to Pernilla they're here somewhere."

"I can't keep this up day and night! It's exhausting. I'm going to take a break."

With those words, two men suddenly appeared in the middle of the road.

Kylen guessed who they were even before he saw a group of others trailing behind them. Somehow the Tantellans had found them again.

And they were capable of making themselves invisible. The illusion apparently didn't extend to sound, though, and they were finding the effort tiring. Perhaps Trisanna possessed mage taste ability more powerful than the person responsible for illusion among her Tantellan pursuers.

Was he still being hidden by Trisanna? It had never occurred to him to ask how close to her he needed to be to remain hidden.

His ghostly visitor could clearly see him, which suggested he was visible. Then it occurred to him that illusions might only be effective on the living. Either way, he could not risk being seen by their pursuers.

Returning his attention to the Tantellans, he peered forward cautiously. He saw at once that the wraith-girl had vanished.

If he had continued on to the mansion he would almost certainly have been exposed. Her warning had saved him. He frowned in puzzlement. Why had she done it? Who was she?

Invisibility was not the only reason he had failed to detect the Tantellans. They had managed to hide their glimmer as well. He suddenly discovered how much comfort he had derived from the obviously mistaken belief that Dalthinir was the only mage capable of hiding his aura.

Then he noticed what seemed to be flickers of magical aura from several of the passing mages. For some reason, whoever was masking their glimmer apparently wasn't able to do it perfectly.

The Tantellans were moving quickly. They were almost past him now, heading back toward the square. He began to sweat. He had to warn the others. How could he, though? The foreigners were between him and the inn. He would never make it past them unseen.

As he watched them go, he noticed for the first time how weary many of them appeared to be. Having lost their horses, they must have decided to press on almost without sleeping. It had allowed them to make up for lost time, and he wondered if avoiding sleep had also spared them the night terrors experienced by the mages in Dalthinir's party.

The most baffling question was how they had been able to track Trisanna so effectively. The comment he had overheard suggested they were far from certain exactly where she was. They had never actually seen Trisanna or her companions. Yet they kept reappearing.

The group was far enough ahead that he was willing to take the chance of following them from a distance. The greatest risk was that the mage who had been hiding them would decide it was time to resume the illusion. If they suddenly disappeared again at the wrong moment, being able to hear what they were saying wouldn't be enough. He would have no idea which direction they might be facing. It was possible they might spot him without him knowing.

What choice did he have though? Keeping within cover as much as he could, he set off after them.

Dawn hadn't arrived soon enough for Trisanna. She was still reeling from the nightmare that had haunted her dreams the previous night.

Her previously uncomplicated life had been in almost constant upheaval from the moment her magical ability first asserted itself. It had been hard enough when the parents who fostered her had revealed her true origins and the legacy of danger that came with her heritage. She had been forced to flee, leaving behind the peaceful farm she had called home for her entire life. The mages hadn't caught her, but they had thrust her within reach of the terrifying monsters in the lake.

Her life had taken a momentary turn for the better when Inga found her. Yet within days she was first a prisoner, then an escaped fugitive. At that point she might have been excused for believing her life couldn't become more complicated. Yet somehow the Tantellans had learned she was still alive. Now mages from two kingdoms were pursuing her. The most bitter blow of all had been the revelation that her much-loved foster parents had been tortured and killed because of her.

As if all of this wasn't enough, having escaped the terrors of the lake, she was being chased into Methesia—into the very heart of madness.

Difficult as it had been to bear the seemingly endless trials she had faced, nothing compared with the guilt she carried over the lives disrupted, and even horribly destroyed, solely because of a selfless desire to help her. Her parents, Zeke, Inga and her aunt, now Dalthinir, Kylen, and the twins. Where would it end?

In her nightmare, all of them had lined up, staring at her accusingly. The sight of her foster parents had undone her. Their faces were drawn with pain, their bodies torn with many wounds. The others bore no visible scars, but she didn't doubt their suffering was barely beginning.

None of them had spoken a word. If they had railed at her it couldn't have been worse than enduring their silence. She had wailed her apologies. They had remained unmoved.

When she had woken she could barely face the others. Although she knew it was only a dream, the knowledge didn't blunt its impact. She hadn't caused the deaths of Dalthinir and his friends. Not yet. But it wouldn't be long before she did.

Dalthinir seemed untroubled by the burden of protecting her. Maybe he truly wasn't concerned. He had been hunted for so long it had become normal. He had always managed to avoid capture and death. But his charmed life couldn't continue. Not if she remained with him.

As for Kylen, he hadn't seemed upset about sharing his mentor and the twins with her. But he surely could never have guessed at the trouble she would bring down upon them. She sensed, too, that he was silently bearing burdens of his own. All she was going to do was make his life more difficult. She was cursed.

Bella seemed to understand better than anyone, perhaps because she herself had suffered pain and loss. She was a remarkable person, no less than her brother. Both of the twins exuded life. She could not allow them to die for her.

But what could she do? If she headed off on her own, her friends would be exposed. They needed her ability with illusion as much as she needed them. It was the only thing preventing her from slipping away from them while they slept.

Glancing around she noticed that Kylen was missing. He'd probably left the inn for fresh air and sunshine.

Stepping outside, she glanced around, but she could see no sign of him.

Relieved to find herself in the sunshine, she decided to explore the area. Heading around the side of the inn she gasped, coming to a dead stop. Before her stood the girl Kylen had described. She was dressed in a brown smock, not unlike any normal girl, but light passed completely through her. She was staring at Trisanna fixedly, a grave look on her face.

Realizing that her mouth was open wide, Trisanna clamped it shut. Her first instinct had been to scream, but so far the ghostly figure had made no threatening moves.

The girl stepped out from the shadows. In bright sunlight she was more insubstantial than ever. Turning away, she headed into the square, pausing long enough to look back and beckon.

Although she didn't seem threatening, Trisanna hesitated, unsure what to do. The sensible thing was to return to the inn to alert Dalthinir, but the girl had already crossed most of the square. She was clearly in a hurry. Beckoning urgently one more time, she pressed on without waiting for a response.

The girl was disappearing around a building onto the main road. Trisanna came to a decision. Whether she was comfortable with it or not, the bizarre was becoming commonplace. Dalthinir was masking her magical aura continuously, but in the safety of the inn she had allowed her illusion to lapse. Quickly reinstating it, she made sure to include her friends as well as herself. She would add Kylen as soon as she located him.

Then, taking a deep breath, she set off after the wraith.

CHAPTER 20

Striding forward grimly, Pernilla brooded on the mission assigned to her by Tantel's chief master. It was bad enough that he was sitting at home in comfort while she was roughing it in Periton. He expected her to find and dispose of Trisanna. What was more galling was his demand that she retrieve the Amulet of Zinth and hand it over to him. The talisman was a prize without equal, and Kharkin had freely acknowledged his own greediness. He had also hinted that something more was involved. She couldn't help wondering what he might be referring to.

One thing was certain—she would do the hard work, and he would take the glory. That was no surprise. He'd operated like that for as long as she had known him.

When would her time come? Would she ever see a day when she was the one honored and admired for what she achieved? Maybe someday she'd shock herself and everyone else by acting in her own interest instead of Kharkin's.

She shook her head. This wasn't the moment for daydreams. She needed to stay focused on the challenges before her.

Reaching absently beneath her clothing, she fingered the tiny talisman suspended on a fine chain around her neck. Her father had also been a mage, and she had inherited it from him. Mounted in silver, it supposedly held a small piece of a dragon's claw. If the tiny fragment had magical properties she was not aware of them. She had brought it more for good luck than anything. Thus far she had encountered very little that could reasonably be construed as good luck.

The pursuit of Trisanna had become an increasingly bitter experience for Pernilla. After the satisfaction of breaking free of the Peritonian mages, everything had started to go wrong.

From the beginning she had felt overwhelmingly confident about where to find their quarry. Now, with no rational basis for that certainty and with not so much as a glimpse of the girl, she was beginning to doubt herself. Yet, frustrating as it might be, she couldn't ignore the inner guide that tugged relentlessly at her senses.

The incident with the wasps had been unusual enough, but then their horses had disappeared from under their noses. Given that four saddles had gone as well, there could be no doubt they had been stolen, presumably by a party of four.

How thieves had escaped the notice of twelve alert mages was a question she couldn't answer. The Peritonian mages must surely be hunting for them, but a bold and effective action of that kind was beyond their capability from the little she'd seen of them.

She had considered the possibility that Trisanna and her companions were responsible, but she quickly rejected the notion. Considerable power would have been required to make them invisible. And they hadn't made a sound. Even her own much vaunted team couldn't create an invisibility illusion that masked sound. Further, the thieves would have needed to hide their magical auras and all use of power.

Magic wasn't always the answer, of course. No magic of any kind had been necessary to escape the Peritonian mages. The success of that maneuver had depended solely on finding a suitable river. The water had hidden their glimmer and the current had quickly carried them out of sight.

Her team was by no means lacking in magical skills, though. Those among her companions with mage touch ability had been poised to provide both people and horses with protective shields if the river had become overly turbulent. And the moment they found a suitable location to leave the water, two of her mages had made the entire team invisible. There had never been any real risk of them being detected by the Peritonians.

Making the team invisible was far from simple, of course. Her two mages with mage taste ability found it extremely taxing. They couldn't keep it up for long, and she only called on them when there was pressing need. And while they were able to provide invisibility, masking sound and smell was beyond them.

As for masking magical auras, she knew of no mage capable of achieving such a thing. Once again, though, magic was not the only answer. Her team had access to a clever alternative that did the job well enough. Other mages in Tantel had constructed thin waterproof garments that, with magical assistance, trapped a thin layer of water. Worn under a cloak, a garment of that type was surprisingly effective at hiding a mage's aura. Unfortunately, the garments were heavy and uncomfortable. But their usefulness was indisputable.

She had no solution for masking the use of magical power. It was simply out of the question. She had never heard of a mage who could achieve such a feat.

Taking everything into consideration, the horses must have been stolen by non-magical thieves. Their loss had been a heavy blow, and her team had been forced to work hard to make up for lost time. She would have gladly taken advantage of a river if one had been available. But nothing suitable presented itself.

At least only four of the saddlebags had disappeared with the horses. They still had the provisions from the other eight. The remaining supplies were now being carefully rationed.

Reduced to traveling by foot, they nevertheless made good progress. Her team members had not been chosen solely for their magical abilities. No mage was allowed to join the team unless they were mentally tough and in excellent physical condition. This mission was providing ample opportunity for them to demonstrate it.

Every team member shared another important quality—none of them were squeamish. She didn't doubt that a time for ruthlessness would arrive sooner or later.

Her immediate priority was to establish the team's current location.

If she was accurately recalling the maps she'd studied before leaving Tantel, they had arrived in the abandoned town of Flaxendell. She felt sure that Trisanna and her companions were close at hand. If so they were most likely hiding somewhere in the town. Accordingly, she had ignored the protests of her team and insisted on them wearing the special garments that masked their glimmer. She had also called on the two mages with mage taste ability to make them all invisible.

She wondered why the fugitives had crossed the border into the ruined land. If they were hoping to throw off the pursuit, their attempt was futile.

Or did they have another reason?

Perhaps they didn't understand the risks they were taking. She had done considerable research into the dangers associated with traveling in the old kingdom of Methesia. In the decades since the Great Desolation many had attempted it, for a range of reasons. Treasure seekers sought plunder. Others craved knowledge. The library of the Compact in Ettaran had been unequalled, and some mages were willing to risk anything to gain access to it.

In the border region, mages suffered nightmares and visions whenever they slept. Every report described the experience as extremely disturbing. A few who were not sufficiently resilient had gone mad. For reasons that were not understood, common people were little affected. Not surprisingly, anything of value in the region had long since been carried off by looters.

Everything changed for anyone foolish enough to draw closer to the old capital of Ettaran. Adverse manifestations became worse— much worse. Mages and commoners alike invariably yielded to insanity, whatever they tried to do to protect themselves. It happened very quickly too.

Once they entered the border region, Pernilla had prevented her team members from sleeping for more than a few minutes at a time. None of them had thanked her, even though she'd made it clear what would happen if she let them give in to their weariness. How long they could get by without proper sleep was unknown, but they had managed so far.

If Trisanna hadn't known better, she might already have slept. If she had, Pernilla wasn't hopeful about her having been incapacitated. Based on the evidence thus far, she was considerably more resilient than most.

At the very least the girl might have lost track of time. Mages who did surrender to sleep sometimes didn't wake for days. Eventually some of them became incapable of distinguishing between dreams and reality.

If her team had merely been tasked with disposing of Trisanna, they would only have needed to drive her further into the desolation. But Pernilla had personally been charged with recovering the amulet. That meant they needed to find her. And they needed to do it soon, before their quarry wandered in so far they couldn't reach her.

It was time to seize the initiative. If witnessing the ineptitude of the Peritonians had made her overconfident, any complacency had been thoroughly expunged. The brazen theft of their horses had seen to that.

She was angry now. Trisanna would pay, along with anyone else who dared to hinder her.

THE VAST MAJORITY of Kothlar's party had spent little time in the saddle in the recent past, and all of them were feeling sore and uncomfortable when they settled for their first night on the road. They had gradually been adapting in the days that followed, but he nevertheless heard many sighs of relief whenever he halted the column for a break.

On that particular occasion, Ramond rode back toward Kothlar as soon as the column came to a halt.

"We've almost reached the border with Methesia."

"Have you seen any sign of other travelers?"

Ramond shook his head. "Not yet. Are you planning to continue?"

"Yes. Have you traveled across the border before?"

"I have, on several occasions. I've been to Flaxendell a couple of times. It isn't too far from the border."

"Did you experience any ill effects?"

"No. My men and I are not likely to be affected. Not for a while. Horses don't like it, though." His face turned grim. "I once traveled across the border with a mage. He was badly shaken. We got him out safely, but he is still affected by what happened to him."

Kothlar nodded. "I know the mage you're speaking of. I did some research the day before we left. We will be most at risk if we sleep."

"How can you avoid sleeping?"

"We can allow ourselves brief naps. Thirty minutes at the most. That approach has worked for others in the past. Only in the border region, though. It won't be safe for any of us beyond that, mage or not."

"What do you propose?" asked Ramond.

"We will stop for the night before crossing the border. Every mage in the party will be allowed to sleep for as long as they can. When we set out, half of our number will remain behind."

"A wise precaution," agreed Ramond.

"Since you and your men will not be in immediate danger," Kothlar continued, "I would be grateful if you would ride ahead. Return as soon as you find indications of recent travelers. And don't go into Flaxendell—not under any circumstances. I'm almost certain that other mages have reached there already."

Ramond nodded.

"One word of warning. You should assume that you are under constant observation, even when there is no possible location where observers could conceal themselves."

The mercenary captain stared at him curiously.

"Speculation is likely to be confusing rather than helpful, so I won't say more. I simply want to encourage you to be extremely cautious at all times. We will remain here until you return with a report."

When Kothlar questioned other members of his party the following morning, he learned that most of them had slept well. It was also obvious they were appreciating a break from continuous riding.

Ramond rode in with his men a couple of hours before noon. Kothlar was sitting with Alexis when he found them.

"We went almost as far as Flaxendell, although we turned back before we came in sight of it," he reported. "The signs were confused, but we saw clear evidence that other travelers have recently passed that way. One was a large party—ten or a dozen people on foot. Their number must have included one or more mages, because they had made an effort to cover their tracks magically. Their efforts were ineffective—or perhaps half-hearted. We had no difficulty reading the signs."

He paused. "We did see other indicators too. I hesitate to mention them, because they were confusing at best."

Kothlar worked hard at concealing his eagerness. "Tell me everything," he urged. "However bizarre it might seem."

"There were signs that a smaller party of four or five had passed that way before the larger group. The odd thing was that apart from one location there was no sign of them at all."

His brows drew together. "I closely examined the location with my best tracker. I have never seen anything like it. I have little understanding of magic, but if I had to make a wild guess I would say that the smaller party succeeded completely in erasing their tracks, and they did so using magic. The magic used by the later party interacted with theirs in such a way that in one location the original signs were exposed."

Kothlar was careful to conceal his elation. "Thank you, Ramond. Your information confirms precisely what I might have expected. Once more you have amply repaid our faith in you. Please notify everyone that we will leave at dawn tomorrow. I have already let my party know who will be going and who will be staying behind."

Ramond left after dipping his head in acknowledgment.

"What do you make of his report?" Kothlar asked Alexis.

"I would say it means that the Tantellans are ahead of us. We'll undoubtedly find them in Flaxendell. Or, perhaps more accurately, we'd find them there if we were able to see them."

Kothlar nodded, a sly smile on his face. "I agree. It also means that Dalthinir got there first, along with a few others."

"Why are you so happy about that? We'll have two invisible groups of mages waiting for us. One group will be foreigners we know we can't trust, and the other will be renegades who have no more love for us than we have for them."

"I agree with your assessment of the Tantellans. We can't trust them even for a minute. But you have encountered Dalthinir once, and Kylen twice. Have they ever shown any indication at all of wanting to harm you?"

"No, none whatever."

"We know that the Tantellans are pursuing Trisanna. I believe she is with Dalthinir. That will put the two groups in conflict."

Alexis frowned at him. "And you're hoping it will give us an opportunity to connect with Dalthinir? What do you imagine the chief master is going to think of that?"

"I already know that he won't be happy. But if my guesses are correct, we have important lessons to learn from Dalthinir."

"What makes you think he'll be willing to share that knowledge with us?"

"It won't harm him in any way. He'll still be able to hide from us. And I never believed Lars and Petria. He's on the run because for him the only alternative is death. But I don't think he's ever intended harm to the kingdom, or to the Compact. He's put himself in danger more than once to rescue Compact mages, including you."

Alexis nodded tightly. "I'm willing to take the risk of supporting you. But you'd better hope Emmela isn't around when it happens."

The smaller group had been riding hard. Kothlar had positioned himself at the head of the column beside Ramond.

"We're very close to Flaxendell," Ramond informed him. "If we continue for another five minutes we should be in sight of it."

"It's time to leave the horses, then," Kothlar replied.

By arrangement, several mages from the group remaining behind had ridden with them. They would be riding back to the border with the horses once the town was within reach. They would then return to the current location with the horses an hour before sunset.

Ramond had suggested the arrangement, and Kothlar was increasingly seeing the sense of it. The further they went from the border, the more skittish and difficult to handle the horses were becoming. It would have been a major distraction to have them in Flaxendell.

Those among them intending to continue paused to dismount and replace reins with halters. Then they handed the halters to the riders returning to the campsite. All of them stood watching as they rode away.

Kothlar saw the tension on the faces of the mages. They were entering a place with an evil reputation to face mages with potentially hostile intentions.

"Gather around!" Kothlar called.

He spotted Emmela in the group. "Have you made progress?" he asked.

She nodded.

"Please demonstrate," he invited her.

Three other mages were standing near her. "Now," she told them.

Ramond and his group disappeared. Then several mages vanished as well, followed by several more.

"Each of you should only be able to see the people sharing the same illusion," said Emmela. "The fact that everyone can still hear me indicates that the illusion does not extend to sound. So you will need to remain quiet."

"Were you able to cover everyone?" asked Kothlar.

He suddenly found himself alone.

"Can you see anyone else?" Emmela asked.

"No, I can't."

"Then it's working. I removed you from your group, so you were no longer covered by any of the illusions."

"You can drop the illusions for now," Kothlar said. "Well done to all of you with mage taste abilities!"

There was an instant buzz from the assembled mages. They were clearly impressed.

Emmela looked pleased, and he didn't begrudge her the attention, especially given the lack of respect so often shown to her and others with illusion ability.

"Kaspra and Ellis?" he called.

The two mages stepped forward, somewhat shamefacedly.

"Anything to report on hiding auras?" he asked.

They shook their heads.

"Don't be too disappointed," he said. "Keep working on it."

He wasn't too concerned. Although he didn't say so, he had high hopes of getting some tips from Dalthinir, who had apparently mastered the skill.

More quietly, he said to them, "It mightn't even be an issue. They might not have anyone like Inga or Pellistri who can smell magical auras."

Holding up his hands for attention, he called, "We're about to head into the town of Flaxendell. There are a few things you need to be aware of. First, we're now within the borders of Methesia. If you go to sleep for any length of time you will experience disturbing visions and nightmares. While we're across the border, never let each other sleep for longer than thirty minutes at a time. Second, as you know, we're looking for twelve Tantellan mages. You've just witnessed the effectiveness of illusion as a way of hiding a group of people. We believe they routinely practice the same tactic. You will all be hidden as well—don't expect to see anyone apart from the others in the same illusion group. To make sure we don't bump into each other, a member of Ramond's team will lead each group. They will be responsible for coordinating the groups. They won't be able to see each other, but they will be able to hear each other. They plan to use audible sounds as signals when it isn't safe to talk. Make sure you know who is leading your group. One final thing about hiding. Although we have Pellistri with us, there might be little she can do to identify the Tantellan mages. We suspect they might be able to hide magical auras as well."

Loud muttering broke out at these words, and he held up his hands for silence again.

"We don't know what to expect from the Tantellans. Make sure you are never far from someone who can shield you should the need arise. Finally, there is reason to think that Dalthinir might be in Flaxendell. If you encounter him—or Kylen, who seems to be his apprentice—I want to speak with them. Do not, and I repeat, DO NOT attempt to apprehend them. If you encounter Trisanna, I want to speak with her as well. I should warn you that the renegades are also likely to be invisible."

Before they could begin muttering again, he added, "These are highly unusual circumstances, and we are in an unfamiliar place. If you get into trouble, don't be slow about asking for help."

He turned to Emmela. "Could you and your colleagues please hide us?"

As people began to disappear before his eyes, he added, "Lead on, Ramond. We are in the hands of you and your team."

CHAPTER 21

Hurrying after the phantom girl, Trisanna reached the main road to Ettaran at the point where it left the square. It took a few moments before she spotted the girl.

When she did so, she gasped. Beyond her were two mages, with a larger group behind them. Her heart began to race. She had no doubt that she was looking at Tantellans. A shiver of fear shook her when she realized that the mages who killed her parents and chased her to the lake must be among them. Taking a deep breath, she reminded herself she was invisible, with her magical aura masked.

The two mages came to a sudden halt, looking alarmed. They had clearly seen the phantom. The larger group hurried forward to join them, and they briefly conferred before all turning to face her.

A fireball sailed suddenly toward the ghostly figure, quickly followed by several more. Rocks began to fly in her direction, and a fierce wind sprang up to buffet her. Apparently the Tantellans had decided to find out whether this particular ghost was as insubstantial as she appeared.

The girl abruptly disappeared. However, before she vanished Trisanna thought she caught a glimpse of her collapsing.

The rain of missiles ceased and the wind died down. The Tantellans stood silently for a moment, then a large number of them headed to the place where she had been.

Trisanna got there first. Bending low, she heard ragged breathing punctuated by whimpers of pain. This girl was no ghost. Reaching down, she felt around for the girl's body. Having found her, she gathered her into her arms and ran as swiftly as she could toward the square and the inn that lay beyond it.

"Go find what happened to the phantom girl," ordered Pernilla.

Several mages hurried forward. Reaching the place where she had been, they groped around on the ground, trying to find her.

"There's no one here!" one of them eventually called.

After a glare in their direction, Pernilla ignored them. "The girl doesn't matter—she was a distraction. Move forward, and stay alert. Remember that our only goal is to find Trisanna."

She caught a glimpse of the face of Gharvil, one of the two team members with mage taste ability. "Don't look so sour," she growled. "I'm not about to ask you to make the group invisible."

Gharvil didn't try to hide his relief.

The square stood before them, and they moved into it, glancing about for any sign of others. Finding it empty, Pernilla decided it was time to hunt. The only member of the group able to detect magical auras was Gharvil. His ability was effective provided he used it over relatively short distances. Unfortunately, that meant he'd be unable to detect other mages if they weren't quite close to the square.

"Gharvil, take a look around. Trisanna and her new friends must be somewhere nearby. See if you can sniff out any glimmer. Make yourself invisible and you shouldn't get into trouble."

With a nod, Gharvil turned away. Then he simply disappeared. One moment he was there, then he had vanished.

Pernilla shook her head. Perhaps one day the mystery of it might grow stale. It hadn't happened so far.

As she settled down to wait she glanced at her group. Every one of them showed signs of weariness. Mistakes crept in when people were tired. She would need to be especially vigilant.

THE LAST THING Gharvil needed was a new search. He couldn't remember ever feeling as tired as he did at that moment. He had been expected to help keep the group invisible while also remaining constantly alert for magical auras. It was exhausting. And Pernilla had refused to let him sleep. No one could reasonably be expected to continue for long under such conditions.

Traveling to Periton was one thing. But no one had told him they would be heading into Methesia. He personally knew of a mage who had ventured too far into the ruined kingdom. The poor fool had gone completely insane. Pernilla could talk as much as she liked about skipping sleep to avoid the danger. The only real solution was to leave Methesia before all of them went crazy.

Perhaps Pernilla thought the threat of madness would increase her team's determination to capture Trisanna. If so, she was pulling the wrong lever, at least as far as Gharvil was concerned.

Beyond all that, a bigger issue had been preying on his mind. Among the Tantellan mages, Pernilla's team was recognized as the best of the best, and he had been flattered when first admitted to their ranks. But of late the tasks assigned to the team had been unusually disturbing. It hadn't sat easily with him to see the girl's foster parents tortured at the farm. His companions might have become hardened to such things, but the same could not be said for him.

It was easy to guess what Pernilla would say—the team was serving a higher purpose, and it was about time he toughened up. He supposed she was right. He shook his head wearily. The struggle to overcome his own feebleness didn't lessen his exhaustion.

Coming to a dwelling that appeared largely intact, he carefully pushed open the door and peered inside. He wasn't sure why he was bothering. If a mage was in there, he would have already detected glimmer. But at least he could claim to have done some searching.

The dust covering the floor made it clear no one had entered the house in many years. The front room boasted a very comfortable-looking armchair covered with a large blanket. Clouds of dust rose in the air when he pulled off the covering. After he had recovered from his coughing he discovered that the armchair was still in surprisingly good condition. In fact it looked incredibly appealing. Lowering himself into it he released a sigh of satisfaction. It felt even more comfortable than it had looked.

There could be no harm in sitting quietly for a few minutes. He deserved a short break. He wouldn't stay for long. When he returned he'd tell Pernilla he searched high and low. No one would know any different. Not when he was invisible and none of the others were capable of sensing his aura.

His eyelids began to close of their own volition. For a few moments he fought to keep them open. Then, surrendering to the inevitable, he allowed them to ease shut. Just for a moment.

He was sound asleep within seconds.

Trisanna burst into the inn, gasping from the effort of carrying the limp form. The girl was alive, although her breathing was noticeably ragged. There was little she could do for the injured child. She could only hope that Dalthinir could help in some way.

Dalthinir and the twins looked at her strangely, providing an abrupt reminder that they could see nothing more than her empty arms.

"It's the ghost girl!" she panted. "She's no ghost—she was just partially visible, which made her look like a wraith. Now she's completely invisible. The Tantellan mages have found us again. They sent rocks and fireballs at her, and she's been hit! I think she's badly hurt!"

Hurrying forward, Dalthinir bent low to listen to her breathing. He touched her head lightly, and his hand came away with blood on it. "It's hard to know how to treat her when I can't see her," he said.

"I can see her," said a voice. "Thank you for rescuing her!"

Trisanna started, quickly feeling foolish for her reaction—there was surely no mystery about what had happened. The person who made the girl invisible must have followed them into the inn.

"Her injuries don't appear to be too severe," said the voice. "My wife is on her way, and she has some skill as a healer. In the meantime, could I suggest that all of us manage without illusion for a while?"

Abruptly both the speaker and the girl became visible. A man with a gray beard stood before them. He was no longer young, although Trisanna saw that the light hadn't dimmed from his eye.

In response, she dropped her own illusion.

"I can usually see through illusions, but yours is more robust than most," he said, with a quick bow to Trisanna.

The inn door opened abruptly to admit a spindly woman of senior years. She exuded an air of quiet competence. Kneeling beside the girl, she felt her gently, her hand lingering on the girl's head.

After a few moments the girl stirred and opened her eyes. "Grandma, Grandpa," she said. "You found me."

"Of course we did, dearie!" exclaimed the woman. "We always keep an eye out for you." She glanced up at the newcomers. "We do get people wandering around in Flaxendell from time to time. Our granddaughter has a bad habit of putting herself in danger for their sakes!" she explained.

The girl's grandfather was shaking his head. "We guessed you might be in trouble when we sensed multiple bursts of power. I immediately made you fully invisible, just in case. Apparently my instinct was right." His voice became grim. "It's about time I stopped letting you wander around half visible."

"Someone needs to warn people," the girl protested weakly. "Not everyone seems to know that it's dangerous for mages here. And it's unusual for them to be as cruel as the ones that attacked me."

"We do know something of the dangers that mages face in Methesia," Dalthinir assured her. "We had a reason for taking the risk of coming to Flaxendell. The other mages have been pursuing us, and unfortunately they followed us here."

"There's no need for any of you to suffer ill effects from being here," observed the man. "Not with the talisman she's carrying." He nodded toward Trisanna. "But I should introduce us. I'm Sorren, and this is my wife Vennia. Our bold little adventurer here is our grand-daughter, Marigold."

Dalthinir briefly introduced the members of his party. "One of our number is missing. He's a mage too, and his name is Kylen."

"It's a dangerous time to be wandering about at the moment. A second group of mages will soon be arriving."

"I've detected them as well," Dalthinir confirmed. "I'm not too concerned about Kylen. His farsense is stronger than mine, and he can detect magical auras. He is also well able to shield himself if the need arises."

"He must be the one I saw when you all arrived in Flaxendell," said Marigold. "I saw him again earlier this morning."

"He thought you were a ghost!" said Dalthinir with a wry smile.

"I just wanted to warn him," she said.

"You did warn him," Trisanna assured her. "Me too! Thank you!"

"I think you can trust them, Grandpa," said Marigold. "I felt sure of it the moment I met them."

Her comment prompted a glow of pride from Vennia.

"She seems to have inherited her grandmother's insight," said Sorren with a wink.

"Where have you come from?" Dalthinir asked Sorren and Vennia.

"We both grew up here," Vennia told him.

"Isn't it dangerous?" asked Trisanna. "We had some bad dreams last night."

"We're protected by a powerful talisman. Not unlike the one you're carrying," Sorren told her.

"How do you know about that?" she asked in wonder.

"The illusion was a nice piece of work, but there's no hiding your talisman," he replied. "It drew us to you. The more powerful dragon talismans exert quite a tug on anyone who has a dragon talisman of their own, provided they're not too far away."

"Were you able to sense their talisman?" Dalthinir asked Trisanna.

"Not at all," she said.

"It isn't surprising," Sorren told them. "Our talisman is not as powerful. But you'll have no difficulty detecting it once you activate the one you have."

"We haven't been able to understand how the other group could find us so consistently," mused Dalthinir. "Perhaps the amulet has been drawing them."

Sorren nodded. "I wouldn't be surprised. The amulet is unusually powerful. It's like a beacon on a dark night."

Trisanna was horrified. "I'll throw it away if it means the Tantellans won't be able to find us!"

"I wouldn't recommend that, dearie!" said Vennia in alarm. "It would almost certainly end up in the wrong hands."

"You're better off using it to protect you," added Sorren.

"But I don't know how to use it!" she protested. She gazed hopefully at Sorren. "Would you be willing to teach me?"

He gazed back. "Not until I know what you intend to do with it."

"I have no particular plans. I'd like to protect us from bad dreams. And from going mad."

He looked unconvinced.

"Ask me anything you like!" she offered.

"What is your purpose in coming here?"

"I was born in Tantel. I came to Periton because the Tantellans want to kill me."

"Because you're a renegade?"

"Yes, although that isn't by any choice of mine. Their Compact was not involved in my magical awakening. That's the reason they see me as a renegade."

Sorren glanced at his wife.

Vennia nodded her head slowly. "She's telling the truth. She isn't telling us everything, though."

After exchanging a glance with Dalthinir, Trisanna sighed. "You might as well know the rest. Late in his life, my father had an affair. He was king of Tantel at the time. I was conceived as a result, although he never learned of it. My half-brother is now on the throne. It seems that as soon as he found out about me, he ordered me killed."

Both pairs of eyebrows went up.

"The fact that my mother was a mage only makes it worse. I'm the most despised of mages, because I have royal blood."

"It's small wonder that so many people want you dead!" exclaimed Vennia. "I feel for you very much, my dear!"

"How do you come to have a dragon talisman?" asked Sorren.

Trisanna pulled the jewel out from under her clothing and held it up for inspection.

"My foster parents gave me this when I fled Tantel. I had no idea what it was."

"That is the Amulet of Zinth! They gave you a treasure beyond price!" Sorren told her. "Are you hoping to use it to take revenge on your enemies?"

She looked startled. "I don't think I've ever truly wished ill on anyone."

"And what of you, Dalthinir? Have you wished ill on others?"

"I cannot pretend to be as untarnished as Trisanna," he said frankly. "But I'm not looking for revenge. And I have never sought power for its own sake."

When Sorren glanced at Vennia, she nodded again.

"It seems you are a most unusual group of people," he conceded.

"What about me?" asked Jonno indignantly. "Don't I get to be questioned? For all you know I could be a demon in disguise!"

Vennia snorted. "If I'm reading you right, you're more like the pussy cat I had when I was a child," she said. "He was very effective at dealing with rats when the need arose and even dangerous snakes on occasion. He was also surprisingly good company when he wasn't preening himself."

Her assessment drew a laugh from the others. Even Bella joined in.

"She has you figured out," said Dalthinir with a smile.

Jonno's face wore a wounded expression, but he took it with good grace, providing further evidence of the resilience of the twins.

CHAPTER 22

It was obvious to Trisanna that Sorren had thawed noticeably since questioning her motives and Dalthinir's.

"I'll be happy to work with you on activating the amulet whenever you like," he told her.

Dalthinir broke into the conversation. "Before you talk talismans with Trisanna, I'd be interested to hear something of your story if you're willing to share it. You said you both grew up here. How is that possible?"

"There isn't a great deal to tell," Sorren replied. "Our forebears were mages who left Periton three generations ago due to conflict in the Compact at the time. I'm sure they're long forgotten now. Everyone will have assumed they perished years ago. There were four families, and the only reason they survived was the talisman I referred to. They were able to establish a farm in a hidden valley, protected from the blight that covers these lands. We were born in the valley to two of the families and grew up there side by side. After we married we had two children. Our oldest daughter married into one of the other families. She gave birth to our granddaughter, Marigold, who lives with us. Our other child, a son, was unusually headstrong. He insisted on going to Ettaran. He wanted to explore its fabled treasures. He'd spent many hours in the library in Flaxendell and hunted down anything that talked about dragon talismans. I think he'd convinced himself he could find a talisman of his own there."

Vennia took up the tale. "He refused to accept the seriousness of the danger. He'd grown up under the protection of the talisman, so he was unaffected by the blight. We tried to convince him, and he wouldn't listen. We wanted to go after him with the talisman, but the others refused to allow it. They were right, of course. We'd agreed that anyone who left our community would be on their own. Our son never returned."

"That's horrible!" said Trisanna.

"Most of the descendants of the original families failed to thrive," Vennia continued. "Many died quite young, including our daughter and her husband."

Sorren nodded. "The community began with high hopes, but over time it became insular—too insular to survive for long. All these years later, the three of us are the only ones who remain."

"Marigold isn't insular," said Vennia. "She has always been keenly interested in the outside world."

A grim expression had come over Sorren's face. "When we're gone, Marigold will need to make some difficult decisions. By then I expect she'll be a mage herself, and she'll have the talisman, of course. But she can't stay here on her own."

"Perhaps she could join us when she's ready," offered Bella with a grin.

"An excellent suggestion," agreed Jonno. "Dalthinir seems willing to tolerate new additions to his merry band."

"I'm not leaving you!" Marigold told her grandparents emphatically.

"There is certainly no urgency about such matters," said Vennia brightly. "In the meantime, I'm guessing that none of you have much fresh food with you." When no one disagreed, she nodded. "I'll be back soon," she told them as she left the inn.

"You said your son hunted down documents that talk about dragon talismans," said Dalthinir. "Does that mean no such documents can be found in the library here?"

"They're all gone," Sorren confirmed. "Our son took them with him."

Dalthinir shook his head. "Those documents are the main reason we came here."

"Were you hoping to confirm whether or not it's the Amulet of Zinth?"

"Yes, I was. We need to know. If you're right, and it is the amulet, we can't let it fall into the wrong hands."

"There's no question about its identity. Our son located a document that described it, and he showed me a sketch of it. It's the Amulet of Zinth—there can be no doubt about it. You certainly need to stop it falling into the wrong hands. It's extremely powerful—much more so than my own talisman."

Dalthinir seemed to accept Sorren's assertion. "Thank you, Sorren. You've confirmed my suspicions." He had his answer, if not quite in the manner he'd expected.

Sorren had a final observation to share. "My son learned in his research that the Great Library in Ettaran is the place to go to find out everything that's ever been known about dragon talismans. It was a key reason why he wanted to go there."

With Dalthinir's immediate questions answered, Sorren beckoned Trisanna over. "Would you like some instruction about that talisman now?"

"Yes, please!" she replied. "Especially if it means we're able to sleep peacefully tonight."

He nodded. "You'll find talismans of this type remarkably useful. They don't grant new abilities, but they greatly boost existing abilities, even before they're activated. I find I'm able to use my magic continuously, without tiring. Talismans are also useful for a range of other purposes. Protecting people from going mad is only one of them. Mine has a way of presenting me with useful actions it can take—actions relevant to my situation at the time."

Trisanna listened wide-eyed. She'd regarded the amulet as nothing more than a valuable jewel.

"The first thing to understand, though, is that a dragon talisman isn't a tool to be wielded at your pleasure. To appropriate its power you need to grant it access to your magical core—the magical part of your inner being."

Seeing Trisanna's surprise and alarm, Sorren smiled grimly. "Did you imagine it would be like a knife—you pick it up whenever you want to cut something?"

"I...I'm not sure what I thought. You speak of granting access to my magical core—what does that mean in practice?"

"Perhaps a simple illustration might help. A sword is not intelligent. It is an object under the control of a warrior. But it cannot be used effectively until it becomes almost an extension of the warrior's arm. It must be embraced wholeheartedly. In doing so, the warrior is introduced to opportunities and challenges that would have otherwise been out of reach. And so it brings about change, unthinking as it is."

She nodded. "I understand that. Do you mean that in embracing the sword, the warrior grants it access to the core of their being?"

"In some small measure that is true. Sooner or later it will present the warrior with ethical dilemmas—challenges never faced before. A magical artifact does the same, but it is much more far-reaching in its effect. It is not like a sword that can be bent to the will of the warrior. It is infused with dragon magic. It encapsulates magic that originates from a different and incompatible species. You must allow it to settle into your magical being before you can draw upon it."

"Granting dragon magic access to your inner being surely can't be safe!" protested Dalthinir.

"You seem to be laying claim to a great deal of knowledge about dragons," said Sorren mildly.

"Do you doubt that dragons turned on humankind?" Dalthinir retorted.

"I do not question it," replied Sorren. "But saying that some dragons turned on humankind is not the same as saying dragon magic is unsafe. That would suggest that all dragons are evil. You are a renegade, are you not?"

Dalthinir nodded.

"Some renegade mages have caused great evil. Does that make all renegades evil?"

"Of course not. But we're talking about dragon magic. It is perilous —in ways that human magic is not."

"Dragon magic is powerful, and for humans, any kind of power is perilous."

"You are saying that dragon magic is *not* evil by its very nature?" asked Trisanna.

"Is human magic evil by its very nature?" asked Sorren.

She paused before shaking her head.

"Then dragon magic isn't either. It can't be, given that human magic is derived from dragon magic."

Dalthinir wasn't satisfied. "What if the dragon that infused this amulet with magical power was thoroughly evil? What would be the implications of Trisanna granting that dragon access to her inner being, even indirectly through an amulet?"

"I can't say," Sorren admitted. "The talisman I inherited has not led to evil in any who have held it. But the history of the amulet is not known to me." He turned to Trisanna. "Only you can decide whether you will grant it access to your inner being. I will not try to advise you. If you decide to proceed, though, you must reach down into your gut and draw in the magic of the talisman."

Trisanna wasn't at all sure what to think about the issue. Dalthinir clearly had serious reservations. But the mages who taught him had shown themselves to be unfairly prejudiced—against renegades at least. Perhaps they had been wrong about these matters too.

She had no opportunity to explore it further. At that moment Vennia returned, laden down with food in a large woven basket. She had dried meat of some kind, cheeses, bread, and other things Dalthinir couldn't immediately identify.

"I hope you're all hungry!" she exclaimed, setting the food on a large table.

They gathered around eagerly. Everything went quiet as they attacked the food with enthusiasm.

She had brought enough to satisfy them all. Almost.

"That was a delicious appetizer," said Jonno hopefully.

Vennia raised an eyebrow. "I haven't entirely forgotten the appetites of young males." Rummaging around in the basket, she retrieved an apple and tossed it to Jonno. Catching it gleefully, he set to work on it at once.

None of the others had been forgotten. When Vennia offered an apple to each of them, no one refused her.

Dalthinir was becoming restless. "Kylen hasn't returned. I'm starting to become concerned."

Trisanna nodded. "We need to find him. Exploring the amulet can wait a little longer."

"We'll come too," said Jonno immediately.

"Please don't!" replied Dalthinir. "I won't be able to keep track of too many people at once."

"I'll be staying with Marigold and my wife," Sorren told him. "I can provide illusion for your twins as well as for us if you like."

Dalthinir looked relieved. "Thank you. We will return as soon as we can. Trisanna, could you please hide us?"

"It's done."

Trisanna led the way to the square, closely followed by Dalthinir.

Scurrying from cover to cover, Kylen tailed the Tantellans as they headed back toward the square.

Uppermost in his mind was the need to warn his friends. He pictured the buildings that surrounded the square. It might be possible to get past the Tantellans by skirting around them.

The next time he peered around from behind his cover, he noticed the two leading mages come to a halt. His heart missed a beat when he saw the reason for them stopping. Ahead of them stood the phantom girl.

The larger group hurried forward to join the leaders. After a brief consultation, they faced the girl together. Then they began assaulting her with fire, earth, and wind.

Why were they attacking her? Everyone knew you couldn't harm a ghost.

Yet he heaved a sigh of relief when she disappeared. He frowned, trying to understand his own reaction. Why had his heart been sinking when she was at risk? Concern for the vulnerable made no sense in this case.

Then he was confronted with a question that had been niggling away in the back of his mind from the moment she set out to warn him. If illusion could make someone invisible, why couldn't it make someone appear ghost-like?

He realized with a start she was no ghost. She was much too young to be a mage. That meant someone else was doing it for her.

His concern for her came rushing back. The mage hiding her clearly had mage taste abilities. But did they have mage touch abilities as well? Had they also been able to protect her from the deadly barrage launched by the Tantellans?

Distracted by his sudden alarm, he had stepped away from his cover to peer forward in the hope of catching a glimpse of the girl. Suddenly sensing someone behind him, he spun around.

He was too slow. A heavy blow to his head sent him crashing to the ground. Everything went black.

"MASTER PERNILLA!"

Hearing the call, Pernilla glanced behind her. She had instructed two mages to follow the main group from a distance. The strategy appeared to have yielded a reward. A limp form lay at their feet. Could they have captured Trisanna?

Hurrying back to join them, she saw at once it was a male—a youth of similar age to the girl she sought.

"Is he a mage?" she asked. As the words left her lips, she remembered that Gharvil was off hunting mages. She'd sent away the one mage in her group capable of sensing magical auras. Until he returned there would be no way to confirm the boy's status.

Whoever he was, though, he must have been traveling with Trisanna and her friends. She couldn't imagine why anyone else would be wandering around in Flaxendell.

"Where did you find him?"

"He was following you from behind, trying to stay out of sight."

Pernilla peered at the prone figure thoughtfully. "Trisanna was locked up, and a young male mage broke her out. If this is the youth in question, she's undoubtedly nearby. Having him might give us some leverage."

She nodded to Agalar, the other mage. "You know what to do."

"It's already done," Agalar assured her.

"Keep him alive and in good condition, at least for now," Pernilla told him. "He's your responsibility. That means you'll be carrying him until he wakes up."

Taking the hint, Agalar detached a waterskin from his belt and splashed water over the boy's face.

Coughing and spluttering, the captive opened his eyes. He lay dazed for a few moments, squinting up at the unfamiliar faces. Then he frowned, reaching with both hands for his neck.

"That's right, boy," growled Agalar. "You've acquired a magical noose. Don't bother trying to remove it—it's protected by a shield. The other end is tied to my belt. It's my invention, so I know how to keep it secure. Whether or not you're a mage you'd better stay close, or the noose will tighten."

So saying, he stepped back a couple of paces. Choking helplessly, the boy clutched at his neck.

Agalar stepped forward again, easing the pressure. "You can see how it is. Now get on your feet! And don't try anything clever. The noose is designed to strangle you unless I prevent it. So you'd better hope I want to keep preventing it."

Struggling to his feet, the boy cowered at Agalar's side.

"Excellent," said Pernilla, "Now let's rejoin the others. Then we'll see if we can find your companions."

She walked swiftly forward, not waiting for them.

Agalar soon joined her, the captive with him. The boy was sticking to Agalar's side like molasses.

"We have one of Trisanna's companions," Pernilla told them. "She can't be far away."

She looked at the boy. "Where are they?" she demanded.

He glared back at her without speaking.

She nodded to Agalar, who immediately tightened the invisible noose.

The boy fell to his knees, gasping for air. Agalar remained unmoved, watching dispassionately as his victim collapsed, losing consciousness.

"I said alive and in good condition!" snapped Pernilla.

Agalar immediately eased the pressure. They watched for a long moment as he lay there without breathing. Then he sucked in a shuddering breath of air. Several more minutes had been wasted before he was capable of standing unaided.

Pernilla glowered at Agalar. "Don't try a stunt like that again," she growled.

She peered around restlessly. "Where is Gharvil? If he doesn't return soon I'll have his hide!"

Pernilla was becoming increasingly annoyed. Without Gharvil's ability to detect magical auras, she was effectively blind. Worse, he was one of only two mages in the group with mage taste capabilities. Without him only half of them could be invisible. Where was he?

Clearly it had been unwise to send him off alone. While it was possible he had come to grief, it seemed far more likely he was having a nap somewhere in a quiet corner. If so, the man was a fool. Glancing around, she saw others struggling with weariness. Several of them were almost asleep on their feet.

She had no sympathy for them. She was no less tired, but she'd managed to keep herself awake.

If she thought she had problems, it immediately became apparent they were only beginning. One moment she was shaking her head at her fellow Tantellans. The next moment her group was surrounded.

A large number of people in mage attire had appeared out of nowhere. She saw at once they were Peritonians. Thanks to the absence of Gharvil, there'd been no warning of their approach.

"Shields!" Pernilla shouted belatedly.

So the Peritonians too had mastered the art of making their group invisible. She couldn't pretend it wasn't unsettling to have lost her imagined advantage.

She found herself facing Kothlar, the Peritonian mage supposedly in charge of the joint mission.

"You seem to have a propensity for getting lost, Pernilla," said Kothlar dryly. He didn't sound happy.

"A mere mishap in the river," Pernilla replied curtly. "By the time we made it to dry land we couldn't find you anywhere."

The Peritonian clearly wasn't impressed by the explanation. "We seem to have found you, in spite of your best efforts to lose us. I wonder why you feel the need for shields."

"I find it's an instinctive reaction whenever someone sneaks up on me," countered Pernilla.

"I see you have a fugitive we have been looking for," said Kothlar, pointing at the boy. "We'll take him from here."

"You're welcome to him, Kothlar—as soon as we have Trisanna in our custody. Not before."

Kothlar was peering at the boy. "Is that a magical restraint around his neck?" he asked incredulously.

"He's dangerous," snarled Pernilla. "Rabid animals bite if you don't control them."

"It's barbaric! Release him immediately!"

"In case I haven't already made it clear," snarled Pernilla, "he isn't yours until you hand over Trisanna."

"We don't have Trisanna."

"Then you can't have the boy."

Kothlar, with his eyes narrowing, took a step back. There was nothing encouraging in that particular move.

It was impossible to guess what might happen next. The only thing Pernilla knew with certainty was that the situation was becoming extremely volatile.

CHAPTER 23

Trisanna arrived with Dalthinir to see Kylen standing among a group of mages, positioned at the side of one of them. He appeared to have something around his neck. It was like a cord, except that it was shimmering. The Tantellan clearly had the other end of it. There was so much magic around that the atmosphere almost crackled with it. But she could still sense the malign magical stench of the cord encircling his neck.

Knowing she could talk freely without the Tantellans hearing, she asked Dalthinir anxiously, "Should I include Kylen in our illusion?"

"Not yet," he warned. "Not until we find a way to free him. There's no telling what they'll do if he suddenly disappears."

Trisanna looked on fretfully. Kylen had rescued her from the lockup. Now he was the one who needed rescuing, and she had nothing to offer. She was reduced to looking on helplessly.

Dalthinir broke into her thoughts. "We need to move to the edge of the square at once! Another group of mages will be here very soon."

She followed him to what he deemed a safe location. A few minutes later a whole group of mages suddenly appeared out of nowhere to surround the Tantellans. Invisibility had become very popular all of a sudden.

"A group of Peritonian mages has joined us," said Dalthinir calmly.

Trisanna watched wide-eyed as the two groups faced off. The mage called Kothlar clearly wanted the Tantellans to free Kylen, but only so he could take him into custody. The politics of the situation were of no interest to her. All she cared about was freeing her rescuer.

"I'm going to get closer to Kylen to see if there's something I can do," Dalthinir told her, moving quickly toward the Tantellans.

He threaded his way through the mages, dodging right and left in his attempts to avoid making contact with them. With Peritonians on every side, the Tantellan mages were clustered together tightly, Kylen in the middle of them.

It quickly became apparent to Trisanna that Dalthinir would not be able to reach him, and Dalthinir himself soon reached the same conclusion. Weaving back through the people in his path, the mage returned to Trisanna's side.

"This situation is impossible," he told her, frustration evident on his face. "We'll have to try again later."

"What do you think the Tantellans will do next?" she asked anxiously.

"They'll keep searching for you. If you can find a way to protect us with the amulet, we can draw them further in. Without protection, they'll eventually go mad. Whatever happens though, we'll need to watch for the right moment to get Kylen back."

So it all depended on her. The prospect of giving herself to the amulet filled her with apprehension. But Kylen had rescued her. How could she deny him in his hour of need?

It was becoming clear to Kothlar that he was only seeing a part of what was going on before him. At some point during the confrontation with the Tantellans, Pellistri leaned toward him and murmured, "A couple of the Tantellans don't have magical auras. And both of them are wearing some kind of strange garment under their cloaks."

Scanning the group carefully, Kothlar spotted the mages she must be referring to. How could a garment mask glimmer? He immediately remembered that water masked auras. Was it possible the Tantellans had come up with a way to trap a layer of water inside an item of clothing?

Most of the Tantellans were not wearing similar garments. But they were wearing backpacks that might conceal such clothing.

His eyes narrowed. This new information changed everything for the Peritonian leader. He had imagined the Tantellan mages to be much more capable than they were. Pernilla and her thugs clearly had no greater magical ability than his own team. They were relying on cleverly designed clothing to give them an edge.

He waved his fellow mages back to his side before addressing Pernilla one last time.

"I still want the youth Kylen. Since you apparently have nothing useful to contribute on that subject, I'm going to leave you in Methesia. Assuming you're fool enough to remain here. If you decide to return to Periton, you'll find the border well guarded. Don't think you can continue to wander around freely. We know how you hide your magical auras now, and we'll be waiting for you. I'll be advising King Durvaryn to proclaim that you're no longer welcome. And you'd better expect that a strongly worded protest will be sent to your own king and your chief master about your conduct since your arrival."

At a word from Kothlar, the Peritonians disappeared.

Angry shouts from Pernilla and her mages accompanied their withdrawal. Kothlar didn't care. He had no interest in the bleating of the Tantellans. As far as he was concerned, finding a way to connect with Dalthinir had just become his most pressing priority.

Dalthinir and Trisanna had witnessed the interchange between Kothlar and Pernilla.

"What did the Peritonian mean about knowing how they hide their magical auras now?" Trisanna asked.

"I've been wondering the same thing," he replied. "Two of the Tantellans are wearing something under their cloaks, and the same two are showing very little glimmer."

"Very little, rather than none?"

He nodded. "I can detect traces from them, and I'm sure Kylen could too. Someone with a weaker ability to detect magical auras might sense nothing. I'm guessing that the Peritonians have concluded they're using some kind of garment to hide their glimmer. Perhaps something that surrounds them with a thin layer of water. It's an interesting idea. I'm surprised no one else has thought of it."

"Kylen isn't wearing anything unusual. Does that mean you will easily be able to sense his aura?"

"Yes. Unless they have a spare garment, they won't be able to hide him. That should make our task easier."

"What do you think we should do?" she asked.

"Let's return to the inn. Our most important priority now is releasing Kylen. Once we've collected the twins we should move on, drawing the Tantellans toward Ettaran."

Upon arriving, Dalthinir pushed through the door with Trisanna close behind him.

The inn appeared to be empty, although Dalthinir's farsense told him that Sorren and Vennia were in the same place they had left them. Invisibility certainly had a way of complicating social interaction.

"For the moment we don't need to be invisible," he told Trisanna.

Sorren responded in kind. He was sitting beside his wife, with their granddaughter lying beside them. The twins were sitting near them.

Jonno looked bemused. "Didn't you find Kylen?"

"We found him," replied Dalthinir grimly. "The Tantellans have taken him captive. It wasn't possible to immediately release him."

"What can we do to help?" asked Bella.

"We'll need to choose our moment. In the meantime, we'll be tracking him."

Vennia made an effort to lighten the mood. "Your youngsters have been hard at work while you were gone. They've constructed a stretcher for our Marigold!"

"Would you like us to help you return her to your home?" asked Dalthinir. "Its location might be exposed to the Tantellans if we go there with the amulet, though."

"It won't be necessary," Sorren assured him. "We have a donkey cart nearby. We only need to get her onto it."

Protected by illusion, all of them accompanied the injured girl to the cart. "Thank you for your help!" Vennia exclaimed. The cart held other provisions, and she gave them as much as they could carry.

"Thank you!" Dalthinir responded. "You've been very generous, and you've also answered a lot of our questions."

"Please visit us if ever you come back this way," Sorren told them.

After promising to do so, they returned to the inn to gather their few possessions in preparation for departure.

TRISANNA HAD PROVIDED the entire party with illusion on their way to the cart. Then she had removed Sorren, Vennia, and Marigold, allowing Sorren to provide an illusion of his own for his little group. The end result was that the three of them became invisible to Dalthinir and his companions.

"Are we invisible?" asked Bella. "I'm confused about it most of the time."

Jonno nodded vigorously. "Me too. Especially whenever we're around other mages!"

"It's a good point," Dalthinir told them. "Trisanna, when we're near other people, could you please let us know when you make us invisible or end an illusion?"

She nodded. "Of course. We don't want to be taken by surprise."

"Thank you," Dalthinir replied. "Both the Tantellans and the Peritonians have figured out how to make themselves invisible, which means we need to be doubly careful. I'll let you know whenever I'm detecting magical auras."

"Just to let you know, I'll be providing us all with invisibility until further notice," Trisanna announced.

Dalthinir dipped his head. "And I'm masking our glimmer. I've also thrown up a shield, just as a precaution. No other magical auras are nearby at the moment."

They hadn't long returned to the inn when Dalthinir detected a magical aura approaching the building. With no other glimmer nearby, he was not too alarmed when the door of the inn opened briefly, then closed again.

Every head turned in that direction, although no one could be seen.

"Is anyone in here?" asked a tentative voice. The visitor's invisibility illusion apparently didn't extend to sound.

"Can you remove just my voice from our illusion?" Dalthinir asked Trisanna.

She nodded. "It's done."

She'd attained true mastery over her ability, and he smiled in appreciation.

"Hello?" persisted the voice.

Invisible or not, the intruder's magical aura had readily identified him. Dalthinir sighed. "What do you want, Kothlar?" he asked.

"Is that you, Dalthinir?" Kothlar asked. He sounded relieved. "I was hoping to discuss some matters with you."

"How did you find us?"

"It wasn't difficult," Kothlar returned. "I asked my people to watch for signs of habitation. Doors opening and closing, for example, when no one appeared to be going in or out. It led me to this inn."

"Very clever, I'm sure," said Dalthinir dryly. "What possible reason could you have for wanting a discussion with a renegade? And why should I trust you even for a minute? By now you probably have the inn surrounded with soldiers with no glimmer to detect."

"I don't blame you for not trusting me. But I can assure you that no one came here except me. I have no agenda beyond speaking with you."

"What do you think Adrastas will have to say about that?"

"He knows I was planning to talk to you if an opportunity arose. He wasn't happy about it, but he accepted it."

Dalthinir threw a glance in Trisanna's direction.

She took his meaning. "Would you like me to remove you from the illusion?"

He nodded.

"Thank you!" said Kothlar. "It helps to be able to see you. If you would be willing to wait for me here, I will arrange to have myself removed from the invisibility illusion."

Dalthinir hesitated for a moment before agreeing. "Just so you know, I have shields in place."

"I understand. You won't need them."

Having lost the shelter of invisibility, Dalthinir felt exposed, even inside the inn. After ten years of hiding without the benefit of illusion, it was surprising how quickly he'd come to rely on it.

"We're right here beside you," said Trisanna's disembodied voice. "If you'd like me to make you invisible again, just raise one of your arms."

"Could you please arrange invisibility, including sound, for me and Kothlar?" he replied. "I suspect he means what he says about being trustworthy, but I'd rather not take any chances."

Only a few minutes passed before Kothlar returned, fully visible this time. "Where would you prefer to talk?" he asked. "With the Tantellans wandering around Flaxendell, it might be safest right here inside the inn."

"Let's go for a walk," countered Dalthinir, pushing the door open and heading outside. "We should be safe enough. I've arranged for us to be invisible, and no one will hear us either. Both of us are also capable of shielding ourselves if the need arises."

Kothlar was clearly impressed. "So the illusion covers sound as well? Is Trisanna the only mage in your group with mage taste ability?" After a moment, he added, "Are you hiding our magical auras too?" He was bursting with questions.

"Did you come here to talk or to interrogate me?"

Kothlar shot him a glance. "Sorry. I can't help being curious. If you're worried about me, let me say again that I haven't sought you out to apprehend you."

"It isn't just you. If I'm testy, it's because the Tantellans have Kylen."

"Yes, the Tantellans. Where they're concerned, our interests coincide. They're a problem for all of us. It's the reason I wanted to talk with you." He glanced at Dalthinir. "I don't believe you want to see the kingdom of Periton come to harm. You went to a lot of effort to stop Lars and Petria, and you did it at considerable risk to yourself."

"You mean someone actually noticed?" Dalthinir wasn't normally given to sarcasm; on this occasion he couldn't resist. "Is it possible you've come to thank me on behalf of the Compact?"

If Kothlar registered his irony, he gave no indication of it. "We're at a disadvantage compared to the Tantellans. They've figured out how to mask their magical auras." After hesitating for a moment, he added, "It seems to involve a specially designed garment."

So Kothlar and his companions had noticed it too. Dalthinir was curious to see where this conversation might be going.

"We're aware that you've found a way to do the same thing by magic. We would like you to teach us how to do it."

"And if I did that, would you teach it to the Tantellans?"

"Of course not!"

"So you want to gain an advantage over them. What would you do with it?"

"We wouldn't use it against Tantel. We just want it for our protection."

"That might be true of you, Kothlar. But what about Adrastas? And can you speak for whoever will come after him?"

There were no satisfying answers to such questions, and both men knew it. Dalthinir couldn't resist adding, "Perhaps you're looking for an edge in your war against renegades."

Kothlar looked shocked. "Why would you think that?"

"Being pursued for ten years has that effect on a person. Especially when getting caught means execution."

"It was your choice to leave the Compact! You knew what it meant."

"Is that how Adrastas presents it? Banadin tried to murder me, and Adrastas refused to believe it. His version of justice involved protecting Banadin's followers while sanctioning me. I only left because he was actively preventing me from keeping Lars and Petria under observation. In the end, my warnings about Banadin's followers were shown to be well founded. Lars and Petria were always the real threat, not me."

Kothlar had gone silent.

"If I'd done what Adrastas wanted me to do, we wouldn't be alive to have this conversation. Curiously, I haven't received an apology from him yet. He's still just as intent on seeing me killed. You said earlier that our interests coincide. But you surely don't expect me to further whatever interests Adrastas might happen to adopt."

"Adrastas isn't always right, but he isn't a bad man. Would you return to the Compact if Adrastas offered you the opportunity?"

"Would such an offer extend to Kylen and Trisanna as well?"

"No actual offer exists, of course. But if there was one, I suspect it would apply only to you."

"Then I'm not interested. Nor am I willing to hand Adrastas a weapon to use against me and my friends."

"How would it harm you if we were able to block our glimmer?"

"Are you serious? We'd never see you coming, however much we watched over our shoulders."

Disappointment was evident on Kothlar's face. Incredible as it seemed to Dalthinir, he'd truly been hoping for a different outcome.

"Don't try to force us into your mold, Kothlar. We're outcasts. *You* made us that. If you want to accommodate us and our skills, it's your rules that need to change." He shook his head helplessly. "If it's any comfort to you, we're not going to stop doing what we believe to be right, even at risk to ourselves."

Raising an arm, Dalthinir signaled to Trisanna that he was ready to leave the conversation. Trisanna and the twins immediately became visible. Turning his back on Kothlar, he returned to his friends.

VOLUME 3—THE PERILS OF ETTARAN

CHAPTER 24

Trisanna and her companions had relocated to a deserted house in Flaxendell, their move spurred by Kothlar's almost effortless discovery that the inn was in active use. They were now based in what had once been a comfortable home of modest size. To avoid detection, they were limiting their comings and goings to a rear entrance hidden from plain view.

Enough traces of the original occupants remained to make the dwelling eerie. Personal effects still haunted the empty rooms—a hairbrush resting before a cracked mirror; a toy horse carved from wood lying abandoned on the floor; a faded painting hanging askew on a wall. Trisanna ached to think of the countless lives that had ended so abruptly as a result of the Great Desolation. Was it possible that such a disaster could ever be repeated? The thought terrified her.

Trisanna looked up as the door opened and Dalthinir re-entered the dwelling.

"The Peritonian mages have returned to the border," he announced.

She peered at him anxiously. "Are the Tantellans still in Flaxendell?"

Even before he confirmed it, she knew what the answer would be. With a sniff of their quarry in their nostrils and re-energized by their capture of Kylen, her pursuers wouldn't be leaving while she was in the area.

"They're still wandering around. Half of them are invisible. They're wearing the garments that cloak their magical auras again. I can only pick up traces if I'm quite close to them. The worst thing is that they've put one of the garments on Kylen. I can't detect his glimmer anymore. And they've apparently included him in the group that's invisible. I don't know where he is!"

He was unusually restless. It was painfully obvious to Trisanna that the capture of his apprentice had come as a body blow to him, not least because he believed himself to be responsible.

A fierce scowl had twisted his features. "I'm going to find a way to get him back!" He looked toward Trisanna. "And they won't get you. I don't care how determined they are to kill you and to capture the amulet. It won't happen while I'm still alive!"

The twins exchanged a glance. "We'll do whatever we can," said Jonno.

Dalthinir nodded. "Thank you. It won't be straightforward, unfortunately. It will be important to choose the right moment. Our best hope will be to draw them further in, toward the heart of Methesia."

"Won't they go mad?" asked Jonno.

"They eventually will. Once we get beyond The Spine—one of the mountain ranges that helped shelter Periton from the worst effects of the Great Desolation—it won't be long before they find the effort of simply surviving has become more than enough of a challenge."

"What about us going mad?" Bella's tone of voice belied the seriousness of her question.

Dalthinir's only response was a brief glance toward Trisanna.

She sighed. "I haven't forgotten that our safety depends on me mastering the power of the amulet." With the acknowledgment, she hurried from the room, eager to be gone before they could ask questions.

What she most needed at that moment was solitude. Having managed to find a small room of her own in the house, she headed for it. Situated near the front of the dwelling, the room boasted a small bed and a wooden rocking chair. It was located far enough from the others to hold promise of becoming a haven whenever she felt the need to be alone.

Arriving in the room, she sank into the rocking chair. The time had come. Appropriating the power of the amulet could be deferred no longer.

The interaction between Dalthinir and Sorren had left her wary about allowing the amulet access to her inner being. However, she didn't see that she had a choice. Not when the safety of the others depended entirely on her.

Coming to a sudden decision, she withdrew the talisman from beneath her clothing and closed a hand around it. Her heart began to pound within her chest. Then, with the words of Sorren in her mind, she thrust down, deep into her gut, to the source of her magic. Closing her eyes tightly, she reached out to the amulet and drew its power into herself.

As it responded, some part of her inner being rose up in resistance. The talisman rushed in, overwhelming her defenses and yielding up its treasures before she could prevent it. Awash with power, she saw at once how to surround herself and her companions with the protection they needed. The prospect of it was irresistible.

Deciding that her reticence was nothing more than foolishness, she acted immediately. Mages were especially vulnerable, and she defended Dalthinir, Kylen, and herself first. The twins needed a different kind of shielding, but she also achieved that without difficulty. It was the work of a moment.

As she was releasing the amulet's power, she glimpsed a way to use it to hit back at the mages who lusted after the amulet and sought her life. Permanently incapacitating the Tantellans would be a trivial task. She could picture their twisted bodies, writhing in agony. The torture they had visited upon her parents would rebound on them.

She drew back in horror. Much as the mages might deserve it, the very idea of visiting such cruelty on another person sickened her.

Her emphatic rejection of the offered torture seemed to have the desired effect—the impulse diminished quickly. Long after the pressure had eased, though, she remained in the rocking chair, trying without success to recover her composure.

She thrust the amulet beneath her clothing once more. It might be hidden from view, but it had gained access to her inner being. What had she done? Sorren had granted the same access to his talisman. Did it torment him in similar ways?

She couldn't immediately ask Sorren, but a trusted confidant was close at hand. Poking her head out of the door of her room, she called down the hallway, her voice quavering. "Dalthinir? Could I please speak with you for a moment?"

The mage appeared in the door, eyebrows raised inquiringly. Seeing her sitting rigid in the rocking chair, he positioned himself on the bed opposite.

She poked at the talisman beneath her clothing. "I've done it," she told him. "We're all protected from the madness. Kylen as well."

"That's heartening news!" He looked at her uncertainly. "You look distressed. Is there a problem?"

"It's the amulet." Her heart was beginning to pound, her breath coming in rapid gasps. "The Tantellans out there hunting me—it showed me how to destroy them. It was...terrible!" She covered her face with her hands. "I can't get it out of my head."

Never had Kylen been in such peril. He had already seen that Agalar, the mage who had captured and restrained him, was brutal and heartless. The life of a captive apparently meant nothing to him.

All of the Tantellans were extremely edgy. Every one of them seemed ready to drop with weariness. Their leader, Pernilla, was determined to prevent them sleeping for more than a few minutes at a time. How she herself was managing to stay upright was not clear. It surely must have been by force of will alone.

There had been no sign of Dalthinir and the others, but Kylen didn't doubt they would be watching for an opportunity to free him. How they might do it was far from certain. The magically protected noose around his neck was a diabolical device. Kylen had been trying for hours to think of a way of freeing himself. He was no closer to a solution.

"Where is Gharvil?" snapped Pernilla. It had become a repeated refrain. Apparently the missing mage was the only member of the group capable of detecting magical auras with farsense. It made no difference, of course. The Tantellans clearly didn't know that Dalthinir was capable of hiding glimmer. There would be no auras for anyone to see.

It seemed that Gharvil also had mage taste ability. Without him, only half the foreigners were able to become magically invisible. The limitation was one small thing worth celebrating. It would make the Tantellans easier for his friends to avoid.

Kylen wondered if Dalthinir knew about the garments the Tantellans had designed to hide magical auras. They were only partially effective. His own farsense allowed him to detect their glimmer without difficulty when he was close enough. Given Dalthinir's strong farsense ability, it seemed unlikely that he would be fooled either, provided he wasn't too far away. Unfortunately, detecting them at a distance was likely to prove more difficult.

A barked command from Pernilla interrupted his musing. "All of you! Stop everything you're doing and find Gharvil!" the Tantellan shouted. "And don't think this is an opportunity for a quiet nap in some hidden corner! I have ways to make you suffer."

People scattered in every direction, leaving only Pernilla, Agalar, and Kylen.

Agalar, a stocky man with light brown hair, was apparently the other person responsible for providing invisibility for the group. He was not happy. "I should be hiding us! We're far too exposed here!" He pulled irritably on the noose until Kylen began to choke.

"We'll stay as we are," Pernilla retorted. "The fools out searching for Gharvil won't be able to find us if we're invisible. And I want Trisanna and her friends to see our hostage."

"How can you be certain he's a part of their band? Without Gharvil we have no way to confirm that he even has a magical aura."

"The Peritonians recognized him. They only care about him because he's a renegade."

Many minutes passed without a single mage reappearing.

Pernilla became increasingly agitated. "I'll have the hides of every one of them!" she spat.

Agalar snorted. "Both of us are barely managing to stay awake, and there's no shortage of places to stretch out in those abandoned houses. You're a fool sending them off like that."

"Watch your lip!" warned Pernilla. "Don't think I won't make an example of you."

"You've got bigger problems than me to deal with," Agalar replied sourly.

The return of some of the searchers interrupted their squabble.

"Well?" demanded Pernilla.

"We found no sign of him," one of them told her wearily. "He could be anywhere. We could search every house and still miss him, especially if he's made himself invisible. Without someone who can detect magical auras I don't know how we can find him."

Pernilla turned to Kylen with a glower. "How's your farsense, boy? Can you detect glimmer?"

Kylen made no reply, even when Agalar jerked his noose.

Over the next few minutes the others slowly trickled in.

"We'll find somewhere to rest," said Pernilla. "Catnaps only. Do it in pairs. One will sleep, the other will wake them up in thirty minutes. After that no one will be sleeping for two hours, so get used to it."

"How will Gharvil find us?" someone asked.

"Using farsense, you idiot!" barked Pernilla. She jerked her head toward Kylen. "We believe our new friend here is a mage. There's no spare garment, and I don't want his aura to be visible. That means he'll be using yours. Take it off!"

The mage wasn't happy, but he complied. Agalar temporarily removed the end of the noose from his belt, retrieving it from the back of the garment as Kylen struggled into it. He then retied it firmly on his belt as before.

"From now on we're going to be invisible again. Until Gharvil gets back, that will only apply to half of us. That will include me, Agalar, and our new friend here. Agalar, you can choose the others."

The invisibility must have been put in place immediately judging from the irritation that appeared on several faces. The mages in question were presumably among those Agalar had not included.

The group set off to find somewhere to rest. Kylen was swept along with them, struggling to match Agalar's stride. After a brief search they settled on a mansion on the main road that boasted a large number of rooms with beds. The Tantellans were so desperate to sleep that Pernilla was hard pressed to prevent all of them from succumbing at once. She was forced to hand select the ones who would stay awake for the first thirty minutes.

She had no reason to worry about anyone exceeding their time allocation. Those left awake would never permit it—not with their own turn on hold until their companions had been roused.

The greater risk was that everyone would immediately embark on a second cycle. With that in mind, she apparently intended to sleep with the first group to ensure she was in full possession of her faculties when the second group reached their time limit.

Gharvil's absence left an odd number of mages. Identifying an unallocated mage, Pernilla arranged for him to watch her and Agalar. Then both of them threw themselves down, immediately falling into a deep sleep.

Wondering if his moment had finally arrived, Kylen began to slowly move toward the end of the noose attached to Agalar's belt. Before he reached it, the mage left to monitor the two sleepers spoke sharply to him. "Don't get ideas about messing with your noose while Agalar is asleep! I'll make sure he's awake before you go anywhere near it. And he won't be happy!"

Kylen backed away hastily.

"You won't achieve anything by staying awake," the other mage told him. "You might as well sleep."

He didn't bother to reply. He hadn't forgotten what happened the last time he'd slept.

To him, half an hour felt like an eternity. It must have felt impossibly brief to the mages who were awakened from deep sleep. All of them, Pernilla included, were only roused with great difficulty.

It came as no surprise to Kylen when none of them emerged in a good mood. For the next thirty minutes he greatly feared for his life.

Agalar seemed intent on choking him purely out of spite. He was saved only because Pernilla finally became enraged.

"If the captive dies, you die!" she spat. From the look on her face, she meant it.

Agalar subsided after that, at least while Pernilla was nearby. But as soon as she was gone, Agalar took an opportunity to whisper into Kylen's ear. "Your time will come! And when it does I'm going to make you pay!"

It was looking increasingly likely that if Dalthinir didn't rescue him soon it would be too late.

Pernilla reappeared, an unreadable expression on her face.

"It's time to move!" she announced.

"Why?" asked one of the mages.

"Trisanna has left Flaxendell."

"How do you know?" another asked.

"The same way I tracked her here. We're going to follow her."

This time the voices were a chorus. "Where?"

"East. Toward Ettaran."

The Tantellans seemed to have reached some kind of tipping point.

"We can't go there! We'll go mad!"

"We need to sleep!"

With the atmosphere almost crackling with tension, Pernilla faced the others calmly. "If you're with me, join me here."

Agalar came immediately, Kylen shuffling along behind him. Others followed in ones and twos until only three mages remained.

"This is your final chance," Pernilla told them. "I'll put nooses around your necks myself if I need to."

The threat decided them. She watched with narrowed eyes as they moved forward to join her. "I'll be watching you," she growled.

At this crucial moment another mage stumbled into the building. The missing Gharvil had finally returned.

"Where have you been?" demanded Pernilla.

"I fell asleep," he replied, a haunted look on his face. "It was terrible!"

"Do it again and I'll deal with you myself," Pernilla promised him.

She turned to the others. "Take a good look at Gharvil! You're getting a tiny whiff of what will happen to you if you don't follow through *exactly* on what I tell you to do!"

With that she led them out of the building onto the main road. Then she turned her back on the safety of the distant border with Periton and headed east.

With his head bowed dejectedly, Kylen followed her into the madness.

CHAPTER 25

The sun set over Pernilla's miserable band of Tantellans and their captive. Thanks largely to her threats, they had made steady progress. Most of them were simply too exhausted to fight her. They were almost through the mountains that separated Flaxendell from the vast lowlands of Methesia, once the bread basket of the kingdom.

The Tantellan leader had been forced to pay special attention to Agalar. The fool would have choked his captive if he'd been allowed. That would have eliminated their leverage over Trisanna and her friends. Assuming they had any leverage. The girl was on the move again, heading deeper into Methesia. Apparently she had abandoned the captive. Or was pretending to have done so.

She couldn't say how she knew Trisanna had left, but she was certain of it. Her inner compass had led her to the girl, and now it was pointing unerringly eastward.

No one else was happy about where they were heading. Nerves were fraying all around her. No one showed any interest in the meager amount of food that still remained to them. The others had been whispering incessantly, and when they stopped for the night, she discovered the reason.

"We want to sleep," one of the mages told her. "And we want to do it at the same time. It's pointless for half of us to watch the other half. You can stay awake, and get the rest of us up after thirty minutes."

Pernilla snorted. "Do you think I'm stupid? Once I'm asleep, you'll all just lie down again!"

"I won't," said Gharvil emphatically. "Not after last time."

Voices rose in his support. "We saw how he was. We're not stupid!"

Scanning the faces before her, Pernilla decided this was not a battle worth fighting. "Have it your own way. But you'd better bestir yourselves when I come to wake you up!"

Lying down where they were, the mages fell asleep immediately.

Peering across at the captive in the semi-dark, Pernilla spoke to him gruffly. "You'd better get some sleep while you can."

The only response was a stubborn shake of the boy's head.

Pernilla shrugged. "Suit yourself."

Sitting down, she positioned herself against a tree. Thirty minutes wasn't long to wait, but she might as well make herself comfortable. Resting even for a moment made her aware of how tense and weary she was. She was bearing alone the burden of accomplishing their mission while protecting the group from going mad. The others could complain as much as they liked about lack of sleep. She was getting no more of it than they were.

Her eyes were sagging with weariness. It was all she could do to keep them open. She shot a glance toward the captive. It was dark enough that she could barely see him. He was sitting with his head in his hands.

As she looked away, she found her eyes wouldn't focus. With a struggle she returned to alertness. Then her chin nodded forward involuntarily, startling her into wakefulness. An eternity lay ahead before she could rouse the others and take her turn at sleeping. Twenty five minutes of torture.

Leaning back against the tree, she tried once more to make herself comfortable.

FOR REASONS he couldn't understand, Kylen did not feel especially tired. Nor did he have any reason to believe himself at risk of losing his mind. When offered the chance to sleep, he refused for one simple reason—he anticipated his first real opportunity to escape. With the behavior of his captor, Agalar, becoming increasingly erratic, Kylen had been constantly fearing for his life.

His hopes began to rise when Pernilla agreed to watch while the others slept. If the Tantellan's struggle to keep her eyes open was any indication, she would succumb within a few minutes.

Kylen immediately began watching Pernilla out of the corner of his eye. It was almost comical observing the woman's attempts to keep herself awake. She even resorted to slapping herself on the face a few times. None of it made any difference. Overcome by weariness, she was soon sleeping as soundly as her companions.

Kylen's opportunity had arrived. He knew that the rope around his neck passed through a slip knot, allowing it to tighten whenever he pulled away from Agalar. That should also allow him to loosen it until the loop was wide enough to pass over his head.

Reaching up to take hold of the noose, he discovered that he was unable to widen it sufficiently to remove it. After placing the loop over his head, Agalar had apparently tied a thick knot in the rope just below the slip knot and pulled it extremely tight. The result was that rope could pass through the slip knot to tighten the noose, but there was a limit to how much rope could be retracted to widen it.

He was not overly disheartened. The other obvious option was to untie the end of the rope from Agalar's belt, allowing him to escape with the noose still around his neck. Dalthinir should be able to help him remove it later.

Agalar had gone to sleep lying face down, and it was only when he bent lower that Kylen discovered the mage's posture obscured the location where the noose was tied to his belt. Should he try to roll Agalar over? He agonized for several minutes, undecided if such an attempt would wake him.

He could not afford to rouse Agalar. The mage had been on the brink of throttling his prisoner more than once, and Kylen might not still be alive if the Tantellan leader hadn't restrained him.

A single glance at Pernilla confirmed she was soundly asleep. If Agalar woke to find his captive trying to free himself, he would be beside himself. Pernilla might not be able to intervene in time.

Kylen couldn't afford to risk it.

Even so, how could he stand by passively without making the smallest attempt to free himself? It would be simple if he was capable of rendering someone unconscious as Dalthinir had done to Lars and Petria on the mountain. His own attempts had been less than useful.

There would be no better moment for Dalthinir to appear and help him out. But there was no sign of him.

He wondered where his friends were. His farsense hadn't revealed the smallest glimmer of Dalthinir or Trisanna, although that was hardly surprising since Dalthinir was undoubtedly masking their magical auras. They were probably far away. The Tantellans were on the move again, and they had always been the pursuers.

For a moment his mind wandered, wondering once more how Pernilla and her team had repeatedly been able to locate them. He wondered if Dalthinir or Trisanna had solved the puzzle during his absence.

The reality of his current situation quickly reasserted itself. He sighed, returning his attention to the problem before him.

In the end, he decided he could never live with himself if he didn't at least make an attempt to roll Agalar over. Reaching down, he carefully lifted one shoulder. His efforts had no effect. The sleeping mage had become a dead weight. Trying again more vigorously, he managed to get a shoulder completely off the ground. Agalar frowned, grunting loudly. An eye squinted open and he twisted his head around in an attempt to see what had disturbed him. Releasing him hastily, Kylen stepped away. With another loud grunt, the mage slumped back to his original position and resumed his snoring.

This latest attempt unnerved Kylen. It was impossible to guess how close Agalar had been to waking, but he wasn't willing to risk another attempt. Sitting down in disgust, he settled in for a long wait.

WANDERING ALONE IN A DESOLATE LANDSCAPE, Pernilla could see nothing she recognized and no sign of life. She knew she was dreaming, although it wasn't clear to her how she could be certain. Without warning, she found herself inside a building in the dark. No windows were anywhere in sight, making it impossible to tell if it was day or night outside.

She felt sure no living creature had entered this place for uncounted years. The atmosphere had the feel of barren lifelessness. Noticing a glow at one end of the space, she set off toward it. The glow increased in strength until she stood before a huge sphere, alive with color. Within the sphere she saw small concentrations of colored light, darting about vigorously.

No voice spoke, but somehow she sensed it was not safe to touch the sphere. Desire welled up in her to shatter it, to release the streaks of color into the wild. Where such an impulse came from she could not guess.

Once more the scene changed. She stood on a road, and gazing forward she saw a young woman ahead of her, walking away. The young woman stopped briefly, and turned to stare at her. A dazzling jewel hung from her neck. Then, spinning around, she resumed her journey.

Feeling something tugging at her neck, she glanced down to see her own talisman straining, as if on a leash. Was it an attempt to reach the jewel she had glimpsed around the girl's neck?

Prompted by an urge she could not understand, she reached down into her gut to the heart of her magical power. Then she grasped hold of the talisman.

ABRUPTLY THE DREAM ENDED. She realized she had been lying with her back to a tree. Her neck hurt.

Climbing unsteadily to her feet, she peered about her in the darkness. As far as she could tell, every mage in her party lay asleep. The only sign of movement was from the captive, still positioned beside Agalar.

Pernilla suddenly wondered how long she had been sleeping. Alarmed, she opened her mouth to shout at the others to rouse themselves. Then she remembered the final sensation in her dream. She snapped her mouth shut without uttering a word.

There was something she was supposed to learn from the dream. Pulling the dragon claw on its chain from beneath her clothing, she held it up. Then, reaching down into her gut, she connected with the talisman.

She gasped in astonishment. The talisman was no mere good luck charm. It almost seemed to be alive. Sensing that she needed to draw it into herself, she opened her inner being to admit it. She experienced a moment of self-doubt as it wormed its way in and made itself at home, but she quickly dismissed her reaction. This was not a time for squeamishness.

The talisman immediately rewarded her receptivity. Her jaw opened wide as a surge of understanding flooded through her. So much became clear at last. She saw that the jewel around the neck of the girl she had seen in her dream was the amulet she had been searching for, and that the girl was Trisanna. She realized that her talisman had been guiding her to the amulet. The jewel was being carried away from her, and she knew exactly where to find it.

She sensed, too, that another talisman lay behind her in the region of Flaxendell. Though more powerful than her own, it paled beside the amulet. She ignored it.

Much else was revealed to her as well. Seeing what she needed to do to protect herself from the madness in Methesia, she did so immediately. The available protection hadn't been entirely exhausted—she could stretch it to cover one other member of her party. At one time she might have chosen Gharvil for his farsense ability, but no longer. Magical auras held little interest for her now that she could track the amulet directly.

Choosing Agalar instead, she covered him with protection as well.

Apart from Agalar's ability to use mage taste to provide invisibility, the man was useful for one reason only—Pernilla needed him to guard the captive. The captive's usefulness was less than certain, aside from a vague possibility he could be used for leverage, yet Pernilla felt compelled to preserve him. She shrugged. Making sense of it could be deferred to a later time.

The Tantellan leader did not have the capacity to protect the captive as well as herself and Agalar, but it did not trouble her. She cared nothing for the boy's sanity.

The only thing that mattered now was to find the girl and retrieve the prize she bore.

She would keep the amulet for herself, of course. There was no question of delivering it to the grasping Kharkin. Having long since grown tired of doing the bidding of others, it was exhilarating to have a mission of her own to fulfill at last. She would locate the shining sphere and destroy it, releasing to the world the energy it held captive. And when she succeeded, the credit would be hers and hers alone.

Her new sense of purpose had come as a side effect of the dream. She was not following the dream blindly. It had proven itself. She had already appropriated what she learned from it, using her talisman to protect her against insanity. She sensed, too, the talisman's potential for new power she had not begun to tap. It was also pointing the way to a much greater and more significant source of power—the amulet.

The vigorous pursuit of Trisanna had again become her key priority. The other members of her group might still have a role. If there was to be a confrontation, she might need to call upon them, perhaps for their combined magical power—provided they survived long enough to use it. She foresaw that they would go mad before many more days had passed. Unfortunate as it might be, there was nothing she could do to prevent it. Perhaps she might be able to reverse their madness once she had acquired the amulet. Time alone would tell.

The first hint of dawn had begun to appear in the sky. The road beckoned.

Clapping her hands loudly, she shouted for her team to get up. They came to life slowly and resentfully, and loud grumbling soon filled the air. Many of them looked deeply troubled.

She didn't care what they thought or felt. Like it or not, they would do as she said. She had access to a new source of power now, and she would not hesitate to use it against them if she needed to.

Brimming with newfound confidence, she addressed her bleary-eyed audience. "All of us are here to fulfill a higher purpose! Don't trouble yourselves if grasping it is beyond you. I understand well enough, and for now that's all you need to know."

She stepped onto the road, beckoning them forward. "Time to go!" she called resolutely.

CHAPTER 26

The decision to leave Flaxendell with Kylen still in captivity was not easy for Dalthinir. But Kylen was invisible and his magical aura was masked. Even if Dalthinir knew his whereabouts, it would be close to impossible to release him if he wasn't able to see him.

Until something changed, Dalthinir could foresee no opportunity to free his apprentice. Drawing the Tantellans deeper into Methesia offered hope of change. Once madness took hold of them, it would be harder for them to maintain their invisibility and their discipline. When that happened, an opportunity should arise to free Kylen.

The strategy was not without risk, but Trisanna was actively protecting Kylen from madness. And Dalthinir intended to make sure he was never too far away.

That didn't mean he was satisfied with the situation. The safety and welfare of his apprentice had always been his responsibility, and he had failed in his duty. As a result, he was forced to choose between unsavory alternatives.

Although no one else was proposing solutions, he didn't expect them to. Freeing his apprentice was up to him, as was choosing the appropriate time and place.

Leaving Flaxendell seemed to suit Trisanna. Restless and distracted, she needed to be doing something.

It wasn't hard to guess what was on her mind. Dragon talismans were dangerous and unpredictable, and he had freely expressed his reservations about allowing one of them to invade her inner being. At the same time, he had left her in no doubt they needed the protection provided by the amulet.

As a result, Dalthinir felt compromised. He had nothing to offer when she called on him for support and comfort. What could he possibly say with any credibility?

There were other reasons for his dour mood. When they stopped a little before sundown, he announced the latest piece of bad news.

"I've decided to ration our food. The provisions provided by Sorren and Vennia were generous. But we have no way of knowing how long it will be before we can replenish our supplies."

Bella peered at him hopefully. "Will we find food of any kind in Ettaran?"

Dalthinir shook his head. "Unless we have the opportunity to visit Sorren and Vennia again, we shouldn't expect to find anything that's safe for us to eat until we return to the border."

Jonno pulled a face. "I'm hungry enough to eat a dragon."

"Dragons are not a subject for jesting," Dalthinir told him grimly.

After a less than satisfying meal they prepared to sleep.

Trisanna appeared beside him. "The Tantellans have a dragon talisman," she said, speaking quietly.

"How do you know?"

"The amulet showed me. The talismans are somehow aware of each other."

He shrugged. "It's no real surprise after what Sorren told us. It must be how they've been able to track us. But now you'll always know where they are, with or without them masking their auras."

Something else was bothering her. "What's wrong?" he asked.

"There's been a change since I first became aware of their talisman."

"What kind of a change?"

"I'm not sure, but I think the mage who's carrying it has done something to wake it up. It has power of some kind. I can tell it isn't as powerful as the amulet, although I'm not exactly sure how I know."

The news was alarming. "Is it possible it can offer them protection like the amulet is doing for us?" He needed to know, because, gruesome as his plan was, it was dependent on the Tantellans losing their sanity.

Her brows drew together. "I don't know. I'd be surprised if it could protect all of them, but I'm only guessing."

There were other concerns. "Whatever power it has, they'll probably try to use it to take the amulet from you. Do you think you'll be able to stop them?"

Her expression was bleak. "Without killing or maiming them? I'm not sure."

He gave her a puzzled look.

"I could destroy them all right now. Easily." She passed an unsteady hand over her face. "The amulet has been eager to present me with endless ways of doing it. All of them equally horrible." She grimaced. "It croons to me, Dalthinir! It wants me to give myself over to it completely. It promises all kinds of things. I won't do it! It's burrowed its way deep inside me, but it doesn't belong there!"

Dalthinir abruptly decided he'd had enough of being compromised. It had gone too far. "You need to get rid of it," he said firmly.

"What would become of us? Our protection would end. And how will we free Kylen?" She threw up her hands in helpless appeal. "If I reject the amulet, I'll lose access to its power. That means there'll be no way to prevent the Tantellans from taking it. It wouldn't end well for anyone." She shook her head sadly. "It's too late. Now that I've let it in, I'm not sure it's even possible to remove it."

He ground his teeth in frustration. "Then we will go to Ettaran, and I will search the library until I discover how to free you from it. Don't lose hope, Trisanna. We'll find a way!"

With her face pale, she stared at him. "I've heard you talk about Providence. How you were rescued from certain death, and you were convinced it was because there was something you were supposed to achieve. I hope there's something I'm supposed to do. Because now I'm the one who needs rescuing!"

❋

WITH NO SIGN of his friends and with his attempts to escape ending in frustration, Kylen was becoming increasingly despondent.

Where was Dalthinir? Why hadn't he mounted some kind of rescue attempt? The answer was probably very simple. Pernilla had made Kylen wear one of the garments that masked magical auras, and Agalar had been instructed to keep them invisible all the time. Dalthinir might not know where he was. Even if he knew Kylen's location, it wouldn't be practical to free him without being able to see him.

His own helplessness wasn't Kylen's only source of discouragement. Watching the men and women around him slowly descend into madness was also taking a toll.

It was confronting to watch as the sanity of the other mages steadily crumbled. Apparently engrossed in otherworldly hallucinations, they were wandering about aimlessly, conversing with people or creatures unseen, sometimes shouting aloud, occasionally cringing fearfully away from some hidden terror. None of them were engaging with each other any more.

To his growing astonishment, he himself had not yielded to the madness. Nor had Pernilla or Agalar.

That did not mean any of them remained unaffected.

Pernilla in particular seemed to be changing before their eyes. There was something profoundly unsettling about her demeanor and behavior. Kylen had heard of people being described as driven, and the Tantellan leader now fit the description closely. Yet she seemed elated and full of confidence. Kylen could make no sense of it.

The woman's energy was astonishing. She might not be insane, but there was a mad intensity about her. She showed little interest in sleeping or eating.

Remarkably, although the people most affected by madness were members of Pernilla's team, their leader seemed entirely unaffected by what she was witnessing.

By contrast, Agalar was visibly impacted by his companions' deterioration. Pernilla's complete indifference to their fate must surely have magnified the effect.

224

It was hardly surprising that it had become too much for Agalar. His leader had turned into a fanatic—one with an agenda that made sense to no one but herself—and he was surrounded by people who had lost touch with reality. He must be wondering what possible future there could be for him.

Having been on the receiving end of Agalar's brutality, Kylen could hardly have anticipated the effect on the Tantellan of the demise of his friends. Surprisingly, the man had not bullied his captive for some time. He actually seemed reassured by Kylen's presence. Perhaps it was because he was the only other person still behaving normally.

"It's close! I can feel it!" breathed Pernilla.

Looking at her, Kylen saw only ecstatic fervor. She appeared to be a woman possessed.

It felt wrong. He didn't know what she might be planning, but it couldn't be good.

"Follow me!" called Pernilla.

Agalar and Kylen reluctantly complied, a deranged assortment of once-feared mages strung out behind them.

As THE DAYS WORE ON, Agalar became almost friendly. Before Gharvil had succumbed to the creeping madness, he was able to confirm Pernilla's suspicion that Kylen was a mage. That meant Agalar had at least something in common with his captive.

There'd been no opportunity for Kylen to make use of it, though. From the beginning he had refused to talk with his captors, and he continued to rebuff Agalar's attempts to draw him out.

The Tantellan eventually became reconciled to his silence. With no one else to talk to, he had resorted to chattering away to Kylen. As time wore on, he began to do it with increasing abandon.

At first Kylen couldn't bear it. Of late he had begun to recognize its value as a diversion. And he desperately needed a diversion. He was beginning to wonder if the waking nightmare of his captivity would never end.

No one could continue such a journey without sleep. Kylen and

Agalar certainly slept. Even Pernilla had taken to resting at night. Sometimes she lay with her eyes open. At other times she slept deeply.

Kylen had learned to dread the arrival of dawn. Apparently Agalar had a similar reaction.

"I don't know what happens while she's sleeping," the Tantellan confided, "She seems to get a new dose of whatever's spurring her on, and it always makes her worse. I can't believe her energy!"

It was true. Pernilla emerged newly energized and more intense than ever. She continued to speak and function relatively normally, provided her euphoria could be ignored. Nevertheless, in Kylen's opinion she was lurching steadily toward outright madness.

"We've lost five members of our original group!" Agalar threw up his hands. "They've disappeared completely from sight. I wonder if they even know or care that they're wandering around in a wilderness without food or water!"

In spite of everything, several mages were still trailing along behind them. Kylen couldn't understand why.

Pernilla had told Agalar to keep them invisible. That meant half of the group, since that was all he could cover. It might help explain why some of the wandering mages had lost touch with the main group entirely. Even if he was still complying with the instruction, Kylen knew he wasn't capable of keeping it up indefinitely. He'd heard Agalar complain often enough about how tired it left him.

The complaints had eased of late, which probably meant that Agalar was no longer bothering at all. Kylen could have quickly satisfied his curiosity by asking Agalar, but he had no intention of speaking a word.

Agalar was shaking his head hopelessly. "The one piece of good news is that we're unlikely to run out of supplies. No one apart from me and you is interested in them anymore. And occasionally Pernilla, of course." He gave Kylen a wink.

With almost complete indifference from the others toward the supplies, the burden of carrying them fell entirely to Agalar and Kylen. That meant it fell to Kylen. Fortunately, while they were in Flaxendell the Tantellans had found a working version of a small wheeled wagon with a handle. It wasn't difficult to pull—the main challenge was to remain close to Agalar while doing so. Far too often Agalar moved thoughtlessly away, causing the noose to choke him.

Another thing had been playing on his mind. What was the situation of his friends? He himself had seen no hint of their glimmer. That was probably because Dalthinir was masking it, but without contact of any kind and with no way of tracking them, he could only hope that nothing had happened to them.

When they next settled for the night, Kylen slept fitfully. Waking in complete darkness, he found everyone else sleeping, even Pernilla.

Looking up, he saw a brilliant display of stars. Positioned just above the horizon, the moon looked larger than usual.

A huge shape momentarily blotted out the tiny lights, and Kylen watched in alarm as a gigantic creature swooped down, heading directly for him. Constrained by the noose, fleeing was not a possibility. Before he could blink, he found himself face to face with a dragon.

He stared wide-eyed.

"Well met, young Kalmithien."

Even without its greeting he would have recognized the creature. The darkness did not entirely hide the mottled green scales or the purple streaks on its folded wings. The same terrifying claws protruded from its feet. He was keenly aware of how puny he was beside the majestic creature.

Strangest of all, for the first time he sensed a magical glimmer about the dragon, a powerful scent quite unlike the glimmer of any human mage. Had it been masked when they first met? Or was the smell instead an indicator of the growing sensitivity of his own senses?

No better informed than at their first meeting about how to address a dragon, he mumbled a weak greeting.

The dragon seemed to be studying him.

Feeling compelled to somehow fill the silence, he sputtered, "I don't know your name." The comment seemed feeble even to him, and he was taken completely by surprise when he received a courteous response.

"You may call me Elef'nissar." The dragon dipped its head solemnly.

Emboldened by the reply, Kylen asked, "Have you come to free me, Elef'nissar?"

The dragon ignored his question. "Your companion is intent on great evil," it said, swinging its mighty head in the direction of Pernilla.

"She isn't exactly my companion," grunted Kylen.

"You must prevent her," persisted the creature.

Kylen stared up at the huge visage in bemusement. "Me? I'm a prisoner!"

The intruder appeared to view his response as irrelevant. "You will find a way."

It made no sense. Why him? Such a task would surely be effortless for a dragon.

"Why can't you do it?" demanded Kylen.

A hint of smoke swirled about its face. "Humans have many questions," it growled.

"You are so much more powerful than me!" the little human protested. "It would be simple for you!"

Elef'nissar gazed somberly at him before replying. "It is not permitted." The dragon spoke as though nothing further needed to be said.

"Not permitted?" Kylen's brows drew together. "What does that mean?"

The ancient creature tilted its head slightly, staring down at him in its unnerving way. Kylen worked hard at keeping his composure.

Finally it spoke. "The prohibition is as ancient as life itself. Dragonkind may not directly interfere with humankind."

Kylen screwed up his face. "What about the Winged Death? I was told that vicious dragons once roamed the skies, killing people freely!"

"Lawbreakers paid the due penalty," the dragon growled, its shoulders twitching with what might have been a shrug. "Has it not always been so?" Its tone seemed to suggest that such outcomes ought to be self-evident.

This interaction was proving more puzzling by the minute. Even if he could understand what the creature was saying, it occurred to Kylen to wonder if he should believe any of it.

Feeling bolder, he asked, "You told me you awakened my magic! Isn't that interfering?"

"I did not deem it to be such."

"You get to decide things like that?" he asked in bemusement.

Receiving no response, he added hopefully. "Even if you're not permitted to interfere directly, you seem to be allowed to interfere indirectly."

A whiff of smoke escaped the creature's nostrils.

Kylen was apparently becoming too bold for his own good. It was time to head for safer ground. "You're saying Pernilla has to be stopped before she does great evil. There must be something you can do."

The huge orbs peered down at him. "Indeed. And I have done it."

Apparently the interaction was at an end. Rising high on its haunches, Elef'nissar once more addressed him courteously. "Fare well, Kalmithien." Then it was gone.

Kylen was left reeling. What sense could he make of what had just happened?

It came as no surprise to hear that the Tantellan leader was heading for trouble. But why should it be Kylen's responsibility to stop her? Apparently the dragon believed it had fulfilled its duty when it handed the problem to Kylen.

Why hadn't the creature simply fried Pernilla where she slept?

It wasn't difficult to figure out the answer, of course. It wasn't permitted. Such prohibitions hadn't stopped the Winged Death. Why was it that exercising restraint only seemed to apply to those intent on doing good?

He tried to gather his scattered thoughts. There was a great deal for him to ponder. Elef'nissar had apparently come solely with a warning about Pernilla. And it had told him its name! He gazed up at the heavens in wonder.

Harsh realities soon brought him abruptly back to earth. This was the same creature that had tainted him with dragon magic. And yet such considerations seemed of little consequence in its presence. Why was that so?

He had been led to believe that dragons were wholly evil. Was it true? Kylen couldn't deny that Elef'nissar had intervened on the mountain in time to restrain him from doing great evil. And now it claimed to be trying to prevent Pernilla from doing the same.

His reservations about the taint of its magic had not dissipated. Yet dragons were not as he had imagined. He was confused as never before.

One thing was clear to him, though. He could not afford to ignore Elef'nissar's warning. The dragon had reinforced what he already sensed himself—Pernilla was heading for trouble. She had to be stopped, and he had no one else to turn to.

CHAPTER 27

"I'm going to climb up there." Dalthinir pointed to a tall upthrust of rock towering beside the road ahead of them. "I need to find out where we are."

"I'll come too." Bella and Jonno spoke almost in unison.

Trisanna swung in behind them without comment.

Climbing the rock face would have been out of the question, but it wasn't necessary. The summit was accessible using a path that wound back and forth up the slope.

Dalthinir led them onto a seemingly endless line of steps that stretched ahead of him. The steps had been carved out of the rock, with regularly placed landings to ease the climb. Fragile remnants of metal railings still stood on the outer side of the steps, presumably placed there in happier times for the benefit of sightseers. The ascent was steep, but it wasn't particularly dangerous, even with the railings largely rusted away.

Stopping for breath more than once on the way up, Dalthinir was breathing hard by the time he reached the small plateau at the top. The climb was worth it. The lookout commanded an uninterrupted view in every direction.

He immediately directed his attention back in the direction they had come. Kylen was out there, and not too far away. Peering along the road, he searched for the tiniest hint of the Tantellans pursuing them. There was nothing to see.

Even though Dalthinir could not see the Tantellans at that moment, he was by no means ignorant of their movements. At the first opportunity after leaving Flaxendell he had sent Trisanna on toward Ettaran, the twins traveling with her, while he remained behind. It wasn't feasible for her to wait with him. Whether she was invisible or not, the Tantellans would sense the amulet.

Eventually the pursuers had caught up with him. Hidden as he was by Trisanna's illusion, they couldn't see him, and he was masking his glimmer.

They had also been invisible when they reached him, although he could detect their glimmer faintly through the special garments they were wearing. He even detected traces of Kylen's aura.

Dalthinir had tailed them closely, eager for an opportunity to free Kylen. The Tantellan mage providing the illusion had soon needed a rest, leaving Kylen visible as a result. His apprentice didn't look happy, but he appeared unharmed.

It might have been possible to free him there and then in spite of the mages around him. But Trisanna had told him that one of the Tantellans had a dragon talisman. Dalthinir had no idea who the person was, and he could only guess at what it might be capable of. For his own safety, Kylen would need to be made invisible the moment he was freed. And without Trisanna on hand, there was no way to achieve that.

It was intensely frustrating. It occurred to him that at the least he could briefly unmask his own glimmer, just to let Kylen know he was there. But the Tantellans might sense it too. And what if Kylen became excited at the prospect of imminent rescue and attempted something rash? He quickly decided it wasn't worth the risk. The safest strategy was simply to keep an eye on them.

His hopes of staging a rescue had quickly degenerated into an exercise in frustration. The one encouragement was that cracks were already showing in the sanity of the Tantellans. It reinforced his decision to bide his time.

Since then he had limited himself to monitoring the situation on a daily basis. If he had ever seen clear signs that Kylen was at risk, he would have acted immediately. Up to that point, intervention hadn't proven necessary. He had been left waiting for a safe opportunity to free his apprentice.

Dragging his thoughts back to the plateau, he turned with a sigh and joined the others.

Facing forward, Dalthinir saw that the view ahead of them was nothing short of spectacular. They were positioned on the smaller of several mountain upthrusts that marched around the outer reaches of the one-time capital of Ettaran. The city lay spread out before them. Even in its decline it took his breath away.

From a distance the buildings appeared intact, and water still glistened in the river that wound its way beside streets and under bridges. Nevertheless, Dalthinir knew they would find no living thing in the desolation. Ettaran stood abandoned and empty.

The city, the glittering jewel of the kingdom of Methesia, had once teemed with life. Now, nothing stirred apart from dust clouds. No vegetation could be seen anywhere in the vista before them.

Nothing about the place was in any way welcoming, and Dalthinir peered down in distaste at the greenish haze that hung over the city like a noxious cloud. Although he planned to enter the city, he knew that no normal person could do so without surrendering their sanity. He and his companions were safe due only to the amulet. And Trisanna was paying an unacceptably high price for that protection.

Leaning closer to her, he jerked his head back the way they had come. "How far behind are the Tantellans?"

She gazed along the empty road toward Flaxendell. "Not far. We shouldn't stay here too long."

With a nod of acknowledgment, Dalthinir turned toward the stairs.

He frowned all the way back down to the road. It was an instinctive response to the uncomfortable prickling sensation that had been fraying his nerves for the previous few days.

There was something oppressive about the atmosphere of the place. Flaxendell had been devoid of animal and bird life, but he'd slowly grown accustomed to the absence of living creatures and their sounds.

This environment was different. Even plants were nowhere to be found. Barren of any kind of life, it was unnerving.

Nevertheless, Dalthinir had no intention of turning aside. He now had two pressing goals. He needed to free Kylen, and he needed to find a way to release Trisanna from the amulet.

Beyond that, he was beginning to wonder if something much more significant was in the wind. Was there a reason why, in spite of commonsense and against every expectation, they had arrived safely in Ettaran? Was there something they needed to do there, something more consequential than freeing a captive and relieving a burden? He had always believed in Providence. And he was as willing as ever to play his part, whatever that might involve.

He shrugged. He had no immediate answers to such questions. No doubt it would all become clear in time.

Having reached the bottom of the steps, he led the others once more onto the road that stretched out ahead of them. It plotted a direct course for the center of Ettaran.

By nightfall they'd reached the outskirts of the city. Finding a suitable dwelling to sleep in wasn't difficult. They moved inside and prepared to settle for the night.

"Do you think they'll catch us if we pause to sleep?" Dalthinir asked Trisanna.

She shook her head slowly. "They seem to have stopped for the night themselves. And they're not moving quickly. As long as I stay alert we should be safe enough, at least until dawn."

"You're no less tired than the rest of us," he told her. "Let me sit up for a while to watch. I'll wake you partway through the night and you can take a turn. You can confirm their location when you get up."

Accepting his offer, Trisanna went to the room she had selected to sleep in. She emerged a couple of minutes later.

"Look what I found on the floor of the bedroom!" she said, holding up a necklace. It was a green jewel mounted on a gold clasp and suspended on a fine gold chain.

"You should keep it," Dalthinir told her. "There's no point leaving it here."

She shook her head. "It isn't my style. It makes me think more of

Inga." A gentle smile twisted her lips—the first that had visited her face for many days. "It would look wonderful on her."

After laying it out carefully on a sideboard, she waved goodnight and returned to her room.

Peering at the necklace, Dalthinir wondered how people were able to tell what would look good on someone else. He was hopeless at it.

After staring at it for several minutes, he got up and retrieved a small rag from his sack. Then, feeling his face redden self-consciously, he picked up the necklace, wrapped it carefully in the rag, and secured it in one of his pockets. Having done so, he steered his thoughts once more to the present.

Weary though he was, Dalthinir didn't find it difficult to stay awake. He sat musing, pondering the state of Ettaran. The houses in the city appeared little different from those in Flaxendell. If anything, they were better preserved since none of them had been overrun with vegetation.

He knew so little about the cause of the desolation. Not for the first time, he found himself wondering exactly what had happened. Whatever form the catastrophe had taken, it hadn't involved a blast that flattened the buildings.

He knew from studying old scrolls that the Great Desolation had ended all life in the capital and across the plains that surrounded it. The two outlying provinces—Periton to the west and the more heavily populated Tantel to the east—had remained unaffected. Scholars had suggested that the mountain ranges that separated the provinces from the Methesian central plains provided some kind of shielding effect.

Flaxendell was a special case. Although the region around it was empty of animal life, it still supported plants. Perhaps the town had benefited from limited protection. That made sense, since its location meant it would have been at least partially shielded by mountains.

In any event, the destruction of Methesia had long been presented as a cautionary tale. It had delivered a spectacular demonstration that playing with dragon magic led to extreme consequences. Yet as the years passed, the lesson seemed to have been forgotten. Dalthinir could only shake his head in wonder at the short attention span of his kind.

After a few hours had passed, he roused Trisanna as agreed and lay down to sleep.

Dalthinir woke with the dawn. The others were already awake, and as soon as they had broken their fast, he led them onto the road once more. This time he didn't try to hang back to monitor the Tantellans. He sensed that a confrontation between the two groups would not be long delayed.

As the capital drew ever nearer, Dalthinir faced the uncomfortable truth. Releasing Trisanna from the entanglement of the amulet was likely to be no more straightforward than freeing his invisible apprentice.

Never had he been confronted by such a challenging set of complexities.

With a wistful sigh he reflected on the months since acquiring an apprentice. As before, he had been a renegade and an outcast, always at risk of discovery. But his world had changed in other ways. Of late his simple and relatively predictable life had benefited from Kylen's companionship.

The twins were wildly unpredictable, of course, but he had developed great affection for them. His life had been drab at times in the years since he left the Compact, and he had every reason to appreciate their zest and the color they brought with their chaotic antics. He would miss them whenever they decided to move on.

But everything had changed with the arrival of Trisanna. The upheavals that followed her were not her fault, and he had no regrets about allowing her to join them. Nevertheless, her pursuers had complicated all of their lives dramatically.

He had gradually come to the conclusion that keeping the amulet from the Tantellans was no less important than freeing Kylen. Some might insist it was more important, and perhaps they would be right. Nevertheless, under no circumstances would he consider abandoning his apprentice.

He had lured the Tantellans closer to Ettaran with the intention of weakening them. What that meant for them was horrifying, but it was their own choice to hunt Trisanna deep into Methesia. The responsibility lay with them.

And how else could he stop them?

Learning that the Tantellans were carrying a dragon talisman of their own had been a setback. The suggestion that the talisman had the potential to be used aggressively was especially alarming. Still, it wasn't the first time he'd been forced to confront a crisis with no certainty of the outcome.

He had learned to approach life with hope, even when situations appeared hopeless. If the day ever came when hope truly did fail, he would simply have to manage without it.

A CITY STOOD BEFORE KYLEN, vast and silent. This was no mere sibling of Flaxendell. They must surely have reached Ettaran, the former capital of Methesia.

As they plodded forward, Kylen glanced curiously at the buildings that lined the well-ordered streets, trying to imagine what it had been like when the city had been thronged with people. He quickly abandoned the attempt. With streets and walkways empty and parks barren of life, it was simply too difficult. Not even weeds had retained a foothold.

Glorious as Ettaran must once have been, the glory was gone.

For reasons Kylen couldn't grasp, the Tantellan leader was more excited than ever. Agalar was his usual self, although Kylen had the impression his demeanor was as much forced as it was real.

"Pernilla's mumbling to herself again." Agalar shook his head in disgust. "Where's it going to end?"

He peered at Kylen curiously, and for a moment he seemed troubled. "Why is it that neither of us has gone mad?"

Quickly recovering himself, he continued almost without a pause. "You don't act like you're mad, anyway. Apart from the fact that you never speak." He concluded his little speech with a grating laugh.

Kylen could see nothing to laugh about.

Four other members of the original group were still with them. They were becoming noticeably gaunt, which wasn't surprising since all of them had stopped eating entirely. Occasionally they drank small quantities of water. If they were managing to sleep, he wasn't aware of it. Every one of them appeared to be completely insane, apart from an unusual fixation on Pernilla. Was some semblance of duty appearing through the haze that clouded their minds, or was it something else?

Pernilla herself was an unusual case. She hadn't been afflicted like the others, but she certainly wasn't behaving normally. She must be experiencing thirst, because she was still regularly drinking water, but she rarely ate. While able to speak coherently and respond to her surroundings, she seemed to have lost interest in the mages for whom she was supposedly responsible. The mysterious mission she often babbled about had become all consuming.

Why had neither of them gone mad? Agalar's question was a good one. Why were they the only ones eating and drinking and the only ones consistently getting any sleep? Kylen could think of no reason to account for them having been spared.

Sane or not, Kylen was thoroughly tired of the Tantellans and everything to do with them. He was beginning to wonder how much longer he could bear his captivity. Where was Dalthinir?

Had his friends managed to escape the creeping madness? It was a question that increasingly troubled him, and he refused to dwell on it for long.

The more he pondered it, the more he recognized that expecting to be rescued by someone else was neither realistic nor fair. Even if his friends were safe and well, they probably had little or no idea how to find him. And beyond that, it was no one's fault but his own that he'd been captured. It was therefore his responsibility to free himself.

His task might have been easier if Agalar hadn't taken to sleeping so lightly. He himself was no different. How could any one expect restful sleep under such circumstances? On more than one occasion he had set out to untie the other end of the noose while Agalar was asleep. It was a hopeless cause. Each time, the Tantellan woke before Kylen could get anywhere near the belt to which it was secured. The smallest disturbance seemed to be enough to cause Agalar to stir.

If freeing himself magically was a possibility, the mechanism had thus far eluded Kylen completely.

With no other options on offer, he began to focus his attention on

Agalar. The Tantellan had definitely thawed in his attitude to his prisoner. Could he somehow be persuaded to release Kylen?

Persuading Agalar wouldn't be possible without talking to him. After remaining silent for so long, he knew it would seem strange to suddenly begin speaking. But he could think of no good reason not to do it. His earlier refusal owed as much to stubbornness as anything. With his life at stake, it was time to be pragmatic.

Having made a decision, he knew he needed to think long and hard about the best way to approach the subject. Appealing to Agalar's humanity would probably be a waste of his time. Flattery might work, although he wasn't confident he could do it credibly. In the end, he decided the best approach was to focus on Agalar's self-interest.

After waiting a considerable time for Pernilla to be well out of earshot, he made a beginning. "You asked where this is going to end."

The shocked face of Agalar turned toward him. "He has a voice!" he pronounced grandly, raising his arms heavenward. "Pernilla will want hear about this!"

"Wait! You'll be wasting your time if you tell Pernilla! I won't say a single word while she's around."

Agalar paused, frowning.

"Just hear me out!" Kylen urged.

The Tantellan glared at him moodily. "Well? What can you possibly say that's worth listening to?"

"Your friends have gone insane. Except for Pernilla. I can't begin to guess at what's happening to her, but she's clearly in trouble herself. You want to know why neither of us has been affected."

There was no response.

"Perhaps you think Providence is preserving you. Even though you came to Periton to murder a member of the royal family." He pointed bitterly to the noose around his neck. "Even in spite of this."

Agalar was glaring at him with narrowed eyes, but he still hadn't spoken.

"If you think it's Pernilla who's somehow preserving your life, why is she doing it? Were you her favorite? Perhaps she has some kind of plan for you before she goes mad. If so, do you expect it to be something that will benefit you?"

Kylen took a deep breath. "The smart thing would be to get away. Now, while you still can."

"And how am I going to do that?" Agalar asked mockingly. "Do you think Pernilla will smile and wave goodbye? If she is the one preserving us, how is she doing it? What other power does she have that neither of us knows about?"

"You can make yourself invisible."

"And how will I protect myself?"

"I can protect you. If you release me."

The Tantellan snorted. "How are you going to protect me when you can't even protect yourself?"

"We can work together! We have food. You can hide us and I can shield us. As soon as we're clear, you can head for the border or do whatever you want."

Kylen had used his best arguments, and Agalar clearly wasn't convinced. He decided to make one last attempt.

"Pernilla is apparently keeping me alive so she can get what she wants from Trisanna. Maybe she only needs you to guard me. Once I've been disposed of one way or another, why will she need you?"

Watching Agalar's face, he saw that his final sally had more impact than anything else he'd said.

"That's enough!" The Tantellan waved his end of the noose threateningly. "Stop talking now, or I'll dispose of you—for good this time!"

At that moment Pernilla appeared. Either she hadn't noticed or she didn't care that the captive had been talking with Agalar.

"The amulet is within reach!" she said excitedly. "The time has come!"

CHAPTER 28

Trisanna glanced at her companions. "They've arrived in the outskirts of Ettaran. They're not far away."

She watched Dalthinir's face set hard with determination. She knew what he was thinking—he wanted to free Kylen. Her mind was on other things. The amulet was almost salivating within her, anticipating a confrontation.

"Shall I lead you to them?" she asked him.

He nodded tightly.

Remembering her promise to let the twins know whenever she was hiding them, she announced, "All of us are invisible."

They arrived to discover their pursuers making no effort to hide themselves.

Dalthinir confirmed it. "The only mage auras I can detect belong to the people we can see," he growled.

Pernilla appeared to be staring right at them. "I know you're here, Trisanna! Invisible or not, I've always known where to find you. Come closer!"

The Tantellan leader spoke with unnatural energy, a rictus smile covering her face. Trisanna could tell that she was the one with the dragon talisman. Kylen stood beside her, his head down. The magical noose remained around his neck, the other end of it still under the control of the mage who had captured him.

Several other mages bustled about nearby. All of them were completely insane if their appearance and behavior offered any indication.

A strange compulsion drew Trisanna forward, her companions keeping pace beside her.

Even though she remained invisible, she knew the Tantellan had spoken the truth. She couldn't hide from her. Not while she held the amulet.

She clearly saw that the compulsion had its origin in the amulet, and she shook her head in denial, determined to master her own impulses. Was there to be no freedom from the thing? It poked and prodded at her, excited by the prospect of deadly conflict. She responded by thrusting it away fiercely, refusing it ready access to her thoughts and her will.

The Tantellan was sounding excited. "I'm glad you have come! You'll be able to watch your friend die!" She turned to the other mage. "Give him a tug, Agalar."

The mage with the noose hesitated, and Kylen looked up, his face alight with hope. Then the Tantellan shrugged. With an expression that might have been regret, he pulled hard on the noose.

Kylen fell to his knees, gagging horribly.

Unable to bear it, Trisanna turned away. Dalthinir stiffened beside her, his face red with anger. He straightened, ready to act.

Then abruptly the leader waved her hand, and the other mage allowed the noose to go slack.

Swaying unsteadily, Kylen sucked in a long rattling breath. Then he struggled to his feet again, a look of defiance on his face.

An idea abruptly came into Trisanna's mind. It owed nothing to the amulet. It was prompted by her rescue from the lockup. When Kylen had knocked a hole in the wall, Emmela had responded with an illusion that made it appear the wall was still intact. Kylen had needed to enter the lockup and lead her out through what appeared to be a solid wall.

It was time for her to apply a similar trick herself. "Dalthinir, I'm going to include Kylen in our illusion so we can talk with him."

Dalthinir's immediate response was a frown, but before he could speak she added, "I'm also going to create a second illusion. One that makes it appear he's silent and hasn't moved."

"Are you sure you can do it?" Dalthinir asked uncertainly.

She nodded. "I already have."

It must have been working, because none of the Tantellans were reacting in any way.

"How would we manage without you?" asked Dalthinir in wonder. "I need you to do one thing more. Can you add Kylen's captor to your second illusion? Have him standing still as well, just as he is now."

"I can, but I'll also need a third illusion to make him invisible. It won't help us if people can still see the real him as well as an illusion."

It was the work of a moment. "I've done all of that," she reported. "Kylen is part of our invisibility illusion and his captor has an invisibility illusion of his own. The other Tantellans are only seeing images of them—provided by a different illusion."

Dalthinir was looking thoughtful. "You've made Kylen's captor invisible, so I'm only seeing your illusion of him," he said. "I'm going to try to disable him. Once he collapses, I need to be able to see both ends of the noose. If you see me raise both of my arms, can you please add him to our invisibility illusion so I can see the real person? As soon as I've freed Kylen and we're clear of the area, you can switch him back to his own invisibility illusion."

She nodded readily.

"You're remarkable, Trisanna! It's up to me now."

She watched apprehensively as the mage began striding purposefully toward Kylen and his captor.

GRITTING HIS TEETH WITH DETERMINATION, Dalthinir headed for Kylen. Furious as he was with the Tantellans, he was also vexed with himself for having failed to keep a closer check on his apprentice in the first place. He should never have allowed any of them to go wandering about Flaxendell on their own. The environment had been far too dangerous.

Weaving his way between the mad mages, he drew closer to Kylen and his captor.

Seeing him coming, Kylen's eyes went wide. He kept his eyes averted, presumably not wanting to give Dalthinir away. Quickly deciding it would be too difficult to explain what was happening, Dalthinir ignored him.

Kylen still had the magical noose around his throat. As before, he had been forced to position himself close beside his captor to prevent it from strangling him.

Dalthinir scowled. Cruelty of this type had no place in a civilized society. It made him more determined than ever.

He also intended to do everything in his power to prevent these people from getting their hands on Trisanna. In this situation he would have been lost without her. Her illusions offered the first real chance of freeing Kylen.

He faced two unknowns. He needed to assume that Kylen's captor was protected by a shield. The strength of the shield would have a big bearing on the options available to him. The other unknown related to the magical noose around Kylen's neck. After examining it carefully, Dalthinir detected a tiny shield tightly around it. Would the shield persist if he managed to disable Kylen's captor? He could only guess.

He sighed. There were too many unknowns. He had no choice but to make an attempt.

The noose around his apprentice's neck was tied to the other man's belt. If he succeeded in disabling the Tantellan, it might be simplest to untie the noose. Kylen could walk away with it still around his neck.

Tantellans were on every side now, and Dalthinir began to feel increasingly edgy. Most of them were insane, and there was no telling what they might do. Things could deteriorate very rapidly. He needed to act at once.

Gently probing the captor's shield, Dalthinir wondered why he had hesitated. Penetrating the Tantellan's defenses was ridiculously easy.

"Kylen, I need you to bend low right now!"

His apprentice obeyed without hesitation.

Using his mage touch ability, Dalthinir quickly rendered Kylen's captor unconscious, just as he had once done to Lars during the confrontation in the Drakkenridge Mountains. The man slumped to the ground. He wasn't likely to regain consciousness anytime soon.

The moment the Tantellan began to collapse, Dalthinir had raised his arms high. He then watched as the man went down—Trisanna had switched him to their illusion so quickly and smoothly Dalthinir didn't even notice a flicker. He shook his head in wonder.

No one appeared to notice him lying there. The illusions were working.

With Kylen bending low, the noose hadn't stretched tight when the Tantellan went down. Quickly kneeling, Dalthinir untied the other end of it from the man's belt.

"It's time for us to go, Kylen!" he said, straightening. He began picking his way around the Tantellans, Kylen close behind him. The moment they were clear, Dalthinir worked on the knot that had been preventing the noose from being widened. In his eagerness he became unusually clumsy, and it took several minutes before he finally loosened it. By the time he succeeded he was barely able to prevent himself from shaking with nervous energy.

He pulled the loop over Kylen's head. "I'm not going to throw this away, Kylen. The Tantellans can't be allowed to get their hands on it. It needs to be destroyed so it can never be used again."

Kylen was almost speechless with relief. "I was beginning to wonder if you'd ever come, Dalthinir!" He grimaced. "The situation wasn't good back there. Most of the Tantellans have lost their minds, and Pernilla, their leader, is a different kind of crazy."

Kylen wasn't railing at his mentor, even though he had every right to do so. Dalthinir peered at him shamefacedly. "I'm sorry it took us so long."

It must have sounded feeble, but the arrival of Trisanna and the twins prevented him from saying more. All of them were talking at once, enthusiastically congratulating Kylen on his escape.

"It's Dalthinir who needs to be congratulated!" Kylen insisted.

"You need to thank Trisanna more than me," Dalthinir replied. "Without her illusions, I would never have been able to free you."

Kylen thanked her so effusively she began to blush.

"Please stop!" she urged. "It's no more than you've already done for me!"

Bella was flicking her eyes between Kylen and the Tantellans. "This is so weird!" she said. "There's a Kylen here, and one over there as well."

All of them looked back at the illusion of Kylen standing beside his captor.

Dalthinir smiled wryly. "Once the illusion ends, the Tantellans will discover that the real you has disappeared entirely, Kylen. Trisanna is hiding you, and I'm masking your magical aura. We'll leave them to figure out what's happened. If they can."

"We won't be able to shake them off, whatever masking and illusions we use," observed Trisanna grimly. "As long as I have the amulet, she'll be able to find me."

Dalthinir nodded. Although he had achieved his first goal, this was not a time for celebration. "Now that we've freed Kylen, our priority is releasing you from the amulet. It's time to visit the library."

"WAKE UP, AGALAR!"

With a groan, Agalar opened his eyes. Someone had been shaking him. Pernilla was bending low over him, a strange look in her eye.

"What are you doing?" Agalar mumbled. "Leave me alone!"

Pernilla stood up abruptly. "It's time! Our destination is nearby at last. We need to find Trisanna." Turning away, she set off down the road, heading deeper into the heart of the city. She appeared to have lost interest in Agalar entirely.

The four remaining mages tramped slowly after her.

Sitting up, Agalar tried to remember why he'd gone to sleep. The last thing he remembered was Pernilla commanding him to pull the noose tight. He belatedly realized that his captive was missing. With his heart racing, he glanced down at his belt. The noose was no longer tied to it. It had disappeared, along with the youth.

What had happened? Had his captive escaped, or had Pernilla somehow disposed of him?

An aching sense of loss washed over him. He knew he was a fool for mourning the disappearance of a Peritonian renegade. Especially when they had barely spoken. But with the captive gone he felt more alone than ever.

The youth's words came to him. *Maybe Pernilla only needs you to guard me. Once I've been disposed of one way or another, why will she need you?*

A shiver of fear traveled up Agalar's spine. What *did* it mean for him? His options had been outlined neatly by the missing captive. He could continue to follow Pernilla to an unknown end, or he could turn himself invisible and scurry back to the border. Faced with a momentous decision, he was bemused to find the most trivial of thoughts foremost in his mind: whichever path he took, he would be reduced to pulling the food cart himself.

Shaking his head at his own folly, he considered his future. He saw nothing even vaguely appealing about following Pernilla. His gut told him that things were not likely to end well.

Fleeing to the border was no better, though. Returning to Antilin would not be an option. Whether or not Pernilla survived and returned to Tantel, both the king and Chief Master Kharkin would treat Agalar as a deserter. Deserters were executed. Nor could he remain in Periton. After everything that had happened, the Peritonians would be sure to arrest him. At best he would be forced to become a renegade.

Glancing down the road, he saw that Pernilla was in a hurry. She was already a long way ahead. Agalar needed to decide, and decide quickly.

With a disgruntled growl, he took hold of the cart and set off after the others.

It didn't take long to reach the laggards. As he passed them he sped up, intent on minimizing his contact with them. He needn't have worried. They ignored him completely.

A shiver went up his spine. Each of the mages had names—he had known them for years. Now they were no more than empty shells.

It reminded him of times when he had seen a corpse. The features were familiar, but the person wasn't there anymore. He was seeing the same thing. The people he had known were absent. It wasn't right.

Picking up his pace he hurried forward, determined to rejoin Pernilla as soon as possible. When he drew level with her, the leader failed to acknowledge him. Whatever was on her mind had absorbed her completely.

Eventually she noticed Agalar. "Our destination is almost within reach," she announced. "It is as it should be."

She spoke as if the meaning of her words was self-evident. Agalar could only roll his eyes.

A bridge appeared ahead of them, the road continuing across it. A river ran noisily beneath it—the only sound in the otherwise deathly silence. When she reached it, Pernilla turned aside and scrambled down to the water's edge to bury her face in the water for a moment. Then she cupped her hand and drank deeply before climbing back up to the road and resuming her journey.

Agalar watched wide-eyed. Everyone knew it wasn't safe to drink from rivers flowing through cities. Then it occurred to him to wonder what could possibly contaminate the water. With nothing alive in the entire region, there could be no bodies of dead animals or fish, no human or animal waste, and no rotting vegetation. Unless the water still preserved lingering traces of whatever had caused the Great Desolation, it should be safe to drink.

Had he been lugging water in the cart for no reason? A self-mocking laugh burst from his lips. Then, after studying the river for a long minute, he reached down with a shrug and retrieved a waterskin from the cart.

Dusk had crept upon them, and with a brief glance toward the setting sun, Pernilla abruptly stopped walking. Lying down by the roadside, she fell immediately asleep.

There was no shortage of abandoned houses nearby, but exploring them in the semidarkness held little appeal to Agalar. After satisfying his hunger from the gradually diminishing pile of supplies, he lay down beside the cart and tried to sleep.

• • •

As he slept, he found himself in a dream. He was wandering in a broad grassland bounded by dense forests. Birds flew overhead, their cries deafening in his ears. Strips of cultivated land lay ahead, bearing crops ripe for harvest. Smoke drifted into the air from a farmhouse beside the fertile fields.

A blinding flash blotted out the sun, forcing him to cover his face with his hands. When his eyes finally adjusted, every trace of life had vanished. He stood alone in a barren wilderness.

Night fell and he spun around, trying to get his bearings in the darkness. A small figure appeared, heading toward him. Light seemed to emanate from it, driving back the darkness. As the figure drew near, he saw that it was Pernilla. The manic look had disappeared from her face, and she strode forward boldly and with purpose. She passed Agalar without a sideways glance. Four others were hurrying along behind her. Although they came close enough to touch him, they ignored him completely. No madness warped their features or their behavior. They were simply intent on following the glowing figure beyond them.

Some great purpose was driving Pernilla and her followers, and it came as a shock to recognize he was entirely ignorant of it. He had no part in what they were doing. The grief of it felt almost like physical pain.

He woke to find Pernilla and her band of followers gone.

For all the apparent madness of the four mages, they had never been wandering aimlessly. He saw that now. They had come to Ettaran for a reason. The details of the purpose still eluded him, but he could not afford to remain passive any longer.

Leaping up, he hurried after them, the food cart lying forgotten behind him.

CHAPTER 29

Trisanna was not at peace, even with Kylen newly released.

From the moment she had acted to defend the boy with club-foot, the amulet had begun to intrude upon her awareness. She hadn't fully grasped what was happening at first. It wasn't until she granted it access to her inner self that she began to understand. Since then it had been creeping inward ever more insidiously, hungering to possess her.

The experience made no sense, not least because she knew the amulet had no conscious will of its own. Nevertheless, it had been created with magic that was powerful beyond measure and with a subtlety that defied understanding.

In her innocence she had imagined that the amulet was an implement she could use to her own advantage. Now she was beginning to see she had been a fool to think she could ever bend it to her will.

There was nothing simple about it. Sorren had said as much, likening it to a sword in its effect. She wondered if a flaming torch might be closer to the mark. Useful as fire might be, anyone who used it understood the difficulties of containing it. All too frequently it turned on the one who had nursed it to life.

Was the talisman much more than a sword or a torch, though? Was it somehow capable of channeling the will and power of another sentient being—a being that was alive and very much interested in the affairs of humankind? If it was indeed the agent of another intelligence, it might be more accurate to call it a parasite than an implement.

She was caught. She needed the amulet, but she had never been willing to yield up her soul in return. Every day she had been wrestling with it. Now it was every night, too, because it increasingly invaded her dreams.

Perhaps she might be able to extract from it some kind of a truce. Perhaps. The longer she spent with it, the less she liked her chances.

AFTER FREEING KYLEN, the party had pressed on deeper into Ettaran. Dalthinir was determined to find the Great Library.

"She's getting close again," Trisanna announced dejectedly.

"And the other Tantellans are following her," added Kylen. "They're making no effort to hide their glimmer."

Dalthinir's face was grim. "Then we need to keep moving. We might as well drop the illusions. Pernilla knows where the amulet is. There isn't a lot of point in being invisible anymore."

They hurried forward, with Dalthinir in the lead.

He turned to Kylen. "Do you have any idea what she might be planning to do?"

Kylen shook his head. "She's pursuing the amulet, and she seems to have a definite purpose beyond that, although I never heard her say what it was. She mostly mumbled to herself. But whatever it is must be important. She has no interest in anything else."

They appeared to be approaching the center of the city. The streets had become wider and the buildings taller.

Kylen had grown up in Cambrick, the capital of Periton. Built around a castle, the city had slowly spread outward until it filled the space within the enclosing wall that surrounded it. The layout of the city had not been planned in advance—it had emerged haphazardly. Consequently, the end result was chaotic.

Ettaran looked nothing like it. It was orderly, spacious, and attractive.

Kylen gazed about in wonder. The public buildings in Flaxendell had seemed grand to him, but they paled into insignificance beside their counterparts in Ettaran.

The most magnificent of the structures featured a large building circular in shape and capped by a huge dome. Elegant towers stood on either side of it. A broad marble stairway led to a graceful entranceway.

Kylen was staring at it in admiration when Dalthinir joined him.

"You're looking at the Great Library of Ettaran!" his mentor breathed. "A large section of it was maintained by the Compact. It houses the most extensive collection of books and scrolls ever assembled on the topic of magic. Almost every mage I've ever known has wanted to cast their eyes upon the library, and longed even more to enter it."

Trisanna approached them, restless and unsettled. "She isn't far behind us now."

Dalthinir frowned. "We'll have to hurry, then. To have any hope of releasing you from that talisman, I'm going to need time to search the records."

The solution was immediately obvious to Kylen. "Go and do your search. We'll draw them away."

"That isn't going to happen," Dalthinir replied flatly. "Now that we've finally freed you, I'm not letting you out of my sight!"

"They caught me by surprise last time. They won't do it again. Besides, Trisanna will be with me, and she has the amulet."

Dalthinir was not convinced, but Trisanna came to his support. "Kylen is right. This is the opportunity you wanted. It's the amulet they're chasing. They'll follow us and leave you to do what you need to do."

Seeing that the mage was still hesitating, she added, "I don't want to see Kylen come to harm, either. The amulet is more powerful than all of us combined, and I promise you I won't hesitate to use it if I need to."

Kylen pressed home the point. "You've freed *me*. It's time to free Trisanna!"

His mentor yielded, albeit reluctantly. "Very well. As long as you rejoin me the moment you get into any kind of trouble!"

"The twins are probably safer with you," Kylen suggested.

Dalthinir nodded. Having made his choice, he wasted no time hurrying up the steps. Reaching the entrance, he stepped inside, Jonno and Bella at his heels.

Trisanna turned to Kylen. "Where shall we go?"

"We'll need to stay in the open," he replied. "We don't want to be backed into a corner. If they get close it might be useful to become invisible. That won't stop Pernilla from finding us, but it might make it difficult for the others."

They set off, moving as quickly as they could away from the Tantellans.

Before long they came to a bridge. The river below it seemed to wind its way around the city, and as Kylen glanced down at it a memory came to his mind.

He pointed to a small boat pulled up on the riverbank. "I know your recent experience with boats hasn't been entirely encouraging, Trisanna. Even so, I'd like to suggest we take to the water."

She looked doubtful, but she joined him as he scrambled down the riverbank and made his way to the little vessel.

"Help me get it to the water," said Kylen.

"The wood's rotten!" she exclaimed uncertainly.

"Trust me, that won't be a problem," he said with a grin.

Using his mage touch abilities, he made the boat lighter, allowing them to launch it. To Trisanna's astonishment, no water poured in, in spite of several gaping holes in the bottom of the boat. Stepping into it, Kylen reached out a hand to Trisanna. She joined him tentatively, sitting down on one of the thwarts and staring wide-eyed at the flimsy hull of the craft.

"Can I offer a suggestion?" asked Kylen.

She nodded.

"Why don't you do something about the holes?"

It took her a moment to understand his meaning. When she did, a smile lit up her face. In an instant the boat was transformed. No holes remained anywhere, and a bright coat of paint adorned the hull. A mast towered over them, supporting a small sail that billowed merrily in spite of the almost complete absence of a breeze.

No sail was necessary, of course. The boat was moving steadily through the water, propelled entirely by Kylen's magic.

"They're following us," he observed. "But we're pulling away from them."

The strategy was working. They sailed on, the Tantellans never drawing near enough to pose a serious threat.

The sun passed its zenith and still the strange chase continued. Then, in the early afternoon, Trisanna stiffened suddenly. "They're getting closer!"

Kylen frowned in puzzlement. "How is that possible?"

Abruptly it came to him. "It isn't them! It's us! The river has been bending steadily, and it's taking us back the way we came."

"We don't have much time," said Kylen. "We're heading right for Pernilla. Shall I turn the boat around?"

"No!" Trisanna replied fiercely. "We should probably rejoin the others. And I'm sick of running!"

As they rounded the bend, they saw that Pernilla and her remaining mages were ready for them. They had found a couple of old wagons somewhere and pushed them into the water at a point where the river narrowed significantly. There was no way their little craft would make it past their barrier.

To Kylen's astonishment, the boat beneath them abruptly disappeared. In its place appeared a creature of nightmare. Shaped like a giant eel, the monster was bigger than the river was wide. Its mouth yawned menacingly to reveal dagger-like teeth, as it writhed back and forth in search of prey.

Standing rigid on the riverbank, Pernilla stared at it open-mouthed. Beside her, Agalar fell to his knees, covering his face with his hands. Even the mad mages seemed abashed.

To Kylen's astonishment, the monster smashed through the wagons blocking the river, howling its rage. The sound of its voice set Kylen's flesh crawling.

As they rounded another bend in the river, the apparition vanished.

Trisanna's illusion of the boat was gone, too, leaving only the stark reality of an old and rotten vessel.

Pulling the boat in to the riverbank, Kylen helped Trisanna onto dry land. He gazed at her with mingled awe and horror. "Where did you dream that up?" The monster might have been an illusion, but he had been profoundly shaken by it.

"It was no dream," she assured him. She passed a shaking hand across her face. "Zeke and I encountered two of them on the Lake of Death."

He stared at her, shocked speechless.

"For a moment I was afraid that the amulet had brought the creature to life," she told him. "I could sense its hunger!"

He nodded uneasily. "I started to think it was alive, too. Especially when we crashed through the barrier. It wasn't me doing that."

"No," she confirmed. "It was the amulet."

The two of them sat down on the riverbank, struggling to recover their composure. The lifeless city surrounded them on every side, its oppressive silence sapping at Kylen's spirit.

Several minutes had passed before he looked up in alarm. "Where has Pernilla gone?"

Trisanna roused herself with an effort. "Away from us." She caught her breath. "Is it possible she's heading for the library?"

Kylen leaped to his feet. "She can't be aware that Dalthinir is there, can she?" He peered off into the distance. "There must be a reason for her to go there. I know she has a purpose beyond claiming the amulet."

"Perhaps it somehow involves the library," suggested Trisanna.

Kylen had come fully to life at last. "Whether it does or not, we need to get back to Dalthinir!"

As he entered the Great Library, Dalthinir held his breath involuntarily. To him, the tales of this place that had drifted down from the distant past had seemed fanciful. He saw now that the reports had failed to do justice to the reality.

Glancing ahead into the entrance porch, he saw long lines of display cabinets, each constructed with a glass top and sides. Few of the exotic objects on display were recognizable to him. The inscriptions mounted beside each cabinet would have satisfied his curiosity, but he was not willing to pause long enough to examine them.

"This is the way," he said, pointing toward the far end of the entrance hall. He strode off at once, Jonno and Bella hurrying along beside him.

Reaching the rear of the great entrance hall, they found a doorway leading into another broad hall. A sign still hung in place, announcing it as the Annex Dedicated to the Library of the Compact. Dalthinir stared wide-eyed as they entered the hall. Seemingly endless lines of shelves surrounded him, laden with books and scrolls.

The vastness of the accumulated knowledge was breathtaking. He would have given a great deal to come here at his leisure—to spend entire days wandering among the shelves, soaking it all in.

Instead, he must focus. How could he hope to find what he was searching for among this vast outpouring of knowledge?

He knew that every library of any size had some kind of index, and he hunted until he found it. Soon he was racing feverishly about the annex, removing books, scrolls, and parchments and handing them to the twins.

A set of stairs lay at one end of the annex with a sign pointing upward to the Reading Room. When the three of them had filled their arms with as much as they could carry, he led them up the stairs.

Reaching the top, they found themselves in a large and well-lit room. Sunlight was streaming in through windows that overlooked the city in every direction. The circular roof appeared to form the base of the large dome that crowned the building.

Armchairs and tables had been positioned throughout the space in an orderly fashion. Evidence still remained of the area's role as a reading room. Scrolls and books could be seen lying on some of the tables.

"Please put them here," he told the twins, pointing to the nearest table. As soon as they had deposited their loads, he sat down to make a beginning.

. . .

BOOKS AND SCROLLS lay strewn around Dalthinir. He had been at it for what seemed an eternity when at last he picked up a book entitled simply *Dragon Talismans*. Flipping open the cover, his eye was caught by a sketch of the Amulet of Zinth. With heart pounding, he began to read.

> *As the name suggests, a dragon talisman owes its existence to a dragon, although how dragons infuse talismans with magical power is not known. The Amulet of Zinth, preeminent among such relics, is believed to have originated with the dragon Zin'thelestar. Notwithstanding the evil reputation of that creature, the amulet has unquestionably been an extraordinary gift to humankind. Traditionally held by the Chief Master of Methesia, the amulet has played its part in the prosperity and stability of the kingdom.*

HE PAUSED, tempted to wonder if the role of this particular amulet might be a great deal less benign than the writer imagined. He wondered, too, how the amulet had escaped the ruin of Methesia and found its way into the hands of Trisanna. He couldn't begin to guess at the path it must have taken.

Bending down once more, he skipped over sections of the book that described other dragon talismans and their properties. He resumed reading when he came to an overview of the general characteristics of talismans.

> *Dragon talismans do not provide the bearer with new mage abilities. They instead enhance the strength of existing abilities while relieving the mage of weariness resulting from the exer-*

cise of those abilities. However, they come into full effect only when activated by the bearer.

After activation they deliver a range of other benefits. No comprehensive list of such benefits has ever been compiled for any talisman. Such a list would be impossible to complete, since one of the most remarkable characteristics of talismans is that they respond differently to different situations, offering the bearer a range of magical responses both familiar and unexpected.

A talisman makes the bearer aware of the presence of other talismans. Such awareness is greatly enhanced by activation.

A talisman might appear to the bearer to have its own consciousness. In my opinion, this view is mistaken. Some mages have gone further and suggested that a talisman expresses the will and intent—for good or ill—of the dragon that created it. Such a view seems equally implausible.

Occasionally a bearer has felt sufficiently uncomfortable with the effect of a talisman to want to discard or even destroy it. Attempts at destruction have proven ineffectual. The general view is that a dragon talisman can be destroyed only by a dragon. This writer is aware of no recorded cases of a dragon having done so.

IF THIS REPORT WAS ACCURATE, destroying the amulet would not be an option. Beyond that, intriguing though the information might be, it offered nothing that would help release Trisanna.

Turning the page, he continued reading. After some minutes, he came upon something that set his heart pounding.

A talisman can be discarded, provided the bearer is willing to suffer the consequences. Ill effects increase with the length of time that has elapsed since activation.

Chief masters have never needed to relinquish the Amulet

of Zinth, the most powerful talisman of all. Head mages are appointed for life, so they retain the amulet until death.

DALTHINIR HEAVED a huge sigh of relief. He had his answer. It *was* possible for a bearer to be released from a dragon talisman. And in view of the limited amount of time that had passed since Trisanna activated the amulet, it should be realistic for her to discard it without suffering significantly as a result.

There seemed no reason she couldn't wait until they had left Methesia. That would allow them to preserve their sanity.

Disposing of it would be more problematic. They would need to do any unusually thorough job of hiding it. A solution could wait for another day, though.

In the act of returning the book to the table, he noticed a separate note that had been slipped into the back cover. Removing it, he unfolded it carefully. The document was fragile with age, but its writing was still legible. It took him a while to decipher the scrawl.

Arbilis is becoming ever more erratic since his appointment as chief master. It is that cursed amulet he now bears, I am certain of it. The dragon, Zin'thelestar, has been twisting his mind. And I believed Arbilis to be so strong!

It has long been known that previous chief masters rarely drew upon the power of the amulet. They were wise enough to limit their exposure to it. Not so Arbilis. He seems obsessed.

I know of no one I can turn to.

I fear for what will become of him—for what will become of us all!

FOR THE FIRST time Dalthinir wondered if dragons might not solely be responsible for the catastrophe known as the Great Desolation. Was it possible that Master Arbilis—Chief Master Arbilis apparently—had played a role, inspired by a malevolent dragon?

A memory came to him of Kylen asking about Master Arbilis. It had been after the incident with Lars and Petria on the mountain. Where had his apprentice heard that name? Dalthinir's brows drew together thoughtfully.

Mage smell interrupted his thoughts, alerting him to the approach of mages. Kylen and Trisanna were joining him. They couldn't have timed it better.

But where were the Tantellans?

CHAPTER 30

Having reached the library building at last, Kylen and Trisanna paused for breath.

A confrontation was brewing. Any possible uncertainty about it in Kylen's mind had long since been dispelled by the warning from the dragon, Elef'nissar. *Your companion is intent on great evil. You must prevent her.*

How could he be expected to deal with Pernilla? It made no sense. He had never been so aware of his limitations. He hadn't even been able to free himself.

Nor was he the one with a powerful amulet. Not that he would have wanted it—not after what it had done to Trisanna. She had seemed remarkably serene when he first met her, in spite of her harrowing journey from Tantel and her confrontation with the monsters in the lake. Having just caught a tiny glimpse of the true horror of that encounter, he could only be in awe of her fortitude.

Everything had changed for her, though. Since Kylen had been freed, he had seen at a glance that Trisanna was restless and distressed. Her serenity had abandoned her.

He understood now why he hadn't gone mad. It was only thanks to Trisanna. She had been carrying the fabled Amulet of Zinth—a relic that granted its bearer magical power beyond imagining. But the power had come at a cost. In granting the amulet access to her inner being, she had been left carrying an intolerable burden. Her wretchedness troubled him no less than it did Dalthinir.

He had also learned that Pernilla was herself carrying a dragon talisman. That surely explained how she had been able to protect herself and Agalar, and it no doubt accounted for her mood and behavior as well, at least in part.

Compromised by the amulet, Trisanna was clearly distracted. She might have little to offer in a crisis.

Surely Dalthinir was the best person to take responsibility for dealing with Pernilla. His mentor had far more experience than Kylen, and the wisdom of years to go with it.

Although Elef'nissar had approached him rather than Dalthinir, it was probably only because Dalthinir didn't have mage hearing ability and wouldn't have understood a word the dragon was saying.

A tremulous voice broke into his musing.

"She's in there!" murmured Trisanna. Restless and unsettled, she was staring at the library building.

Although he could sense no magical auras apart from Dalthinir's, Kylen did not doubt Trisanna. Glimmer could be masked, but Pernilla's talisman could not hide from the amulet.

He sighed. He knew what needed to be done, and he couldn't leave others to do it, whatever his inadequacies. The twins had little more than their courage to fall back on, but they hadn't shied away from the coming conflict.

All any of them could do was stand firm against the fear. Whatever might come, they would face it together.

Climbing the steps, he entered the building. Trisanna followed, dragging herself across the threshold.

Having set foot in the fabled library at last, Kylen took the opportunity to peer around curiously. Much as he would have loved to examine the display cabinets, he walked resolutely past them.

Wide openings on either side of the entranceway offered a glimpse of vast halls lined with orderly rows of shelves. Even from a distance he could see that the shelves were stacked with scrolls, books, and parchments.

Impressive as Flaxendell's library had been, this place had been built on an entirely different scale. He was standing where mages everywhere wanted to stand, and he now understood why. It was impossible to resist a brief glance into the halls as he passed, but he didn't turn aside.

Locating the mages' annex, they hurried through it and headed for the stairs. Dalthinir was up there.

So, apparently, was Pernilla. A glance at Trisanna's face showed it taut with tension. She, too, seemed to sense that conflict was imminent.

It was impossible to guess what a confrontation with Pernilla might involve. In spite of intense exposure to the Tantellan leader in recent days, she remained a complete mystery to Kylen. Her motivations and intentions were beyond the understanding of any normal person. And Kylen wasn't alone in seeing it that way. Agalar had known Pernilla for years, and he had seemed no less bemused by his leader's behavior.

Placing one hand on the rail beside the stairs, Kylen began to climb. Trisanna followed, trembling uncontrollably and hugging her chest as if she was in pain. Kylen would have done something if he could. At their first meeting he had rescued her from a lockup. This time he had little to offer.

One step at a time, Kylen ascended, alert for any sign of trouble. When he reached the top, he immediately saw Dalthinir and the twins sitting in a broad and well-lit room filled with tables and chairs. All of them tensed when they saw Kylen and Trisanna's expressions.

"Have you found anything?" Kylen asked.

Undoubtedly sensing his apprentice's edginess, Dalthinir limited himself to a tight nod. "Pernilla?" he asked.

"She's here. Somewhere." Even as Kylen said it, he was scanning the room.

Across the tables and seats at the opposite end of the room he spotted another stairway leading upward. Before he could begin to guess what might lie beyond the stairs, Pernilla flickered into view. She was not alone. Four insane Tantellan mages had apparently followed their leader into the building. Agalar was nowhere to be seen, but he must surely be somewhere nearby. He would have been the one who had made them invisible.

Trisanna had warned him that Pernilla was there, but it was still disconcerting. Six Tantellan mages were close at hand, yet he could discern no scent of magical auras. The garments the Tantellans had used to mask their glimmer were not responsible. The four mages had long since discarded them, and at that moment Pernilla was not wearing one either. Was Pernilla's talisman capable of masking glimmer?

The Tantellan leader spread her arms wide. "Ah, Trisanna. You have come to give me the amulet," she crooned.

"Never!" cried Trisanna.

Pernilla shook her head sadly, as if scolding a headstrong child. "Please don't make me take it from you."

When Trisanna failed to respond, she thrust out a hand imperiously. "Give it to me!"

A crazed laugh issued from Trisanna's lips. "You think you can control it? You are a fool! It wants me to tear you apart!"

Unmoved, Pernilla reached for a fine chain around her neck, drawing out a small object that hung from it.

Kylen realized he was looking at Pernilla's talisman. It was certainly a dragon relic. While in no way reminiscent of Elef'nissar, its lingering scent spoke to him of dragons.

Something about this environment was stimulating his mage smell ability. Even without glancing at Trisanna, he could sense the Amulet of Zinth. He sensed that it, too, bore traces of a dragon. It pulsed with suppressed energy as if possessing a life of its own.

With the dragon artifacts now exposed to his senses, he guessed that Pernilla's talisman had been responsible for masking the glimmer of the Tantellan mages. He wondered uneasily what else it might be capable of.

The Tantellan leader held her talisman aloft. In response a chorus of low moans echoed in the emptiness. Dark figures shuffled from her side, heading for Trisanna with arms outstretched.

Dalthinir had risen to his feet, and he stepped in front of Trisanna.

"Kylen can protect you while I deal with the Tantellans," he told her firmly. "You need to back away, for all of our sakes!"

Stumbling uncertainly, Trisanna edged backward, her face buried in her hands. Kylen wasted no time wrapping her in a shield.

The mad mages were coming for Dalthinir. Kylen sensed his mentor's shield as he activated it. The mages didn't seem to care. Surrounding him, they shoved him aside with astonishing ease. In their weakened state Kylen had expected they would have few reserves of physical strength to call upon, yet they possessed astonishing vigor. Crashing into one of the desks, Dalthinir lay stunned on the floor. His shield had not protected him. Pernilla's talisman must somehow have compromised it.

Lurching past him, the mages pressed on toward Trisanna.

Standing in their path, Kylen did the first thing that occurred to him. Wrapping a shield around the legs of the mad mages, he pulled it tight. Swaying drunkenly for a moment, the whole group came crashing to the floor. It happened too quickly for Pernilla to interfere.

Then all at once the mad mages and Pernilla disappeared once more. This time Trisanna disappeared with them. It must have been the work of Agalar.

Unseen hands began grabbing at him. He could neither see them nor detect their magical auras, but he knew they would be able to see him. He was soon engaged in a desperate struggle.

Invisible hands pushed him with incredible force, knocking him from his feet. His head hit hard on the leg of an armchair, and everything went dark.

THE FRENZY around Kylen was gone. Once more he found himself underground and in darkness. He had experienced this vision before, and his detachment felt familiar. He walked slowly forward, expecting to encounter a dim light.

But events did not follow their previous pattern. His dream-world abruptly shimmered, flickering wildly back and forth between competing scenes. Thoroughly disoriented, his head began to spin. Distant cries penetrated his awareness—too faint to recognize as words. Anger pulsed red around him. Then solidity gradually returned.

The blackness had been replaced by bright sunlight.

A form he recognized appeared before him, confirmed by an unmistakable glimmer. The commanding visage of Elef'nissar swung toward him, the great orbed eyes whirling wrathfully. Thick smoke the color of charcoal billowed from the dragon's nostrils.

"I have wrested you from the creature's grip," growled Elef'nissar.

Kylen stared back uncomprehendingly.

No further explanation was on offer. The dragon clearly had something pressing on its mind. "The Great Desolation"—it almost spat the words—"was triggered by an act of supreme folly." It glared at him fiercely, as if daring him to disagree, although it did not wait for a response. "That act could not be undone, but a force possessing great power limited the damage. A part of the dark magic was bound in protective magic and placed in a safe place."

Kylen's forehead wrinkled as he tried to understand. "The mages of Ettaran achieved that before they were destroyed?"

The orbs gyrated more fiercely than ever, and clouds of smoke streamed from its nostrils. The dragon's voice came as a guttural growl from deep in its throat. "Human mages achieved *nothing*—apart from an unimaginable act of lunacy! No greater betrayal has been visited upon the world, save one." A different kind of anger sent its eyes spinning.

Kylen swallowed convulsively as he stared at the creature. Could this account be accurate? Had human mages truly been responsible for the devastation?

"You said that a powerful force limited the damage. Why can't that happen again now?"

The dragon's eyes flashed dangerously. "Do you imagine I peddle words for your entertainment? Would this burden fall to me if the Eldest was stirring?"

Kylen clamped his mouth shut tight.

The great head was swinging back and forth in agitation. "The abomination you call the Amulet of Zinth has found its way at last to the dark magic!" Clouds of smoke issued from the great nostrils, eventually clearing as the dragon mastered its anger. "If the imprisoned magic is released, what humankind refers to as the Great Desolation will become the Final Desolation," it told him fiercely. "It will usher in the climax—the irrevocable culmination of humankind's appetite for self-destruction. Life will be extinguished from the world. Only the dragons will remain, doomed to linger, silent and alone."

The great face drew closer, its voice becoming a low rumble. "*You must prevent it, Kalmithien.*"

CHAPTER 31

Kylen awoke to the soft light of the reading room. He could see no one anywhere near him.

How long had he been unconscious?

The vision remained clear in his mind. He had glimpsed a battle between Elef'nissar and the creature that dwelt in the dark—a battle for his attention. After repeated exposure to both creatures, he had no doubt that only Elef'nissar was worthy of his trust. The dragon had said that dark magic had been bound in protective magic and placed somewhere safe, and that the amulet had found its way to the dark magic. Since the amulet was in the library, that could only mean that the trapped magic was located somewhere nearby, too. And having made it clear that the stakes had never been higher, the dragon had declared him responsible for ensuring that the dark magic was not released.

How could he stop Pernilla? If he'd harbored doubts about the threat she posed, the dragon's palpable alarm had dispelled it. And he had already witnessed the power of her talisman.

There had to be something he could do.

A voice echoed in his mind. *The child of prophecy has awakened! Our doom rests upon his shoulders—deliverance if he stands; destruction and ruin if he falls!* He shook his head, determined not to fall.

Noises that sounded like a scuffle reached him. Clambering onto his knees, he peered around in an effort to orient himself. Partway across the huge room he saw two figures he recognized as Jonno and Bella wrestling an unseen opponent. The twins had no magic to call upon, yet they had not shrunk from the conflict.

As he watched, Dalthinir picked himself up from the floor and threw his weight into the struggle. His intervention must have turned the tide, because the prone form of Agalar winked suddenly into view at their feet. He was holding his head and moaning.

With Agalar's illusion shattered, Kylen spotted a cluster of mages ascending the staircase at the other end of the room. They were bearing the unresisting form of Trisanna. Pernilla appeared to have lost interest in Dalthinir and his companions.

Climbing unsteadily to his feet, he called a warning to the others.

Following his pointing hand, Dalthinir spoke rapidly to the twins. "I've put a shield around Kylen's captor. It will let him use his feet, but nothing else. Get him out of the building, and guard him well. Do whatever you want to him if he tries any more invisibility illusions!"

As they hurried away, Kylen turned to his mentor. "I know what this is about now!" he said.

Dalthinir looked at him quizzically.

"Dark magic is located somewhere near here. It's trapped in protective magic. Pernilla wants the amulet so she can release it. The whole world will be destroyed if she succeeds!"

"How do you know?"

"From a dragon."

"A dragon? You mean in a dream?"

"Yes. But I trust it! I've met it face to face. More than once. It awakened my magic."

Dalthinir was staring at him, too astonished to speak.

"There isn't time to explain! We have to hurry!"

Kylen ran toward the staircase, now empty of figures. To his relief, Dalthinir was right behind him.

Reaching it, they clambered up the stairs as quickly as they were able.

A door stood ajar on the landing at the top. A sign above the lintel identified the room as the 'Observatory.' Pushing cautiously inside they found themselves in a spacious area that was almost completely dark. It appeared empty, although in the enveloping darkness it was impossible to be certain.

Dalthinir must have called upon his elements ability with fire, because a small glowing fireball appeared, suspended in the air above their heads. As his eyes adjusted, Kylen saw Pernilla standing almost in the middle of the observatory. Beyond her he glimpsed a dim light at the far end of the room. There was no sign of furniture. The only visible object was a large and strangely shaped device above them, poking through the top of the dome.

Refusing to be distracted, he searched for Trisanna. He located her in time to see her break free of the mages who had been carrying her, pushing away from them with effort. She managed a tight nod of gratitude to Dalthinir and Kylen as they hurried to her side.

Standing beside Trisanna, Kylen's attention was drawn to the faint glow beyond Pernilla. It was emanating from a huge sphere. Tiny beams of colored light danced and whirled inside it, dazzling him in the otherwise total darkness. At the sight of it, a chill ran up his spine.

The glow became partially obscured as Pernilla stepped in front of the sphere.

"It is beautiful, is it not?" she enthused in a high-pitched voice. "It is even more remarkable up close!"

"Don't go anywhere near it," growled Kylen.

"There is nothing to fear," crooned the Tantellan. "Come and touch it! You will be filled to overflowing with pure magic."

"Don't listen to her!" Trisanna warned shrilly. "It's evil!"

Pernilla was unmoved. "You speak in ignorance. There is no evil here. An unimaginable amount of magic was removed from the kingdom during the Great Desolation—trapped within this sphere. That magic needs to take its proper place in the world again. But it can be released only by destroying the orb that imprisons it." She raised her arms exultantly. "I have seen a vision! The kingdom as it was intended to be—radiant, powerful, and rich with grandeur!" She eyed them hungrily. "It is my destiny to free the magic. I have foreseen it! The Amulet of Zinth is the key." In the dim light she seemed to be licking her lips. "I will offer you one last chance, Trisanna! Give me the amulet!"

Trisanna shook her head stubbornly. Tense and downcast she might be, but her spirit had refused to yield.

The Tantellan leader didn't seem surprised. Raising her talisman high once more, she began to visibly tremble. As if in response to her agitation, a blaze of light burst from the relic clasped in her hand. For an instant it banished the darkness completely.

Kylen stared at Pernilla anxiously. In the brief moment of brightness he had seen only madness in her eyes.

With a cry, she thrust forward her talisman, singling out her target. Trisanna made no effort to block her. A narrow beam of power shot from the relic, but it wasn't quick enough. Kylen and Dalthinir got in first, wrapping Trisanna in layered shields. Pernilla's talisman had broken through Dalthinir's shield in the reading room, but their combined effort turned back the attack.

Frustrated, Pernilla turned and directed her beam at the orb. Kylen watched with horror as it beat upon the protective barrier surrounding the trapped magic. But her efforts were in vain. The talisman was not powerful enough to overcome the orb's defenses.

In growing fury the Tantellan directed the power at a new target— the Amulet of Zinth. For a few anxious moments Kylen and Dalthinir's combined shield held, then the beam bored through it, connecting with the amulet. In response to the beam's stimulation, the amulet began to glow.

To Kylen's alarm, a combined beam emerged. He watched anxiously as it grew noticeably brighter and broader. Apparently responding to Pernilla's direction, the amulet began to turn, directing the beam straight onto the orb.

Glancing in dismay at the glowing ball, Kylen saw the tiny fingers of light spinning in a frenzy. He knew what would happen if they were released. The prospect of it horrified him.

"Trisanna! You have to stop it!" he screamed.

"I'm trying!" she cried desperately.

Her efforts were not visible, but she found a way to reassert her mastery. The amulet wobbled, then moved away from the orb, taking the beam with it. Pernilla shouted in anger, straining to wrest back control.

While they fought their desperate battle, the beam wandered randomly about the conservatory building, wreaking destruction.

At one point Kylen saw it heading for him. Throwing himself frantically to the ground, he watched wide-eyed as it passed directly through the point where he had been standing.

Chunks of masonry began falling around them. A huge piece headed directly for Dalthinir. "Look out!" yelled Kylen.

Barely seeing the danger in time, Dalthinir threw himself to one side as the rubble smashed into the floor.

A pile of debris now separated him from Kylen and Trisanna. He tried climbing over it, but the mound shifted and the floor below it creaked ominously. Backing away, he looked for a way around it, testing the floor gingerly as he went.

Exhausted by her battle for control of the combined beam of power, Trisanna was groaning with the effort. "The amulet is fighting me!" she ground out through clenched teeth.

Kylen hurried to her side. She was barely managing to keep the beam pointed away from the sphere.

The dragon had charged him with preventing Pernilla from achieving her purpose. How could he do it when his shield had proven ineffective against her talisman?

None of his magical abilities offered him an obvious way forward. But he refused to give up—there had to be something he could do.

Then he remembered Dalthinir's words when they were building the bridge. *Some mages think magic is the right tool for every job. It isn't true. Every mage has muscles, and most mages have brains as well. There's no reason to be shy about using them.*

Even if his magical power was helpless, strength remained in his body.

Grasping the amulet carefully in his hands, he physically pointed it away from the orb. To his relief, the beam moved with it.

Large pieces of the dome were crashing down now. A couple of huge chunks barely missed them. "Can you shut off the beam?" he called urgently.

She shook her head tightly.

He steered the beam off to the side instead of upward. It caused even more damage, punching a massive hole in the side of the dome.

At that moment the Tantellan leader strode forward, her own talisman held high in one hand. Her wrathful face filled Kylen's vision. "The trapped magic *must* be released!" she stormed. "Give the amulet to me now!"

Receiving no response, she reached down with her free hand, insistent in her attempts to wrest the amulet from his grasp. As they struggled back and forth Pernilla lost her footing, stumbling forward directly into the path of the beam. A flow of power washed over her, bathing her in a brilliant light. Her body disintegrated, leaving nothing more than a thin layer of ash that settled gently to the ground. No trace remained of her talisman.

Kylen stared in horrified fascination. With Pernilla's interference at an end, the flow of power ceased at once. He immediately released the amulet.

In a single movement, Trisanna pulled it over her head and cast it away. Then she collapsed onto the floor, weeping uncontrollably.

One of the mad mages shuffled into view, heading for the amulet. Kylen got there first. Scooping it up, he clutched it protectively in his hand.

A huge piece of metal from the roof of the dome came crashing down, barely missing Kylen as it tore a great hole in the floor and crashed through to the room below.

The other mage was not so fortunate. Tottering for a moment on the edge, the Tantellan tumbled into the void, disappearing without a sound.

A heavy slab of masonry slammed into the orb, and for a moment Kylen feared disaster might overtake them in spite of everything. But the orb rolled aside unharmed. It didn't even appear dented, and the little fingers of light showed no sign of excitement.

It was becoming clear that the orb was well protected. Only powerful magic could destroy it.

Blocks of stone and lumps of metal were falling almost continuously now. A memory came to his mind of Marta recounting the story of their house collapsing. Dalthinir had held up the roof while her husband rescued their two-year-old child. Spinning around, he bellowed, "Dalthinir! You need to get Trisanna out of here!"

Clambering over some rubble, Dalthinir finally reached them. "I'll take her! You need to come too!"

His words were almost drowned out by an ominous grinding sound. The stability of the dome must surely have been irretrievably compromised. It sounded as if the entire structure was about to collapse.

"I have to stop the dome collapsing," replied Kylen through gritted teeth. "I'll follow as soon as you're clear."

The roof required his full attention. This time, his magic could help. He had already placed a shield beneath the dome to support its weight.

According to Dalthinir, his power was almost unrivaled. Remembering that, he reached down into his gut for every ounce he could find. Even as he reinforced his shield he sensed it was being strengthened from outside—the departing Dalthinir had lent power to it as well. Bolstered by the support, he gave it everything he had.

The weight of the domed roof was beyond imagining. He knew at once that his own power would not be enough, even with Dalthinir's help. The collapse of his shield was imminent. Somehow he had to hold it for long enough to allow their escape.

In his extremity a disembodied voice spoke calmly to him. "The amulet can save you, Kalmithien! Grant it access to your inner being, and it will enhance your power beyond mortal imagining."

For a moment an image came unbidden to Kylen's mind. He saw himself thrusting out his hands, and the dome being restored dramatically to its original state. Then, powerful and wise beyond other mortals, he pictured himself striding forward to right the wrongs of the world.

Reality reasserted itself. The amulet's power came at a price. It had made Trisanna strong, but it had also robbed her of peace. He had not forgotten, either, the moment in the mountains when the forbidden book had lain within his grasp. He had come frighteningly close to yielding to its allure.

He had no intention of stumbling at the second test.

The voice wasn't giving up. "The amulet could never answer to the girl. There has only ever been one mage capable of mastering it! *You* are the child of prophecy! It is *your* destiny."

The voice was known to him. It had spoken to him in his visions of the dark place below the earth. Refusing to be distracted, he did his best to ignore it.

"Use the amulet to release the magic trapped in the orb!" it insisted with growing urgency. "The magic will boost your powers—more than you dream possible."

He offered no reply.

The voice grew hard. "There is no other way to save your friends. No other way to save yourself."

The longer the creature persisted, the better he was able to recognize its smell. He knew now that he was speaking with a dragon.

"No," he said quietly. He had reached his limit, but he had resisted the voice and its seductive promises.

"Then die here, as you deserve, craven fool!"

The weight pressing down on his shield was more than he could bear. He'd promised he would follow the others, but it was too late for that now. He could only hope he'd bought them enough time to escape.

The collapse of his shield was heralded by a portentous groan as the dome came crashing down.

A voice cried out in anguish. He dimly recognized it as his own.

DALTHINIR STUMBLED out of the library entrance, Trisanna leaning heavily on his arm. The twins waited anxiously at the bottom of the marble steps, their Tantellan captive between them.

Hurrying down the steps as quickly as he could, Dalthinir led Trisanna to them.

"Stay with the twins," he told her. "I'm going back for Kylen."

As he set foot on the lowest step, a loud rumbling sound grew in volume. He watched in horror as the dome collapsed completely, casting debris outward. Wreckage hit the towers on each side of the building, forcing the graceful structures to lean precariously until they slowly toppled, crashing to the ground.

A wall of dust poured from the building's entrance, blanketing them all. Having experienced a similar situation on a smaller scale, Dalthinir hastily erected a shield to protect the group. He was in time to safeguard them against debris, but he didn't act quickly enough to prevent dust and other particles from contaminating the air inside the shield. All of them were reduced to coughing and wheezing helplessly until the air gradually cleared.

The sight before them was beyond description. They had savored firsthand the wonders of the library of Ettaran. Imposing and awe-inspiring, it had endured as a monument to the pride and glory of a lost kingdom. Now they had witnessed its complete and final destruction.

Dalthinir gazed at the ruins in numbed perplexity, unable and unwilling to acknowledge the loss of Kylen. Lost he must be—Dalthinir could detect no trace of his glimmer. He knew that a mage's glimmer sometimes faded in the moments before death, but he refused to dwell on the appalling reality. The thought of Kylen suffering alone in the rubble as he waited for death was more than he could bear.

The faces of the others mirrored his horror and dismay. They were not obliged to shoulder the guilt he must carry to his grave, though. The responsibility for the safety and well-being of his apprentice had lain entirely with him. Twice on this calamitous journey he had failed Kylen. This time there was nothing he could do to set it right.

As he stood isolated and forlorn, a high-pitched keening filled the air. Every eye followed his gaze as he looked up to see a huge dragon, mottled green in color and with purple streaks on its wings, hovering over the ruined building. He watched stupefied. All his life he had believed that dragons were extinct. So much of what he'd been told must be wrong. He was too stunned to be terrified.

Could this be the dragon Kylen had referred to? Why was it there, and what was it doing? He dimly remembered reading that, in days gone by, dragons had appeared in the skies to acknowledge the passing of the greatest mages.

"Could it know of Kylen's sacrifice?" he breathed. "Has it come to honor him?"

The possibility that a dragon had emerged from days of legend to acknowledge the passing of his friend caused his breath to hitch. Hastily he forced down his emotions, refusing to grant himself release. Kylen must be the sole focus of his attention.

His apprentice had never sought glory or honor. His life had been one of hardship and difficulty, yet he had cultivated a habit of cheerfully placing the needs of others before his own. Some people demanded respect due solely to the unearned legacy of their birth. Others basked in acclaim for their achievements, the bulk of which flowed from abilities received through their heredity. Kylen deserved honor ahead of them all.

Dalthinir stood rigid, unable and unwilling to embrace the loss of his apprentice and friend.

Kylen lay broken and dying in the rubble, a tiny piece of wreckage amid the shattered legacy of forgotten artisans. Through a haze of unspeakable pain he registered the arrival of Elef'nissar. The majestic creature swooped down, hovering above him. As it lifted him tenderly in its great claws, it bent low and breathed on him. His agony slowly receded, giving way to an overwhelming weariness.

"You came for me," he whispered. "Doesn't that count as interfering?"

"I did not deem it to be such," Elef'nissar replied calmly.

Kylen was incapable of hearing the response.

Soaring high above the deserted city, the dragon wheeled northward.

CHAPTER 32

Dalthinir peered at the dragon. After grasping something in its claws, it opened its great jaws and poured fire into the rubble. Then it bore its burden aloft, disappearing into the distance.

He stared after it. "Could you see what it had in its claws?"

They shook their heads.

"Did you hear what it said as it flew over us?" asked Trisanna in wonder.

"The dragon? You heard it speak?" he asked incredulously.

She nodded.

He stared at her in surprise. "Then you must have mage hearing ability."

She nodded again, more slowly this time. "I think you must be right. I never understood how I could recognize meaning in the hideous cries of the monsters in the lake. This explains it."

"What did the dragon say?" pressed Dalthinir.

"It said, *Kalmithien has fulfilled the charge placed upon him! All honor to him for his valor, his resolve, and his sacrifice!*"

"Who is Kalmithien?"

"I don't know."

They stood in silence, struggling to comprehend what it might mean.

Jonno spoke first. "Do you think we could find Kylen's body? So we can bury him properly?"

Dalthinir did not immediately respond. As he considered the question, a loud rumble sounded and the ground shook. Debris from the building settled further into the rubble.

"We have our answer," Dalthinir replied, staring at the cloud of dust raised by the movement. "Any search would be extremely dangerous and almost certainly fruitless. It isn't worth the risk of more lives."

None of them protested his conclusion.

"Do you still have the amulet?" asked Bella suddenly.

Trisanna shook her head.

"I suppose that means we'll go mad fairly soon." Jonno sounded uncharacteristically gloomy. The loss of Kylen had clearly hit him hard.

No one offered comment. What could any of them say? They had stopped Pernilla, but at what cost? Perhaps they might soon come to think of Kylen as fortunate.

Trisanna had been staring absently into the distance. "What's that?" she asked, pointing along the broad avenue that ran westward.

Bella squinted in that direction. "It looks like a couple of people with a cart."

Jonno shook his head in bafflement. "Who would be crazy enough to wander around Ettaran—with or without a cart?"

"Whoever it is seems to be heading toward us," said Dalthinir calmly. "Let's wait here and find out."

The interlopers didn't seem in a hurry, and the twins became increasingly restless as the minutes passed.

"It's a short person with two others," offered Bella.

"Perfect. They brought a pixie with them. That's just what we needed," said Jonno moodily.

As they drew nearer, the shorter person began running toward them.

"It's Marigold!" said Bella joyfully, racing forward to meet her.

"That must be Sorren and Vennia behind her," concluded Trisanna.

Bella and Marigold met and embraced, then walked arm in arm back toward the others. The two groups had joined before many minutes passed.

"It's so good to see you again," enthused Vennia.

"None of you appear to be mad," said Sorren with a wink. He smiled at Trisanna. "That must mean you mastered the amulet. I'm not sensing it, though. What's become of it?"

"And what happened there?" asked Vennia, pointing at the cloud of dust still hanging over the remains of the library.

Before any of them could attempt an answer, Marigold pointed at Agalar. "This isn't your friend! I mean the one who was captured by the Tantellans. Where is he?"

Dalthinir opened his mouth to answer, but he couldn't find the words. He snapped it shut again.

"I can see that all of you are greatly troubled," said Vennia. "Our questions can wait until later. Let's find somewhere to rest and eat. We brought enough food for everyone."

"And please don't concern yourself about your sanity," added Sorren. "My talisman will protect us all. I have already done what's necessary."

Marigold headed off with the twins to find somewhere suitable for the whole party to rest.

"We've never visited Ettaran before," explained Sorren. "We lost our son because of his determination to see the place, and it has soured us on the idea of ever coming here. But Marigold insisted we come. She had a feeling we might be needed."

"She was right," Dalthinir murmured. He waved a hand toward the remains of the library. "If anything is left of the amulet, it's buried somewhere in there. It can't help us now. Things would not have ended well for us if you hadn't come."

The two of them stood together staring at the ruins.

"I've heard that the library was magnificent," ventured Sorren.

"It was." Feeling his throat tightening, he said no more.

Sensing his reaction, Sorren didn't push for further information.

Vennia called, drawing their attention away. "Here come the young ones!"

"We've found somewhere we think might be suitable," said Marigold brightly. "It's a bit further along the road. We should be able to spend the night there."

She led the party to a medium-sized building that featured a large common area with armchairs scattered about. A table stood off to one side with a dozen chairs pulled up to it. Beyond the common room, a similar number of small bedrooms ran off a central corridor.

After each of them had chosen a bedroom, they sat around the table.

Dalthinir faced Agalar. "I'm willing to release you, provided you promise not to harm us in any way."

"You have my word," Agalar returned gruffly.

"Very well, then. Be aware that there's nowhere for you to go out there. If you decide to run, we won't chase you. It will be on your own head."

Agalar glared back at him as the shield that had been constraining him disappeared. "No one should have to endure that."

Dalthinir scowled at him angrily. "You dare to complain after what you did to Kylen? That magical noose was barbaric!"

Agalar quickly subsided.

Recognizing he needed to calm down, Dalthinir remained silent for a couple of minutes. When he had recovered himself, he added, "You'd better understand that I intend to restrain you again as soon as we get closer to the border. I'm planning to turn you over to the Peritonian mages. I imagine they'll send you home to give an account to the authorities in Tantel."

Agalar was wise enough to say nothing.

"And in case you're wondering, I'm well aware that you have mage taste ability," Dalthinir told him. "If you imagine you can hide by making yourself invisible, you'd better think again. You won't be able to conceal your glimmer from me. Visible or not, I'll know where you are."

Trisanna hadn't spoken a word for some time. Even the twins were uncharacteristically silent. Dalthinir needed no explanation.

"Where are the other Tantellans?" asked Vennia.

With no answer forthcoming, Agalar apparently decided it was time he had his say.

"You're all miserable about losing one person." Seeing their reaction, he hastily added, "I'm not speaking ill of the departed! I became acquainted with your friend myself. We were the only two sane people in the whole Tantellan group. He was a decent kid, and I regret what I did to him. I truly do! Coming to Methesia changed all of us, me as much as anyone. I'll never treat another person that way again as long as I live, whatever the circumstances. And no matter what I'm ordered to do."

His eyes grew red as he glared at them. "I'm sorry he's gone too. But he isn't the only one who's been lost! I've known Pernilla and the others for years. Good or bad, they were my friends. Now they're dead —every one of them! It isn't pretty watching your friends go insane. You'd better hope you never have to do it." He buried his head in his hands.

Dalthinir sighed. "Every one of us has been diminished by what happened." He turned to Sorren, Vennia, and Marigold. "Thank you again for coming. We are deeply in your debt."

Sorren nodded. "As we've already said, you can thank Marigold."

All of them thanked her sincerely.

"It's because of a dream," she told them. "I saw a street with buildings, except there was a big building with a dome on top and tall towers on each side."

"That was the library!" exclaimed Bella.

"You were all there, and you were calling my name, pleading for me to help."

Dalthinir and the others looked at each other, speechless. Finally Dalthinir said, "It would seem that your arrival, and even the timing of it, is no accident. Providence has been at work once more."

"What has been happening?" asked Marigold.

Trisanna finally found her voice. "I should answer this question. I suspect I was privy to information none of the rest of you had. You deserve to know it too."

Every face turned intently toward her, Agalar no less so than the others.

"I'd better start at the end. The reason for all of this horror and destruction was the orb located in the observatory at the top of the library building."

"Do you know what it was?" asked Dalthinir.

She nodded. "Pernilla told us that a vast amount of magic had been trapped within it during the Great Desolation. That much was true. She demanded I hand over the amulet, because she needed it to free the magic trapped by the orb. She claimed that the magic had to be released to restore the world to normal. I think she believed it, too. She thought she had been chosen to do a great act that would bring her undying renown from a grateful world. I know what she was told because a voice whispered the same thing to me. At first I thought the amulet had a voice, even though I knew it was just an inanimate object. Later I realized that some other being was speaking through the amulet, in an attempt to influence me. I'm sure the same being was influencing Pernilla too, perhaps through her dragon talisman. I don't know what this being is, but it is extremely powerful. Without Kylen's help at the end, I might not have prevented the orb from being destroyed by the amulet, even though I didn't actually want that."

"What do you believe would have happened if it had been destroyed?" asked Vennia.

"There was another voice as well. I heard it more than once in my dreams. It said that a portion of the dark magic released during the Great Desolation had been trapped inside the orb before the destruction could be completed. It claimed that if the magic was released, life as we know it would end. The entire world would become like Ettaran —lifeless and empty."

Sorren gazed at her thoughtfully. "How did you decide which voice was speaking the truth?"

"For a long time I wasn't certain. But I came to see that the voice speaking through the amulet lusted after destruction. It longed for conflict. It wanted to destroy the orb, but it also wanted me to tear Pernilla apart, along with all of the Tantellan mages. It made sure the amulet offered me many ways of doing it, every one of them equally terrible. Even before I activated the amulet, I sensed it wanted me to destroy some bullies who were persecuting a boy with clubfoot. After a while I came to refer to that voice as the 'Destroyer'. The other voice —the one that warned about what would happen if the orb was destroyed—seemed more interested in preserving than destroying. So I called it the 'Preserver.'"

A flash of insight came to Dalthinir. "The voice you heard earlier, when the dragon flew over us. Was it one of the voices?"

She gave him a lopsided smile. "You don't miss much, Dalthinir. Yes, you're right. The dragon we saw spoke with the voice of the Preserver."

"So you have mage hearing ability," said Vennia.

"Yes, it seems I do," she agreed.

"I have the ability as well," said Vennia with a smile. "It's a wonderful gift, especially when it allows you to communicate directly with dragons." She caught Sorren's eye. "It seems the dragons have been very much involved in all of this."

"Apparently so," he agreed.

Dalthinir was shocked. "You speak as if you have seen and communicated with dragons."

"Of course. What mage hasn't?"

"Dragons haven't been seen in Periton for generations," Dalthinir exclaimed. His head was spinning. He would have a lot of questions for Sorren and Vennia when the moment was right.

As he said it, the great gold dragon of his visions came to mind. They were just visions, though. They weren't real. Were they?

"Everyone believes dragons are extinct," he concluded self-consciously.

"The same can be said for Tantel," confirmed Agalar. Trisanna nodded agreement.

"It seems we are quite unusual, my dear," Sorren told his wife.

She shot him a wry smile. "In more ways than one, I imagine." Then she returned her attention to Trisanna. "Please continue with your account!"

Trisanna outlined the events that led them to the observatory, and what happened after they arrived. She left no doubt about the significance of Kylen's role, but she became too emotional to continue when speaking of his final moments.

After she had recovered herself, she continued. "There's no need to go into every detail. It's enough to say that everything revolved around the orb in the observatory. It was a huge transparent ball, filled with wildly spinning fingers of light. It excited Pernilla enormously."

"Did she have mage hearing?" asked Sorren.

Agalar shook his head. "None of our team did."

"But she had a dragon talisman, and she activated it," said Vennia.

"That should have allowed her to protect at least some of her team from going mad," observed Sorren.

"She didn't protect the whole team," said Agalar. "Just her and me. And Kylen."

Dalthinir shook his head. "She wasn't the one who protected Kylen. Trisanna used the amulet to do that."

The face of Agalar darkened as he glared at Trisanna. "So you could have protected our team as well. You chose to let them go mad instead."

Seeing her mouth beginning to open, he sighed. "Don't bother saying anything. Pernilla saw what was happening, and she did nothing to help them. She could have sent them back across the border, but she didn't seem to care about them. Why should you have saved any of us? We were sent here to kill you. And to take the amulet by force." He shot a glance at Dalthinir. "Don't expect me to be this frank with the Peritonians."

Sorren deftly changed the subject. "Dragons have other ways of communicating apart from mage hearing. They sometimes use dreams and visions."

Agalar nodded. "Pernilla was having plenty of those. So were the others—the ones who went mad. I had one myself, toward the end. It showed Pernilla doing something momentous and wonderful. The dream convinced me I needed to be part of it." His eyes scanned the faces around the table. "How can you be certain my vision wasn't true?"

"We know something of the creature Trisanna refers to as the Destroyer," Vennia replied. "It is a dragon, one that is ancient and very evil. It cares about one thing only—annihilating the human race. It was imprisoned long ago, so now it enlists humans to do its work for it."

Agalar stared at her skeptically. "You're saying it gets humans to work toward their own destruction?"

"It seems ironic, doesn't it? The creature is very sparing with the truth, of course. It presents itself as appealing to the nobler instincts of its victims. All the while it plays to their vanity and greed. It very nearly succeeded in its purpose during the Great Desolation."

"What will it do now?" asked Trisanna.

"It won't give up, if that's what you're wondering," replied Sorren. "It seems from what you've said that the Amulet of Zinth was crucial to destroying the orb and releasing the magic trapped within it. The orb is now buried under a mountain of rubble, and I can no longer detect any sign of the amulet. Or of the other dragon talisman held by the Tantellan leader for that matter. I can only conclude that they were destroyed along with the library. The creature will need to find another way."

"I found a book in the library," Dalthinir told them. "It claimed that dragon talismans could only be destroyed by a dragon. We saw the dragon directing flame into the ruins before it left. It must have been destroying the amulet."

"That makes sense," agreed Trisanna. "It would explain why Sorren can't detect it anymore."

"Perhaps the dragon destroyed the lesser talisman as well," Sorren added.

Trisanna shook her head. "Pernilla stumbled into the beam of power created by the two talismans. It was horrible. There was no trace of her talisman from that moment. It apparently perished with her."

"Then a dragon wasn't involved," mused Sorren. "Although what happened might have amounted to the same thing."

All of them fell silent.

Eventually Vennia spoke again. "I'm confident your instincts were right about the dragon you know as the Preserver. I'm glad to say that such creatures are not unique among dragonkind. I can't tell you exactly which dragon it was. Dragons seem to develop an affinity with particular humans. Did your Kylen have mage hearing ability?"

"He did," confirmed Dalthinir.

"Then from what you've said, this dragon was almost certainly in direct communication with him. Most likely it warned him about Pernilla and tasked him with preventing her from destroying the orb."

"Why couldn't it have just stopped her itself?" asked Trisanna.

Sorren and Vennia exchanged knowing glances before Vennia replied. "Your Preserver would tell you that dragons are not permitted to interfere with humans."

Seeing the puzzled looks on their faces, she continued. "The prohibition is apparently real, although any reasonable human would see the actions of the Destroyer as a clear case of interference. Arguably the Preserver was also interfering if it enlisted Kylen's help. Dragons don't think like us, though. They have their own ways of interpreting what they are—and are not—permitted to do under the prohibition. It doesn't always make sense to us. And the Destroyer was never above violating the prohibition anyway. That seems to be the reason it was imprisoned."

At that moment the conversation was interrupted by a loud yawn from Jonno. Everyone laughed.

Recognizing the laughter as a release of tension, Dalthinir decided they all needed a break from the relentless intensity they had been subjected to.

"It seems to be getting dark outside," he told them. "I don't doubt we could all benefit from a good night's sleep."

CHAPTER 33

Utterly weary in body, mind, and spirit, Trisanna fell at once into deep slumber. Dalthinir might have been hoping for a good night's sleep, but for her there was nothing good about it. Even without the toehold presented by the amulet, the Destroyer managed to invade her dreams.

A dark and desolate location provided the backdrop to its tirade. "You might have known glory and immortal honor. But you chose death and destruction instead," it hissed. "Now your pitiful life—the little that remains of it—will be known for nothing else!"

Then a scream of agony and terror filled her senses. The voice reminded her of Kylen. "You did this!" roared the Destroyer. "You left him to die!"

The screaming went on and on, leaving her distraught and quivering.

Just when she began to think she might lose her sanity, the dream seemed to shudder, the blackness replaced by the face of a dragon and the sound of a familiar voice. "Pay no heed to the creature you know as the Destroyer. It has no power to harm you, in spite of what it says."

The words were undoubtedly intended to be comforting. But the dragon was standing in a dimly lit cave, and behind it Trisanna caught a faint glimpse of a slab with a body stretched out on it. It reminded her of Kylen.

She woke panting to find her bedclothes soaked with perspiration. Eventually she lay down once more. The lonely hours of the morning slipped slowly away as she remained there sleepless.

Many of the others emerged from their rooms subdued. After a quick look at her, Dalthinir asked, "Were you troubled by a dream?"

She nodded miserably. "And you?"

He nodded as well. When she raised her eyebrows inquiringly, he added, "I will not speak of it."

After they had broken their fast, Jonno ventured, "I'm more than ready to leave this place."

Bella chimed in immediately. "I never want to hear the word 'Ettaran' again!"

Their remarks were greeted with an overwhelming chorus of assent.

The party left without delay.

The return journey proved to be a frustrating experience for Trisanna and her companions.

Not surprisingly, the closer they came to the border, the more moody Agalar became. He kept apart from the others as much as he could, which suited everyone, not least because he had taken to mumbling to himself almost continuously.

Dalthinir seemed to have withdrawn into himself. He had always been the leader of their little party. Now, he showed no interest in leading anyone.

Trisanna was at a complete loss about her own future. She had developed great affection for Dalthinir and the twins, but the prospect of spending the rest of her life as a fugitive seemed impossibly bleak. From the time she fled Tantel, every experience had left a new set of scars. Never more so than in Ettaran. Above all else, she needed an opportunity to heal.

She could at least look forward to a future free of the amulet and its pernicious influence. That was worth celebrating.

As the days passed, the twins slowly returned to something close to normal. They were not unchanged, though. Their jauntiness and brashness eventually rebounded, but their behavior had mellowed. They seemed to have aged.

Thankfully Sorren and Vennia were fully present and available. Having weathered more than their share of storms and disappointments throughout their lives, they had emerged solid and reliable. It was a relief to be able to lean on them for purpose and direction.

As for Marigold, she was nothing short of a delight. Her childhood might have been bereft of human companionship, yet she seemed to know when to speak and when to remain silent. She quickly became everyone's favorite walking partner.

As Flaxendell drew closer, the seeds of an idea took root in Trisanna's mind. Not knowing what to do with it, she left it alone, allowing it opportunity to either grow strong or wither and die.

When they were one day out from Flaxendell, the old Dalthinir briefly reappeared. Knowing he could not leave Agalar's situation to chance, he prepared a plan to hand the Tantellan over to the Peritonian authorities. The process would not be straightforward. He had no desire to alert the world to the existence of Sorren and Vennia and their little community, and he could not risk exposing either himself or Trisanna to capture. He made his plans accordingly.

Passing through Flaxendell, Dalthinir led Trisanna and the twins toward the border, with Agalar in tow. The Tantellan was once more constrained by a shield, although less restrictively than before.

As they approached the border, Dalthinir detected faint signs of glimmer. There was something unusual about it, and it took him a while to put his finger on it. He eventually guessed that the Peritonians must have constructed their own version of the Tantellan garment that masked a mage's magical aura. The end result wasn't entirely able to fool him, and it wouldn't have fooled Inga. Kylen would have seen through it even more easily, he added to himself dully.

Being forewarned, he put in place the second phase of his plan. Trisanna made both Dalthinir and herself invisible while he masked their glimmer. Then the party continued on its way. The twins led Agalar forward with a rope tied around his waist. Dalthinir's shield remained in place, although he was masking the power used to maintain it, along with Trisanna's illusion.

After thirty minutes the party of three was challenged. Guards emerged, ordering them to stay where they were while mages were fetched. They hadn't been waiting long when Master Kothlar himself appeared.

"I recognize you!" he cried when he spotted Agalar. "You're one of the Tantellan mages—the one who put a magical noose around the renegade, Kylen!"

Agalar winced, but didn't speak.

"We were instructed to give you this," announced Jonno, handing Kothlar a parchment. The document contained the following brief message.

To Chief Master Adrastas or his representative,

I am hereby returning to you Master Agalar, the last surviving member of the mage delegation sent by Tantel. The Tantellans penetrated deep into Methesia pursuing Trisanna. They were also eager to seize a certain talisman she was carrying. I regret to say that all of them lost both their minds and their lives as a result. The only two unaffected were Master Pernilla and Master Agalar.

Master Pernilla attempted an action that would have caused the destruction of the entire world had she succeeded. It need hardly be said that she failed. Her attempt resulted in two deaths, one of them being her own. It grieves me to say that the other casualty was our friend and companion, Kylen, who lost his life preventing this act of destruction. Trisanna's talisman was destroyed in the process.

It is important to convey to you that Master Pernilla's actions could not have been anticipated by the authorities in Antilin. You therefore have no reason to suppose that her conduct was sanctioned by them. Master Agalar is also inno-

cent of any role in these matters. I am content to leave it to him to explain the details of what happened. Be aware that he has mage taste ability, so it might take more than a usual amount of effort to keep him in custody.

With regret,

Dalthinir

A GALAR WAS aware of the content of Dalthinir's document, and he seemed reconciled to it. Trisanna could only wonder what he would tell both the Peritonian and Tantellan authorities. She did not envy him.

The twins waited until Master Kothlar had scanned the document, then they bowed.

"We have carried out our instructions. We will now bid you farewell," said Jonno.

"Not so fast!" cried Kothlar. "You will be accompanying us to Cambrick. There will be many questions you will need to answer."

"We thank you for your most gracious invitation," Bella replied with a second bow. "Sadly, we must decline."

With that, the twins disappeared.

"Where did they go?" demanded Kothlar.

"There's no smell of power, so it can't be an illusion," responded one of his companions.

"This is the work of Dalthinir," growled Kothlar.

People began milling around, groping about fruitlessly for the missing twins. Through it all, Kothlar had enough presence of mind to keep a firm grip on Agalar.

"It's about time we rejoined Sorren and Vennia," said Dalthinir.

"Don't you want to stay and watch the excitement?" asked Jonno.

"I think I've had enough excitement to last me a lifetime," returned Dalthinir grimly. He turned his face eastward.

• • •

After they were reunited in Flaxendell, Sorren and Vennia led them to a quiet valley not far from the abandoned town. From the moment they entered it, the valley seemed like a paradise—a sharp contrast to the barren emptiness of the town. With its lush vegetation, the song of birds, and the lowing of cows, it was a haven worth celebrating. The seedling nurtured in Trisanna's mind burst into sudden life. This was the place.

"You are all welcome to stay for as long as you choose," Vennia told them.

As soon as a suitable moment arrived, Trisanna spoke to Sorren, Vennia, and Marigold. "I would like to make this my home, if you are willing."

The older couple smiled warmly. "Of course! We would be delighted to have you."

Marigold was ecstatic. "It will be like having an older sister!"

"You had better speak to Dalthinir," Vennia advised her. "I'm not sure how he'll feel about losing you."

"I suspect he'll be relieved. But I will make it a priority to discuss it with him."

She didn't need to wait long for an opportunity.

"It's good to see you thriving in this place," Dalthinir told her. "You're coming to life again."

"There's a long way to go, but I do feel like I am starting to come alive." She glanced at him tentatively. "I think I will remain here. If you have no objection."

"How could I possibly object?" He smiled sadly. "I know I'm not exactly good company these days."

Stepping forward impulsively, she threw her arms around him. "I will never be able to repay your kindness, Dalthinir! You've been my rock—from the moment I met you."

She paused, drawing back and gazing up at him candidly. "You need a break from heavy burdens. You've been strong for everyone else for far too long. It's time for you to let others care for you. Why don't you stay here with us—at least for a while?"

"I'm sure I would benefit from it," he replied. "I'll certainly stay for a week or two. Not for longer, though. I think I'd like to go somewhere out of the way—somewhere I don't have to interact with people too much."

"What about the twins?"

"They will need to make their own choice."

"Of course."

On Dalthinir's final night in the valley, Sorren and Vennia hosted a farewell party.

All of them were feeling the loss of Kylen keenly. For Dalthinir, it was still too raw to discuss. "It's been more than two weeks since Kylen's passing, and I know it's important to grieve his loss," he told them. "I'm not ready, though. Not yet."

Out of consideration for him, the others avoided any reference to the events of the recent past. Earlier days weren't safe either. It was impossible to reminisce without bumping into anecdotes that involved Kylen. They therefore focused on the present and the future.

"What do you think Agalar is doing right now?" asked Trisanna.

Dalthinir snorted. "Probably working out what he's going to say. I left him plenty of scope in my letter. He'll need to explain to the Chief Master and the king of Tantel how he managed to lose an entire group of his fellow mages. That will be hard enough. Accounting for how he alone emerged unscathed will be even more difficult."

"I feel a little sorry for him," Vennia told them.

"That's because you didn't see what he did to Kylen," said Trisanna.

And there it was. In spite of every attempt to avoid it, they had stumbled onto the taboo topic.

Sorren quickly changed the subject. Turning to the twins, he asked, "Have you come to a decision about your future?"

"The future sounds like an awfully long time," Bella told him, raising her eyes heavenward and rolling her head.

"There was never any real doubt about what we would do," Jonno added. "Someone has to look after old Dalthinir."

Dalthinir screwed up his face. "They've always been trouble, but I imagine I'll somehow find a way to put up with them." In spite of his words, he didn't look at all unhappy about the prospect of traveling with the twins again.

"You've been very kind to us. I'm grateful for your generous hospitality," he continued. "And I know you'll take good care of Trisanna."

"It will be our pleasure," Vennia told him. "I hope the three of you know you'll always be welcome here—whatever happens."

After thanking her sincerely they retired for the night.

The travelers assembled at dawn, laden down with supplies to last for a couple of weeks if they were careful. Trisanna hugged each of them in turn, tears running unashamedly down her face. "I don't know how to thank you all!" she breathed. "I can't imagine what I would have done without you."

And then they were gone, heading west, chased by the rising sun.

"WHERE ARE WE GOING?" asked Dalthinir moodily. They had been wandering for several days—aimlessly as far as he was concerned. But he had the feeling that the twins might have something a bit more definite in mind.

"Mostly south," Jonno told him. "Away from Cambrick and its friendly mages."

Returning a grunt, he put his head down and continued to plod forward. He was more than content to let someone else lead.

It hadn't escaped him that the twins could easily have stayed with Trisanna, or even gone off on their own. He had seen plenty of evidence of the welcome they received whenever they visited a farm. And he was well aware that in the days since leaving Ettaran he could lay no claim to being an agreeable traveling companion. Their decision to travel with him had encouraged him enormously, even if he'd said little about it.

WITH UNLIMITED TIME TO REFLECT, Dalthinir had been carefully re-examining everything that had taken place from the moment they rescued Trisanna in Sengin to the destruction of the library in Ettaran. Many times he had returned to Kylen's perplexing comments about a dragon. Could a dragon truly have been responsible for his magical awakening? It was difficult to make sense of it all.

It was clear that dragons had communicated directly with both Kylen and Trisanna, undoubtedly aided by the fact that they had mage hearing ability. He himself had been bypassed.

It didn't bother him. Many years previously he had been accused of envy because he didn't have mage hearing. It was no more true now than it had been then.

He recognized that his role had been peripheral in other respects too. He had not anticipated the looming crisis involving the orb. How could he? The consequences had been dire. He'd been so busy drawing the Tantellans deeper into Methesia that he failed to see he was doing exactly what Pernilla wanted.

With the wisdom of hindsight, they should have done everything in their power to keep the amulet far from Ettaran and the orb. Such a task would not have been straightforward. Not with the Tantellans constantly hounding them. He hadn't attempted it because he hadn't known what was at stake.

In retrospect, there had been a certain inevitability about the amulet finding its way to the orb.

He had at least played a part in keeping Trisanna safe. That in turn had prevented Pernilla from getting her hands on the amulet. Beyond that, he freely acknowledged that his contribution to the final outcome had been minor.

It hadn't mattered. Thanks to Kylen, Trisanna, and a dragon, the orb had been preserved and the amulet destroyed.

One issue remained unresolved and unresolvable: Kylen was dead.

Dalthinir couldn't shake free of his guilt. His mind told him he was not responsible for what had happened. But the rest of him wouldn't listen. Blaming himself had become a daily ritual—a cycle he couldn't break.

He expected he would get over it in time, but he wasn't willing to let himself off easily. Life had become miserable for him as a result, and he had become miserable company.

Fortunately for him the twins were doing much more than taking the lead. They were trapping food, locating campsites, and building fires. He would have been lost without them.

DALTHINIR'S SUSPICIONS about the direction the twins were taking began to solidify as the days went by. Eventually he confronted his companions.

"We're heading for Sengin!" he told them bluntly.

"You finally noticed," said Bella with a grin.

"Why Sengin?" he demanded.

"We wanted to examine the town lockup more closely," Jonno replied. "We only saw it from the outside last time."

He frowned at them. "Tell me this isn't about Inga."

"This isn't about Inga," they said in perfect unison, chortling in satisfaction at the achievement.

"I didn't ask you to take me to Inga!" he protested fiercely.

Jonno shook his head sadly. "Dalthinir, Dalthinir. Why does everything always have to be about you?"

The mage scowled back at him.

"Bella has wanted to see Inga for a very long time. As you know, I was not especially supportive of the relationship in the early days. But I have since abandoned my grumpy ways."

He turned to Bella. "Others could learn from my approach, don't you think?"

"Certainly!" she added solemnly. "No one we know, of course."

"Definitely not. I was speaking in general terms."

The two of them burst out laughing, which made him even more irritable.

Bella eventually calmed down enough to say, "We'll probably discover that Inga is long gone. She might have decided her future lies with the Compact in Cambrick."

"Even if she is still there," added Jonno, "there's no need for you to see her. In fact I'm not honestly convinced that seeing you would do anything to brighten her day."

He followed up his statement with a wink, but it didn't help Dalthinir's mood. Turning away, the mage stomped off to find some solitude.

When he later rejoined them, he made no reference to the earlier conversation. Thankfully they didn't either.

If Bella wanted to see Inga, he certainly wasn't going to stand in her way. And it was true that Inga wouldn't want to see him. Not in the mood he was in. Maybe not ever.

Nevertheless, as Sengin drew closer, it was increasingly difficult not to think about her. Deep down he wanted to see her very much, but he had no intention of acknowledging that to the twins. It was enough of a struggle to honestly admit it to himself. It wasn't at all difficult to convince himself he didn't deserve it.

Before long he was able to detect Inga's glimmer. He confirmed to the twins she was still at her aunt's house some distance from Sengin. After going to great lengths to skirt around the town, they approached the house from the seaward side.

Bella was becoming visibly eager. The moment they were close enough, she left the others and hurried toward the house.

"Don't worry, Dalthinir," said Jonno brightly. "You still have me to keep you company."

Glaring back at him, Dalthinir bit his tongue. With nothing better to do, he sought out a comfortable place to sit and settled down to wait for Bella's return.

CHAPTER 34

A soft knock on the back door of the house pulled Inga away from her long anticipated cup of tea. Upon opening the door she squealed with surprise and delight.

"Bella!" she cried, enfolding the girl in a warm embrace.

Then she stood back anxiously, holding the visitor at arm's length. "Is there a problem?"

"I suppose there is," Bella acknowledged seriously, brushing at the happy tears trickling down her face.

"My aunt is staying with her sister on a farm some distance from here, so I'm alone," Inga told her. "Come in. I want to hear all about it."

The afternoon wore away as Bella recounted everything that had happened since they left Sengin with Trisanna. Inga's eyes grew ever wider as she heard of the journey into Methesia, the pursuit by the Tantellans, the discovery of the orb, and the final confrontation in the observatory.

Bella described Kylen's bravery in holding up the dome while Dalthinir helped Trisanna to safety, and the price he paid as a result. Finally, she told of their rescue by the Methesian mages and the brief stay in their secluded valley. She concluded by passing on whatever she had learned about the Amulet of Zinth, the orb, and the role of the dragons.

When she eventually finished, Inga could only shake her head with wonder. "That is an astonishing story. It seems that every one of us has had another narrow escape. And not only do dragons live on, they still involve themselves in human affairs—for better and for worse." She lowered her eyes. "The loss of Kylen is especially grievous."

The fire in the oven was going out, and she paused long enough to throw in more wood. "I took a big risk when I chose not to hand Trisanna over to the authorities. As far as I'm concerned, my decision has been thoroughly vindicated. Once more the task of saving us all from ruin has fallen to a group of renegades. And once more they will receive neither honor nor thanks for their sacrifices on our behalf, even though it has come at enormous cost to themselves."

She returned her full attention to Bella. "So Trisanna has remained with the mages in their hidden valley. Are Jonno and Dalthinir here with you?"

Bella nodded. Inga's heart skipped a beat at the prospect of seeing Dalthinir again. "Then it's time we went to see them," she said solemnly.

"Before you go," Bella replied tentatively, "there's something you need to know about Dalthinir."

Inga stopped cold, her eyebrows rising inquiringly.

After hesitating for a moment, Bella threw up her hands in frustration. "There's no point slathering honey over it. He's been impossible! He blames himself for Kylen's death, even though all of us have told him time and time again it isn't his fault. He's been acting like a bear with a thorn in its paw!"

Inga rolled her eyes. Dalthinir was an intelligent man. Except when it came to dealing with emotions.

"I see," she said quietly. "Thank you, Bella. I appreciate the warning. Let's go find Jonno and your injured bear."

INGA FOLLOWED Bella toward the sea, coming to a halt in a hollow nestled among the sand dunes. Both Jonno and Dalthinir jumped up when they saw her arrive.

She greeted Jonno first.

"Hello, Inga, This time I truly am happy to see you," he replied a little shamefacedly.

Next she greeted Dalthinir.

Although he made an attempt to return her greeting, words seemed to desert him. He barely managed more than a grunt.

She gave them a little bow. "I understand your lives have been eventful since you were last here. It seems that along with the entire world, I owe you a huge debt of gratitude."

Jonno dipped his head in return. Dalthinir didn't seem to know what to do.

"Please come with me. There's no one else staying at my aunt's house right now, and we won't be disturbed."

They set off, Bella walking alongside her and chatting eagerly, the others trailing behind.

When they arrived she served them hot tea and bread fresh from the oven that morning. With a cheeky wink at Bella, she slathered honey on Dalthinir's bread before serving it. Then she asked questions, gently drawing them out on matters both minor and significant until they began to relax.

An hour had passed when Jonno said abruptly, "There's bound to be work that needs doing around this place."

Both of the twins jumped up and disappeared outside before Inga or Dalthinir could say a word.

After a silence that was quickly becoming uncomfortable, Dalthinir waved a hand vaguely around the room. "You seem happy here, Inga."

She found his comment bewildering. Was he being ironic or just making conversation? He couldn't be that lacking in perception, could he? She stared at him quizzically for long enough that he started to become restless.

His lack of awareness decided her. There were things that had never been said between them, and another opportunity might not arise. "I knew a man once," she said evenly. "He was convinced he needed to save the world, and he was willing to throw away every-thing—his reputation, his future, maybe even his life—to do what he believed was right." Her brows drew together. "To the astonishment of everyone, myself included, it turned out he was right all along! He *was* the only one who fully understood what was at stake, and he *did* actually manage to save the world."

He was looking more uncomfortable than ever. Now she'd started, though, she intended to finish. "There were, of course, other conse-quences when he disappeared into nowhere. I've often wondered whether breaking my heart featured in his thinking at all. Did he simply see it as the price both of us had to pay? Or was he so engrossed in his own view of the world that the impact of his choices on other people didn't even register with him?"

Dalthinir was wincing, but she had no intention of sparing him. She peered at him unflinchingly.

"What do you think, Dalthinir? Do you have an opinion on the matter?"

He found nothing to say.

"I didn't see or hear from this particular person for ten long years. Curiously, I later learned that for two of those years he wasn't far from me in Cambrick. But not a word, not even a letter." She shrugged again. "He might have been dead for all I knew. I might never have seen him again if I hadn't happened to be on hand the first time he was saving the world."

Dalthinir's face had begun to glow bright red.

"Now he's suddenly appeared at my door. I can only wonder why."

At that moment Jonno and Bella burst in, both of them talking at once.

She'd said what she needed to say, and it had felt good to get it out. It had also been painful for Dalthinir, and the time had come to let go of her hurt and disappointment.

Although she hadn't been easy on him, she wasn't nearly as unsympathetic as he probably thought. Dalthinir wouldn't have been able to stop Lars and Petria if it weren't for his willingness to turn aside from everything except his duty.

It was true he was susceptible to becoming engrossed in his own view of the world. It was both his greatest strength and his greatest weakness. And it was almost certainly a prime contributor to his sometimes remarkable cluelessness when it came to emotions.

He had appeared at her door at a time when his emotional disconnection was causing him considerable distress. Perhaps she could help him. She was more than willing to make an attempt.

As soon as the time was right. Turning to the twins with a smile, she steered the subject in a different direction.

DALTHINIR WANTED nothing more than to leave. He should never have come to this place.

"We mustn't intrude on Inga's hospitality any longer," he said, the moment an opportunity arose.

"Are you serious?" asked Jonno.

"I'm not going anywhere!" Bella told him. "I've been offered the chance to sleep in a real bed tonight!"

Inga was watching him appraisingly. Realizing that any insistence on his part would only make matters worse, he quickly backed down. They could leave first thing in the morning.

THE EVENING DRAGGED SLOWLY AWAY. It felt like an eternity before Dalthinir could reasonably excuse himself and retire for the night.

His bed was more than comfortable, but he couldn't sleep. Inga's words repeated endlessly in his mind. Everything she had said was true. She had every reason to be upset with him. He'd told himself it was safer for both of them if he avoided contact, and maybe he'd been right. But then, after ten long years, they'd met on the mountain, and she'd tended his injuries. It had felt as if nothing had ever changed between them. But once they parted, he'd behaved no differently from before. He'd continued to rigidly maintain his distance and his silence.

Not long ago he'd come to Sengin, knowing she was there. Bella had spent time with her. He hadn't even sent a message. Then, fully absorbed with his mission to rescue Trisanna from the lockup, he'd left without making the tiniest effort to communicate with her.

From the moment he became a renegade he'd behaved abominably. There was no other way to describe it. And yet to his complete amazement, she had never stopped thinking about him over the years they'd been apart. Not only had she confessed he'd broken her heart when he left the Compact, she'd made it clear she would have welcomed ongoing contact. It was both astonishing and excruciating at the same time.

He didn't dare derive any hope from it. He'd bungled the relationship far too badly for that.

How could he face her again?

After the sun rose he left it longer than was comfortable before getting up. It didn't help, because when he emerged the twins were nowhere to be seen.

Inga was boiling a kettle. "Jonno and Bella were up with the dawn," she said over her shoulder. "They've eaten already. They're out working on the property."

He sat silently at the kitchen table, wishing he were anywhere but alone with Inga.

After filling a plate with freshly cooked eggs and toast, she placed it in front of him. Then she poured a hot cup of tea for both of them and sat down opposite him. "You had almost nothing to say last night, Dalthinir," she observed. "Perhaps I shouldn't have spoken my mind so freely. It's been brewing for a very long time, though, and I must admit it was a relief to get it out."

He groaned inside. By directly raising the subject she'd left him no way to maintain a polite silence. He reluctantly acknowledged it was for the best. It was only right to at least try to make amends.

"I deserved it," he managed. "I owe you an apology, Inga. I convinced myself it wasn't safe to communicate with you. It didn't take long before I persuaded myself you wouldn't welcome it anyway. I never had a valid reason for not trying, though."

She nodded an acknowledgment. "Thank you for saying that. I hope you understand I wasn't setting out to add to your misery."

He didn't reply.

Her voice grew gentle. "The loss of Kylen has clearly been devastating for you, Dalthinir. It's distressing to see the state you're in. You haven't been able to find a way through it, have you?"

She'd switched completely—from anger to sensitivity. He shouldn't have been surprised.

Stealing a glance at her, he momentarily caught her eyes. His alarm began to rise. Perhaps he could have kept her at arm's length if she'd stayed angry with him, but he wasn't sure he had the resources to cope with her empathy.

He pushed himself to his feet, his food untouched. Almost unconsciously, he began pacing about the kitchen.

She stood up, too, positioning herself directly in front of him. "I'm sure you know you need to grieve. I think you're here because you need help to do it. Maybe coming here wasn't entirely your idea, but however it came about, you've found your way to a person who knows you and cares about you."

Her face turned upward to his. "That's me, Dalthinir—I'm that person. I know you. And I've never stopped caring about you."

Stunned into stillness, he peered into her eyes. The compassion he saw there shook his protective barriers to their foundations. His breath hitched, and before he could prevent it a teardrop escaped his control, rolling down his cheek. Then came a sob, followed by another. Before long his whole body began to heave. Abandoning any attempt to restrain himself, he started to weep, ever more loudly. Soon he was howling his grief to the heavens, his tears flowing in a torrent.

It was more than the loss of Kylen. Dalthinir was giving voice at last to the helpless frustration that had driven him from the Compact. He was venting the wretchedness of a hunted fugitive, under sentence of death for no good reason—bewailing ten lonely years of exile, cut off from the life he had known and torn apart from the woman he loved.

As the anguish poured out, Inga drew close and wrapped her arms around him.

When finally he began to grow calm again, she rested her head on his chest. "It's going to be all right," she whispered. "The difficult part is behind you now. We'll make it through this."

❋

TRISANNA AND SORREN were perched on three-legged stools, milking cows. For Trisanna, it brought back memories of happier times as a child in Tantel.

They had almost finished when Sorren abruptly halted his milking. He was peering into the distance, a wary look on his face. "It appears we're about to have company."

Standing up, Trisanna pushed back her stool and stared in the direction he was pointing. "That looks like the twins! And Inga! And is that Dalthinir with them? I wouldn't have recognized him!"

Calling loudly for Vennia and Marigold, they set off to greet the new arrivals.

AFTER AN EVENING OVERFLOWING with food and merriment, they made themselves comfortable around the fire. Leaning toward Dalthinir, Trisanna whispered, "I'm delighted to see you didn't leave that necklace in Ettaran! It looks every bit as good on Inga as I expected!"

Dalthinir blushed, causing her to laugh merrily. Thankfully for him, everyone's attention was elsewhere.

"I hear you've decided to stay with us, at least for a while!" Sorren told the twins with a delighted smile.

Bella nodded seriously. "It's been far too long since we experienced the joys of mucking out manure."

"Not that we're suggesting it was anything other than delightful to wander the world with Dalthinir," chipped in Jonno.

That drew a laugh from everyone, including Dalthinir.

Vennia turned to Inga and Dalthinir. "And what about you two?"

"We were wondering,..." Dalthinir began tentatively.

"If we would host a wedding celebration?" asked Vennia with a knowing grin.

Both of them smiled through their shyness while everyone else clapped and cheered.

"I've never stopped imagining how Inga would be as a bride," said Dalthinir awkwardly.

"It isn't my fault you've waited so long to find out!" retorted Inga.

"It would be a great delight," Sorren assured them with a laugh. "It will bring back many happy memories."

"And after that?" Vennia asked them.

"I'm not needed in Sengin," Inga replied. "My aunt has her daughter and grandchildren nearby. Her sister also lost her husband recently, and she's planning to leave the farm and move in with my aunt."

"What about the Compact?" asked Jonno.

"They won't miss me. I was never able to contribute to anything practical like agriculture or the guilds. My ability was mostly useful for hunting down renegades." She aimed a grin at Dalthinir. "Thankfully, I wasn't very successful at it."

Trisanna redirected her gaze to Dalthinir. She had never seen him so content, although he had a wistfulness about him. It wasn't surprising. The loss of his apprentice had hit him hard.

"As for me, I've done more than my share of roaming about the kingdom," Dalthinir was saying. "Both of us are looking forward to the opportunity to settle down for a while. Here, if you're willing to have us."

"We'd be delighted!" said Sorren and Vennia in unison.

"We'll be a real community again," enthused Marigold.

"You're not going to miss saving the world?" teased Inga.

Dalthinir snorted. "As far as I'm concerned, it can save itself from now on."

EPILOGUE

A mage burst in on Master Kothlar, alarm on his face. "The prisoner! He's disappeared!"

Kothlar raised his eyes heavenward. "We haven't even delivered Agalar to Cambrick and we've lost him? You were warned about his mage taste ability."

"No one told us he has mage touch abilities as well! He punched a hole in his prison wall, and used it to escape."

"We'll catch him before long. He won't be able to hide his glimmer from Pellistri."

"Yes he will!"

"What are you talking about?"

"He stole one of our new glimmer-masking garments."

"How did he even know they existed?"

"Everyone's been talking about them. He must have overheard us."

Kothlar scowled in irritation. "How am I going to explain this to Chief Master Adrastas and the king? The Tantellan authorities will be furious!"

Quickly recovering himself, he began rapidly barking out orders. "Get some patrols out looking for him! He can't have gone far. And call for the trackers."

"Master Kothlar," the mage called awkwardly.

"Well?"

"He took a horse as well. He'll be far away by now."

Kothlar buried his head in his hands and groaned. It was hard to imagine how the outcome could have been worse. "Find me some parchment. Someone needs to inform the Chief Master there's a new renegade loose in Periton."

CHIEF MASTER KHARKIN knew it was going to be a bad day when he received an immediate summons to attend King Garneth. He arrived to find the king in a foul mood.

"This morning I received an official message from the Chief Master in Periton," spat the king. "He claims that the entire Tantellan delegation of mages has perished, with the exception of Master Agalar."

Kharkin struggled to believe it. He had sent his best mages. "How is that possible?"

"Adrastas claims they traveled all the way to Ettaran."

Kharkin caught his breath, unable to catch himself. Had the king noticed his slip?

Realizing immediately that there had been no reason for alarm, he berated himself for his own folly. The king couldn't know that a charge had been given to Kharkin in a dream to go to Ettaran. Once the amulet was in his hands.

"The capital of Methesia?" he managed. "They would have gone mad if they went there!"

"Adrastas attached a document purportedly written by one of their renegades who claimed to have been directly involved in whatever happened. I don't believe a word of it."

There was ice in the sovereign's voice. "Then a second communication arrived this afternoon. It was sent several days after the last one, but the ship carrying the first message was delayed, with the result that both messages arrived the same day."

Could the news get any worse? "What does the message say?"

"It claims that Agalar escaped custody and went renegade in Periton! What game do the Peritonians think they're playing?" stormed the monarch. "Do they dare to pretend they're not responsible for any of this?"

Kharkin was reeling, but the king hadn't finished.

"I ordered you to deal with my darling half-sister, and your people botched it! Now my agents are telling me she wasn't the only love child spawned by my idiot father. There was a boy as well! Also born to a mage! And can you guess where he was sent for protection as a baby?"

"To Periton?" Kharkin offered, hoping it wasn't true.

"To Periton!" the king roared back.

"These people dare to harbor not one, but two illegitimate pretenders to my throne! And they wipe out an entire group of my best mages! Any one of these outrages amounts to an act of war!" He slammed his fist down on the table beside his chair, sending his goblet crashing to the floor.

The king slowly grew calm and measured. His servants had learned to fear such a mood. "Who can I turn to in my hour of need?" His eyes drilled into his chief master. "Not you, Kharkin! Not my esteemed Chief Master! If I know you, you distracted your team with an agenda of your own. Whether you did or not, you were responsible for them, and they botched the job! Be careful, Kharkin. Be very careful. You are dismissed!"

Tired, irritable, and fearful, Chief Master Kharkin retreated to his tower room to lick his wounds.

The cold seemed to penetrate his bones. He couldn't remember when his joints had ached so much.

Had Pernilla retrieved the amulet? Had she dared to claim it for herself? How had the king come to suspect he had a secret agenda? He would almost certainly never know.

Many hours passed before he managed to sleep. He quickly regretted it, because the moment he slept he dreamed.

ONCE MORE HE found himself in the abandoned city of Ettaran. This time he stood before a pile of rubble. Looking around, he recognized the location. He was facing the remains of the fabled library.

"You have failed," intoned a harsh voice. "The amulet has been lost —without releasing the magic." The voice laughed. "I am already working on ways of retrieving the situation. However, my patience has limits. Consider yourself discarded."

A figure came shuffling into view, then another, and finally a whole group of them. Looking at them intently he recognized the ravaged faces of his team. Last of all he spotted Pernilla, a mad light in her eyes. Moving closer, she stared right through him.

KHARKIN WOKE FEELING MORE desolate than at any time in his life. What would become of him? What would become of Tantel?

AWAY IN A HIDDEN valley near Flaxendell, Trisanna lay down to sleep. She felt more content than she had in a long time. In the dark watches of the night she had a dream.

ONCE MORE SHE found herself gazing at a dragon. It was the Preserver, the creature that had wrested control of her earlier dream away from the Destroyer. This time its face was turned aside.

Once more in the background she saw the slab with a body laid out upon it. Staring intently at it, she felt sure she recognized the figure on the slab. A voice spoke, too quietly for her to make out words. Then to her astonishment the head lolled slowly to one side, offering her a clear view of the face.

It was Kylen. She was certain of it.

He hadn't opened his eyes, although his head had moved. He must be gravely injured, but he wasn't dead. And he wasn't alone. He was being cared for.

The great head of the dragon swung around until the creature was looking directly at her. It regarded her silently, opening its mouth in what might have been a smile.

TRISANNA WOKE WITH A GASP, scarcely able to believe what she had seen. It couldn't have been merely a dream—it must surely have been real. Scrambling out of bed, she fumbled awkwardly in her haste to pull on a robe in the dark.

It was still the middle of the night, but she didn't care. With mounting excitement, she raced off to wake Dalthinir.

The End

The saga continues with

The Weight of Interference
Book 3 of Allan N. Packer's
The Ruptured Kingdom series

LIST OF CHARACTERS

- *Adrastas* - Chief Master (head mage) of the Peritonian Compact
- *Agalar* - Tantellan mage with mage taste (illusion) abilities as well as moderate mage touch abilities
- *Alexis* - Peritonian mage
- *Arbilis* - Methesian mage at the time of the Great Desolation
- *Banadin* - Peritonian mage who died some years previously; a key factor in driving Dalthinir away from the Compact
- *Bella* - twin of Jonno and companion of Dalthinir and Kylen
- *Dalthinir* - renegade Peritonian mage
- *Dibson* - Peritonian mage
- *Durvaryn* - king of Periton; married to Karolin with two children: Firan, a son, and Layla, a daughter
- *Emmela* - Peritonian mage with illusionary magic ability; friend of Inga
- *Ellis* - Peritonian mage
- *Felicia* - cousin of Inga, daughter of Jemilla; lives in the town of Sengin in the southeastern corner of Periton
- *Garneth* - king of Tantel; son of King Nolan
- *Gharvil* - Tantellan mage capable of detecting magical auras

- *Inga* - mage with the Compact's strongest farsense ability; friend of Dalthinir prior to him becoming a renegade
- *Jemilla* - aunt of Master Inga; lives in the town of Sengin in the southeastern corner of Periton
- *Jonno* - twin of Bella and companion of Dalthinir and Kylen
- *Kalmithien* - name given to Kylen by the dragon
- *Kaspra* - Peritonian mage
- *Kharkin* - chief master of Tantellan Compact
- *Kothlar* - Peritonian mage
- *Kylen* - renegade mage and companion of Dalthinir and the twins
- *Lars* - Peritonian mage who has become a renegade
- *Marigold* - granddaughter of Sorren and Vennia
- *Marta* - wife of Grudem and friend of Dalthinir, living in Camberton, the town outside the walls of Cambrick
- *Nolan* - previous king of Tantel; father of Garneth
- *Olatiren* - Kylen's tutor in his early years on the streets.
- *Petria* - Peritonian mage who has become a renegade
- *Pernilla* - Tantellan mage; head of special mage group
- *Pellistri* - Peritonian mage
- *Ramond* - mercenary leader; childhood friend of Adrastas
- *Sorren* - Methesian mage; husband to Vennia
- *Trisanna* - Tantellan mage fleeing her home country
- *Vennia* - Methesian mage; wife to Sorren
- *Zeke* - Tantellan fisherman

NOTE FROM THE AUTHOR

Thank you for reading *The Riven Land*—I hope you enjoyed it. Please consider leaving a review. Reviews make a huge difference to me as well as benefiting other readers.

I also very much appreciate feedback from my readers. I'd love to hear from you—please feel free to send me an email.

The saga of the Ruptured Kingdom continues in *The Weight of Interference (The Ruptured Kingdom Book 3)*. See below for an outline of the book.

To be kept up to date on new releases, sign up to my newsletter mailing list at *www.allanpacker.com*. New subscribers will receive an exclusive bonus novelette—a prequel to *The Hard Edge of Magic*. The novelette, *The Renegade*, provides important background to the wider story, revealing the beginnings of Dalthinir's relationship with Inga and portraying the process that led to him becoming a renegade. The novelette is described below.

A second exclusive bonus novelette is also available to subscribers —a prequel to *The Cost of Knowing* from my first epic fantasy series, *The Stone Cycle*. The novelette, *The Rending*, is a complete story that can be read independently from other books in the series.

Is anything worth being hunted and despised?

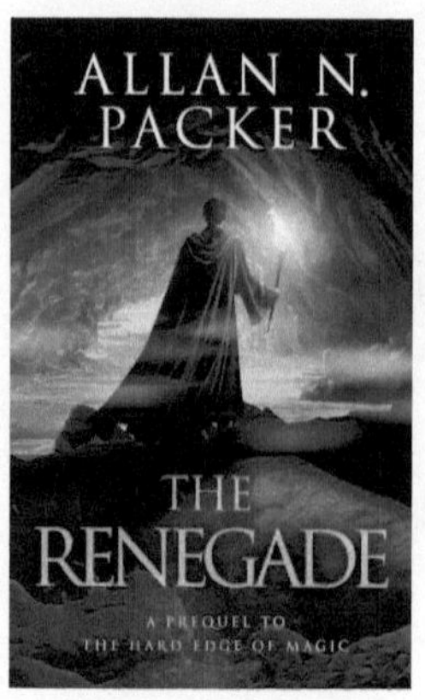

Dalthinir's life quickly unravels when he acts on suspicions about a fellow mage. After desperately using magic to escape an attempt on his life, he finds himself on trial for murder.

But more is at stake than his reputation. In their greed for power, reckless mages are willing to risk a release of magic so powerful it will destroy the kingdom. He alone recognizes the peril.

Prohibited from taking action, Dalthinir must decide what he is prepared to lose for the sake of the kingdom. Can he sacrifice everything he cares about to become a scorned and hunted renegade?

The Renegade is also available in print and audiobook editions at online bookstores.

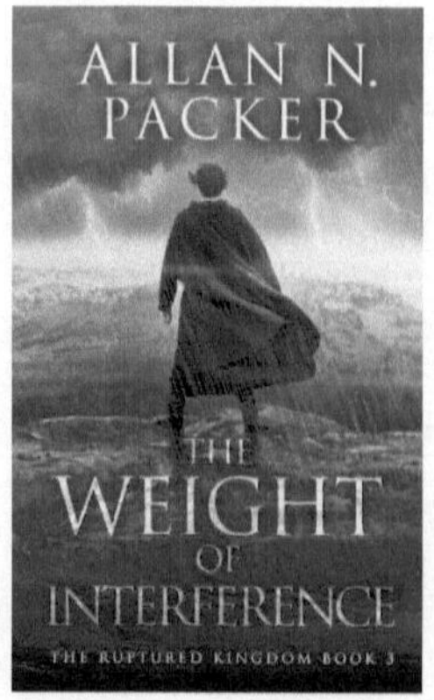

Confusion reigns in both Tantel and Periton as King Garneth of Tantel prepares for war. But a new upheaval looms when foreigners known as the Exiles are unmasked. Settled covertly within easy reach of both kingdoms, their numbers include powerful mages hiding momentous secrets.

Caught up in the turmoil, Dalthinir, Inga, and Trisanna seek answers, not least to Dalthinir's most pressing question: what has become of Kylen?

Underlying it all is a more alarming concern. Have dragons found new ways to interfere with humankind, in defiance of the prohibition?

The Weight of Interference is available in ebook, print, and audiobook editions at online bookstores.

AN OUTLINE OF MAGICAL SENSES

The magical senses are magical analogues of the physical senses of touch, sight, hearing, smell and taste.

Unlike physical senses, where most people possess all five senses, no mage possesses the full range of abilities that correspond to magical senses. Further, different mages possess the same ability in varying strengths. Some mages possess only a single magical sense. Most mages possess a couple of magical senses, although the strength of one sense is almost always greater than the other. A small number of mages possess more than two magical senses.

For any magical sense, the power possessed by a particular mage is typically characterized as strong, medium, or weak, although wide variations are observed within each of those levels. The Compact maintains standards that define the minimum power level for each magical sense. A mage is not recognized as having a magical sense unless they are capable of expressing power that meets or exceeds the minimum standard.

The magical senses can be loosely characterized as follows:
1. *Mage smell*, better known as farsense.

- This ability is most akin to the physical sense of smell.
- Magical power has a unique scent for each mage, and every mage can sense the use of it. Just as animals mark their territories with urine sprays, mages uniquely reveal their presence when giving expression to magical power. (Note that dragons were traditionally regarded as able to mask their use of magic. Dalthinir is also able to mask his expressions of magic).
- An unusual aspect of mage smell (farsense) is that the exercise of it is not detectable by other mages. It may reasonably be asked how a person possessing only mage smell ability (for example, Inga) can be a mage if they never exercise magical power in any detectable way. The answer is that the ability to discern the use of magical power in others is by definition what makes a person a mage.
- A more focused kind of farsense allows a mage to sense the unique magical aura, also known as glimmer, that belongs to every mage (including mages who possess only mage smell ability). The distance over which glimmer is detectable depends on the strength of the mage's ability. (Note that dragons were traditionally regarded as able to mask their magical aura. Dalthinir is also able to mask/hide his magical aura.)
- A mage with the ability to detect glimmer may also be able to sense the presence of nearby non-magical creatures, including humans. The most adept practitioners can also sense the mood and intent of a creature they detect (whether the creature is hostile, for example). This ability is extremely rare.
- Mages with no magical sense apart from mage smell are rare.

2. *Mage touch* takes a number of forms:

- Pushing/thrusting/pulling power. A form of telekinesis (the ability to control, manipulate, or move objects with magic).

- Shielding ability is often used to deflect arrows or other missiles. It is also used to deflect magical attacks. A different form of shielding ability blocks farsense by masking the use of magical abilities. An extremely rare form of shielding masks magical auras.
- Healing ability works by manipulating parts of the body without the need to use an incision to expose them.
- Elemental magic involves harnessing the elements such as earth, air, fire, and water, to produce magical results. An example is pyrokinesis (heating a mass of air).

3. *Mage taste,* or manipulating the 'taste buds of the imagination' with illusionary magic.

- The link between illusionary magic and taste might seem tenuous, but it is nonetheless well established. The notion was popularized by Master Ella, a past mage who drew attention to the way spices and similar flavorings masked or enhanced the taste of food, drawing parallels with the way illusion masks or enhances the appearance of reality. Note that at the time of Dalthinir and Kylen, some mages were dismissive of mage taste as being somehow lesser than other magical senses since its effects are only transitory.
- Illusionary magic is able to make something appear different from how it actually is.
- Another form of illusionary magic is the power to make something disappear. In reality, the object is not gone; it just appears to be.
- Strong illusionary magic affects more than one of the physical senses. For example, if a dog is made to appear to be a skunk, it might smell like a skunk as well as appearing to be a skunk. Equally, if a skunk is made to disappear, no trace of its smell might linger either.

4. *Mage hearing* is the rare ability to understand and communicate in any language, including non-human languages.

- The mage becomes a linguist or polyglot by magical means.
- This ability allows a mage to communicate in any language (which may not involve speaking if the communication does not rely on the voice box).
- Curiously, a literate mage with this ability is also able to read and write foreign languages. Once literacy has trained the mage to perceive meaning in the scrawl of written words, magical comprehension of written language is unlocked as well. Those possessing mage hearing invariably learn to read and write more quickly than others.
- Note that draconic speech can also be transcribed as a written language. In Dalthinir's time, draconic texts of any kind were declared extremely dangerous and strictly forbidden. By law, any scrolls or parchments in draconic language were required to be destroyed by burning immediately upon discovery.

5. *Mage sight* is the rare ability to borrow the senses of non-human creatures.

- This ability allows the mage to see through the creature's eyes.
- More adept mages are also able to hear through their ears as well as smelling, tasting, and touching as they do.
- A unique form of telepathy, mage sight is not related to astral travel, since neither the mage's soul nor mind travel outside their body.

Limits on the Use of Power

Just as mages have magical abilities that differ in strength, they have differing abilities to sustain the use of power. One mage might be able to deliver a burst of power for a short period, while another might be capable of delivering magic less powerfully over a sustained period. To use a physical analogy, some runners do better at sprints and others at marathons. The most powerful mages are capable of both.

Curiously, unlike physical strength, magical strength does not degrade with age.

No mage can use power without experiencing weariness (unless they possess a dragon talisman). Physical weariness is the primary symptom, although greater physical fitness does not boost magical endurance. Rest, or more precisely the passage of time, restores power. The most powerful mages succumb more slowly and recover more quickly.

As well as possessing greater strength magically, dragons were believed to possess unending power, which allowed them to use power without interruption.

ACKNOWLEDGMENTS

Writing would be a lot more challenging for me without my wife, Merilyn, who accepts my drafts in their raw state and provides invaluable insights. I'm greatly in her debt.

My beta readers are also a key part of the process. Thanks to Adrian Herber, Roly Edwardes, Alison George, Samuel Pryor, and Stephen for their great feedback, and to Arpenny Hart who patiently works through my audiobook drafts.

Mary Novak, my developmental editor plays a key role, ferreting out issues of every kind. And James polishes the end result with his thorough proofread. I am grateful to them both.

Brian Plush is a legend—I'm loving his map. And 100 Covers remains as responsive as ever with multiple revisions to the cover design.

Finally, I'm grateful to God, the author and sustainer, who never abandons us no matter what.

ABOUT THE AUTHOR

Allan Packer writes epic fantasy. *The Ruptured Kingdom* is his second series.

Allan grew up surrounded by books and became an avid reader during his childhood. In his university years fantasy displaced science fiction as his favorite genre, thanks primarily to J. R. R. Tolkien. He later shared this love with his four children by reading *The Lord of the Rings* to them aloud—a three-month marathon he completed twice during their formative years.

Born in Australia, Allan has lived and worked on three continents, and spent one quarter of his working years abroad. Having worked as an IT professional throughout his career, he was first published as a technical author.

Today he lives with his wife in Adelaide, South Australia, at the heart of a growing and geographically distributed extended family.

Allan is currently working on the latest installment in his series *The Ruptured Kingdom*.